Physician: The Life of Paul Beeson

Physician

The Life of Paul Beeson

Richard Rapport, M.D.

BARRICADE BOOKS, INC.

FORT LEE, NEW JERSEY

Published by Barricade Books Inc.
185 Bridge Plaza North
Suite 308-A
Ft. Lee, NJ 07024

Library of Congress Cataloging-in-Publication Data

This information can be obtained from the Library of
Congress.

Printed in the United States of America.

10 9 8 7 6 5 4 3 2 1

"And a doctor has very much to be thankful for also. Don't you ever forget it. It is such a pleasure to do a little good that a man should pay for the privilege instead of being paid for it. . . . It is a noble, generous, kindly profession, and you youngsters have got to see that it remains so."

Arthur Conan Doyle, 1894

CONTENTS

For Valerie and Daniel

ACKNOWLEDGMENTS

Like Paul Beeson, my father was a doctor, and from him I learned to value the dedication to patients that characterized Beeson's life. This book is an effort to preserve that ethic as well as to tell the story of a heroic, fortunate man. Of the dozens of people I interviewed, or who otherwise helped me with the research, Paul himself was the most generous, allowing me access to all his papers, files, books and memories. For more than two years, I spent two or three Sunday mornings a month with him in his study, looking out over a horse pasture toward the Cascade Mountains, and listening to the story of a life that both describes and helps to define medicine in the twentieth century. This was, I think, a joyful process for us both. Barbara Beeson tolerated the intrusion, and interviews with her seasoned the soup. Their children Judy Beeson Assirrelli, Peter and John Beeson helped to remember details and to add perspectives of their own through interviews and letters.

Doris Whithorn, archivist at the Park County Museum in Livingston, Montana unearthed long-buried information about the Beeson and Ash families that I otherwise would never have found. Archivists at the University of Washington, Northwestern University, McGill University, the University of Pennsylvania, Harvard University, and Rockefeller University all provided helpful information.

I am indebted to Philip and Robert Hocker for giving me Bernadine Prince's book on the history of the Alaska Railroad, a rich and loving description of the Alaska frontier including some of John Beeson's life there at the turn of the century. Mrs. Prince's daughter, Marcia Caillier, generously allowed me to use photographs from that book. J. Willis Hurst, M.D., kindly sent me first the typescript and then a copy of his book on the history of the Department of Medicine at Emory. Philip Bondy, M.D., gave me his memoir concerning his family, including the beautifully written section describing his house staff days at Grady Hospital. My two wonderful partners, John Howe, M.D., and Ken Peirce, M.D., lent me important books and helped make time available for me to write.

Robert Petersdorf, M.D., a man who terrified me and most of the rest of the house staff when I was a resident at the University of Washington, was considerate and kind. When I first interviewed him in his office at the Seattle V.A. Hospital where he is now the Distinguished Physician, I reminded him of his power over the residents twenty-five years earlier. "Well," he said, "I've mellowed, and most of it was show anyhow." Bob Petersdorf, a participant in much of Beeson's career, helped me enormously. The rest of the faculty from Yale were just as generous: Drs. Robert Levine, Gerard Burrow, Dorothy Horstmann, Gilbert Glaser, Howard Spiro, John Forrest, Aaron Lerner, Thomas (and his wife Barbara) Amatruda, and Fred Kantor all were interviewed in New Haven. Drs. Arthur Ebbert and Alvan Feinstein were especially helpful in making their time and files available, and extended themselves more than they had to in order to help record Beeson's life.

Drs. Richard Root and Petersdorf invited me to the 1997 Port Ludlow meeting of the Interplanetary Society where I interviewed Drs. Vincent Andriole, Elisha Atkins and his wife Elizabeth, David Durack, Robert Fekety, Lawrence and Rina Freedman, Edward Hook, Stephen Malawista, and Robert

Wagner. I have also benefited from some of the papers presented by other speakers at that meeting.

Janet Watt arranged my interviews at Oxford, and found the minutes of the Nuffield Committee stashed unseen for many years in an office at the Institute of Medicine. Drs. Sir David Weatherall, James Holt, Derek Hockaday, Bent Juel-Jensen and Mr. John Potter agreed to interviews and explained the unique Oxford system. Phyl Woolford invited me to her house near Oxford for tea, and described the Nuffield Department of Medicine during Beeson's tenure, as well as its history.

Professor Elias Clark of the Yale Law School sent me an unpublished paper he read at a meeting for attorneys and judges about John Peters' conflict with the Supreme Court. Drs. Halstead Holman and Franklin Epstein also sent me material about Peters otherwise not available. Arnold Relman, M.D. was interviewed by phone on this same subject.

Charles Dinarello, M.D. was extremely generous in writing to me several times concerning Paul Beeson's scientific contributions to the understanding of cytokine biology.

Dozens of others wrote or talked to me on the telephone about Beeson and the several institutions where they knew him. Most notably, these include: Harold Beeson's daughter Sarah Cutler, Drs. Robert Glaser, Lewis Landsberg, Thomas Ferris, Charles Cook, Gene Stollerman, Daniel Hankey, Linton Bishop, Lisa Steiner, Thomas Stamey and Kenneth Johnson. Dr. Eugene and Evelyn Selby Stead both wrote and phoned me about their memories of Beeson, Soma Weiss, and Emory University. My thanks to the more than fifty others who wrote to me between 1996 and 1998 about this work.

Sherwin Nuland, M.D., the Yale surgeon and fine writer, did me several kindnesses. He wrote to me about his own brief encounter with Beeson as a patient when he was a medical student, and he both praised and promoted my non-fiction. I am grateful.

Paul Ramsey, M.D., current Dean at the University of Washington School of Medicine, made it possible for me to use archived material in the library when that proved difficult. Shalamar Pedersen flawlessly transcribed nearly one hundred hours of taped interviews. Drs. Petersdorf, Feinstein and Hurst read early drafts of several chapters, and their editing and comments have assured correct details.

Craig Rothstein, my editor at Barricade, recognized the value of this story when he acquired the manuscript, and his edits improved the writing.

My wife Valerie Trueblood helped me as she always does by reading and editing several drafts of this book. Our son Daniel put up with the process, and allowed me to write using his computer. Both of them, and my brother and sister-in-law Pat Soden and Marilyn Trueblood and my niece Cassie Soden tolerated the probably too long and frequent discussion of the topic over several years.

PREFACE

Writing from Oxford in 1924, Harvey Cushing, one of the founders of modern neurological surgery, finished recording the life of Sir William Osler who had died five years earlier. It is slightly coincidental that seventy-five years later another neurosurgeon should write the biography of Paul Beeson, who may be said to have continued the tradition of Osler's humanism in medicine during the remainder of the twentieth century.

While Cushing was certainly an innovator in the surgical treatment of diseases of the nervous system, and an able writer, this three-hundred-page biography of Beeson is probably an improvement on the thirteen hundred and seventy-two pages of detail it took Dr. Cushing to describe the life of Osler. A complete record of Dr. Beeson's every activity has not been my goal.

I have tried to describe faithfully the life of a good, dedicated and fortunate man who, by the example of his life, characterized the academic physician. Born during an era of medical practice when doctors could many times offer only rudimentary treatments but sometimes great comfort to patients, physicians like became teachers when the science was new, the money for research abundant and the hope limitless. As medicine has changed from a healers' art into a technologically dependent industry, such teachers have vanished, in part because they were so successful.

Those of us who were students and house officers during the era when medicine was taught by academics like Paul Beeson (and others mentioned in this book) were improved by the experience beyond any ability to repay their dedication to us and to their patients. Paul Beeson's life has been so fortunate, so unique and so influential that I have attempted to write about him in a way that shows his quiet, pervasive influence without reciting, as J.P. Peters once accused a visitor of doing at Yale Grand Rounds, a "catalog of ships."

Paul's father John Beeson entered medical school in 1898, and so the story told of his son's life includes one hundred years of medicine. Each of the chapters is introduced by a quote, a sign-post erected in an attempt to illustrate either the state of knowledge of human biology about that time, or the place of medical practice in contemporary society. The date given with the quotation refers to when it was first written, or to when the events described occurred, not necessarily the publication date of the source.

While this book is no more a complete history of medicine in the twentieth century than a microscopic examination of Paul Beeson's life, the maturation of the healers art into science and then its amalgamation into business is an important theme in the account.

Richard Rapport
Seattle, 1999

PROLOGUE

$\mathcal{M}$idway through the fall term of 1950 at Emory, eight third-year medical students on the internal medicine clinical rotation gathered outside one of the wards at Grady Hospital. Although they were still inexperienced clinicians, having been permitted on the wards for only a few months, they were nonetheless sophisticated observers of medicine and of the staff that instructed them. They were excited, a little anxious, but ready to begin treating patients.

The anticipated moment was exhilarating for the seven men and one woman as they waited, stethoscopes hanging from their pockets, for their new attending physician to take them on teaching rounds. They had spent the first three weeks of the rotation under the competent guidance of an internist from Atlanta, who came two afternoons a week to the big public wards at Grady to see uninsured patients sick with cancer, diabetes, heart disease, and infection of every kind.

The students studied these illnesses, and most of internal medicine, from Harrison's just-published *Principles of Internal Medicine*, and they were expected to know at least something about each of the diseases cataloged in the nearly two-thousand page volume. In the preceding few weeks, they had learned pages of written description of illnesses as well as more practical medicine than in all of their first two years in medical school.

The man these eight students eagerly awaited was Paul Beeson, one of the editors of Harrison's text and Chairman of the Department of Medicine at Emory. Just forty-one years old, Beeson was already well known, not only in the South but around the world, for his work in the developing field of Infectious Disease. The students all knew the subjects of Beeson's basic research. They anticipated rounds with him not only for what he would teach them about infection, but because of the stories they had heard about him from classmates and older students.

Beeson would show them how to examine a patient and how to interpret their laboratory and x-ray studies, finding their way to a diagnosis. This was not uncommon among the capable Emory faculty. But they were waiting for Beeson with excitement because he had a special quality that the students and house staff all talked about and admired but could not quite define.

In October it was still warm in Atlanta and the students sweated while they stood in the cramped conference room outside the twenty-four bed male ward. The senior medical resident, assistant resident and intern hurried in at nine o'clock, carrying stacks of x-rays and laboratory reports harvested from earlier rounds that began at six-thirty. Their short white coats, buttoned at the shoulder, were already damp.

The previous day, the senior resident had assigned each student a case for presentation. He wanted to be certain that they all understood the data and had their topics thoroughly rehearsed before introducing the patients to Professor Beeson. He lingered over the problem of a nineteen-year-old man with subacute bacterial endocarditis, an infection of the heart valves, making certain that the student assigned to discuss that case knew the disease well.

Paul Beeson appeared at exactly nine-thirty. The students and house staff stood when he came in the room. Standing was not necessarily expected any longer by faculty members. It was an act of admiration accorded to few, but Beeson was different. "Good morning," said their teacher. "What do we have to talk about today?"

The house staff, all individually picked by Beeson to train at Emory, were as anxious as the students to start rounds this particular morning. Making rounds with an attending in practice was usually instructive, but now they all had the opportunity to learn from an accomplished scientist and teacher, an academic physician doing work on the frontier of science.

Technology, the child of basic research, had not yet come to dominate medicine. A few years earlier, Beeson had published new work on the sites of removal of bacteria from the blood of patients with endocarditis, and he had more experience with penicillin in treating this condition than anyone else in the South. Everybody was aware of the young patient with this illness on the ward and had carefully studied the chapter in Harrison's book that discussed bacterial vegetations on heart valves. They wanted to show Beeson what they knew, and to learn from him the details of an illness often fatal prior to the advent of antibiotics.

Dr. Beeson took a chair at the head of the conference table and the others stood or sat, filling the little room. The senior resident read the list of the patients to be presented that morning, along with their diagnoses. Beeson asked for a few particulars of some of the cases. The students said nothing.

"Before we begin rounds," Beeson said to the one sitting next to him, "tell me what you know about the patient who had diabetic ketoacidosis." The student hesitantly described carbohydrate metabolism in the absence of adequate insulin levels, accumulation of ketone bodies, dehydration, and shifts of cellular sodium and potassium.

When he stumbled over details, Dr. Beeson gently corrected his errors and then added, "You know, these patients are very sick and frightened; sometimes they rapidly become comatose and die. Their families are worried for them. Diabetes is a chronic, often progressive disease, and while we can treat diabetics now with insulin, we cannot cure them. We must do what we can for their sugar metabolism, but we should also work as hard as we can to ease their fears and control their suffering. If we do all of these things properly, then we will be of some help to that patient."

The students were prepared to hear this from the department chairman. Although his work on infection was influential and the research on endocarditis, the mode of transmission of hepatitis and causes of fever were published in the world's best medical journals, it was his quiet attention to each individual patient that had earned him a unique kind of respect among students, staff and faculty at Emory. Because he was a shy man, often saying little at rounds or in meetings, sometimes nearly diffident, it was unclear just how he projected such a powerful sense of caring. It was, someone suggested, Shakespeare's "quality of mercy."

The dozen or so people stood to follow Beeson out of the conference room, the residents beside him and the students trailing closely behind. No one hurried. The intern led the way through the open doorway onto the ward and the group entered a one-hundred-fifty foot long room with twelve beds perpendicular to the wall on each side. Big windows opened above the beds, nearly reaching the high ceiling; the floor was linoleum. Apart from the nurses' station stacked with charts and cluttered with a dressing cart, blood pressure cuffs and stethoscopes, mercury thermometers, and a few basic drugs, there was little other equipment on the ward. An odor of alcohol and antiseptic clung to everything. The nurse in charge greeted them and directed the group to the bedside of the first of eight patients to be presented for discussion that morning.

A nervous twenty-four year old year medical student began to recite the history and physical findings: "This eighty-two year old white male farmer from Tallapoosa started to notice ease of fatigue and slight shortness of breath about six months ago. Two months ago, he became short of breath at rest and found that he couldn't milk his cows. A month later, he could not go to bed at night, but began to sleep sitting up in a chair. Two weeks ago, he was admitted with pulmonary edema and ascites. His chest x-ray shows an enlarged heart and prominent vasculature."

As the young man spoke, Dr. Beeson did something so unusual that none of the students or residents had even heard of it, much less seen an attending physician behave in this way; he sat on a chair at the bedside. The frail older man was propped up on two pillows in the white, metal frame bed and breathed with effort. He looked gratefully at Beeson, who focused his entire attention on the man as one of the residents pulled up a rolling curtain to close off the group from the other patients. The student took about ten minutes to present the details of the farmer's illness and discuss all of the laboratory and x-ray findings, only occasionally requiring guidance from one of the residents when he faltered or rambled. When the student had finished, Beeson put his hand on the patient's thin, bruised arm, carefully avoiding an IV plugged into a tiny vein and asked: "Can you tell me when you first felt ill? What was the first thing that happened before you started to become so short of breath? Take your time; we have all morning to learn about your problem."

The old man sighed deeply, sat up a little higher in the bed, and in a meandering Southern cadence began to tell his story. "It started to hit me when the wife passed, doctor, and my legs swelled up," he began. "We was married sixty-four years last November." When he had finished talking, he smiled only slightly as Beeson told him that they all were going to discuss his illness and treatment so that they could help him feel better.

"What is the differential diagnosis?" Beeson stood up and asked the student who had presented the case. "Well," began the amply prepared novice, "dyspnea at rest can be associated with severe anemia, but the patient has a normal blood count. Thyrotoxicosis can rarely present this way, and so can metabolic acidosis, but his labs don't fit. He could have shortness of breath due to pulmonary disease, but the most likely diagnosis is congestive heart failure because of the history, ascites, ankle edema and x-ray picture."

Professor Beeson nodded agreement. "And how did you treat him?" The student hesitated long enough for one of the residents to mention having prescribed mercurial diuretics, digitalis and sedation. The old man looked reassured as Dr. Beeson thanked him, and the entire group moved three beds down the row, preparing to discuss bacterial infections of the heart valves.

While Paul Beeson did not invent this method for making teaching rounds with house staff and students, he learned it from the man who did. One of the several unexpected turns in his life had taken him to Peter Bent Brigham Hospital in Boston just as Soma Weiss assumed the chair of medicine at Harvard. Weiss possessed a curious and inventive mind, as well as a comprehensive knowledge of general internal medicine. Through his behavior and language, he communicated his wisdom so artistically and completely that his students flourished. Furthermore, he was without the burden of ego in caring for the sick; the patients were of foremost importance.

Weiss took morning report himself, hearing the details of each newly admitted patient's illness before making rounds with Beeson, who was his first Chief Resident, and the rest of the house staff and students on his service. In Boston, making rounds with Soma Weiss was an event that often drew an audience of more than a hundred doctors and students.

Beeson's journey to the Harvard Medicine Service had passed through Wooster, Ohio. Following medical school and internship, he had spent two years in general practice with his father and brother in the Midwest. While not a traditional beginning to an important academic career, he saw in Wooster a broad canvas of human disease and behavior. Beeson's father, an independent frontier surgeon, had thirty years' experience of this kind of medical practice by the time his sons joined him, and Paul profited not only from that education, but from hearing the life and death stories of frightened sick people. He learned to listen. However, he never learned to operate—a skill then required for successful general practice.

In part because he was a poor surgeon, Beeson moved from the pastures of Ohio to the Rockefeller Institute for Medical Research where he began both the clinical and experimental study of infection. By the time he was chosen to direct the Harvard-Red Cross Epidemiological Hospital in England during World War II, he already had a rising reputation in academic medicine. At Emory, his work on infection and fever moved into the front ranks of research.

At a time when American culture permitted a more narrow range of behaviors, the rules governing what the ill could expect from their doctors were fundamental to the culture of medicine. The guardians of these tenets were, in general, professors in medical schools (nearly all associated with universities after 1945), and chief among these were internists. Professors of Internal Medicine had as their exemplar Sir William Osler, an Emersonian man who not only wrote the first modern classification of disease, but who passionately taught a nineteenth century humanism that eased physicians from their barber-surgeon ancestry into a scientific profession. In addition to the guidance of Osler, academic internists were usually thoughtful people like Beeson with intellectual interests in the laboratory and time enough to consider the needs of their patients as well as their students.

For most of the twentieth century, medical students and house staff were taught to provide the most current treatment available to every patient, anticipating the best results for the least risk, without regard to cost. Nor was the price of treatment always calculated in dollars. In 1965, after Beeson had moved to New Haven, a pulmonary specialist at Yale told his charges on rounds that, even if they knew a patient who was-n't breathing had active tuberculosis, they must give mouth to mouth resuscitation anyway, or they weren't fit to be doctors and should drop out of medical school right then.

All patients, even the uninsured or indigent who received care in charity hospitals staffed by medical schools, expected help but not necessarily a guarantee of complete success. Prior to the discovery of the sulfa drugs in the nineteen thirties, and the rediscovery of penicillin during the early years of World War II, doctors and their septic patients often measured success only by the alleviation of suffering. Cure of infection deep in tissue or in organs sometimes occurred when a surgeon could drain an abscess, but more often it did not.

Micro-organisms were known to be the cause of infection from the mid-nineteenth century following the work of Pasteur and Lister. Antisepsis was an accepted method of preventing such illness but there was little treatment until antibiotics. While sanitation and public health measures controlled pandemics such as the bubonic plague that ravaged the population of Europe in the middle-ages, there were still epidemics.

The "Spanish" influenza of 1918 spread around the world. In cities large and small, polio outbreaks occurred each summer, and every winter lobar pneumonia killed more patients than were cured. Sepsis was usually fatal prior to penicillin. Just at the time useful treatments for infectious diseases were being discovered, Beeson was studying infection as a resident in New York City.

Oswald Avery and others at Rockefeller had devised ingenious methods for the treatment of pneumococcal pneumonia just prior to wide spread use of sulfa drugs. These innovators first learned that the several types of pneumococci could be categorized according to their polysaccharide membranes. Then, antibodies against each type were raised in horses. Antigen-antibody reaction was by then understood and the sera collected could be used to treat patients once their specific type of infection was known. The reclusive Dr. Avery was at the same time in the process of discovering that DNA was the chemical machinery of genetics. These various early experiments in cellular metabolism prepared Beeson the scientist to exploit a rational basis for treating infection with antibiotics. Once it was learned that the metabolism of micro-organisms could be manipulated chemically, the development of specific drugs to interfere with the cellular metabolism of bacteria, and later of viruses, was underway. The discovery of antibiotics, it has been argued, is the most important contribution that medicine has made to human health.

With the technology for isolating, growing and chemically manipulating micro-organisms came at least the possibility for a cure. It was this understanding that Beeson offered to his students on the wards and in the labs at Emory that fall in 1950. He would continue later at Yale, then Oxford, and finally around the world as an editor of both of the great textbooks of medicine, Harrison's *Principles of Internal Medicine* and Cecil and Loeb's *Textbook of Medicine*. Important as these contributions were, however, Beeson's scientific discoveries were only a small part of what he gave to students, colleagues, and patients.

Paul's father began to treat sick people on the American frontier as medicine was becoming science and when doctors were not necessarily highly regarded nor greatly rewarded. As the medical profession grew more confident of scientific certainty, the advertised value of the product increased and health care became a marketable commodity. As a consequence, physicians in practice often developed a certain aloof separation from their patients, and academics retreated from the care of the sick into research and administration. Since it is difficult to maintain in the same mind a profound sense of the value of the work being done and, at the same time, a realization that doing the work is its own reward, fame and wealth sometimes became ends in themselves. Humility is easily overwhelmed by advertising.

By the example of his life, Paul Beeson taught his students

never to forget their grand opportunities, nor that their principal duty was to each sick patient placed before them. These simple traits were the distilled essence of Beeson's own teachers—his father John and his mother Martha, Oswald Avery, and Soma Weiss—who taught him dedication to his profession.

CHAPTER 1

And from the standpoint of medicine as an art for the prevention and cure of disease, the man who translates the hieroglyphics of science into plain language is certainly the more useful.

William Osler, 1892(1)

As the autumn cold fell out of the Rocky Mountains onto windy Livingston, Montana in October of 1908, Dr. John Beeson put on his heavy coat, picked up his black bag and started down the empty street to begin making his rounds. Taking care of sick people began early, before his wife Martha and eight-year-old son Harold were awake, and often continued until well after dinner was finished. Most mornings he walked (and later drove a buggy, then a Buick) around the small town calling on elderly patients and stopping at households filled with childhood diseases. By mid-morning he arrived at his office.

At the turn of the century, when a remnant of the Montana frontier still lurked at the edges of Livingston, not so long cleared of mountain men, Dr. Beeson's pharmacopoeia was limited to very few items. In his bag were antiseptics, laudanum, cathartics, and digitalis-leaf, as well as a few surgical instruments and bandages.

This was the age of Osler in medicine and physicians were only decades removed from their barber-surgeon ancestry; the Flexner Report codifying *Medical Education in the United States and Canada* was still to be written.(2) Real medical science was little known beyond the lessons of innovators like Roentgen, Pasteur and Curie, and there were few drugs other than those Dr. Beeson carried with him. Neither was there much therapy available other than straightforward surgery and simple treatments based on observation.

The *art* of medicine was what could be offered, and the written word of Sir William Osler, himself a product of the North American frontier, was the final authority on almost every medical subject. But with his small selection of medicines, a few instruments, a careful understanding of anatomy, dedication to his profession and common sense, John Beeson managed to comfort many and heal some. He was, therefore, a central figure in the community that depended on him.

Dr. Beeson and his family lived at 112 South Sixth Street in a house they had built near the one owned by Martha's father, Thomas Ash. Martha was born in 1878, the third child in a family from rural Missouri. Her father fought for the Confederacy in the Civil War and survived incarceration in a dismal Union prison. Afterwards, he moved the family around until finding success in business in Livingston, Montana.

After finishing school in Livingston, Martha went to Chicago for a year where she studied at the Cumnock School of Oratory. Her three-term curriculum included rhetoric (with Professor Cumnock himself), essays, meter and elocution. This sort of limited education was a common practice for young women who wished to teach grade school in the west at the turn of the century. In 1896, she returned home to instruct the primary grades in Livingston and soon met another young teacher just arrived from Iowa, John Beeson.

A good deal is known about the Beeson family in America, all of whom seem to have sprouted from the seed of Edward Beeson and his wife Rachel Pennington.(3) These two, from Lancaster, England, traveled sometime between 1682 and 1684 with the Penn emigrants to Chester County, Pennsylvania where they had four children, including Richard who married Charity Grubb. The family was Quaker, and Richard became a Quaker preacher moving often to towns in Pennsylvania, Virginia and as far south as North Carolina. Richard and Charity had a son, also named Richard, who married Ann Brown. These were the great great grandparents of Wilson Bruce Beeson, the father of Dr. John Beeson of Livingston, Montana.

Wilson (called Bruce) lived most of his life near Marshalltown, Iowa. He too fought in the Civil War, but on the side of the Union, and was released to return to Iowa from the notorious Georgia prison at Andersonville in 1865. Working his way back across the mid-west, Bruce Beeson stopped in the eastern Ohio county of Columbiana where he hired on as a farm hand for the Binford family and, after what must have been a brief courtship, married their quiet daughter Hannah. Apparently her Quaker parents had some misgivings in consenting to the marriage of their daughter to a soldier, but the union occurred and the newlyweds managed to cross Ohio, Indiana, and Illinois to settle again outside Marshalltown.

These two farm children became the parents of five offspring including John, who was to father Paul and Harold Beeson. Harold recalled that thirty-three years after the end of the Civil War, when Bruce Beeson met Thomas Ash in Montana while both were visiting their children, these two surviving representatives of opposing points of view never progressed beyond addressing each other with a distant "Mr. Beeson" and "Mr. Ash."(4)

John Bradley Beeson was born in Marshalltown in 1872 and spent his boyhood attending the local schools and working on the family farm as well as hiring himself out to other nearby farmers. The end of the nineteenth century was, of course, well before mechanized farming so John and his oldest brother Orin were valuable labor, plowing, making hay and harvesting corn.

Sam, younger than his two brothers by many years, was apparently less successful as a farm hand. As a child, Sam was once given a brand new bicycle which he promptly traded for a horse, convinced he had struck an excellent bargain. However, as the animal was led for the first time into the Beeson barn, it ran its head into the top of the door, thereby allowing the youngest son's wiser father Bruce to observe that the horse was blind.

Sam was a much more successful salesman than farmer and eventually became the General Sales Manager for Walkover shoes. His wife, a devout Christian Scientist, did not allow Sam medical treatment following his eventually fatal myocardial infarction. The eldest brother, Orin, practiced dentistry in Beatrice, Nebraska and also married a strong-willed and ardent Christian Scientist; these two women may have influenced their sister-in-law Alice to become a Christian Science healer following the death of her husband.

> Christian Science was born in the East, near Boston, and like homeopathy picked up adherents in urban areas among the well-to-do classes. Mary Baker Eddy, an obscure New England mystagogue who founded the group, altogether denied the reality of matter and claimed that disease, like all else, was purely a function of mind and spirit. Christian Science was, in a sense, homeopathy taken to the final dilution, the point where the world dissolved into idea. But, while Mrs. Eddy thought medicine and nourishment of no use . . . she did not deny the value of money. Like Osteopathy, Christian Science was run in a very business-like fashion and earned its founder a substantial fortune.(5)

After John went to medical school, the anti-medical beliefs of his brothers and sister caused some family discomfort.

At about age eighteen, John Beeson decided he was not a farmer and enrolled at Valparaiso University where he studied pre-medical subjects for two years. However, needing money, he did not go directly to medical school but instead qualified as a teacher. In 1895 or 1896, he secured an initial job teaching the seventh and eighth grades in Livingston. An article in the June 19, 1897 *Livingston Enterprise* notes that J.B. Beeson was hired as the principal of the Big Timber School.

The *Enterprise*, which seems to have investigated the new teacher's activities carefully along with the other routine events of a small frontier town without many distractions, reported that John Beeson and Martha Ash were issued a marriage license in September of 1898. Shortly after getting married at the Episcopal Church in Livingston on September 20th, the Beesons honeymooned aboard the transcontinental train the Empire Builder on their way to Chicago where John entered the Rush Graduate School of Medicine, then part of the University of Chicago.

In order to finance this education, the newlyweds borrowed $5,000 at 6% interest from John's father. The debt was faithfully repaid in small amounts until John and Martha settled in Anchorage, Alaska still owing his father about $2,000, which was then forgiven by the older man. Martha taught secondary school in Chicago for the first two years, then became pregnant and Harold was born in 1900.

John learned the art and primitive science of medicine during the required four years as a student at Rush. He had about as much training as was possible before the Flexner Report. After graduation, the Beesons moved for six months to Columbia, South Dakota before settling again in Livingston where John began a general practice.

Dr. Beeson opened his office as Physician and Surgeon in Livingston, probably in 1904. The community of about five thousand inhabitants had been founded in 1832 as Clark City. Herman Clark was the principal contractor of the Northern Pacific Railroad from "the Missouri to the proposed last spike," but the town was named for him only as long as it took for the name to be recorded. It seems that between the time the five hundred inhabitants decided what to call the place and the several days it took to travel one hundred miles east to record it, the honor of the town name went to the largest stockholder of the railroad rather than its builder.

Livingston is located just outside Yellowstone National Park, and "when the first construction train reached the town there were two hotels, one hardware store, two restaurants, two watchmakers, three blacksmiths, two wholesale liquor dealers, two meat markets, six general merchandise stores, two drug stores and thirty saloons."(6) Civilization came promptly, however, and by 1900 several prominent Livingston citizens were physicians. Dr. and Mrs. Beeson were soon well established in this society and quickly saved the five thousand dollars needed to build the comfortable wooden house on Sixth Street near Martha's parents.

Paul Beeson was born in that house on October 18, 1908, in a second floor alcove off the front master bedroom later used as a nursery. He was delivered by his father's colleague, Dr. B.L. Pampel, who signed the Certificate of Birth.

A few weeks prior to the birth of his brother, eight-year-old Harold found a large, newly constructed bassinet in the bathroom. In spite of the change in shape of his mother's body, pregnancy and birth were not then discussed with children. Harold, interpreting the new construction as a place to put dirty clothes, promptly dumped in his pants. Then, putting on a clean pair of overalls (the brand name "Levis" not yet in use), he took down the shoe hook, fastened his high-button shoes, put the elastic bands around the knees of his short trousers and went to school.

On the morning she began to labor, Harold's mother took him to the front door, gave him a little money and a push, and sent him around the corner to Second Street with the instruction that he stay overnight with her sister's family. Harold was very much excited by this prospect because his Aunt Annie and Uncle John King had three teenage children who were greatly admired by their younger cousin. At dinner that night, Harold was especially impressed at the scientific response given by his eldest cousin Russell who, when reproached by his father for putting his own used spoon into the sugar bowl, replied "What's the problem—any sugar touched sticks to the spoon, doesn't it?"(7)

The next morning when he returned home, Harold was greeted at the door by a nurse who announced that his mother was "lying in" and that he was in possession of a baby brother. She told him that his mother and brother were both well, but did not mention the slight congenital anomaly with which the baby had been born.

Harold was a little disappointed by the red-faced creature in the nursery, but raced across the street to share the good fortune with his best friend, seven-year-old George Van Fleet, an only child. While Mrs. Van Fleet wept, George put up a wail demanding that she produce a brother for him, which a year later she did. Following the excitement of that October morning, both Harold and George returned to school and the newborn had a small surgical procedure done at home by his father, partially correcting the anomaly.

On this particular day, John Beeson probably did not go to his comfortable three-room office that sat on the second floor of the Park Building near the center of downtown Livingston. He would not, however, have missed more than a day or two of caring for his patients.

Dr. Beeson's patients sat in the front room of the office waiting to be seen in the small consultation room, or to be taken into the third room for physical examination or x-ray by a primitive, unshielded Roentgen tube. This device produced a "frightening, chattering noise, bluish light and the smell of ozone. Photographs were not made; only a hand-held fluoroscopic screen—about 10x12 inches."(8)

Dr. Beeson didn't know of Marie Curie's leukemia and did not appreciate the potential harm of radiation, so he "calibrated" the instrument by holding his left hand in front of the tube to check the image. This practice resulted in the chronic irradiation of several fingers on that hand and eventually a cancer requiring amputation of the ends of those digits. Years later, while still practicing medicine in Wooster, Ohio, Dr. Beeson had special surgical gloves made to fit his deformed left hand so that he could continue to operate.

John Beeson was accustomed to hardship; a few finger tips gone was simply an inconvenience. Real pain was making house calls at country homes by horse and buggy during the Montana winter. If the case was obstetrical, he might be away for an entire day or even overnight. His life became a little easier in 1908 when the family acquired a white Buick equipped with four seats, a canvas top, right-hand drive and a crank. Harold was required to assist his father in starting the wonderful new machine by depressing the spark lever in the middle of the steering wheel while Dr. Beeson cranked the engine by hand. As the motor caught and turned over, the young assistant advanced the spark and hoped that the whirling crank did not break his fathers hand.

The car had carbide lights, but no doors. While holding the baby, Martha Beeson always placed a protective arm on her eldest son's shoulder as they traveled the rutted, unpaved streets of Livingston or the rough, usually empty mountain roads. There were no service stations outside the town and the routine mechanical failures, broken springs and axles or frequent flat tires had to be repaired by the driver. The road outside Livingston on the way to Helena, Montana was especially dangerous because it followed the surface of an abandoned rail bed full of metal and broken glass.

Fortunately, John Beeson, remembered by his older son as "a square shouldered, rugged and taciturn man with little interest outside his profession" maintained the physique of a farm hand. When a blow-out occurred he jacked up the car, removed the rims from the wooden wheels, peeled off the tire and took the inner tube out of the casing. The site of the puncture had to be identified and then "vulcanized"—chemically treated so that the rubber patch would stick. Then the process was reversed, the tire put back on the wheel and inflated with a single-barrel hand pump. Such an outing was not for the frail or for talkers, but for someone who said little and did what was required.

These family trips, which often included the King cousins, had rewards as well as hardships. The natural hot springs at Hunter's and Chico included hotels, dining rooms and swimming pools. On the 4th of July in 1910, thirty thousand fans in Reno watched Heavyweight Champion of the World Jack Johnson defeat Jim Jeffries in what was prematurely called "The Fight of the Century." The ring action was sent round by round over telegraph from Nevada to an eager holiday audience at Hunter's Hot Springs.

As "Johnson battered the aging Jeffries into a helpless pulp," all the members of the Beeson and King families, except for Russell King, listened to the news around a balcony of the indoor pool. This most playful of the King cousins, masquerading as a woman with her face shaded by a parasol, pretended to fall off the high-diving board and flounder in the water. Her several rescuers were surprised when the woman surfaced from the depth of the pool as a male in a bathing suit.

No doubt, this did not amuse Russell's gruff and fearsome father, the Chief of Livingston Police, any more than had his dipping a wet spoon into the sugar bowl. Russell, high-spirited and adventuresome, left Montana at age twenty to travel with the Red Cross to a U.S. military operation in Eastern Siberia. There he became sick with an undiagnosable illness, returned home and died.

Life in Montana in 1908 was not gentle. John Beeson labored long hours for his patients as a general practitioner, a term that included what are now the specialties of obstetrics, general surgery, orthopedics and urology, as well as family medicine. He did not have an internship or residency, but did get advanced training especially in surgery at the Mayo Clinic, as well as studying for six months at the New York Post Graduate School.

In Livingston, Dr. Beeson set broken bones, took out gall bladders, treated renal stones and delivered babies. Outside the town he had responsibility for the occupants of "the poor farm," a collection of unfortunates who were old, disabled or so poor that they could not care for themselves. He periodically drove the five miles out of Livingston to the two-story building in a lonely valley off the road to that led to Hunter's Hot Springs where Harold Beeson remembered the "musty smell of antiseptics, body odor and stale cooking. There was a general atmosphere of resignation and despair."(9) Away from the main building was a "pesthouse" and occasionally Dr. Beeson put on gown and gloves, cap and surgical mask to visit patients with smallpox who were confined to this little house and left it only when removed by death.(10)

Life was spare and even though John worked long hours and had to be available to his patients at any time, the Beeson family was always able to find some diversion in Livingston. John and Martha enjoyed bowling and joined the local club which, in one of those mysterious transformations of club life, became a bridge society while retaining "bowling club" as its title. Bridge games were frequent in the evenings and were often held at the house on Sixth Street. Paul and Harold learned the game watching their parents and friends play and were both to enjoy the strategies of bridge as adults themselves.

By this time, Dr. Beeson's practice was so successful that he earned as much as ten thousand dollars annually, and was able to afford thirty dollars a month to pay a Scandinavian live-in "hired girl" who, once a week, baked bread on a large, coal-burning stove in the kitchen. This delicious treat was put in the long, narrow pantry off the kitchen, the loaves covered with tea towels and left overnight to rise. The next night at dinner, hungry boys were treated to fresh bread smeared with butter. After such a meal one night in 1910, John Beeson called Harold out on the lawn and asked him to look up at the huge, clear Montana sky; it was a night that gives the "Big Sky Country" its name. John pointed out Halley's comet to his older son and told him, "When you're an old man, you'll see that again."

There was also time and money for excitement like the Sells-Floto Circus that came to town by rail in the summer. John Beeson roused his wife and children early and took them to the rail-siding illuminated by huge fires while the animals, cages, steam calliope, equipment and circus people were unloaded. Then they followed this parade to a vacant lot and watched the spectacle of the tents going up.

By 1915, however, Dr. and Mrs. Beeson had grown restless in Montana and John believed that he might have a more successful practice in a larger city. In that year, the Beeson family of Livingston, Montana moved to Queen Anne Hill in Seattle. Instead of a horse and buggy or a Buick, the family traveled up and down Temperance Street on the recently rebuilt counterbalance to the Mercer streetcar line. When Harold entered Queen Anne High School and his little brother Paul started the first grade at the local grammar school, there were still huge stands of virgin timber on both sides of Lake Washington.

John opened his office in the Medical Dental Building in downtown Seattle, with the familiar lettering on the door reading "John B. Beeson, M.D.—Physician and Surgeon." He struggled. By that time Seattle had become a sophisticated town, thanks in part to the Alaska gold rush of 1897, and specialty medicine was already becoming established.

Dr. Beeson found that he was unable to attract enough patients to build a respectable general practice, much less do the kind of surgery that he was so skilled at and enjoyed. In fact, he didn't really make a living. This predicament was remedied in 1916 when the Alaska Railroad Company started to build the rail bed from Anchorage in both directions to Seward and Fairbanks. John Beeson accepted a job as House Surgeon for the Railroad Company and moved his family back onto the frontier, this time in Alaska.

◆ ◆ ◆

On his third voyage of discovery in about 1778, Captain James Cook described what is now called Cook Inlet and the Anchorage area of South central Alaska. Russian traders were already well established in the region and for the next hundred years, until Russian America was sold to the United States in 1867 for 7.2 million dollars, Russian trading and culture dominated the region.

The following year, the Alaska Commercial Company built and began to operate dozens of stations along Cook Inlet, and the Alaska Gold Rush of 1897 brought a steady new population to the region. If few men got rich finding gold at the close of the century in Alaska, many died trying to walk or travel by horseback from the embarkation point at Skagway to the gold fields farther north in the Klondike.

On August 24 of 1912, an enterprising Congress authorized President Taft to appoint a commission for investigation of the transportation problems in Alaska. Their 1913 report to the third session of the 62nd Congress recommended:

> That railroad connections with open ports on the Pacific were necessary for utilization of the fertile regions of the Alaska interior and the mineral resources, and to open up a large region to the homesteader, the prospector, and the miner, and that construction of two independent railroad systems to be ultimately connected and supplemented was advisable, one to run from Cordova by way of Chitina to Fairbanks, and the other from Seward around Cook Inlet to the Iditarod River, with a total cost of $35 million for the 733 miles of new construction involved.(11)

Hearings were held, the merits of various routes debated, and on March 12, 1914 the Enabling Act was approved allocating the full amount of money and allowing the President to authorize construction. In May, Woodrow Wilson directed the Secretary of the Interior to begin surveying routes, and the Alaska Railroad Company began its work. "By Executive Order of April 10, 1915, the President chose the Western or Susitna route for the railroad. Starting at Seward, it cut through the Kenai Peninsula, edged around Turnagain and Knik arms, through the Matanuska Valley, up the Susitna Valley, over Broad Pass, along the Nenana River, and up the drainage of the Tanana, to Fairbanks. It was 467 miles long. . . . "(12)

During that first year construction did not proceed especially easily. A stevedore strike on the Pacific Coast and labor problems in Anchorage delayed deliveries. The weather was wet and, not too surprisingly, the price of raw materials increased. It soon became clear to engineers on site that the main line should pass through Anchorage rather than four miles to the east as had been planned. Predictably, these delays resulted in too much idle time for the hundreds of men hired to cook, survey, blast, carry and build the railroad.

Forty men from the 14th Infantry under the command of Lt. C.A. Ross were sent on the steamer "Mariposa" to help maintain order, and arrived in Anchorage on November 17, 1916. In addition to the usual illness in such a collection of people, there were injuries caused by the work itself, carelessness and fights. Recognizing this as a problem in 1916, President Wilson authorized money for hospital services in connection with construction of the railroad including, of course, doctors.

On November 1, 1916, the overnight temperature in Anchorage was ten degrees below zero. That week, thirty-five year old T. Aamodt was killed instantly when he was struck by a boulder while at work two miles below Rainbow Creek on the Turnagain arm of Cook Inlet. Charles Carlson and Ole Sanden, his fellow laborers, hurried down the fifty foot cliff he had fallen from to recover his body. As he was unmarried, Aamodt's father in Norway was awarded twenty-five percent of his approximately sixty-five dollars per month salary under the terms of the Employees' Compensation Act.

During that month of November, four other men were reported missing. At the same time in the Directory of Officials, the Alaskan Engineering Commission (Anchorage Division) listed Dr. J.B. Beeson as Surgeon along with the Chief Surgeon, Dr. E.S. Reedy. Three other doctors were assigned to stations at Moose Creek, Potter Creek and Talkeetna; there was plenty of work for these five physicians.

When John and Martha Beeson arrived in Alaska, Harold was almost sixteen and his brother Paul about seven. Although Livingston had been a small town, it was not primitive, and by 1916 Seattle had become a cosmopolitan city. Therefore, it must have been a shock to the family when they moved into a two-story log house in Anchorage next to the identical log hospital, both lacking electricity. Dr. Beeson was once again practicing frontier medicine.

By this time, roughly two thousand people had found their way to the new town: men, women—some pregnant—and many children. As yet, there was no railroad and the trip to more sophisticated medical care in Seattle took at least a week by dogsled, stagecoach and boat. Drs. Reedy and Beeson were required, therefore, to care for all the medical problems that befell these isolated workers and their families. Life was dangerous for every creature involved in building the railroad, not only the people. Dead Horse Hill, for example, got its name:

> When they were making the survey, they had a Frenchman in charge of the pack horses. They were going around the hillside when they missed a couple of their horses. The Frenchman went back to look for them and found them at the bottom of a slide, both dead. This is one of many versions but this one sounds reasonable.(13)

As John Beeson immediately set about the business of caring for the sick of Anchorage, Martha and her children began accommodating to their new frontier life. Harold, however, stayed with the family only briefly, sharing the drafty bedroom on the second floor with Paul before returning to Queen Anne High School in Seattle. He lived with his Aunt Nellie and Uncle Mike McLennan and, following graduation, secured an appointment to Annapolis through Alaska's representatives to Congress.

Paul, now alone in the bedroom at night, was sometimes frightened by the noises of the wind blowing through chinks in the cabin and by the flickering of downstairs gas lights and candles on the log walls of the staircase leading to the second floor. On June 21, 1916, the day of no night in Alaska, the boy had trouble sleeping at all and stayed awake imagining.

Paul soon made friends in the second grade classroom. One boy became a close enough companion to share a cigarette with the future professor of medicine—the only cigarette in a lifetime—behind the new hospital building constructed across Ship Creek in 1916. This hospital, thought at the time to be the largest and best equipped in the Territory, was completed in December of the Beesons' first year in Alaska and was two stories plus attic and basement, making it a big building of about sixteen thousand square feet. Constructed at a cost of thirty-five thousand dollars, the new hospital housed fifty patients and the office of now Chief Surgeon, John Beeson. The offices and a large, open ward were on the first floor while the operating room, kitchen and smaller wards occupied the second.

Shortly after this hospital opened, Paul and his parents moved into their new, more modern government-built house, Number 31. Dr. Beeson operated in the morning, saw patients in his office in the afternoons, and made house calls late in the day. His younger son often waved good-bye to him as he navigated the wooden boardwalk in front of their new house, black bag in hand, shouting back over his shoulder "I'm off to see a patient."

Although there was occasionally an Assistant Surgeon to help him, most of the operations in the Anchorage Hospital were done by John Beeson with an orderly acting as the anesthesiologist. Patients were put to sleep with ether administered drop after open drop by the orderly onto a mask at the surgeon's direction. When the blood became too blue during the course of a compound fracture's reduction, the removal of a breast, appendix, gall bladder or infected kidney, Dr. Beeson called for a slower rate of the drops. If the blood became so dark that the heart stopped or the patient ceased breathing, little could be done aside from comforting the survivors.

Judging from contemporary photographs taken in the operating room of the Nenana Hospital just south of Fairbanks, the room was spare. It contained a metal-legged operating table that did not go up or down, a large and cumbersome autoclave for sterilizing instruments, two sinks for scrubbing, a goose-necked lamp and several glass-door cabinets containing a sparse collection of surgical tools, all metal and reusable. The floor was linoleum. Most of the light in the room entered naturally, streaming in through large windows on two sides of the fifteen-by-twenty foot room. An ordinary white enamel bucket stood in a corner for disposal of the few items that were thrown away.

Dr. Beeson's continuing education during these years included trips to the Mayo Clinic, which sometimes occupied many weeks, including several days' travel in both directions. Dr. Charles Mayo, an outdoorsman, made the return journey to Alaska for a hunting trip on at least one occasion. However, the major influence on Dr. Beeson, and on all of the medical profession at that time, came not from the Mayo brothers in Rochester, Minnesota but from William Osler first in Philadelphia, then Baltimore and, by 1916, at Oxford, England.

Osler's textbook, *The Principles and Practice of Medicine*, first appeared in 1892 and was sold only by subscription. The authentic first edition was available cloth-bound for $5.50 or "half morocco" for $7.00, and is identified by a misspelling of *Gorgias* attached to a quotation from Plato facing the Contents page. A review in the June 18, 1892 *British Medical Journal* by Dr. Y.J. Pentland noted:

> . . . the announcement that Dr. Wm. Osler had a systematic work on general medicine in the press raised expectation that we might be presented with another real textbook . . . He has done such good work that the reader is prejudiced in his favor; we expect a masterly production . . . Dr. Osler has written throughout of modern pathology and of the most modern methods of clinical examination . . . [He] writes English—not one of his least merits. He has shown once more that the language of Emerson and of Longfellow is sufficiently full and expressive to permit any man, who knows what he wants to say and how to say it, to write so that he may be clearly understanded (sic). . . . (14)

Osler's text quickly dominated the market and, because it contained almost no references, his opinion alone was considered definitive on most medical subjects until the Second World War. It was to this book of Osler's that John Beeson turned for advice throughout his career in Alaska. It was the same Osler who was the final authority for both of his sons when they went to medical school at McGill, where the great clinician had finished his own medical education and joined the faculty.

In 1916, Osler was sixty-seven years old and ending his career as the Regius Professor of Medicine at Oxford. It was a career that had as simple a beginning as Paul Beeson's, when he was born on the frontier just north of Lake Ontario. Osler's early teachers, William Johnson and James Bovell, studied the work of the great categorizers Linneaus, Lyell, Darwin and Wallace.

Even as a student William Osler was interested in observation and taxonomy. When he discovered *Trichina spiralis* in one of the cadavers used in his anatomy course he wrote in his journal, "All the men in the dissecting rooms, teachers included, 'saw' the little specks in the muscles: but I believe that I alone 'looked-at' them and observed them: no one trained in natural history could have failed to do so."(15) Later as a faculty member at McGill, he gave the same attention to vegetations on the heart valves of patients dead of endocarditis.

The nosology formulated in Osler's Textbook is the first systematic cataloging of human diseases; its usefulness was immediately recognized by his readers. John Beeson would certainly have consulted his copy of Osler when he helped obtain and distribute the antitoxin used to contain a diphtheria epidemic that broke out in Nome in January, 1925.(16)

The diphtheria outbreak was not the first time Dr. Beeson had been identified as a hero in Alaska. In January of 1921, popular Iditarod banker Claude Baker wired Anchorage seeking medical treatment for an undiagnosed and extreme illness. The *Anchorage Daily Times* of February 17 reported that this sickness was felt to have resulted from "an old injury received while serving as a guard on gold trains out of Iditarod. He was thrown some distance while holding the gee pole and received internal injuries."

Baker was trying to contact John Beeson who, although already widely known in Alaska as a skilled physician and surgeon, had gained further notoriety the previous summer when he judged the Anchorage Fair "baby show" with almost five hundred entrants, all of whom he had delivered himself.

On January 24, Dr. Beeson left Anchorage by the regular train with thirteen sled dogs and two experienced drivers. They took the "steel" to the end of the line at Nenana, about three hundred miles from Anchorage and seventy miles south of Fairbanks. Arriving about 11 PM, the party was met by a driver fruitlessly named "Scurvy Kid," and planned to go as far as possible in his sleigh. However, an accident forced them all into the forty-degree-below-zero weather to the dogsleds which they drove the remaining four hundred miles to Iditarod.

In all, John Beeson covered the five hundred and twelve miles from Nenana to Iditarod in about one hundred and thirty hours (five and a half days). Even today, using high-tech equipment and training, simply finishing the modern Iditarod dogsled race is respectable.

On February 28, 1921, the *Anchorage Daily Times* reported that "Claude Baker is now on the road to recovery and the name Dr. J.B. Beeson is inscribed among the historical records of the Yukon." Recovery was not to be the outcome, however. Dr. Beeson had undertaken the trip expecting to discover a pleural empyema which he anticipated treating with rib resection and open drainage. He may have known that, almost exactly two years earlier, Osler had died in 1919 at Oxford of just such an empyema following an operation at the old Radcliffe Infirmary.

However, when he finally reached Baker's bedside he found, on physical examination alone, that the banker had advanced pulmonary tuberculosis, a disease he knew well but could not treat. His patient died shortly after Dr. Beeson had returned home by way of a southern route around Mt. McKinley.

As the party left McGrath on the trip back, they were overtaken by Leonard Seppala, a famous Alaska musher and winner of the 1916 Nome Sweepstakes. He was returning with Major Gotwals from an inspection trip for the railroad along the Kuskokwim River. As Seppala later remembered that historic trip:

When we started out from McGrath, Doctor Beeson was on his way back to his patients at the hospital at Anchorage, and though they had a two days' start on us we caught up with them. The trail was through a narrow canyon. A creek ran through it which had frozen over, later drying up and leaving a covering of ice. The creek was steep and made a series of waterfalls under the ice, and as we drove along the sled would break through and fall from four to eight feet to the bottom, men and dogs going down together . . . we traveled down the Southern slope of the Alaska Range, known to be the heaviest snow belt in Alaska. We all traveled close together, taking turns in leading the way, and one man from each outfit going ahead on snowshoes or skis breaking trail. At Susitna Station the doctor found it necessary for him to continue on through the night, as he was in a hurry to get back to Anchorage. His dogs were pretty well used up by this time, so the Major offered to change teams with him, and I was to take the doctor through. The next day we arrived at Anchorage, making the last lap of what was known as the first relay drive ever undertaken in Alaska.(17)

For Anchorage Chief Surgeon John Beeson, not a young man at age 49, that was a " . . . twenty-eight day 'night call' in 1921 he considered just a professional duty. He charged a trivial fee [and] never considered it much of a deal."(18)

One month later, *The Seattle Times* reported on February 20 that "The first of what will become the Anchorage Classic dog-team race will be run on February 27....Among the features of the race will be the entry of Nellie Neil, Deadhorse, who will mush her own team of five malamutes, and is backing them heavily." More than sixty years later, Libby Riddles became the first woman musher to win the modern Iditarod dog-sled race over the one thousand and forty nine miles from Anchorage to Nome, following the first part of the trail John Beeson had driven in 1921. Today, as at the turn of the century, women are as durable as men in Alaska.

Martha Beeson did not return to the classroom after the birth of her children. There was little to distract her from the task of teaching her sons the Victorian manners of the day, and less to prevent them from absorbing these lessons. It was perhaps these personal traits of their mother, who was steadfast, gentle but firm and always fair, that shaped the basic characters of the two boys.

Harold and Paul certainly admired their slightly removed and often absent father, both for his dedication to the sick he tended and his prominence in the community, but their mother taught them consideration, diligence and responsibility to augment their native abilities. Although she maintained membership in the Episcopal Church and was President of the Women's Club (an organization associated with the woman's suffrage movement) both in Anchorage and then the State of Alaska, her principal interest was her husband and two sons.

With his brother away at school in Seattle, and later at Annapolis and Stanford, Paul advanced on his own through the local primary school, skipping the third grade because his teacher considered him exceptional. Often, there were only a few children to a grade and several grades to one classroom and teacher, so students were logically assigned according to their abilities. The teachers were of unusual scholarship and dedication, adventuresome men and women attracted to the rigor and excitement of the last American frontier.

There were few cars and no sort of public transportation, so it wasn't without effort that either the students or their teachers traveled to the school building. Paul often walked the mile or so each way, but in the winter he fashioned his own single dog sled by attaching his pet to a "flexible flyer" and mushing over the unplowed city streets.

Anchorage was then a company town, but the company was the federal government and although there was a feeling of isolation, the inhabitants all felt a sense of community and involvement in the biggest engineering endeavor since the building of the Panama Canal. The only news of life outside the immediate region came from travelers, telegraph or the *Anchorage Daily Times*. Without modern electronic distractions and urban interruptions, Paul's life focused on the big schoolhouse with its large gymnasium and up-to-date laboratory facilities for physics and chemistry. The main winter physical entertainment for the boys was playing basketball in the gym, but since there were no other schools to compete against, the thirteen students in his 1925 graduating class only played amongst themselves.

Occasionally however, Paul did get a peek at the larger world during his difficult trips to Seattle and one long stay in California. His brother had developed an unknown, disabling illness that lasted many weeks during his third year at Annapolis and, rather than repeat the entire year, he abandoned his naval career. He returned to Anchorage where he worked on a survey gang before transferring to Stanford in 1922.

Although Paul did not participate in the discussion with his parents, Martha Beeson decided to spend that winter in Palo Alto with both of her sons. She and Paul took the train one hundred and fourteen miles to Seward, and then a boat for at least seven days through the Inside Passage, stopping at Valdez, Juneau, Petersburg and Ketchikan. The old steamship had serviceable staterooms, each with bunk beds and a bathroom. The trip was both slow and compelling, passing by huge glaciers breaking off into the waters of the Alexander Archipelago, with pods of humpbacked whales often surfacing around the boat.

They arrived at the downtown Seattle waterfront and spent one night at the Atwood Hotel on First Avenue before resuming the rail trip to San Francisco the next morning. Once established in Palo Alto, Paul entered the tenth grade for a semester while Harold finished his junior year at Stanford.

Palo Alto was a sophisticated place and, of course in comparison to Anchorage, Northern California could have been New York or London. Rather than stay in one room visited by different teachers of each subject, the students at Palo Alto High School moved from room to room for their classes. Paul began to study French and was especially impressed by the worldliness and learning of that teacher.

Initially, Harold, Paul and their mother all lived together in an apartment on the Stanford campus near the President's House, but Harold quickly moved into a fraternity. This several-month stay in California expanded Paul's horizons beyond the long days and nights of Anchorage.

The summer after he and his mother returned to Alaska, Paul worked at the local bank. He made occasional bicycle trips with his friends several miles out of town on dirt roads to swim at Lake Spenard, a site now located well within the city, just north of the Anchorage International Airport. They played baseball in vacant city lots.

When they could afford it they went to the Empress Theatre on Forth Avenue. This three story clapboard building opened its front door and large windows onto a boardwalk and dirt street. The big painted Empress Theatre sign stuck out from the third floor between smaller ones announcing an ice cream parlor on one side and a fledgling general store called The Bon Marche on the other. Paul and his friends could listen to band music, watch stage productions and, when it changed on Thursdays, see a silent movie in this theater.

The children were as excited as the adults in the summer of 1923 when President Warren Harding spoke from a covered platform in Anchorage and two days later traveled to Nenana to drive the golden spike into the last rail of the Alaska Railroad. It may have been the elderly President's exertion in doing this on the hot Sunday in July that caused his myocardial infarction (called acute indigestion at the time) and subsequent death in San Francisco during the return trip. Angina was often misinterpreted as gastric in origin during this time, and John Beeson, relying on Osler who seems not to have understood angina either, sometimes made the same error.

On most ordinary evenings, Paul had dinner with both parents before finishing his school work. He was sometimes interrupted when the newly-installed telephone rang and his father instructed a nurse at the hospital a few hundred yards away to give one of his patients "a sixth of morphine." Although he admired his physician father, Paul was, at this point, neither pushed by John Beeson nor pulled by his brother Harold, already in medical school at McGill, to become a doctor. (It may have been, however, that the medical profession was suggested more than once to both boys by their practical and convincing mother.)

In 1925, at the age of sixteen, Paul graduated from the Anchorage High School and made plans to travel back to Seattle to enter the University of Washington, for study in Business Administration.

CHAPTER 2

> The hardest conviction to get into the mind of a beginner is that the education upon which he is engaged is not a college course, not a medical course, but a life course, ending only with death, for which the work of a few years under teachers is but a preparation . . . You can all become good students, a few may become great students, and now and again one of you will be found who does easily and well what others cannot do at all . . .
>
> William Osler, 1905(1)

Sometime during Paul's final year in high school, his mother announced that he would attend the University of Washington. Although he had not really considered becoming an undergraduate anywhere else, there was no discussion about this selection any more than there was doubt that she would accompany him for the first semester.

When they arrived in Seattle by rail and ship, the skyline of the city was dominated by the forty-two story L.C. Smith Building (now the Smith Tower), named in 1913 for an armaments entrepreneur who by then had beaten " . . . his firearms into a typewriter fortune big enough to finance skyscrapers."(2)

Martha Beeson found an apartment in the Wilsonian, a building that even now is a staid Victorian presence, just north of the campus on University Avenue. Bertha Landes, the temperance Mayor of Seattle at the time and one of the first women to be mayor of a major city in the United States, lived in the same building.

Constructing the Aurora Bridge (then called the George Washington Memorial Bridge), heavily promoted by Landes as a link to the Pacific Coast Highway, was still being debated in the State Legislature and a nine-hole golf course occupied the future site of the University's Magnuson Health Science Center. Seattle was a rapidly developing city and even though Paul had lived in Palo Alto while his brother was at Stanford, it was still disquieting for the not-yet-seventeen year old, small town Alaska boy to enter a university with six thousand students. He was glad to have his mother with him for advice.

Paul was registered in business administration because he had enjoyed his summer job at the First National Bank of Anchorage. He had, however, no real knowledge about what this curriculum would teach him. As he prepared to begin classes that September, his mother took him downtown to shop for clothes one overcast afternoon. While the trousers were being fitted, their salesman proudly offered that he was a recent graduate of the University with a degree in business administration. During the slow streetcar ride back to campus, Martha advised her son that, if a degree in business qualified the graduate for a clerk's job, then Paul should change his major to pre-med. He went to the Registrar that afternoon and entered into a course of study that followed that of his father and brother. Even many years later, he remained surprised that he had not thought to question such an enormous change in the direction of his life.

One of Martha Beeson's purposes in coming to Seattle, aside from making sure her young son was able to manage in his new surroundings, (and, one suspects, to encourage the move into pre-med) was to buy a car. During the fraternity rush parties that occupied the first weeks of the school year, Paul was a conspicuous freshman as he traveled from house to house in a new Hudson.

Once he had joined Delta Upsilon, some of his new fraternity brothers were more than a little disappointed when, at the end of the term, the automobile traveled back to Alaska by boat with the new "plebe's" mother. He was several times reminded of the vanished car during the foolish initiation rituals that kept him and his fraternity classmates awake for the week scrubbing floors and washing windows (but not swallowing goldfish). From that time until the end of his three years at the University, the male life of Delta Upsilon in the house at 1818 Northeast 45th Street was the center of Paul's society.

Even though his new brothers arranged a date with a pretty girl for a major holiday event at the Olympic Hotel in downtown that first year, the Alaskan was such a poor dancer that she found it necessary to spend most of the evening with upperclassmen. There were plenty of women around the co-ed campus, but perhaps because of this first experience, Paul preferred to play poker and drink. The prohibition-era beer was smuggled into their fraternity house by hoisting it with a rope to the upper stories and in through a back window.

Other time out of class or the library he spent almost entirely in the University District playing tennis or golf, going to the movies and occasional parties. There were few diversions downtown, no bridges across Lake Washington, and no reason even to look across it much less to take one of the "mosquito fleet" ferries to the tiny east side village of Bellevue.

Although Paul had done well in the Anchorage schools, there were very few other students to measure himself against in Alaska. He was therefore gratified when he scored in the upper five percent on an intelligence test given to the freshman class by the Psychology Department. A memo announcing this success was sent to the fraternity and posted in the living room by the same fellows who had been so disappointed when the Hudson had gone north with Paul's mother.

The new college man had classes in biology, chemistry, mathematics, English and French. His course of study was outlined by a pre-med faculty advisor, and once the decision had been made to trade business administration for medicine, the young student had little choice in his curriculum. Even though sciences were coming to dominate the pre-professional classes at universities like Washington, students were still expected to learn the Victorian humanities.

Such an education was promoted by William Osler, who had advised, "A physician may possess the science of Harvey and the art of Sydenham, and yet there may be lacking in him those finer qualities of heart and head which count for so much in life . . . by the neglect of the studies of the humanities, which has been far to general, the profession loses a very precious quality."(3)

At the beginning of his third year in college, Paul's parents moved back to Seattle, where Dr. Beeson again attempted to capitalize on his prominence in Anchorage and opened an office downtown. There was improved, more rapid travel between the two cities by the middle 1920s, and a significant number of his former patients had moved to Washington.

John and Martha rented a house just south of the Montlake Bridge on Shelby Street close to the University, which provided Paul and his formerly disappointed fraternity brothers occasional access to the much valued Hudson automobile. He remained living at the fraternity, though, and after only three years in college, began to receive letters from Harold in Montreal encouraging him to apply to the McGill Medical School.

McGill had a reputation for accepting students with this abbreviated undergraduate career, especially from the University of Washington. Frank Horsfall, son of a prominent Seattle surgeon and member of the crew team, was known to the Beeson family and had also gone to McGill; the idea appealed to Paul even though he was still only nineteen.

So it happened that a man who was to become full Professor of Medicine and Department Chair by the age of thirty-eight didn't graduate from college.

❖ ❖ ❖

As the stock market dove into disarray in 1929, John Beeson abandoned his second unsuccessful attempt to establish a medical practice in Seattle. Life was as chaotic in the Pacific Northwest as in the rest of the country, and John had not become prosperous enough in downtown Seattle to withstand the economic uncertainty, especially with two sons in medical school.

Fortunately for the Beeson family, it was just then that the general practitioner in Ketchikan died and the isolated town in the most Southeastern corner of Alaska required a versatile doctor. John was able to buy the practice, and he and Martha moved again to a small community where he would attend to essentially all of the inhabitants' health problems.

He was remarkably skilled at this type of practice, and is remembered by William "Handlogger" Jackson who, returning from winter travel in a small boat having survived a severe storm, fell sick with a fever of one hundred and four degrees. "Handlogger" and his wife didn't have money for the hospital stay immediately recommended by Dr. Beeson, and had to remain on the boat. There being little alternative other than no treatment, John agreed to come and make a house call every day. "And that he did. With the floats and the boats sheeted in ice and snow, he came down every day for eight days. Finally he said to Ruth, 'I think we did a good job to pull him through that one.' We always had a soft spot in our hearts for old silver-haired Dr. Beeson."(4) ("Handlogger" and Ruth might have been surprised to know that the "silver hair" was not John Beeson's own, but a toupee.)

In the fall of 1928, Paul boarded a train at the King Street Station near Pioneer Square in Seattle with his clothes and a few books to begin the three thousand mile trip to Montreal. At the end of four days, he was met by Harold who was about to start his final year as a medical student. His brother went out of his way to be good to Paul, giving up some of his prerogatives as an older student, and the two of them shared a dorm room in Strathcona Hall that year. Harold introduced his brother to the cosmopolitan city and to the mysterious workings of the medical school which, at that time, required five years to complete.

The first two years were entirely pre-clinical and included the study of anatomy, histology, pathology and bacteriology. Biochemistry was actually still organic chemistry, although the head of the department was the Nobel Prize winner J.B. Collip. The immunology of the day was simply a discussion of antigens and antibodies. Even the pharmacology course in the late 1920s was limited to a handful of compounds; there were no antibiotics and no chemotherapy for cancer. Molecular biology wasn't even a rumor.

The study of anatomy occupied much of Paul's first year. It was a stuffy affair overseen by an Englishman named Professor Whitnall, who wore a monocle and relied almost entirely on students studying their textbooks. The professor wandered around the dissecting room now and then, doing little enough, and doing nothing at all that was not removed and formal. Although he lectured occasionally, most of the teaching was done by volunteer instructors, usually young surgeons from Montreal General or the Royal Victoria hospitals.

Laboratory was conducted with four students standing around each cadaver, following the anatomy manual. Several days a week were spent in this large, completely open dissecting room saturated with the odor of formaldehyde which passed through the rubber aprons and into the clothing of the first year students, only two of them women and two others black. At night, the cadavers were covered with big sheets of canvas treated with a waterproofing material to keep the preparations from drying out.

Histology lectures were given by a practitioner who went through the textbook chapter by chapter, just keeping ahead of his students. Since all the material was from the book, Paul memorized enough of this purely descriptive science to lead the class on the first examination. He did not lead in anything else, however, until the fourth year, when he shared the top prize for internal medicine.

"The instruction in pre-clinical subjects was pretty standard," remembered Professor Beeson years later while discussing changes in medical education with students at the University of Washington School of Medicine, "with lectures, lab exercises, and textbook assignments. I have little recollection of our teachers referring to recent research, and certainly no recollection that they encouraged us to look at current journals."(5)

Although students were aware that some of their professors went off and did something in offices or laboratories when they weren't teaching, especially those in the biochemistry and pharmacology departments, they weren't exactly sure what it was. In truth, research, and the money to do research, was limited to what was left over in departmental budgets. Though a few private research institutes existed, there were no meaningful government funding sources; significant extra-mural grants from agencies like the National Institutes of Health did not begin until after World War II.

Paul encountered the work of Osler that first year. Trying to figure out his way around the medical school, he discovered the legacy of Osler during his exploration of the medical library shortly after classes began. Although he had a huge collection of books, and left prized volumes to certain people and institutions, Osler had willed part of his library to McGill. The collection was housed in a special section of the medical library where it was carefully overseen by his nephew, the unassuming William Francis.

Without knowing exactly where they were, or the real significance of Osler, Paul and a classmate wandered one morning into this section of the library. Mr. Francis came out to greet them, eager to stimulate interest in the great man's books. This frightened the two first-year students so badly that they backed out of the librarian's reach and fled as quickly as possible, never to return.

Had they stopped, they would have found Sir William's "Bed-side library for medical students" and the following admonishment: "A liberal education may be had for a very slight cost of time and money. . . . Before going to sleep read for half an hour, and in the morning have a book open on your dressing table. You will be surprised to find how much can be accomplished in the course of a year. I have put down a list of ten books which you may make close friends."(6) The list demonstrates Osler's classical tastes and includes The Old and New Testament, Shakespeare, Montaigne, Plutarch's *Lives*, Marcus Aurelius, Epictetus, *Religio Medici, Don Quixote*, Emerson and Oliver Wendell Holmes.

In the late spring of 1929, Harold Beeson was awarded his M.D. from McGill and was elected to the medical honorary society, Alpha Omega Alpha. Paul had become used to fraternity life as an undergraduate and, with his brother an intern in surgery, joined the Alpha Kappa Kappa medical fraternity. He moved into their house near the Royal Victoria Hospital on a hill looking over Montreal, where Harold was to be a house officer. The notable Frank Horsfall from Seattle and the University of Washington was already a member, and Paul's admiration for the older student probably influenced his decision.

As had been the case in Seattle, the fraternity became the focus of Beeson's social life. On weekends, he played poker with the other medical students. They made their own version of "bathtub" gin from whatever alcohol they could collect and seasoned it with juniper berries; the product was inauthentic but produced the desired result.

He began to date some of the nurses, and was especially fond of Helen Misener who had come to Montreal from Nova Scotia. As the campus was near St. Catherine Street, the main road of the town, Paul often took Miss Misener to tea at the elegant Mount Royal Hotel on St. Catherine. But apart from golf, tennis, and occasionally going to tea, social life was secondary to studies, which in the second year included an intensive focus on pathology, pharmacology and physiology.

The Professor of Pathology was a German man named Oertel who held a conference each Saturday morning based on the gross findings at autopsies done the prior week. Although these lectures were still not clinical medicine, and the dissections of gross pathology bore a certain similarity to gross anatomy, it was still a step closer to the wards. This pleased the more confident second-year medical student, anxious to be allowed access to real patients.

An elementary form of pharmacology was also taught; the observed (but not chemically understood) actions of drugs could be learned in addition to indications for their uses and possible side effects. A scientific basis for pharmacological therapeutics was, by this time, widely accepted by the public. However, the battle to distinguish drug therapy with a scientific basis from the claims of patent medicine companies had been hard fought by the American Medical Association, and not easily won.

Probably the most famous investigation of the drug industry in American history began appearing in *Collier's Weekly* in October 1905. In two series—the first on patent medicines, the second on medical quacks—the muckraking reporter Samuel Hopkins Adams explored the cynical deceptions of medicine makers and medicine men who sold dangerous and addictive drugs. Adams attacked 264 individuals and companies by name, giving detailed evidence, such as laboratory reports showing drugs were worthless and burial notices of people who gave testimonials to drug companies and then died from the diseases that were supposed to have been cured....The message underlying the exposes was that commercial interests were dangerous to health and that physicians had to be trusted.(7)

A pharmacology textbook contemporary with the investigation conducted largely in the press but supported by the AMA, listed oxidizing germicides, metals and their salts, acids, alkalis, salts, halogen and aromatic compounds under the heading titled "Drugs acting locally on micro-organisms."(8)

In that same volume there was but a single entry under the heading "Drugs acting on the respiratory mucous membranes"— expectorants. This list of drugs to make patients cough did include potassium iodide, but also such curious remedies as Balsam of Tolu, strychnine, onion, garlic, licorice, sulphur, turpentine, tar and oil of Scotch fir. These exotic substances seem more likely to have been compounded either for cooking or murder than for curing respiratory illnesses, but perhaps they worked better than the patent medicines which always contained a large percentage of alcohol and sometimes opium or cocaine.

Even in the early editions of Russell Cecil's textbook, which began to take over the market about the time of World War II, the brief section on treatment of pneumococcal pneumonia is limited to a discussion of serum therapy and, later, sulfonamides. Treatment remained a small part of the topic, however, which was still limited to a description of the signs, symptoms, epidemiology, and course of the illness.(9)

By the time Beeson began his study of pharmacology in 1929, patients had acquired a trust in their physicians to provide them with drugs that had at least a theoretical relationship to their diseases. And some of the new drugs did work a little: intravenous arsenical and iodide for syphilis, and quinine for malaria. In addition, by about 1930, Avery's exquisitely-designed experiments resulted in the production of type-specific serum (antibodies) for the treatment of pneumococcal pneumonia.(10) Paul himself had been given a German drug called Urotropin, a mixture of formaldehyde and ammonia, by his father for the treatment of the recurrent urinary tract infections that bothered him from childhood to middle life.

Physiology was a well understood subject, and approached clinical medicine closely enough to be of great interest to the second-year students, all of whom longed for the wards and living and dying patients. An academic from Philadelphia, Chevalier Jackson, gave a demonstration one afternoon in the huge amphitheater used for the physiology lectures, on the use of the recently perfected rigid bronchoscope. The second-year students were thrilled by his description of the inside of the normal bronchial tree, and the pathology that could be discovered with this splendid new diagnostic tool. At meals and in the living room of the medical fraternity:

> . . . conversation was usually about clinical experiences and the adventures of upper classmen on the wards of the Royal Victoria or the Montreal General. We members of the first and second years were so interested in these tales. Medical students did not wear white coats in the teaching hospitals, but carried stethoscopes in visible locations in their jacket pockets. How we yearned for the time when we could sport that badge! The senior students kept recounting anecdotes about the clinical teachers, using the nicknames that other clinical teachers used. One of the surgeons, a burly figure, was called "Buck" Keenan, and we felt we knew Buck before we ever saw him. We could hardly wait to begin our clinical work.(11)

Between school years, Beeson returned to his parents' house by train, first in Seattle where he had a summer job selling coal door to door. This approach wasn't very profitable, but his income improved the next summer in Ketchikan when he was hired as a U.S. customs officer aboard a Canadian oil tanker traveling to salmon fisheries between Ketchikan and Petersburg. His duties were to do absolutely nothing; he stood in the wheelhouse talking to the navigator much of the time. He made several hundred dollars those few months, a good income for a summer job at the time.

Though Paul turned all this money over to his father, as he was packing to get on the train and travel back to Montreal, he asked him (a little uncharacteristically) to increase his monthly allowance by one ninth of the total amount. As the older man was already paying four hundred dollars a year tuition in addition to the allowance plus money for travel and books, he was slightly surprised by the request. These were significant costs during the depression. However, because of the still-strong fishing economy, Southeastern Alaska fared better than the continental United States. John and Martha were comfortable in their Ketchikan apartment; the tireless Dr. Beeson was again making a good living as the lone physician for about three thousand people. Paul received the increase in allowance and began the five day trip, first by boat back to Vancouver, and then on the Canadian Pacific Railroad across Canada to Montreal and to the beginning of his career in clinical medicine.

In the third year of medical school at McGill, the world of outpatient clinics and wards stocked with real patients opened to the students. Paul and his classmates began to dangle their new stethoscopes conspicuously from their jacket pockets as they walked from campus to the "Royal Vic" or trekked the three miles across town to Montreal General, only occasionally riding the streetcar.

There still existed a huge social gulf between the students, doctors and the "charity patients" who were cared for in these institutions. The introduction to clinical medicine occurred in the outpatient clinics and on the large, open wards of the teaching hospitals without the benefit of formal instruction in history-taking or physical diagnosis. The younger students learned from the older ones, and from house officers like Harold who was becoming a surgeon. None of the faculty was likely to remind the twenty-four year olds that these patients were individuals with important life stories that influenced their diseases; the illnesses were the focus of study, not the patients. Rounds were conducted entirely on the open wards where beds were separated only by white curtains that could be pulled closed during physical examinations. The students learned to percuss the chest and listen to the lungs with their brand new stethoscopes. They could auscultate, palpate and observe, but the curtained-off bed offered no privacy for conversation had anyone thought to have one.

The hour long rounds were supervised by a junior attending physician who had collected the cases to be seen, and included the participation of house staff. Students then practiced their new skills on each other at home or in the fraternity house, but never on the patients hospitalized on the private service at the Royal Victoria. They were forbidden to enter these wards.

Volumes of information about the nature of diseases were written by 1930, but there was still little to be done about most of them. Rheumatic fever was known to be caused by streptococcus, though no one had any idea how to prevent its occurrence. The exciting discovery of air cholecystography had been made in St. Louis, pyelograms could be done, and chest x-rays saw TB, but treatments for illness of the organs remained primarily surgical if at all.

Paul White, a cardiologist from Massachusetts General Hospital who was later to become President Eisenhower's personal physician, lectured on his own series of five hundred cases of myocardial infarction. An astonished McGill audience was surprised that such a young man had seen so many cases of this one entity. Dr. White promoted treatment of cardiac failure by oxygen and rest, but also advocated the use of digitalis and mercury diuretics. These recommendations departed from Osler who had suggested that, in the management of progressive heart failure, "Alcohol is here our mainstay and can be given freely. Strychnine is most useful and may be given hypodermically in full doses. Whether digitalis is indicated in the failing heart of fevers is not yet settled. Personally, I am by no means convinced that it does good."(12)

These clinical introductions were the focus of conversation for the students as they met for meals or walked together between classes and hospitals. Sometimes there was disapproval of what a certain teacher had said or done, but most of the time they discussed the interesting episodes of the hospital day and were excited about becoming doctors. A few of the students were eager to put on the pants and short white coats worn by house staff, but many more simply wished to finish their basic medical training and start a practice.

Medical students had confidence that their instructors were teaching them everything they needed to know in order to treat diseases. In addition to the ward rounds, instruction was given in:

> . . . an avalanche of lectures, plus clinical teaching in large amphitheaters. The fourth year was devoted almost exclusively to formal lectures—averaging five hours per day. We took extensive notes and studied these notes, along with textbooks, at night. Dr. Meakins, Professor of Medicine at the Royal Victoria, gave us a weekly teaching session, in which a patient was brought to the amphitheater. Nearly always at some point he would suggest that we read certain pages in the Osler textbook in connection with that case. The implication was clear that the corpus of clinical information was established, and we just needed to learn that to prepare ourselves for a lifetime in the profession.(13)

In medicine, pathology and surgery the eleventh edition of Osler's text remained the final authority on almost every subject. Beeson, and most of his fellows, carefully underlined the passages of the text that seemed most significant to those with little experience; the result was a text largely underlined. The inside front cover of Beeson's copy of this 1931 edition is further annotated with an outline of subjects the student found either especially interesting or especially difficult to remember. All of these subjects were of importance to Paul, who at this point anticipated a life in general practice with his father and brother.

Harold finished his two years of surgical internship at the Royal Victoria and obtained a fellowship in urology at the University of Pennsylvania Hospital. He moved to Philadelphia in the summer of 1930, starting two more years of specialty training. During the second year of this instruction he went to see the Dean, William Pepper.

The Pepper family had for many years been in charge of the Medical School at this university, and "It is said of [William] Pepper that, with great dignity but conveying the impression of having no time to spare, he would enter the classroom while taking off his gloves and coat, and immediately begin a brilliant discourse on some topic, not always related to his prescribed subject."(14)

That day he did have time for Harold, however, who must have favorably impressed the Dean, because when Dr. Beeson mentioned that his brother Paul was in the final year at McGill and looking for an internship, William Pepper responded, "Fine, we'll make him our first choice when we start to pick our class." Indeed, the January 25, 1933 minutes of the Board of Managers of the Hospital of the University of Pennsylvania announce the selection of Paul Beeson along with thirteen other men and Miss Jean McAlister to be interns beginning July 1, 1933. There was no matching plan; things were arranged.

In Montreal, Paul and his classmates, including the extraordinary Charles Drew—a black, star student who was later responsible for helping to establish blood banking while at Columbia—were clerking on the wards. Their attendings were largely non-salaried practitioners who spent time with the students teaching them physical examination and the few things that were then possible for aiding diagnosis. They sometimes drew blood using dulled needles that were routinely reground in the basement of the hospital and then reused until too short for further service. Syringes were made of glass.

As a final year student, Paul was now the one admired by his younger fraternity brothers because of his ease of access to the mysterious world of the hospital. One Sunday morning he gave in to his temptation to take four of them on his rounds. This was, of course, forbidden. They passed from bed to curtained-off bed, the senior student doctor not even nodding a greeting to the patients, but simply telling the outline of each diagnosis and treatment plan. In remembering this story long after, Beeson, still chagrined by his own behavior and the younger students' attitudes, recalled:

> Afterward one of them spoke admiringly about my lack of embarrassment in talking about a person within his hearing, and I felt a glow of pride. . . . As I look back, I feel that our teachers, and we medical students, considered ourselves members of a different social class. . . . Indeed [we] almost ignored the patient as a person, acting as though the patient was simply a specimen for teaching. . . . These charity patients were not paying anything, and we felt that they were lucky to be in the care of Montreal's most respected doctors. I am sure the situation was the same in the teaching hospitals of the U.S.—most of them at that time being large county hospitals such as Bellevue, Philadelphia General, Boston City, Cook County, Charity.(15)

Outpatient departments were conducted in a similar impersonal manner. The non-paying patients came from around the city to clinics where they could be seen without appointment after waiting for hours in a room filled with wooden benches. Eventually, their names were shouted out by house officers or students from the doors of small rooms where a history was taken and an examination conducted.

While the medical students became more and more expert at these tasks, there was often little treatment to offer after the history and physical were done. As therapies have improved over the intervening sixty-five years, so, one hopes, have the attitudes of students and young doctors toward caring for sick people with public financing. Certainly in the practice of obtaining consent from patients entering clinical research protocols, the ethics of study design now reflect a more responsible position, demanding that patients are carefully informed about the goals and risks of their participation. Such ideas were not part of the ethos in medical education during the 1930s.

Still planning on a career in general practice like most of his classmates, Beeson paid special attention to the final year rotations in obstetrics and surgery. The senior students found this an especially exciting month during which they were allowed to spend hours waiting with the pregnant women on the OB ward for deliveries.

Once in a while, especially late at night, medical students were permitted to deliver a baby with an attending to monitor them as they were actually "doing something." In the operating room they usually suffered the same fate as do most current students and more junior residents in the surgical specialties—they held retractors. Unscrubbed classmates, watching from the high banked seats of the surgical amphitheater, always laughed when the least senior student was finally pushed completely out of the operative field by someone's shoulder, and left holding his retractor in the air. While Beeson was interested in the idea of surgery, even at this early stage he began to suspect that he was not skilled at the manual tasks required of a dexterous surgeon.

Blood banks did not become common until the late 1930s, making blood loss during surgery or from trauma an enormous hazard. This was one of the reasons that speed in the operating room was then considered an advantage. Giving a patient blood with no ready supply required finding potential donors. Since a proper match was found by trial and error, more than one donor was usually required.

During Paul's final surgery rotation, the surgery chief resident was capable of giving a patient a blood transfusion, an unheard of event for the students. They all watched carefully through the microscope as red cells from the patient were mixed with serum from each potential donor; if agglutination occurred on the slide, indicating an antigen-antibody reaction, that donor was excluded. After two days of searching, a match was finally obtained and the patient, who by this time needed it desperately, was transfused a unit of whole blood, which dripped slowly out of a glass bottle through brown surgical tubing attached to a re-sharpened needle. It was a major event, but not as remarkable to the students as some of the clinical experiments being undertaken by the recently arrived American Professor of Neurosurgery.

Wilder Penfield, the new Chief of Neurosurgery at the Montreal Neurological Institute, which was being established across the street from the Royal Victoria Hospital, was a much admired physician. Penfield was already well known as a student of the great English neurophysiologist Charles Sherrington, and was beginning his own work mapping the cerebral cortex of patients who were operated upon while awake for the treatment of epilepsy.(16) This feat, remarkable even at the end of the twentieth century, was considered nearly magical at its beginning.

Although Paul did not watch any of the hundreds of operations and intra-operative functional cerebral localization experiments done by Penfield in Montreal, Harold, who had both an interest in surgery and more mechanical skill, observed at least once. He reported his astonishment while watching the bone flap being removed and the brain stimulated electrically as the surgeon talked to his conscious patient, mapping out the homunculus for motor and language cortex. The Institute included a special operating room, designed by Penfield, with a gallery above and behind the surgeon allowing both electroencephalography and overhead photography of the awake cerebral cortex. Penfield, surrounded by earnest young residents wearing white cloth surgical caps and large masks, was able to discuss the case as it proceeded with the neurologist Herbert Jasper. Jasper was seated in the glassed-in observation room to Penfield's rear, recording the EEG.

A few of Paul's classmates had decided on specialty residencies, a term first used at Johns Hopkins to describe advanced training following an internship. This medical school was unique early in the century, and its curriculum characterized university control of medical training, a domination that came to completion by World War II.

> The significance of Johns Hopkins Medical School lay in the new relationships it established. It joined science and research more firmly to clinical hospital practice. . . . Hopkins also stood for a new synthesis of medicine and the larger culture—a union vividly represented by the two major figures at the school, William Welch and William Osler. Welch, who had done important work in pathology as a young man, and Osler, the great clinician, were both dedicated to research, but they were also broadly educated and had a lively interest in the history and traditions of their profession.(17)

As the third Dr. Beeson graduated from medical school, well placed in his class but without the distinction his brother had of election to AOA, he prepared to start his postgraduate education at the University of Pennsylvania Hospital as arranged by William Pepper and his brother. Technology was not only expanding in medicine by 1933; more rapid transportation was also possible. For the first time, Paul traveled not by train between Montreal and Philadelphia, but on a sloping, propeller-driven DC-3, and in July he began a two year rotating internship.

CHAPTER 3

My father took me along on house calls whenever I was
around the house, all through my childhood. . . . I'm
quite sure my father always hoped I would want to
become a doctor, and that must have been part of the
reason for taking me along. . . . But the general drift of
his conversation was intended to make clear to me, early
on, the aspect of medicine that troubled him most all
through his professional life; there were so many people needing help, and so little that he could do for any
of them.

Lewis Thomas, 1919(1)

By the time Paul's plane landed in Philadelphia late in June of
1933, his brother and father were already working together in
Wooster. Harold had learned about a general practice for sale
in Ohio during a poker game at Penn, just as he was completing his surgical training in urology. He was concerned about
how he was going to make a living during the depression. As
the poker chips were being collected, one of the other residents
mentioned that his uncle, a doctor in Wooster, had been killed
in an automobile accident and that his practice was being offered
for sale. Harold had considered joining his father in Alaska, but
Ketchikan was too small to support two general practitioners
in any case, and Harold was interested in urological surgery
which required a much bigger patient population.

John and Martha were firmly in middle life, and anxious to leave Alaska. With John's capital and Harold's enthusiasm the practice in Ohio was purchased. As his mother and father made ready to leave Alaska for the final time, Harold moved to Wooster and opened the new office.

Just before leaving Penn, Harold married Mary Leigh Hodges, a nurse who had trained at Johns Hopkins. The young couple packed the bride's Model T Ford and left the cosmopolitan city of Philadelphia for the small town life and corn fields of North Central Ohio. The groom's parents joined them three months later.

In another year, the youngest Dr. Beeson was hard at work as a rotating intern at the Hospital of the University of Pennsylvania. He anticipated joining the family medical practice when he finished.

Dr. Paul Beeson moved into the intern's quarters of the hospital and didn't leave very often for the next two years. This was really a suite of rooms which provided individual sleeping arrangements for each of the fourteen new graduates, including the rarity of one woman. All of the interns were unmarried, like the great majority of medical students and even the more senior residents, so they essentially lived in the hospital. Their quarters included a private dining room where they were served their meals, and a common room where they could play chess and backgammon. Laundry and maid service were provided.

Jean McAlister lived there too, in what must have been an atmosphere not unlike Paul's previous fraternities, making it perhaps a little difficult for her. But she was accepted by her fellow interns and felt comfortable with them at meals and games as well as on the wards.

They took up their duties immediately. In the first year, they were assigned to the specialty wards in six two-month rotations including obstetrics, neurology, radiology, and pediatrics but to none of the sub-specialties which were later to become dominant. Infectious disease was a term used to describe a patient's illness, not an entire discipline.

In addition to "clerking" their newly admitted patients, that is, obtaining the history and doing an initial physical examination, the interns were responsible for the routine basic laboratory tests. Such tests had to be done by hand before the development of automated cell counters and flame ion detectors. They became proficient at urinalysis and complete blood count, learning to differentiate a polymorphonuclear cell from a lymphocyte, and to measure the specific gravity of urine, in the small, often untidy intern laboratories attached to each ward.

Professor Beeson later recalled, "It was a monastic sort of life, but we were happy, spending leisure time reading, playing cards, and talking medicine. I don't recall any use of the hospital's medical library, and certainly none of us subscribed to a journal."(2)

Nurses never started intravenous lines, and there was no such thing as an "IV team." These tasks were part of the province of the interns. While it is true that they were employed as cheap labor by the University, it never occurred to them that they did not profit more than they suffered.

During a gynecological procedure early in this first year, Beeson was summoned to the operating room where an arm had been exposed from under the drapes. It was still not "routine" for patients undergoing operations to begin the procedure with an IV in place since very often there was nothing to be given through it. Furthermore, the clinical importance of fluid balance and electrolytes was not yet well understood as Donald Van Slyke and John Peters had yet to publish methods allowing rapid and accurate clinical chemistry determinations to be performed in hospital laboratories.(3)

This particular patient in the operating room did need an IV however, probably for blood transfusion, and it was the intern's chore to start it. After Beeson's first three or four shaking stabs into the anticubital fossa with the often-used and blunted needle, the nurses behind him began to murmur disapproval, causing the young intern's tremor to become even worse.(4) Eventually, Paul succeeded and glucose and saline locally manufactured in the hospital central supply unit, were running into the patient through the difficult-to-sterilize brown rubber surgical tubing. However, the notice taken by the nurses of his inability had embarrassed the intern.

The faculty available to the house staff were a collection similar to the teachers at McGill. There were a few full-time salaried professors of medicine (O.H.P. Pepper, William's brother, was Chief of Medicine) and surgery, and a part-time faculty of leading practitioners in Philadelphia. They attended not only on the general medical and surgical wards but did all the teaching of the specialties.

This volunteer service was provided not only out of a sense of obligation to the community—certainly part of the motivation—but also because of the prestige to be found in association with the medical school. There was also a desire for the continuing education inherent in the teaching of house staff and medical students. Such volunteerism was largely lost with the advent of all full-time faculty members in medical schools, many of whom became progressively more dependent on reimbursements from clinical work to fund their salaries and research.

The interns were expected to be on call for their assigned ward at all times. If they wished to leave, even for an errand or the rare night off, they were required to notify the hospital operator and sign out to one of the other interns to take their calls. Because they could not be contacted electronically at a distance, the responsible house officer had to be in the building, and was summoned by the operator over a public address system from which there was no escape.

Most of the work they were called upon to do was mundane, described even then by the interns and residents as "scut." Not many of the young doctors appreciated the few, short strides that had been taken in recognition of illnesses and, more importantly, in treatments. Like most medical students and interns, they accepted the body of knowledge available to them as a given.

Over the preceding decade, liver extract (vitamin B-12) had been discovered to cure pernicious anemia and, thanks in part to Dr. Collip, Beeson's biochemistry professor at McGill, insulin had been purified for the treatment of diabetes. The electrocardiogram was in common usage, heart disease was better understood, and the term myocardial infarction had replaced Osler's usage of coronary thrombosis or occlusion; "heart attack" and angina were clinically recognized by most practitioners.

On the other hand, there were still no practical methods for determining serum sodium or potassium, the most common and fundamentally important of the electrolytes, much less calcium or magnesium. There was no way of obtaining measurements of blood gases. Neither hormones nor drugs were measurable in serum. These interns had no renal dialysis to suggest, no cardioversion or pacemakers to provide, no antibiotics, oral diuretics or chemotherapeutics to give. They did not even have useful drug therapy for hypertension or cardiac arrhythmia.

When their inabilities to intervene were exposed, these shortcomings were often simply camouflaged. On ward rounds one morning with one of the city's leading gynecologists, Beeson and the attending physician visited a patient who seemed unhappy. "Dr. Keene," she said miserably, "I've seen my chart and it says I have inoperable cancer." Without stopping to discuss the matter "He responded smoothly, 'That's fine . . . it means you won't have to have an operation,' and we all moved on."(5) Such an attitude was not atypical in 1934, and forthright answers to such patient inquiries were not regularly given for several more decades.

Because there were so few treatments to provide, so little to actually do for the sick who were hospitalized for long periods, the intern's work was not as exhausting as it was to become.

Each intern made morning rounds with the attending physicians, discussed the nature of their patients' illnesses, and made decisions about what little could be done to increase their chances for recovery. Sedatives were given, as well as laxatives, and narcotics for the easing of pain; digitalis leaf and the xanthenes were known. One patient on the University Hospital general medicine ward with bacterial endocarditis was provided the frightening treatment of intravenous acriflavine, an antiseptic, while another with the same condition was treated with radiation to the affected valve. Even giving IV saline or glucose was considered modern therapy.

Beeson did begin to notice a peculiar consequence of patients receiving intravenous solutions while he was an intern; they often developed chills and fever soon after treatment. He returned to this observation later in his training, and his research into the origins of fever became his most important contributions to clinical investigation.

The second year of the internship was spent on the general surgical and medical wards, but daily life was much the same. Out of his twenty-five dollar a month salary, Beeson managed to save one hundred and fifty dollars to buy an old car, which more often than not was left parked on the hospital grounds. On some occasions he found time to invite one of the nurses from among the young women in the Nursing School out to the movies, but rarely. Most of the year was spent in an effort to acquire enough practical experience so that he could be a useful partner to his father and brother when he joined the family medical practice in Wooster.

◆ ◆ ◆

In the summer of 1935, Paul Beeson drove his old Buick coupe through the Pennsylvania Dutch country of Lancaster County to Pittsburgh, then south into what he assumed would be a lifetime of general practice in Wooster. It was a town in the North Central farming country of Ohio not sixty miles from where his grandfather Bruce had found Hannah Binford, Paul's grand-mother, on a Quaker farm. He moved in with his parents, oddly enough just across the street from a young man named James Neal whom he would come to know much later under differ-ent circumstances.

When John Beeson arrived in Wooster, he gave up the toupee recommended by his wife while they lived in Alaska. Both Martha and the Ohio patients accommodated to the baldness that had never bothered John. He continued to wear a coat and tie every day, as did his sons, when they made morning house calls and then went to the original office they inherited from their predecessor in the Peoples Savings and Loan Building.

Wooster was a small town of perhaps twelve thousand peo-ple, home of the State Agricultural Station and the hub of com-merce for the local farming community. There were seven or eight other doctors in town, all generalists, including another group which became the great rival of the Beeson family. John Beeson was recognized as a man of vast experience and skill at relatively sophisticated surgery. He was accustomed to being on his own, which may have contributed to this feeling of com-petition. Harold, newly graduated from a major teaching pro-gram in surgery and with about as much academic training as could then be acquired, was anxious for work. He had a sur-geon's personality, outgoing and certain.

Much of the most effective treatment in 1935 was still sur-gical, and the Beeson group, without their own hospital or oper-ating room at this point, had to share a hospital owned by the other group. This did not work out well; although relations were gentlemanly, they were not cordial. On occasional after-noons when the senior Dr. Beeson and his sons played golf on the same course with the owners of this hospital, they did not play together and only nodded politely as they passed each other on the fairway.

Into this environment Paul entered with a basic medical education and some skill at treating hospitalized patients, but little confidence in his surgical abilities. John and Harold were already well established and, at the age of twenty-six, the youngest Dr. Beeson found himself the last of the family to be requested by new patients. "I'd like to see one of the older doctors," was often an appeal by patients as they checked into the reception desk, especially if they had a problem that might require an operation.

John and Harold were busy delivering babies, fixing hernias, taking out gall bladders and setting fractures. While Paul assisted at many of these procedures, he did not do them himself. More often he spent the late morning and afternoon in conversations with middle-aged and elderly patients about their discomforts, worries and dissatisfactions. He must have been successful at this kind of practice, because many of these patients kept returning. The fee for consulting one of the Beesons in their office during the day was two dollars. House calls were three dollars, unless it was after hours when the rate increased to five dollars a visit.

Several months after Paul arrived in Ohio, it became clear that the shared arrangement of surgical space with the other group of Wooster doctors would not be satisfactory. A new Beeson Clinic was built on North Market Street. It contained a central waiting room inside the entry and, behind that, offices in three corners of the building. John and Harold occupied the front two and Paul was in the one at the rear. In the fourth corner was a minor operating room, and in the center were an x-ray machine and fluoroscope. During the day there was often a technician to do simple lab work and take x-rays, but after hours the doctors did these tasks themselves.

Adjacent to the clinic they built a small hospital: a few patient beds plus an operating room and a delivery room. Dr. Cutright, the wife of a senior man at the Agricultural Station, came to this hospital in the mornings to give the anesthesia, still open drop ether.

Paul's principal responsibility outside of seeing his clinic patients was to assist in the operating room, make post-operative rounds and take much of the night call. Since his father and brother did all of the major surgery and wished to be rested in the morning for scheduled operations, Paul got up more often than the elder two and cared for patients after hours.

One such evening, a young man brought his wife to the clinic for treatment of a laceration. With her husband looking on, Paul began what he found the tedious job of sewing up the cut arm; his hand began to tremble and the husband became more and more anxious and unhappy. So did Paul, remembering the same kind of problem in the operating room at Penn.

Over the next two years, Beeson did learn practical medicine and surgery from watching his father and brother. They subscribed to *The Journal of the American Medical Association* and *The Ohio State Medical Journal*. One of these publications brought to rural Ohio the discovery of the sulfonamides, the first significant medical treatment for infection. This family of antibiotics was discovered in England in the 1930s, and Paul and Harold drove to Cleveland one evening to hear Leonard Colebrook from London describe successful experimental treatment of patients with puerperal infection using this exciting new drug. On the drive back to Wooster, both of them agreed that something very important had occurred in medicine.

Yet for Paul there remained his lack of ability in surgery and obstetrics. In the early morning hours on-call for the family, he was summoned to the hospital by the night nurse. She was looking after a woman whose baby John Beeson had delivered a few days before by cesarean section. The patient's name was Krause and her husband was a senior scientist at the Agricultural Station. The Krause and Beeson families were friends, and Mrs. Krause's difficult pregnancy had been of concern to all the Beeson doctors. She had developed intractable vomiting of pregnancy, didn't eat much and her nutrition had been so poor that she had negative nitrogen balance.

Paul entered the darkened room knowing that something

was terribly wrong, but he was not prepared for what he found. As he lifted off the top blanket, he discovered the contents of her peritoneum spilled out on the bed sheets. He had no idea what to do. Immediately he rushed to the phone, woke his father and then assisted the older man as he repaired the dehisced wound. Miraculously, she did not develop peritonitis, then associated with an almost fifty percent mortality rate, and recovered so completely that she was able to dance with Paul at a country club party three months later.

More than anything else, this late-night experience of helplessness on Paul's part convinced the three partners that he should find a residency for further training in internal medicine and return to Wooster secure in and confined to that specialty.

He had learned things in Wooster, however. His experiences with elderly patients taught him to listen carefully to the complaints of the aged who recounted their stories of the problems that accumulate with years. He became more sympathetic to the suffering of individuals, and less focused on only the disease process as he had been taught in school.

Perhaps most especially, he found the value of honesty and sympathy in his intercourse with the sick. Although his father and brother sometimes didn't tell the entire truth to their patients, they seldom hid it completely as did many of their contemporaries. John Beeson was known for coming out of his small operating room, for example, and telling the patient's family exactly what he had found during the surgery. On more than one occasion, he asked a relative to put on a mask and look at a malignant tumor in the operating room. These were lessons Paul remembered when he moved to a different life.

About the time Mrs. Krause's wound dehisced, Robert Boggs, a classmate and fraternity brother from McGill, was driving through Wooster on his way home to Oregon. Boggs, who was completing a residency at the New York Hospital, stopped overnight with the Beeson family, breaking up his cross-country drive.

In the course of the good conversation that evening, the two young physicians shared their experiences since graduation from medical school. His friend told Paul of a possible opening on the private service at the hospital where he was just finishing. After he returned to New York a few weeks later, Boggs wrote Paul confirming that this position was available, encouraging him to inquire immediately. He wrote to apply and was accepted without interview.

The ease with which he obtained this position should have warned Beeson that it came with a few conditions, but it didn't. So, in the spring of 1937 at age 28, with two years of internship and two more of practical experience, he set out in a newer Buick and headed east to New York City. When he got to Manhattan, Paul parked in a garage under the hospital and moved into the house staff quarters on the twenty-third floor, overlooking the East River.

◆ ◆ ◆

There were two medical services at the New York Hospital, one academic, run by Cornell, and one which was a private service. If it was not apparent to Beeson before he left Ohio why the private service had a residency position so easily available, he soon discovered that the job was not a desirable one. Although he easily moved into the society of unmarried house officers who shared the top floor quarters, he didn't learn much internal medicine.

The private medical service was actually run by the important physicians of New York City such as Russell Cecil, who were the attendings. These well-known, busy doctors took little interest in the residents. They taught them nothing beyond scraps of information and largely ignored them. The attending physicians came to see their patients alone, didn't make rounds with the residents or send for them, but left them occasional notes telling them what they wished to have done. And this was the way the patients wanted it too, of course, as most of them were from wealthy New York society. They wished for as little contact as possible with doctors in general, and none, if it was avoidable, with the young residents on the house staff.

The resident's job was to do an admitting history and physical examination—basically to "clerk" the patient as Paul had done as a medical student—and to write notes in the chart occasionally. After a few weeks of this it became obvious that the experience was unlikely to profit him much more than discussions about anxiety with the elderly of Wooster.

After about four months of this mundane job, Beeson had a call from another old fraternity brother and friend from the University of Washington, the redoubtable Frank Horsfall. Frank had found a residency position at the prestigious Rockefeller Institute across the street from the New York Hospital. He knew that Beeson was there because Paul had been seeing New York City with some of the nurses at Rockefeller. Because of this he also knew that his recently arrived friend had a car, a commodity still in short supply for residents during the last days of the Depression. Horsfall was about to get married; he needed the Buick. "I wonder if I may borrow your car for my wedding trip, Paul?" he asked his friend. Of course Beeson agreed, and was immediately invited to the bachelor party scheduled to take place a few days later.

The party was held at a club on First Avenue, in a room half underground entered by going down a short flight of stairs. The only person Beeson knew in the room filled with young, beer drinking men was the prospective groom, but he was introduced and quickly fell into the progressively boisterous spirit of the evening.

After they had eaten, Paul was sitting at one of the tables when Horsfall left off chatting with an older man and sat down beside him, saying "Don't look up!" With both of the young doctors carefully examining their shoes, Horsfall told his friend that the older man he had just been talking to was Tom Rivers, the new Director of the Rockefeller Institute Hospital, who had replaced Rufus Cole early in 1937. Horsfall said, "Paul, how would you like to move across the street to Rockefeller? There is an opening for an assistant resident on Oswald Avery's pneumonia service!"

If Beeson knew who Avery was or, for that matter, who Dr. Rivers was, he didn't mention it. Instead, still gazing at the floor, he asked "Do you think my future from such a move would be better than from where I am now?" It was such a silly question that Horsfall could only say "yes." He took Beeson over and introduced him to Dr. Rivers. Frank Horsfall had no doubt promoted his younger fraternity brother in his prior conversation with Rivers, because without much hesitation the Director mentioned that the residency was available. The next morning, Paul awoke with a hangover and a new job.

He went the same day to see Mr. Hannon, the Superintendent of the New York Hospital, and resigned. Because the job on the private service was such a poor one, this was a common occurrence and the resignation was accepted without complaint. Paul obtained letters of recommendation from Montreal and Philadelphia, including one from Dr. D.S. Lewis, Acting Physician-in-Chief at the Royal Victoria Hospital, who assured Rivers that Beeson "showed a very intelligent interest in his work. He was one that I felt I always could rely upon. I have made inquiries about him from others here and they all recommend him very highly."

The application form Beeson filled out in July of 1937, titled "Information Desired For Staff Appointment", was only three pages: the first listed demographics and education, the second references and prior publications (left blank) and the third requested "Remarks" (also left blank).

Rivers applied for an assistant resident salary of twelve hundred dollars a year with the expectation that Beeson would start work at Rockefeller on October 1, 1937. Thus, by the same alchemy that had transmogrified the undergraduate Paul Beeson from a student of business into one of medicine, he was now transported from the routine life of a general medical resident in an undistinguished program, across 68th street to the rarefied science and academics of the Rockefeller Institute.

CHAPTER 4

Originally trained as a naturalist, Osler carried this attitude into medicine. Medical science meant to him not experimental science, but clinical information gathered at the bedside. . . . Despite Osler's prestige, the attitude toward medical research changed during his own lifetime. L.F. Barker, who succeeded him in the chair of medicine at [Hopkins], had first had a career in laboratory research. Rufus Cole, who was the first head of Barker's biological laboratory, took advantage of the situation to carry out experimental studies on typhoid fever. From the beginning, the Rockefeller Hospital had been "designed wholly for research in clinical medicine."

Rene Dubos, 1930(1)

Beeson had not been at the Rockefeller Institute very many days when he realized that he would never return to general practice in Wooster. The enthusiasm for his new experience soon began to communicate itself in letters to his family, and the change in his life became known without necessarily having been spoken.

Beeson had arrived just at the time of an exciting new discovery, and the Rockefeller dining room and halls were filled with conversation about the production of improved type-specific antipneumococcal serum for the treatment of pneumcoc-

cal pneumonia, a disease that for Osler had been both dangerous and untreatable. This paper, with Frank Horsfall as first
author, described a significant improvement in making type-
specific antibodies from rabbit rather than horse serum, a much
easier process.(2)

Although Beeson had done well in his academic life at the
University of Washington, McGill and the University of
Pennsylvania Hospital, he had not been the kind of genius that
was always first to grasp a difficult idea and find its application in another construct. Nor would hehave found these new
ideas himself. But now he was entering an environment where
these things did happen, and were all around him; Nobel Prize
winners including Karl Landsteiner, who discovered blood
types, and Alexis Carrel, the first modern cardiovascular surgeon, were likely to be part of the lunchroom discussions. He
immediately recognized this new possibility and, like all of the
opportunities that were placed in his path, he used it to his
advantage without ever using it to promote himself.

If there is one characteristic that summarizes Beeson's career,
it is the ability to recognize and then unselfishly utilize the possibilities made available to him. It is a trait well-defined by
Pasteur's famous quote, "Chance only favors the prepared
mind." Furthermore, it was just at this time when the practice
of medicine was entering a period of rapid change and expansion, which accelerated even faster after World War II for Beeson
and for the country. The age of Osler was ending.

Important as he was, and as dominant in the formulation
of clinical medicine and medical education in the early twentieth century, Osler's influence came at a price. He believed
throughout his life and preached to others that "the wards are
clinical laboratories utilized for the scientific study and treatment of disease."(3) He was first a naturalist, an observer and
categorizer, and his opinion that laboratory science was useful
in medicine only as an aid in specific diagnosis was shared by
much of the medical community during his lifetime. By July of

1937 at the Rockefeller Institute, however, that was certainly not the case.

Before the flowering of the National Institutes of Health just after World War II when research money and laboratories proliferated, the Rockefeller Institute was unique in the United States. From its founding in 1901, the principal mission of the Rockefeller Institute for Medical Research was only that, and the adjoining Rockefeller Hospital was intended solely for research in clinical medicine. Laboratories in the Institute building were used for research on the clinical problems presented by patients occupying the Hospital wards.

The Institute was funded by a philanthropic gift from John D. Rockefeller, who was guided by the opinion of his advisor in such matters, Frederick Gates. Mr. Gates, a Baptist minister and son of a physician, began his investigation into a possible gift for the construction of a medical institute in 1897. Though he was very impressed with Osler and his textbook, he recognized the failure of most available therapies, perhaps especially the futility in the treatment of infections.

Simon Flexner, brother of Abraham, was hired as the first Director and the Institute established its own temporary laboratories on Lexington Avenue in New York in 1903. By 1906 the Rockefeller Institute and Hospital had been built in Manhattan, and in 1908 Rufus Cole moved from Johns Hopkins Medical School to become Physician-in-Chief. Under Cole's direction, the main medical problems then afflicting society were investigated. Illnesses such as heart disease, syphilis, rheumatic fever, metabolism and renal disease as well as lobar pneumonia were studied.

Cole invited not only medical doctors, but also Ph.D.s to join the staff, including Donald Van Slyke, who took care of the patients with renal diseases and who later, along with John Peters at Yale, helped to quantify clinical chemistry. Although Van Slyke could not sign orders or prescribe drugs, he was clearly recognized as the expert in diseases of the kidney at

Rockefeller and directed the care of patients with nephritis and nephrosis on the wards.

On the other hand, Oswald Avery, nominally in charge of the pneumonia service, was an M.D. who behaved most of the time like a Ph.D., and rarely abandoned his lab for the wards. It was to the pneumonia service that Beeson was assigned and where he began to learn what it meant to do clinical and laboratory investigation.

> The Institute was not listed as an educational institution during the first half-century of its existence, but many young men, usually in their twenties, joined it to work under the guidance of its scientists. . . . Thus, although the Institute did not give academic degrees, it helped many young men and women to achieve superior preparation for a career in the field of science they themselves had selected. More importantly, perhaps, it provided an atmosphere in which they could discover themselves by being exposed to the wide range of scientific disciplines and intellectual attitudes represented in the laboratories, during staff conferences, and in the lunch room every day.(4)

By the time Dr. Rivers offered Paul Beeson a residency position in 1937, the small and nearly reclusive Oswald Avery (sometimes called by the residents "Fess," a diminutive for Professor) was firmly established as one of the principal scientists at Rockefeller. He had started his investigations in microbiology at the Hoagland Laboratory, a privately funded institution devoted to bacteriological research, and worked there between 1907 and 1913. He then moved to Rockefeller, continuing a life dedicated to research on the pneumococcus.

Since the introduction of antibiotic drugs about the time of World War II, first sulfonamides in the early 1930s and then penicillin, it is difficult to remember the impossible problem it was to treat pneumonia before such therapy.(5) In the early part of the century:

> "More than 50,000 persons died of the disease annually in the United States. . . . Physicians were so helpless against lobar pneumonia that William Osler referred to it as 'a self-limiting disease which can neither be aborted nor cut short by any means at our command.' The patient either died irrespective of treatment or recovered spontaneously. . . . When Cole became director of the Hospital, he therefore decided that one of his major research goals would be to develop a therapeutic serum for pneumonia, and it was to this end that he appointed Avery as the bacteriologist on the team."(6)

Avery seldom appeared on the wards, however. In July of 1937, all of the clinical decisions for the six or eight patients on the pneumonia service in the Hospital were directed by the senior resident, Colin MacLeod, who had graduated from McGill a few years ahead of Beeson.

When he started as a resident at Rockefeller, Beeson knew a little clinical internal medicine but almost nothing about research. On the wards, he was instructed by MacLeod, whom he remembered vaguely from medical school. They were soon joined by an exceptional intern from Washington University, Charles Hoagland. At the same time he began his clinical duties, Beeson also started his introduction to research.

There was no formal teaching or training in Avery's department. In fact, there was little organization of anything. Avery worked on his problems himself, in his own small laboratory without technicians. He was always attentive to the work of others, though, no matter what their discipline. He was able, through his example, to create a unity of purpose among the staff. His laboratories were in a former hospital ward with high ceilings, and his office was a small room off his own lab.

Into this tiny office Beeson was invited to discuss the general outline of the research efforts underway. By this time, Avery was already well into his study of what he called "the transforming principle," an ability of a sub-cellular material derived from one specific type of pneumococcus to transform another type. Although Beeson didn't understand the significance of this conversation, after the chemist Maclyn McCarty joined the effort, that work became the basis of Avery's discovery that DNA is the engine of genetics.

The great paper describing this research was published with MacLeod and McCarty in 1944.(7) Even within the Institute itself, the simple nature of the DNA molecule and the difficulty in purifying it of proteins made Alfred Mirsky and others working on the biochemistry of genetics skeptical of Avery's research.

The controversy was a matter for public debate at an Institute staff meeting attended by Beeson. It is a commentary on the sometimes approximate nature of reward in the scientific community that, while James Watson and Francis Crick shared the Nobel Prize for their description of the chemical nature of DNA as a double helix, the shy and solitary Avery died in 1955 before he was properly recognized as the real discoverer of DNA as the chemical substance of chromosomes.

Since the Nobel Prize is awarded only to the living, Avery's enormous contribution has been misplaced in scientific history, certainly for the general public as well as almost all medical students. But it was he who "discovered" DNA, not Watson and Crick, who rather described its chemistry and structure in 1953. In his popular book *The Double Helix*, published in 1968, James Watson properly, but rather inconspicuously, credits Avery with first showing that genes are comprised of DNA.

Beeson's afternoon conversation with his new chief included not only the topic of DNA and transformation, but also the work done developing type-specific antibodies for the treatment of lobar pneumonia, a topic much more relevant to the daily lives of the residents. Colin MacLeod remembered how Avery conducted such interviews with his new staff:

> Avery did not assign his associates to problems. His approach was indirect and at times seemed excruciatingly slow. After a week or two in the laboratory, Avery commonly would invite the new assistant into his tiny personal laboratory. . . . A morning or afternoon would be spent in describing the lore of pneumococcus and in tracing the development of knowledge, the problems in which the department was currently concerned and those in which it had an interest. These soliloquies, prose masterpieces of high polish, were widely known as "Red Seal Records" and Avery was prone to repeat them as he sensed the necessity.(8)

It was the responsibility of the residents on the pneumonia service to admit patients from all over New York City already diagnosed with lobar pneumonia. They were to do the history and physical examinations and provide the basic care necessary both to treat them and to obtain the pneumococcus species that the group was trying to understand.

Antigen, antibody and complement interactions were known to be the basic biology of immune response by 1937, and several specific sub-types of pneumococcus were already identified by chemical differences in the polysaccharides of their capsules. As a clinical matter, this allowed identification of the exact organism afflicting a patient by performing the "Neufeld" reaction between the sputum of that patient and a type-specific antiserum obtained by inoculating first horses and later—more economically—rabbits.

A small wire loopful of sputum was smeared onto a glass slide and mixed with one of the specific rabbit antipneumococcal sera in combination with Loeffler's alkaline methyline blue.(9) When the sputum was combined with the correct serum, a microscopic swelling of the polysaccharide capsule could be seen and the type identified. The patient was then treated with an intravenous injection of the correct antiserum containing antibodies to that specific type of pneumococcus.

Here was the Rockefeller Institute at its best: a clinical problem manifested in very sick patients, many of whom would have died before this time without treatment, and a solution found by scientists investigating the causative agent in the laboratory, divining an answer. Beeson and the other residents were enormously excited by this kind of clinical investigation and were anxious to be given an opportunity to participate in the laboratory research as well.

The type-specific antiserum treatment for pneumococcus was the first effective management of lobar pneumonia, and while it worked in treating the disease, there were often side effects. Patients receiving fifty to one hundred cc's of intravenous horse or rabbit serum might, of course, be allergic to the serum itself and develop rapid cardiovascular collapse (shock) requiring epinephrine. While this was not often fatal, it did demand the vigilance of the house staff and occasionally rapid treatment to constrict blood vessels and expand intravascular volume.

Patients also sometimes developed a chill and fever response delayed by thirty to sixty minutes. This observation led to Beeson's first publication, co-authored by Charles Hoagland.(10) The two house officers reasoned that, since calcium salts relaxed tetany and smooth muscle, intravenous calcium chloride might effectively treat chills—and it did.

Their brief initial paper quotes the analytical work of John Peters, whom Beeson was to know much better fifteen years later at Yale. It also led to Beeson's first trip to the prestigious Internal Medicine meetings held each early May in Atlantic City. The observation that patients developed fever and chills following the infusion of serum, which he had initially noticed as a student, stayed with Beeson and went beyond the simple desire to treat the symptoms. The troubling fevers led to work eventually proving it was not the serum itself producing these side effects, but the incomplete sterilization of the brown rubber surgical tubing and glassware still in use for infusions. They were often contaminated by a fever-producing substance—endogenous pyrogen—later studied by Beeson and co-workers at Yale. The final complication of type-specific antipneumococcal therapy was "serum sickness" that resulted in fever, urticaria and joint pains one to two weeks following injection. For this reason, patients remained in the hospital, sometimes for weeks, until it was certain they would not develop this problem. Residents had plenty of experience treating patients with these complications of serum therapy, but they noted the mortality rate from pneumococcal pneumonia declined to about ten percent.(11) Hoagland and Beeson sometimes congratulated each other as they strode the halls of the hospital, comfortable in the realization that not only would the patients recover, but that they themselves were among the few real authorities on the treatment of pneumococcal pneumonia.

Their specialty niche was short-lived, however. As dramatically successful as serum therapy was, it went out of fashion by 1938 following the introduction of sulfapyridine, a specific antibiotic for the treatment of pneumococcal infections, which was both easier to administer and more effective.

The house staff lived at the Rockefeller Hospital, where they were provided food, laundry and maid service, and paid a small wage. At mid-day, they all gathered in the Institute lunch room to discuss both the clinical events of the day and the closely related, exciting research being done in the laboratories.

It was also the custom to have tea in the afternoon in the ground floor lounge of the Hospital, and so the younger staff was continually exposed to more senior scientists like Van Slyke, Avery, Rene Dubos and Walther Goebel. Beeson and his now close friend Charles Hoagland began to read journals and to think about the problems of infection and clinical investigation.

And they soon began to do their own laboratory research.

Beeson's bench research started in the laboratory of Kenneth Goodner, collaborator with Frank Horsfall on the manufacture of type-specific antipneumococcal serum in rabbits and other related projects. Dr. Goodner taught Beeson, who had never before done this kind of work, how to immunize the animals against a certain pneumococcus causing them to make antibodies to that specific polysaccharide type, then to bleed them, pool and store the serum.

While all of the procedures were to be done under sterile conditions, the techniques of the late thirties were limited by equipment and the not-yet-understood problem of endogenous pyrogen, the substance later found to be resistant to the sterilization procedures then being used. Thus, the patients' fevers often continued after treatment for pneumonia.

While he was at work one morning in this lab, several executives from the Lederle Pharmaceutical Company came to see Goodner with an interest in commercial production of antipneumococcal serum. This, of course, pleased the scientist and the residents, but the project was abridged by the superior therapy soon available in the form of sulfapyridine.

It was also about this time that the remarkable Charles Hoagland developed his first problems with hypertension and was hospitalized for hypertensive encephalopathy or perhaps intercerebral hemorrhage—the diagnosis of such illnesses was uncertain before modern imaging techniques. In any case, high blood pressure (not even mentioned by Osler) was still largely untreatable before World War II, and even the 1943 edition of Cecil's *Textbook of Medicine* is not sanguine on this subject.(12)

Hugh Morgan, who wrote the few pages in Cecil's text about hypertension, denounced the continuous infusion of "the nitrates, extracts of mistletoe, garlic or watermelon seed, veratrum viride, aceylcholine and nicotinic acid," as well as the available surgical procedures which he thankfully described as experimental.

However, there was little else to prescribe aside from diet, relaxation and sedatives. Even malignant hypertension, which Hoagland eventually did develop, could be treated only with oxygen, bleeding to reduce blood volume, morphine and digitalis.

At this point neither Beeson nor his friend knew how sick he would become. Though Hoagland was miserable in the hospital, he was anxious to get back to work. He soon did return, and the two residents began to study properties of capsular polysaccharides of the pneumococcus in the lab.

Beeson and Hoagland were now prepared for research beyond the relatively simple manufacture of the antipneumococcal serum and clinical observations such as treating chills with calcium. One of the early investigators in infections diseases, Max Finland of Harvard's Thorndike Laboratories at Boston City Hospital, had observed that there were sometimes serious complications following the intravenous administration of Type XIV antipneumococcal horse serum, including hemoglobinuria and death.

Working in Walther Goebel's laboratory, Hoagland and Beeson showed that "horse sera of this type revealed in every instance agglutinins for human erythrocytes in high titer, whereas only two of 41 specimens of sera of other types agglutinated human red blood cells in dilution of 1:20 or higher."(13)

In this paper and a second published in 1939, the authors demonstrated an immunologic similarity between the capsular polysaccharide of Type XIV pneumococcus and blood Group A. In the complicated preparation processes then available, the polysaccharide was chemically separated through many steps, and then finally purified by dialysis for several hours across large bags of cellophane membrane. Thus it was shown that the complications of giving Type XIV antiserum from immunized horses to patients with Group A blood type resulted from intravascular agglutination and hemolysis. For Beeson, a young resident of thirty, research of this sophistication published in journals of high quality was a far different experience from seeing elderly patients with diffuse complaints in the Wooster clinic.

Although he continued to live in a predominantly male environment, Beeson's social life did broaden at the Rockefeller Institute, both because he was a little older than many of the house staff and because he had a car. Automobiles were still uncommon among the residents, which was why Frank Horsfall had summoned his former fraternity brother in the first place. Now, living right in the middle of New York's East side, Paul began to feel at home, driving to places like Rockefeller Center, and parking right on the street.

Traffic in Manhattan was then modest, and Beeson frequently took nurses from the hospital to concerts and out to dinner. None of these relationships were serious marriage-threatening affairs, however. The diversions were interesting, but the major events of Beeson's life, and of the lives of the other young men and a few women at Rockefeller were still to be found within the Institute itself.

Rene Dubos, more outgoing than Avery and an exciting scientific luminary, sponsored a journal club for the house staff twice a month. Meetings were held after dinner at the Rockefeller Hospital, and Dubos always came and acted as the host for about a dozen residents from the various hospital services. Several recently published papers would be introduced and one of the residents called upon for a detailed summary, followed by a general discussion of the subject. Their enthusiasm for this kind of challenge was increased one evening when Dubos invited Selman Waksman to speak. At the time Waksman was interested in soil bacteria and later was to discover streptomycin.(14)

The research that Waksman and Dubos did for the two decades before World War II—isolating soil microbes that inhibited growth of bacteria—was crucial to the rediscovery of Alexander Fleming's 1929 paper on penicillin. Although Fleming had immediately reported his chance finding that a species of penicillium inhibited growth of staphylococcus both *in vitro* and in animals, the work was ignored.

Twelve years later, antibiotic treatment of sepsis was finally attempted in man on February 12, 1941. Having unearthed Fleming's work, the experimental Pathologist Howard Florey grew the mold in enamel bed pans. Under the direction of Leslie Witts, first Nuffield Professor of Medicine, a house officer named Charles Fletcher injected penicillin into a policeman hospitalized with staphylococcal sepsis at the Radcliffe Infirmary, Oxford. The patient transiently improved, but then soon died because they ran out of the drug. After a second death, they were able to save the next four septic patients.

Waksman's work had prepared Florey for this bold step that soon led to the mass production of penicillin and the Nobel Prize for Fleming, Chain and Florey in 1945. Waksman continued his investigations in soil microbiology, and was awarded the 1952 Nobel Prize for his discovery of streptomycin, the first drug effective against tuberculosis.

The residents were all excited by the idea that more chemical substances might be found for the treatment of infections, a set of problems in medicine that, with the exception of illnesses due to organisms sensitive to sulfa drugs, were still treated rather indirectly.

Beeson also met another young researcher named Barry Wood who came to visit Avery about this time. Wood, a very talented but modest rising star, was already widely known not only for his scientific abilities but also as an All America quarterback on the Harvard football team.

In fact, his undergraduate honors thesis took advantage of several of his skills, measuring the leukocyte response in athletes during exercise. Even though he hadn't yet graduated from Harvard, this work was published in a German physiology journal.(15) It now seems a little comical to imagine the star quarterback drawing blood samples from his teammates during a game, presumably on the sideline while the Harvard defensive team was on the field, but Wood did exactly that experiment.

By 1938, he was already interested in infectious disease, had published papers concerning both serum and sulfa therapy for pneumococcal pneumonia, and was apparently considering a move to Rockefeller. Wood had spent time at Boston City Hospital where he was exposed to teachers like Soma Weiss, Chester Keefer and William Castle, the same great clinicians who were soon to become Beeson's teachers.

Barry Wood did not join the staff at Rockefeller, but soon became the Chief of Medicine at Washington University when he was only thirty-two years old. Beeson already knew Wood's reputation as an athlete and promising clinical investigator when he came to see Avery, and was to know him much more intimately later, as a colleague in the study of infectious disease.

In 1938, Beeson and Hoagland were joined by assistant resident Tom Dublin, who was trained at Bellevue on the Cornell Service and at Boston City Hospital. Although Dublin didn't do much research in the lab with his two senior colleagues, the three doctors took care of the patients on the wards together and became friends.

At about Christmas time, Dublin made a return trip to Boston where he chanced to meet one of his former professors, Soma Weiss. Tom Dublin was well connected in medicine, in part because his father was the Medical Director at the Metropolitan Life Insurance Company, and at the time many decisions in academic medicine were influenced by the opinions of friends. After all, friends could be trusted to provide accurate evaluations of young physicians and scientists at a time when more objective measures were few.

Soma Weiss had just been appointed to succeed Henry Christian as Physician-in-Chief at Peter Bent Brigham Hospital as well as Hersey Professor at Harvard. As he stopped to chat with his former student, he inquired about other residents who were to finish at Rockefeller in the coming summer of 1939.

Dublin mentioned Paul Beeson. Weiss, who apparently valued the opinion of his still young former student, was trying to organize his house staff for the next academic year, and was impressed with Tom Dublin's description of not only the research work Beeson had been doing and his publications, but also with the kind of clinical doctor he was becoming.

It was not much later that Beeson passed Cornelius Rhodes in the hallway of the Institute and learned that the pathologist had had an inquiry from Weiss about him. In fact, Rhodes said, "Dr. Weiss wonders if you might be interested in being his chief resident next year." Remarkably, this didn't mean much to Beeson at the time, possibly because inquiries were not infrequent and actual job offers were another thing altogether. The possibility of going to the Brigham Hospital on the Harvard Service became more tangible, though, when Soma Weiss wrote directly to Beeson asking to meet him for an interview at the Pierre Hotel overlooking New York's Central Park.

CHAPTER 5

The Sixth Edition of the *Textbook of Medicine by American Authors* makes its appearance with extensive changes in both text and format. For example, it contains a number of new articles not covered in previous editions. . . . Another new feature of the book . . . is a list . . . of normal values for the commoner laboratory tests. With the great multiplicity of tests now in use, it becomes more and more difficult to keep the normal values in mind. . . . In planning the Sixth Edition, the editor invited Dr. Soma Weiss, late Hersey Professor of the Theory and Practice of Physic at Harvard University, to act as co-editor.

Russell Cecil, 1941(1)

*B*y the time Beeson arrived at the Central Park hotel to see Dr. Weiss, he already had a job as Chief Resident at the Brigham Hospital—save for one detail. The interviewer wasn't concerned with his qualifications as a physician or a promising investigator. Soma Weiss was a thorough, precise man; when he invited Beeson to the interview he already knew enough about both his achievements and his potential to intend offering him a position. The Hersey Professor wanted to meet Beeson in person not to investigate his character or intelligence, but to determine his religion.

In 1899, Soma Weiss was born in Hungary to a substantial Jewish family. He came to the United States before he was twenty years old, escaping the turmoil as the Austro-Hungarian Empire of Franz Josef collapsed following World War I. His professors at Cornell Medical School considered him their most brilliant student and his reputation as the outstanding young clinician of the era in Boston was already well established as World War II began in Europe.

With his appointment at Harvard, however, came some direction from the University. "He probably had been warned by others not to make many Jewish appointments at the beginning. Remember, this was 1938, 1939, 1940. Later on, as his confidence grew in his job, he made several appointments of Jewish persons."(2)

Early in his tenure, Weiss was not anxious for political problems and so, even with a name as un-semitic-sounding as Beeson, he wanted to make certain that it had not been changed at Ellis Island. Both official and unofficial quota systems for minorities, especially Jews, were a feature of East coast academics between the wars.

> In a day and age when college, particularly in the East, was still largely a gentleman's prerogative, these highly motivated and intelligent young Jews in the eastern cities represented a serious threat to the relaxed 'gentlemanly' college way of life. Shortly after World War I, Harvard University established a 'Sifting Committee,' which placed a quota on Jews. . . . In most schools, admissions committees and officers quietly and unofficially limited the entrance of Jewish applicants. When quota systems were more or less official, it was argued that admitting students on a competitive basis into the private eastern schools might result in a 50 percent Jewish enrollment, a situation thought to be socially unacceptable. . . . As the full horror of the consequences of anti-Semitism in

Germany was revealed in the late 1940s, overt discrim-
ination began to fade.(3)

The brief interview that afternoon included a routine discussion of the applicant's family, education, research and goals. In
addition to answering questions, Beeson felt himself flush with
the infectious quality of the just-appointed chief's intellect and
the excitement for his own new job. He carefully observed Dr.
Weiss' marked accent, impressive vocabulary and European
manners during their half-hour conversation. At the end of the
meeting, Beeson had a position as Chief Resident with instruc-
tions to begin work in the fall of 1939. The next time he saw
Soma Weiss was at a reception for all of the new staff held in
the corridor outside the Chairman's small office at the Peter
Bent Brigham Hospital.

Beeson drove home to visit his family in Wooster and then
back to Boston where he parked under the Brigham Hospital
off Shattuck Street. He would once again live in a hospital with
the rest of the unmarried house staff. When he joined the welcoming celebration outside of Weiss' office, he was introduced
to the rest of the newly-appointed young faculty members: John
Romano, Charles Janeway and Eugene Stead.

He also met Weiss' secretary, the capable Evelyn Selby, who
later married Gene Stead, a union predicted far in advance by
both Weiss and his wife. Over the coming year, Beeson spent
hours sitting in Selby's little office where she typed and ran the
business of the Department of Medicine, while the Chief
Resident waited to make Professor's rounds and fretted that
he might have forgotten an important bit of information about
one of the patients.

Romano, a psychiatrist who would later Chair the
Departments of Psychiatry at Cincinnati and Rochester, was
beginning his faculty career at Harvard in the Department of
Medicine, an unusual appointment. Fifty years later in an interview, he recalled that first day clearly:

> Soma Weiss was a very enthusiastic, charismatic man. He came here as an immigrant. He came to Boston and was put in the research unit, Thorndike Memorial Laboratory, at the Boston City Hospital. . . . He was chosen to become the Hersey Professor in the theory and practice of physic, the oldest and most prestigious medical chair at Harvard. . . . I will never forget the day we started, September 1, 1939, the day that Hitler bombed Warsaw. Soma Weiss got together the old timers . . . [and] said: 'These are my three young men, Stead, Romano and Janeway. I hope you will give them the opportunity to earn your respect.' So they took me on rounds immediately, because I was the one whose throat they were ready to cut, being the psychiatrist.(4)

While the internal medicine faculty at the Brigham had been a distinguished one under his predecessor Henry Christian, Weiss was assembling stars to join him in a different galaxy. Charles Janeway, part of a New York medical family dating from the nineteenth century—including Theodore who followed Osler at Hopkins—was interested in infectious diseases and soon became Professor of Pediatrics at Harvard. Eugene Stead's career took him to Emory as Chair of Medicine just after World War II—where his own first faculty appointment was to be the former Chief Resident Paul Beeson—and then to the Chair at Duke. The other new residents were already skilled and promising physicians with broad interests in clinical investigation.

When Beeson began work that fall as Chief Resident, he discovered that he had greater years but less clinical experience than most of the assistant residents he was supposed to supervise. As a resident at Rockefeller, his own experience had been almost entirely confined to infectious diseases and, specifically, only to the lung. Moreover, the subject he knew best and in which he could be considered an expert, serum therapy for pneumococcal pneumonia, was already outdated by sulfapyridine.

It turned out, though, that it didn't matter. These people were all pushing together against the boundaries of medicine, and they were doing it for teaching, patient care and clinical investigation, glued by their chief and his compelling personality.

Although Weiss was known all over the city by this time as a clinician, he had begun his career in basic science. His first paper, published when he was only seventeen years old, concerned respiratory physiology, and at Cornell he had worked in the pharmacology laboratory of Robert Hatcher. For all of his life, which unhappily wasn't long enough, he was committed to the integrated study of general medical problems as they applied to a specific individual patient.

> In the fall of 1939 Soma Weiss for the first time addressed the Harvard Medical School Faculty and student body in his role as Hersey Professor. The audience expected him to describe one or more of the clinical entities that he had encountered as a brilliant clinician. To their disappointment, the hour was devoted to hard science. The title was 'Chemical structure: Biological Action: Therapeutic Effect.' The era of clinical description was over. Doctors alone could not master disease. . . . The medical service at the Brigham would undergo dramatic and lasting changes.(5)

The choice of Weiss to replace Henry Christian was not without some debate. Chester Keefer and William Castle, both at the Thorndike Laboratory with Weiss, were certainly in consideration for the job. It was Weiss' charismatic personality that set him apart from the others. Castle is reported to have said,

"Soma was our leader. . . . Chester knew everything cold, but Soma knew almost everything and warm."

Beeson and his junior but more broadly experienced residents assembled each day at eight o'clock with Dr. Weiss in his office for morning report. During the next three or four decades, this ritual of the chief of service himself taking morning report with the house staff to discuss all of the admissions from the night before was a cornerstone for the teaching of internal medicine.

An apprenticeship system, medicine residencies were characterized by long hours of thoughtful, demanding work, but the reward was the individual critique of the product of this effort every morning with the master. As circumstances have changed, the administration of huge, sub-specialized departments of medicine is now characterized by committee meetings, applications, university administrative responsibilities, complex research protocols, grants, insurance schemes and public relations, which combine to make the Chair not only unable to conduct morning report, but quite often unqualified to do so.

For Weiss it was a necessity. He consulted about the problems of those who had appeared in the emergency room overnight or had been directly admitted to the wards. He inquired as to the progress of hospitalized patients he already knew. He had the habit of looking directly at the resident to whom he spoke, and sometimes pulled out a black notebook asking his Chief Resident, always addressed as "Beeson", for a patient's name and history number saying, "I'm interested in that disease."

Weiss, of course, had developed interests both broad and deep since the day in 1919 when he arrived in New York and applied for U.S. citizenship. After interning on the Cornell service at Bellevue Hospital he moved to Boston City and the Thorndike Laboratories, where Chester Keefer investigated infection and William Castle worked out the cause and treatment of pernicious anemia.

Although Weiss wrote extensively during that period on hypertension and the cardiovascular system, he also published papers on subjects as specific as the syndrome of esophageal lacerations due to vomiting that—along with Mallory—bears his name, and as general as clinical medicine as a university discipline.(6)

In fact, there wasn't a great deal in clinical medicine that did not interest Dr. Weiss, and his passion for teaching as well as the compelling flair he had for bedside instruction made his Tuesday evening rounds at Boston City spectacular events. Practicing physicians from all over Boston, as well as students and attending physicians assigned to one of the several other university services at the hospital, started with Weiss on the eighth story and descended floor by floor, visiting patients not only on the medicine wards, but also on neurology, obstetrics and surgery. The group included as many as one hundred people, all captivated by Weiss' slight mispronunciations as he focused on the patients being presented and the illnesses dissected.

The genius Soma Weiss had for this kind of instruction was summarized by Eugene DuBois, Chair of the Department of Medicine at Cornell, who at the memorial service held for Weiss remembered:

> There came to the wards of Bellevue all sorts and conditions of men, minor gangsters, major politicians, the black sheep of the best families, the humblest of hoboes. He treated them all with equal kindness and they all trusted him. Soma would become the friend and advisor of the stern hospital administrator, the crusty medical examiner, the exasperating head nurse, and even the floor polisher whose buzz machine would nullify all efforts towards auscultation.(7)

Although Weiss commanded a room when he entered because of an energy and a charismatic persona, Eugene Stead took over with a self-confidence that has been described as "not quite arrogance."(8) Stead came to the Brigham Hospital from medical school at Emory to intern in both the Departments of Medicine in 1932 and then Surgery in 1934; he had a surgeon's demeanor.

Beeson took notice of the fact that Weiss placed great confidence in his "young men," and gave Stead, Janeway and Romano visible assignments and great responsibility on the medicine service. When the Chief was away, for example, Stead usually took morning report. Weiss also put Janeway in charge of the bacteriology laboratory to supervise tasks that had previously been done by interns in labs scattered throughout the hospital. In the newly equipped and reorganized bacteriology laboratory, Janeway examined culture plates himself each day and was often joined by house staff, including the Chief Resident.

It was probably from Weiss that Paul Beeson developed his life-long attitudes about both the ideal structure for a department of medicine and his aversion to more and more narrowly focused sub-specialization. Grand Rounds at the Brigham were held on Saturday morning, and attracted Harvard Professors from other units, as well as physicians from all over Boston.

The focus of these rounds and of the department remained general internal medicine at a time when Weiss complained in his annual report about, "the harmful effect of minute specialization. . . . One of the best examples of this problem is the artificial segregation of medicine from neurology, and in particular psychiatry. . . . As far as medicine is concerned, it became in many respects 'decerebrated.' "(9)

The number of psychiatrists and neurologists in the Department of Medicine continued to increase, and by the time Beeson finished as Chief Resident there were several faculty members representing these disciplines on the staff.

In constructing his department, Weiss seems always to have generalized from the particular patient to a category of illness, remembering that Descartes was mistaken when he viewed the mind and body as separate entities. He was so bold in holding firmly to this view that he included a psychiatrist among his original "young men."

Beeson, and all of the residents, emulated their Chief's manner of introducing himself to each patient when he arrived to see them on rounds. This was certainly a departure from the attitude of attending physicians both at McGill and Penn, but perhaps not so dissimilar from the approach Beeson had observed in Wooster when he worked with his father and brother.

Weiss always took a little time to explain, not only to the residents but to the patient as well, what he was doing and why it might be important in treatment. When the group of residents and students left a bedside, everyone including the patient knew what had been discussed, why it was significant and how it might help the sick person.

As this view of medicine and clinical investigation began to diverge from a medical research more given to molecular biology and genetics, academics divided into two camps. One favored a humanistic approach to the organism as a sick person while the other championed the reduction of illness to biochemistry.

At the end of the century, this schism has produced medical faculties more and more deeply committed to basic research and a public that seeks nurturing from progressively non-traditional healers who provide little treatment but much comfort, thus co-opting the role of physicians in the model of Osler. The teachers in medical schools about the time of the Second World War, and Weiss in particular, characterized a moment in medicine before this separation occurred.

Soma Weiss' interest in people, his compassion, and his dedication extended beyond his patients to his colleagues and students. Just as he asked the sick on the wards about their personalities and situations in life, their jobs and families, he also took notice of his residents' stories. He knew where they came from, who their parents were and what they hoped for in the future. He observed when they slipped out for a tennis game on the Brigham courts in the afternoon, but commented about it so gently that no one resented his noticing. He was interested in their research ideas, and listened seriously to the opinions of the lowliest medical student, gently correcting the mistakes.

> His teaching was not a virtuoso performance, making astonishing diagnoses that the rest of us could hardly aspire to. Instead, he kept everyone's attention on the analysis of a problem and contributed from his own [vast] experience and reading. I'll never forget a remark he made as I was walking back to his office after a teaching session with half a dozen students on a ward. He said, 'You know, Beeson, teaching is hard work. When I finish something like this, I find that my back is aching.' His attitude toward a patient during a teaching visit impressed us all.(10)

Beeson had generous administrative responsibilities as Chief Resident. These included always keeping Dr. Weiss informed about the service, making rounds with both the Chief and various other faculty, scheduling meetings and seminars, and assignments for the residents and interns. The interns were a special problem because of the peculiar system of their entering the program every three months.

In spite of these duties, Beeson had time and energy to continue his research in infectious disease. He collaborated with Charlie Janeway on one paper investigating the antipyretic effects of sulfapyridine and another published in the *New England Journal* concerned with treatment of pneumococcal pneumonia.

Stead was at the same time beginning his important research in the physiology of the cardiovascular system and shock, and Weiss began his collaboration with the physical chemist Edwin Cohn on bovine and human albumin as plasma expanders. This later topic was of serious interest not only to physicians but also to the government, as it became more and more clear that the war in Europe would spread and that blood lost on the battlefields would need to be replaced.

In addition to Weiss' "young men" on the faculty, the residents of that group just prior to World War II all went on to important academic careers. The outstanding clinician Jack Myers became Chief of Medicine at Pittsburgh, Jim Warren who later worked with Stead at Emory became Chief at Ohio State, Lou Hempleman returned to basic science at Washington University and the very funny Max Michael also went to Emory with Stead.

Weiss and many of these residents and junior staff were investigating shock, the vascular system and hypertension at this time, and their work led to an expanded understanding of the cardiovascular system. Stead and Warren were especially important in this field at Emory, but in 1940 no one knew enough about essential hypertension to save Charles Hoagland from a fatal intercerebral hemorrhage. Beeson went to New York to visit his friend during his final hospitalization, just as war became certain.

Beeson found himself deferred from the military, but anxious to serve. In an effort to assist the war struggle, James Conant, the President of the university, had arranged with the Red Cross to form the Harvard-Red Cross Field Unit Hospital at Salisbury for the study of epidemiology. As young men and women were massed together in crowded and sometimes unclean conditions, the risk of uncontrolled spread of infection concerned military planners.

Beeson was appointed the Chief Physician of the Field Unit Hospital and, after about fourteen months as Chief Resident to Weiss, he prepared to leave Boston for England. A farewell party was arranged at a little Cambridge restaurant in the fall of 1940 and Beeson turned over his responsibilities to Jack Myers. After dinner, Weiss stood up and, referring to Beeson for the first time by his first name, said, "I can see war coming for the United States, and I think Paul is one of the first who is going to leave us."

Preparations for an Atlantic crossing by ship began. After a trip back to Ohio where there were still Amish buggies parked among the automobiles outside the clinic in Wooster, Beeson returned to Boston to see Weiss about the continuation of his academic career following the war. The details were left unstated, but it seemed certain that there would be a job at the Brigham if he wished to return. Just before Thanksgiving of 1941, while Beeson was still in Salisbury, Weiss confirmed this in a letter to his first Chief Resident by offering him a faculty job at Harvard with an initial salary of three thousand dollars.

At about the same time, he wrote again telling him that Eugene Stead was moving to a new job as Chair of the Department of Medicine at Emory and also intended to offer him a faculty appointment in Atlanta. Weiss took great care not to influence Beeson in favor of one position or the other, but described what he felt were the advantages of each. He was enthusiastic about the possibilities for clinical research on infectious diseases in the south, and felt that Emory would be an important center for such work following the war. He closed by writing, "I hear very complimentary remarks from many sources about your work and helpfulness in England."

These were two of the last letters Soma Weiss wrote. In January of 1942, he and Edwin Cohn, the physical chemist collaborating with him on the study of bovine and human albumin as blood substitutes, took the train to Washington, D.C. to discuss their research with officials of government and the military. The subject of plasma expanders was, of course, an important topic during the war when the wounded needed blood that was difficult to get and harder to store.

As Weiss, by far the smaller and more agile of the two men, climbed into the upper berth of their sleeper on the trip back home, he developed a sudden, debilitating headache. Unlike most headaches, this one did not abate and even when the train arrived in Boston, Weiss was still sick with pain, nausea and aversion to light. He was taken home where he stayed for two weeks in bed, probably knowing that he had suffered a sub-arachnoid hemorrhage from a cerebral aneurysm. There was no treatment. Soma Weiss died on January 31, 1942, four days after his forty-third birthday.

CHAPTER 6

Clearly, the problem now was one of taking the production of penicillin out of the laboratory, and going into large scale manufacture. It was 1941 . . .Florey and one of his bacteriologist-assistants were brought to America by a grant from the Rockefeller Foundation. The purpose of this mission was to find a way to increase the yield of penicillin from the mold

and to manufacture it on a commercial scale. . . . Starting with a tube of mold from Flemming's original culture, brought over by Florey, penicillin was made to grow in gargantuan fermentation tanks, each with a capacity of 12,000 gallons.

Riedman and Gustafson, 1941(1)

Howard Florey prepared to cross the Atlantic so he could supervise the production of penicillin in the safety of the United States, a task given immediacy by German aggression in Europe and the entry of England into the war. At the same time, Paul Beeson finished making his plans to go in the other direction. After a dusty two-day solitary drive back to Wooster for a farewell visit with his family, he sold his car and took the train to New York. He had already made arrangements to sail on an American freighter bound for Lisbon.

World War II was quickly spreading over Europe so that crossing the Atlantic was already dangerous in 1940, even on a freighter flying the American flag. The young internist's traveling companion was John Gordon, an epidemiologist in the Harvard School of Public Health, who was to be the Director of the American Red Cross-Harvard University Hospital; Beeson had already been named Chief Physician.

Even though the United States had not yet formally entered the war, sentiment strongly favored England and, as German and Italian hostility increased, so did the desire of many Americans to aid the British actively. Two days after Hitler invaded Poland on September 1, 1939, Britain and France declared war on Germany. With the invasion of the Netherlands, Belgium and France in the spring of 1940, and the German defeat in the Battle of Britain, any hope of a rapid conclusion to the conflict held by either side vanished.

When he testified before the Senate, Harvard's President Conant vigorously opposed U.S. isolationism and was outspoken in his enthusiastic support for the British war effort. In conjunction with the American Red Cross, Conant engineered an opportunity for Harvard faculty members to join the conflict early by volunteering as medical staff at an epidemiological hospital to be constructed at Salisbury.

Both British and American epidemiologists, as well as the military planners they advised, knew that the crowding together of troops and civilians from different places, with different immunity and exposure to diseases, increased the risk of epidemics in wartime England. While isolating the infected had been a tradition since the pest house, there still was little specific treatment to offer during epidemics and so more information was sought through clinical investigation.

Nationalism and anti-German feelings were great motivation for sending aid to Europe, but so was a desire to expand the knowledge-base in medicine; wars often produce medical advances. In part to take advantage of opportunities they suspected might be offered during the crowding of conflict, the American Red Cross agreed to furnish a prefabricated field hospital in England with equipment and nurses while the Harvard School of Public Health was to provide medical staff to study infectious diseases.

In a letter to Conant dated March, 1941, Wilson Jameson, the British Minister of Health, described the hospital's function and thanked him for Harvard's participation, writing:

> . . . when your welcome offer of help was conveyed to us by Dr. Gordon, we ourselves proposed, and you readily agreed, that such help should take the form of an infectious disease hospital and laboratory with all necessary staff and equipment. Our greatest need then was for such a unit and our need today is no less. . . . We have none too many hospital beds for cases of infectious disease, and the area in which the Harvard Hospital will be situated is one in which both civil and military demands are great and difficult to meet. The laboratory will be associated intimately with our system of Emergency Public Health Laboratories, and the epidemiological team will be used as though they were members of the staff of the Ministry of Health, in whatever part of the county disease has to be investigated and brought under control. . . .
>
> . . . it is not merely the professional help of this advance party of the Unit that is of value. The very fact that these men have come to our country to work side by side with us in our time of trial stimulates and encourages all of us.(2)

Just after Christmas of 1940, Beeson and John Gordon boarded the lighted freighter that conspicuously flew an American flag. They left New York along with twelve other passengers, among them the movie stars Laurence Olivier and Vivian Leigh who

were returning from Hollywood to their native England. Aside
from a game of dominoes one afternoon, these two colorful figures were completely absorbed in each other and their own
affairs; although they were polite at mealtimes, they otherwise
seldom appeared from their stateroom.

The German submarine attacks had already begun, but only
British ships were then targets and the crossing was uneventful.
When the freighter reached Lisbon, a safer port than Southampton,
Gordon and Beeson flew on a British Air Force transport plane
to London, along with Harry Hopkins, a prominent advisor to
Roosevelt on his way to confer secretly with Churchill.

When the American doctors landed in London, the prefabricated hospital and equipment were still in the United States.
They were not due to arrive—along with the nurses—for almost
six months. The Chief Physician was thirty-two years old, about
twenty years younger than Professor Gordon, and, unlike the
older man, not an experienced traveler.

Gordon, with help from friends among the military advisors who had already been in London for several months, found
a flat near Cavendish Square, close to the center of a city still
under German air attack. During an air raid one night not long
after they moved in, a bomb exploded in the street outside their
darkened building and the blast blew out the windows of their
flat, knocking them both out of their chairs and shooting shards
of glass across the room. They were cut enough to require a trip
to a nearby hospital for sutures, and though not seriously hurt,
they were frightened.

Prior to that night, the Americans often climbed to their
rooftop so they could watch the excitement of bombers, fight-
ers, searchlights and gunfire over the city of London. After surviving the explosion, the "real war" of Clausewitz, both of them
became alarmed at any sound of approaching bombers and
stayed out of the way as much as possible, although it was not
usually necessary for them to dash into the air raid shelters
underground.

While they waited for the medical buildings to arrive and be assembled, Gordon was occupied with the logistical tasks of organizing the unit. Beeson, minus administrative duties without a hospital, spent his first six months in England investigating various outbreaks of infection. Although not a trained epidemiologist, he had learned enough from Gordon to start doing field work.

Late in the winter of 1941, Beeson began traveling by train on behalf of the Ministry of Health to investigate outbreaks of salmonella poisoning. The infection, characterized by gastroenteritis and diarrhea, was the result of eating poorly preserved, contaminated food. While he was doing this work, a British physician reported the unusual occurrence of an epidemic of trichinosis among factory workers in Northampton, and Beeson was sent there next to determine the cause.

Prior to 1937, only twenty-six cases of trichinosis had ever been described in Great Britain.(3) This parasitic infestation is acquired by eating the larvae of the nematode *Trichina spiralis*, often found in undercooked pork. The worms mature and mate in the bowel of the new host, producing larval infestation and migration throughout the body, especially to skeletal muscle. During the single winter of 1940-41, there were more than two hundred cases of trichinosis reported in various parts of Great Britain.

In addition to writing papers detailing the prevalence and clinical manifestations of this infection in humans, Beeson determined that it was the custom of many women factory workers during this time to eat undercooked pork sausage sandwiches that had caused the outbreak.(3,4)

The disease had been unusual in England because British hogs were rarely infected with the nematode. But during the war, hogs were infected with the parasite, possibly transmitted to them by rats (although some felt it had arrived from France in contaminated pork). Either way, it was certainly unknown to the female factory workers who, rushing to manage the start of a busy day for husbands and children before they too left home for wartime jobs, undercooked the sausage they ate for their own mid-day meals.

Fortunately, since it was then untreatable, this illness is rarely fatal. Following a brief period of fever, cough, diarrhea and intense muscle pain during the stage of larval migration, the patient usually recovers, because in humans the encysted larvae may remain viable for many years without producing symptoms.

A key to the laboratory diagnosis of trichinosis is eosinophilia, a large increase in the ratio of the odd, reddish staining cells to the total number of circulating white blood cells. These observations were the beginning of Beeson's long-time interest in this still poorly understood type of leukocyte, "that has both entranced and befuddled investigators for the past century."(5)

Early in the spring of 1941, the components of the hospital buildings began to arrive at Liverpool and were trucked to Salisbury for construction. From a sick bed in the White Hart Hotel in Salisbury, Harvard's touring President Conant wrote to his wife:

> Somewhere last week, I picked up what is called "a throat" in this country. As far as I can tell, it's the equivalent of a "cold" but never reaches your nose!
>
> . . . I met Dr. Gordon, Dr. Beeson (from the School of Public Health), and two regional public health officers in preparation for our inspection of the site of the Harvard-Red Cross Hospital today. Beeson had a look at my throat with the aid of my pocket flashlight and a long-handled spoon. Advised me to take it easy, but couldn't very well advise me to cancel the inspection of the Harvard Unit the next morning. A couple of white patches . . . he allowed were bacterial, and might be streptococci (cheerful man). Anyway, I went to bed early.

> This A.M. I felt as though I had a cold. . . . Beeson thinks
> my throat looks better. . . . (6)

Conant recovered, and later reported that the hospital of one hundred twenty-six beds had opened in September of 1941. This facility was operated jointly by Harvard, the American Red Cross and the British Ministry of Health until July 15, 1942.

To staff the Red Cross-Harvard Hospital, boatloads of nurses began to arrive from the United States. The trip itself was becoming progressively more dangerous because of increasing German submarine attacks on ships crossing the Atlantic. Some of these nurses were killed in the crossing.

Because it took several more months of construction to put the buildings together, the young women who did arrive safely in England were temporarily assigned to London hospitals while they awaited completion of their quarters at Salisbury. Among these was Barbara Neal, a twenty-two year old graduate of St. Luke's School of Nursing in Chicago.

◆ ◆ ◆

The Neal family was from Buffalo, New York. Ray Neal, a prosperous businessman, started selling hardware as a young man and built a successful wholesale machine tool and equipment company in Western New York State. Ray married Margaret White from Hartford; they settled in Buffalo and had four children. When their daughter Barbara was about seven years old, the family moved to Snyder, then a tiny country village accessible either by a two-lane brick road or the one-track Toonerville trolley that ran hourly.

Ray and Margaret Neal were what might be called premature environmentalists; they moved to Snyder to be surrounded by fields and woods, keep animals, raise a garden and teach their children a love of the natural world. The family included dogs, cats, rabbits, guinea pigs, birds and a fish. Margaret Neal had a great interest in biology and health, and she required that her children learn to care for the family pets, and get plenty of fresh air.

When the girls weren't wandering the fields together, learning birds and trees, the farmer next door offered them occasional rides on one of his huge draft horses. The Neals were politically moderate Republicans, but sent Barbara, her sisters and brother all to the relatively liberal Park School. It emphasized values progressive for the era, though it was so small that Barbara graduated from high school with only four others in the class.

Ray and his wife expected their daughters to marry, but emphasized their need to be independent and capable of earning a living themselves. The eldest, named for her mother, became a math teacher and Jane, the youngest, became an artist. Barbara decided she wanted more glamour and intended to become an airline stewardess.

In 1936 when Barbara Neal was eighteen years old, the airlines required that all the stewardesses first be nurses because airsickness was so common. Her parents agreed that it was time for her to leave Snyder, where the only modern entertainment was a radio in the dining room. Her grandfather recommended the School of Nursing at St. Luke's Hospital in Chicago, where he had once been a patient. She applied and in the fall of 1936, Barbara's parents drove her along Lake Erie and across the Midwest to Chicago.

She moved into a room on the eleventh floor of the student nurses' dormitory in Evanston overlooking Lake Michigan. She and her roommate for all three years, a shy young woman from Iowa, eagerly took up their studies but also enjoyed evening walks along the Lake and occasional trips into Chicago on the train. The life of a student nurse before World War II was occupied by work and instruction on the wards. After a month of orientation, these young women were taught by their severe instructors to make beds with proper hospital corners, take temperatures and blood pressures, count respirations, and bathe sick patients in their beds.

Wearing stiffly-starched white uniforms and caps, they worked on each of the traditional eight-hour nursing shifts and were assigned in turn to each of the services—medicine, surgery, obstetrics and pediatrics. All of the students were women recently out of high school, and they were carefully supervised by their instructors; there was no relationship with the doctors (even the youngest ones) beyond formal interactions on the wards during procedures and the business of rounds.

As part of her rotation through an infectious disease hospital, Barbara was sent with some of her classmates to the Chicago stockyards. They got off the buses just outside the holding pens containing hundreds of cattle that were being forced into increasingly narrow chutes onto a conveyor that took them into the slaughter house. At the entry, they were killed, or almost killed, by a hammer blow on the head and then hooked by their bound back feet to an overhead track that moved from station to station as the creatures were disemboweled and dismembered. Most of the nursing students were horrified by the sight and the smell of this spectacle, and several had to leave.

Barbara, though sickened, managed to remain watching and remembers, "by the time they bashed them on the head and slit their throats, they were just about done. To this day, I don't really know why we went to the stockyard. I don't know what we learned." Perhaps Upton Sinclair's *The Jungle*, a novel that exposed the poor sanitation and contamination of meat permitted in the Chicago stockyards at the turn of the century, was still shocking enough in the minds of the nursing school instructors to link the yards to infectious disease and epidemics. By the time Barbara Neal and her classmates visited the stockyards in 1937, government inspection insured that hygiene was no longer an issue.

Following the rotation through the infectious diseases hospital, which included home visits to children with diphtheria and whooping cough where they provided steam treatments by boiling water and erecting tents over the faces of the little ones, the student nurses were encouraged to join the Red Cross. Many of them, including Barbara who had become very interested in public health and infection, did join.

On vacations and at holidays, Barbara, anticipating her life as a stewardess, flew on DC-3 propeller planes back to Buffalo. Most summers, though, she and her siblings traveled two hundred miles north to the middle of Ontario. Ray Neal had built a summer house at Dorset, near Lake of Bays. The family stayed much of the summer in the wild isolation of Central Ontario, canoeing on the lake, camping, fishing and listening to the call of the loons gliding over the water.

In 1939, Barbara graduated cum laude from nursing school and applied for a job with American Airlines. She flew to Long Island to be interviewed for a job as a stewardess, but in spite of her outstanding record at school, she was told she lacked experience. The man who interviewed her suggested that she work for a year in a hospital. Slightly disappointed, Barbara returned to Buffalo and found a job at the Millard-Filmore Hospital—a building with two wings connected by a central supply.

With good organizational skills, but little practical nursing experience, Barbara was placed in charge of the central supply room. She lived at home and worked for a year and a half before reapplying, and being accepted, at American Airlines. After six weeks training at the airline's headquarters on Long Island, she began work as a stewardess on DC-3's flying between Buffalo and Detroit, a job she held for only two months.

Because she had joined the Red Cross, and moreover had been especially interested in infection at St. Luke's, Barbara received a letter from the Red Cross in 1940 describing the Harvard Hospital and offering her a nursing position. Her parents were worried about the danger of the passage to Europe during wartime, but Barbara, like young Paul Beeson, thought it a grand adventure. Although it involved leaving a serious boyfriend, she wanted an opportunity to use the nursing skills which, to her surprise, had interested her much more than she had anticipated when she entered St. Luke's. Barbara and eight other young nurses spent a night at the Roosevelt Hotel in New York City and the next morning sailed on an ancient Dutch freighter, not surprisingly called the Edam.

Because the United States had not yet declared war on Germany, the departure was managed inconspicuously, although the nurses were required to wear their uniforms. The convoy of sixteen ships was blacked out, and in spite of several loud siren warnings and lifeboat drills, they were not attacked.

When they landed at Liverpool three weeks later, however, they learned that some of the ships in another convoy traveling at the same time had been not only attacked, but sunk. Five Red Cross nurses had been lost at sea; several others were finally rescued after bobbing in open lifeboats for a few days on the North Atlantic. The sobered group of young women, confronting the reality of their situation for the first time, took a bus to London where they stayed only a few days before being sent to temporary staff-nurse jobs nearby.

Barbara was assigned to a hospital in the London suburb of Northwood. She lived in a private home there for four months while the ready-made buildings were being assembled at Salisbury. As the day came to open the hospital, the nurses moved back to London where they were permitted by their housemother to stroll the relatively safe streets in the evening before blackout.

Walking home after dinner one night, Barbara and Lucy Church, a nurse who had traveled with her from New York, met Bill Hawley, the Harvard doctor who had come to greet the Edam at Liverpool. Bill introduced the two young women to his companion, the Chief Physician of the new hospital, Paul Beeson. Barbara later recalled being more interested in meeting Dr. Hawley again than in the brief introduction to his boss.

◆　◆　◆

Harmon Hill rises above the City of Salisbury and has a panoramic view of the Salisbury plain and the Cathedral spire. The American Red Cross-Harvard Hospital, a series of buildings connected by colored walkways, was assembled on this hill and admitted its first patients in the fall of 1941, just months before Pearl Harbor was attacked. Up the hill from town there was a parking lot. To the left stood the offices and administrative buildings, and to the right were the hospital wards. Beyond the wards were dormitories, a large dining hall and a recreation building. Some of the English employees lived in town, but all of the Americans lived at the hospital.

As Dr. Beeson began his duties as Chief Physician, Barbara Neal, because of her experience at Millard-Filmore, was placed in charge of central supply located just across from the administrative offices. John Gordon, nominally running the field unit operation, spent a majority of his time in London working on planning with the Ministry of Health. There was a capable Englishwoman director who managed the hospital business affairs and Beeson was responsible for the doctors and patients.

For the few men, it must have been a happy life doing interesting work in a place remote from the bombing and with the companionship of fifty young nurses and other female staff.

Paul Beeson was already much admired by the hospital staff when he and Barbara Neal happened to share a taxi one evening in London. Although they remembered being introduced, and certainly knew each other from chance meetings around the hospital, the attractive Dr. Beeson, it was known, was being pursued by one of the administrative secretaries. In the midst of trying to figure out what to do with the pounds of excess chocolate she kept receiving from the Red Cross, Barbara heard the admiring reports of other nurses, doctors and staff about Beeson's skill as a physician, his beautiful manners and sympathetic heart. She was therefore interested as well as curious when he began to appear rather more frequently than might be expected or required to investigate the central supply room.

After one lingering visit, he suggested that they go to dinner. She said yes. "And to the movies." Again she said, "Yes."

Over the next several months, Paul and Barbara began to spend more and more time together, eating in the dining hall side by side, walking in the country, or picnicking near Salisbury. They went to the recreation building for music and dancing, although Paul was neither an avid nor even a very capable dancer. Barbara, always athletic, tolerated this shortcoming.

On the occasions when nurses from the hospital attended parties at nearby military installations, Paul and the other Harvard doctors conscripted the huge Red Cross lorries to pick them up, seeing to it that the young women were returned safely and at a proper hour. This was, no doubt, a relief to the house-mother assigned to watch over them.

The gentle but ardent secretary was forgotten, although not without some pain. When she learned from Dr. Beeson that he had become engaged, she said, with great feeling but no malice, "I think you ought to un-ask her." By then, Barbara and Paul were committed to each other, though, and their relationship blossomed and ripened along with their work.

Just before the hospital opened to patients, an epidemic of meningococcal meningitis occurred in England. It was exactly the sort of infection planners had been concerned about when Gordon had suggested building the Harvard Unit. Since penicillin was not yet commercially available, and not even really available to the military in useful quantities, most of these people died after only hours or a few days of headache, stiff neck, confusion and coma. Although this particularly violent epidemic had been controlled by September 1941, both military and civilian patients with other infectious diseases from around Salisbury began to be admitted to the Harvard Hospital in about equal numbers.

There were facilities for isolating patients, and a modern bacteriology laboratory was in operation. This enabled Beeson to examine the culture plates for each patient in the morning after rounds, a habit acquired from Charles Janeway at the Brigham. The lab was useful during the investigation of an outbreak of *Paratyphoid B* infection, later reported in the *Lancet* by Scott, Beeson and Hawley, with the finding that the new antibiotic sulphaguanidine was ineffective in its treatment.(7)

There was also an unexpectedly high incidence of mumps at a near-by British training facility, which offered an opportunity to provide new recruits with passive immunization by giving them convalescent serum obtained from infected patients. Beeson was able to report that, while this did eventually control the epidemic, it also resulted in an almost fifty percent incidence of hepatitis among those inoculated, a completely unanticipated complication.(8)

Clinical investigators were beginning to appreciate that biological manipulation, while often solving targeted problems, sometimes introduced unforeseen new ones. The production of highly virulent bacterial species resistant to antibiotics is such a problem. Transmission of viral diseases such as hepatitis is another. Later, as his academic career began at Emory, Beeson remembered this unhappy episode of doing more harm than good, and used the experience when he returned to the investigation of hepatitis transmitted through the transfusion of blood products.

Perhaps as a measure of the surprisingly small numbers of epidemics in England after the meningitis outbreak, Beeson examined the epidemiology of acute myalgia of the neck, a condition that he and co-workers could describe but not transmit or treat.(9) The fact that they even tried to transmit "stiff neck" by injecting volunteers with the uncrossmatched blood of patients recovering from this illness would not be acceptable in today's environment of informed consent. Such a concept was as unknown during the war as it had been while Beeson was a student at McGill.

When this work was presented at the epidemiology section of the Royal Society of Medicine, a member of the audience remarked that, if they had kept up this line of research they would have killed someone. He was probably correct. In fact, Beeson and his colleagues were still relying heavily on the first two hundred and seventy pages of Osler's *Textbook of Medicine*, which carefully described clinical manifestations of the known infections but offered little effective treatment for most. The mold required for the commercial production of penicillin was still growing slowly in huge vats in the agricultural American Midwest.

More and more frequently, as Beeson worked in his office during the evening, he listened for Barbara's distinctive footsteps coming down the hall of the prefabricated building from the direction of central supply. He anticipated her warmth, charm, enthusiasm, and good looks.

When working on the quiet three to eleven evening shift, she sometimes came to sit with him and spend the spring night talking, discussing the hospital, patients and their plans for after the war. Apprehended by the head nurse during one of these visits, she was instructed that she was on duty somewhere else and sent away.

Even so, Paul and Barbara had by this time decided to get married; they decided in the same way they were to determine most things during their lives—together. They took the train into London and bought an engagement ring at a jewelers on Bond Street. They returned to celebrate by climbing the rickety stairs to a second floor Salisbury restaurant, called meatily the Haunch of Venison, for a meal only the English could appreciate—jugged hare.

By the summer of 1942, the United States was at war with Germany and Japan. The original mission of the American Red Cross-Harvard Hospital came to an end. Secretary of War Stimson announced transfer of the twenty-two building Epidemiological Field Unit to the U.S. Army in August, 1942. Members of the Harvard staff were given an opportunity to enlist in the Army and thereby remain at the hospital. As a consequence of the recurrent urinary tract infections related to his congenital anomaly, Beeson was not eligible for military service.

In March of 1942, anticipating transfer of the hospital to the Army, Beeson sent a letter of resignation to Harvard Dean Sidney Burwell. Because he had been slightly uncertain about finding another academic job when departing for England the year before, he had maintained his instructor's position at Harvard.

In his exchange of letters with Soma Weiss during late October of 1941, Beeson had decided not to return to the Brigham, and was waiting to receive cables from Cornell and Emory with final offers of a faculty job. While he had already been named the new Chairman of Medicine at Emory, Eugene Stead was still the acting chief at the Brigham following Weiss' death, before the appointment of George Thorn. Stead remembers contacting Beeson by telegram in Salisbury shortly before he and Evelyn moved to Atlanta:

> I offered Paul the rank of associate professor [actually assistant] and a salary of $4000. Meanwhile David Barr at Cornell had decided to establish an infectious disease unit at New York Hospital and opened negotiations with Beeson. I gave Paul a deadline for my offer and to my great joy he accepted. Shortly thereafter Barr made a definitive offer and upped the salary to $5000. Beeson regretted his acceptance of my Emory offer but being a gentleman as well as a scholar he came to Emory.(10)

In fact, Barr's offer was only forty-five hundred dollars, and arrived by telegram ten hours after Beeson had accepted the Emory job. A few hundred dollars was real money in 1942; a bottle of Coke was still only five cents. Stead, with a total budget of only twenty-three thousand five hundred dollars to run his entire department for the year was not in a position to try to outbid Barr in any case.

The faculty appointment in infectious disease at the more prestigious Cornell-run New York Hospital eventually was taken over by Walsh McDermott (also exempted from military service because of tuberculosis), who was to become Beeson's closest friend and co-editor of Cecil and Loeb's *Textbook of Medicine.* In time, both men thought it fortunate that they had not been placed in competition over the same interests so early in their careers.

Shortly before sending his letter of resignation to Dean Burwell, and not realizing how ill his former chief was, Beeson informed Weiss that he hoped to accept the position at Emory. In a cable dated January 26, 1942 Weiss responded, "Whatever you decide is agreeable with me." Five days later he was dead.

It is perhaps a reflection of the very formal relationships between these doctors that Burwell's letter to Beeson of March 29, written only nine days after the Memorial Service for Weiss at Harvard, doesn't mention either Weiss' death or the events of the heartbreaking service remembering him that Beeson was unable to attend. Just as interesting, especially when compared to the sometimes grand announcements on the stationery of faculty members today, the letterhead reads only "Harvard Medical School, Office of the Dean", and the single page is signed simply C. Sidney Burwell, M.D.

Despite the unexpected loss of his greatly admired chief, Beeson was busy planning to get married and start teaching at Emory. The logistics of arranging a return to the United States, a wedding and a move to Atlanta were begun with Barbara's help.

In June of 1942, when Nazi submarine warfare made trans-Atlantic travel by boat dangerous, Paul and Barbara, plus another nurse returning home to Massachusetts, were the only three passengers on a freighter sailing from Bristol for Boston. Since the German U-boat threat to shipping was at a peak, they crossed the Channel, traveled north around Scotland and Ireland where there was air cover, and joined a military convoy. The ten-day trip across the Atlantic was blacked out at night and, although dangerous, it was uneventful. From Boston, they took trains in different directions, Barbara to Buffalo and Paul to Wooster.

While the prospective groom stayed with his parents and brother, trying to figure out how to become a husband and Assistant Professor of Medicine, Barbara and her family arranged a wedding for July 10, 1942. Even before the couple had returned from England, their families had met, each to be reassured that their child had not made a terrible mistake in England during the excitement of the war and separation from parental influences. Apparently everyone was satisfied, but the twenty-four year old Barbara, on meeting her mother-in-law for the first time just days before her wedding, must have been surprised and apprehensive if not terrified when the older woman said, "If there is such a thing as a perfect person, it would be Paul." Over the next fifty-six years of marriage, Barbara learned why Martha Beeson believed that about her younger child and, with few exceptions, came to agree.

Beeson's parents took the train to Buffalo, and their son, who had gone earlier to be with Barbara and her family, picked them up at the station. As John and Martha Beeson stepped off the Pullman car and made their way down the wooden platform toward him, Paul's eyes suddenly filled with tears as he, in that instant, appreciated the irreversible changes occurring in his life.

A small family wedding was held at the Neal house in Snyder on a hot July day. Leila, a black woman who worked for the Neal family, and her two sons who had grown up with Barbara's brother Pete, were there to join the celebration; it didn't occur to either the bride or groom that the very composition of this bridal party might introduce a problem for them when they moved to the South. Robert Boggs, soon to be named Dean of the New York Postgraduate Medical School, was the best man.

After the ceremony, the newlyweds were officially headed by car (a wedding present from Paul's parents) for Atlanta, but spent the first night in a Buffalo hotel before starting south the next morning. There was still gas rationing along the Atlantic seaboard that summer, but none west of the Alleghenies, so they traveled through Pennsylvania west of the mountains to Atlanta.

On the way, they stopped to rent clubs and play golf, a game Paul had learned from his father and brother in Ohio. Barbara assumed she would be able to play because of her athleticism and schoolgirl career in field hockey. Golf, it turned out, required lessons that the young groom was unable to provide, so the distraction was soon abandoned. Like most newlyweds, they faced days, and then years, of discovery.

During the week-long trip on back roads into the South, Beeson developed another urinary tract infection and was ill for a couple of days. He had taken sulfa and recovered by the time they checked into an Atlanta Hotel and called Gene and Evelyn Stead to report their arrival.

Sometime the first week, they rented a second floor, one bedroom, furnished apartment in a private house on Beach Malley Road near Grady Hospital. Barbara found a part-time job in the blood bank. On August 1, 1942 Dr. Paul Beeson began his academic life as Assistant Professor of Medicine at Emory University.

CHAPTER 7

Seventy-second Meeting [of the Interurban Clinical Club]: Boston, December 7–8, 1945....I.T. Nathanson discussed "Stilbestrol in the Treatment of Cancer of the Breast." Huggins had already made his pioneer observations on the role of the hormones in cancer of the prostate. Then F.D.Moore . . . talked about "Transdiaphragmatic Resection of the Vagus Nerve in the Treatment of Peptic Ulcer"—an innovation of Lester Dragstedt's of the University of Chicago....There was a paper by Lewis Dexter and C.S. Burwell on the use of the new technique of venous catheterization in the "Diagnosis of Congenital Heart Disease."

A. McGehee Harvey, 1945(1)

When Eugene Stead announced to Dr. Weiss that he and Evelyn Selby were engaged and wanted to plan a honeymoon trip, Weiss said, "Fine, take the week-end." After the wedding, at which Weiss stood in for his much-admired secretary's deceased father and gave the bride away, that's just what the newlyweds did.

This commitment to duty was the kind of expectation Weiss had of his staff, from first year medical student to Chief Resident and faculty; the patients and medicine came first. It was the same expectation Stead took with him back to Atlanta when he returned in 1942 as the first full-time Chief of Medicine at Emory.

Gene Stead, born in Georgia, had entered the Emory School of Medicine in 1928. He chose medical school, he later recalled, because "it offered an intellectual challenge . . . [and because] the other graduate schools had no vacancies." Neither of these witticisms seems to have been especially true. Stead, because he graduated with Phi Beta Kappa honors from college, would probably have had his choice of graduate schools.

When Stead was being interviewed for medical school during the depression, "The only question anyone asked me when I applied for admission was, 'Son, can you borrow the money for tuition?' I said that the Atlanta Rotary Club would lend me the money."(2)

During his exceptional career in medical school, Stead developed an early interest in the cardiovascular system. He was influenced by Paul White's work on heart disease—the same White who had so excited Beeson and his classmates at McGill at about the same time.

Several Emory faculty members who had been at Harvard arranged for their outstanding fourth year student to compete for one of the prized and demanding sixteen-month-long internships at the Peter Bent Brigham Hospital. He was appointed. Curiously, and perhaps as an example of Stead's extraordinary commitment to his calling, he wasn't satisfied. Beginning in 1934, he did a second internship at Harvard— this time on the surgery service. He explained seeking this extra burden by saying simply, "I wanted to see the surgical side of practice." He also worked as a research fellow in Henry Christian's laboratory, studying the edema of heart failure, before he moved to Cincinnati and completed his training in internal medicine.

When Soma Weiss visited Cincinnati General Hospital to make teaching rounds in 1936 and found Stead (whom he knew by reputation from his internships) on the ward, he offered him a job at the Thorndike Laboratory of Boston City Hospital for an annual salary of nine hundred dollars. With a gesture of confidence some later misinterpreted as arrogance, Stead replied that he required eighteen hundred and that if Weiss could find it, he would come to Boston. Weiss did so by combining the research fellowship with the job of Chief Resident at the Boston City Hospital, and Stead, who had no wish to go anywhere else, returned to Harvard in 1937.

By the time Beeson arrived at the Brigham Hospital two years later, Stead was firmly established as one of Soma Weiss' "young men." He had published almost a dozen scientific papers, all related to study of the cardiovascular system, and was known for both his commanding presence and his thorough knowledge of clinical medicine. While Beeson had been in Wooster learning bedside manner, Stead, exactly the same age, had gone to Harvard and Cincinnati making a more traditional start to an academic career.

These qualities were not lost on Beeson, and when Soma Weiss wrote to him at Salisbury in 1941, he was prepared to trust his future to Stead. In the October letter, Weiss told him:

> . . . You well know how much I am interested in your future progress, and therefore thought that I would like to write you how I feel about Gene's undertaking. Emory University School of Medicine has always been an important center in the South. . . . You know Gene's ability, so I don't have to add anything on that point. He is taking several younger men from the Brigham in the capacity of assistant residents. . . . The understanding and treatment of infectious diseases have been particularly neglected in the South, and therefore if you decide to go to Emory, you will be certain of a good opportunity to develop yourself clinically. I also believe that if you do good work, you will have no difficulty in getting other even more important positions if that is your ambition.(3)

Stead had joined the Harvard Medical Unit of the Army in 1941, but when he took the job at Emory, the university obtained his release with an understanding that he would neither volunteer for service nor attempt to avoid being drafted in Georgia.

Most of his friends and colleagues in Boston advised against moving to the South, perhaps with the East coast vanity that discounts intellectual activities beyond the Charles River, predicting dire financial constraints and an inability to attract good faculty. Weiss, however, encouraged the move, clearly letting his ambitious protégé know that he felt, ". . . one should go where one was needed and that it was time to determine whether I could move from a man of promise to a man of achievement."(4)

Both Stead and Beeson were carefully counseled by their chief, who seems never to have given either of them advice that wasn't unselfish and entirely in the best interests of the younger men. This quality of Weiss' was preserved in both Stead and Beeson who, although they had very different personalities, became revered by their own students because of their selfless honesty and reliable fairness.

When he arrived at Emory in July of 1942 to take over the Department of Medicine as the first full-time chief of the service, Stead immediately found problems. The most divisive obstacle was the absence of a unified service at a single university hospital.

Before Martin Luther King and the freedom marches that were to come two decades later, Grady Hospital was divided in two by Butler Street. On one side stood the Henry Grady Memorial Hospital, the School of Nursing and an outpatient clinic, all populated by white patients and staff. Across the street was the Emory Division of Grady Hospital, the "colored hospital", with its own dormitory for black nurses, a segregated emergency room and outpatient clinic.

Each of these hospitals had its own chief of medicine, but all of the doctors in both of them were white. Stead, armed with both greater knowledge and depth of purpose, reasoned that he would take charge of the entire operation by remaining in each of the units night and day while the nominal chiefs of the "colored" and "white" hospitals would show up only occasionally. This strategy worked, and by 1943 Stead was named Chief of the Medical Service in both hospitals.

This did not mean, however, that he was completely accepted by the majority of internists in Atlanta, most of whom felt that a local practitioner should have been made the professor and chairman. Since many of these disgruntled physicians helped control the local draft board, their unhappiness resulted in Stead's other early difficulty—keeping his staff.

For the Northerners like Phil Bondy, one of the young residents Stead imported from Boston to finish his training, both the segregation issue and the possibility of being drafted made life difficult. The canny Stead had recruited Bondy because of his several talents and a couple of liabilities. A promising intern at the Brigham, Bondy was deaf in one ear and had severe asthma; the Boston draft board had twice told him that he was unfit for military service. Knowing this, Stead was probably as surprised as his new resident when, three months after he had arrived at Emory, the Fulton-DeKalb County Procurement and Assignment Committee found Dr. Bondy perfectly qualified, drafted him and assigned him to Rome, Georgia for three years of Army service.

When Bondy returned to Grady in 1946, Stead, Beeson, Jack Myers and Jim Warren had already established an excellent clinical medicine service, and all were involved in innovative research. Although the war had ended and with it the threat of residents being stolen by the draft board, the social dilemmas presented by segregation had not changed. Years later, following his retirement from Yale, Bondy wrote about the difficult racial problems at Grady after the war:

First, let me give a social and physical description of the hospital, using the terms that were in use while I worked there, even though some of them are unacceptable today. The color line was clearly drawn in almost everything. When you mentioned a white nurse, she was called "Miss" or "Mrs." Negro nurses were called "Nurse.". . . A white patient you would call "Mrs. Jones" or, if you knew her well, by her first name. Colored patients were usually called "you," "boy" or "girl" but, commonly, "child." It was a sign of respect to call a colored patient by his or her first name. . . .

. . . The hospital was designed and operated with virtually complete separation of the two groups. Linens were marked "Colored" or "White" and were kept separate. There were separate buildings, with separate pharmacies, waiting rooms, operating rooms, clinics, x-ray departments, supply rooms and emergency rooms. There was one laboratory and one blood bank, but blood itself was rigidly segregated. If, in an emergency, one ran out of colored blood of a certain type, it was grudgingly permissible to use white blood, "since this could only improve the colored patient." If the situation were reversed, the party line was that it was better for the white patient to die than to get colored blood! Fortunately, even the most traditional members of the house staff were not crazy enough to go along with this. . . .

In spite of the high quality of the colored nursing students and nurses, the administration refused to give African-Americans full responsibility. Thus the medical colored wards had a white nursing supervisor—a strident, nasty woman who believed in keeping the colored staff in its place—and a black assistant chief nurse who was sensitive, sympathetic and highly skilled. The house staff tried to deal entirely with the assistant. . . . (5)

By the time he was Chief Resident, Bondy did his part to subvert these traditions when he was required to teach both groups of nursing students the basics of internal medicine. He had noticed that, when they worked side by side learning about nutrition in the common kitchen, the black and white students got along just fine. Since he didn't want to waste his time giving the same lecture twice, he put all of them together and, although they sat on opposite sides of the room and considered their instructor a crazy Yankee, the two groups respected each other and there was no trouble.

The Beesons faced the same difficult adjustment to unacceptable traditions after they were settled in Atlanta. Initially these problems were unseen. The task in front of them that late summer was to make a new life together. After they called the Steads from their hotel the night they arrived, Paul and Barbara were invited to their house in the suburb of Decatur.

"Gene remarked in the evening after dinner, 'Paul, I've got a lab for you and a technician.' I was so naive. I hope I didn't show it too much, but I was flabbergasted with the thought that I would be expected to do research."(6)

Along with Stead and the cardiologist Robert Grant, the other full-time internal medicine faculty member, Beeson moved into the departmental office in the basement of what was then called the Colored Nurses Home. It was a consistently damp address that flooded when it rained. Down a few steps from Butler Street, along a single corridor were offices, one for each of the full-time faculty and one for the secretary they all shared. There were also the labs that Beeson was so surprised to discover he would be using, and a small room for housing experimental animals. The department included Stead's friend Art Merrill and several other private internists in Atlanta, part-time faculty who sometimes attended on the wards. In 1942, that was the whole show.

Because Stead, Beeson, Grant and Jack Myers (the great clinician who joined his Boston friends at Emory after the war ended), as well as several of the residents, had all been trained by Soma Weiss, the clinical and teaching programs at Emory quickly acquired the flavor, if not the academic rigor, of Harvard. At exactly eight in the morning, the Chief Resident gathered the other residents and interns for morning report to be heard by Stead in his office.

This early ritual, by which time it was expected that every patient admitted overnight would have been completely worked up by the resident on call, included brief presentations of these new admissions as well as a report on the progress of the sickest patients already on the wards. Focusing on these complex problems, diagnosed primarily by physical examination, plain x-rays or simple lab tests, wasn't easy for the house staff who often had been awake most of the night.

Lack of sleep was not always a consequence of work. Rest was hard to find. There were no phones in the house staff quarters at Grady, which were located just behind the emergency room and near the obstetrics ward of the "colored" hospital. Atlanta at that time was often a violent city and "the ambulance sirens, the shouts of the drunk or injured clinic patients, the yells of the cops shutting them up made a constant racket . . . when a house officer was needed at night the telephone operator would send a colored orderly to wake him up. The orderly usually only had a vague idea of which room to go to, and no clue as to which of the bodies in the room needed wakening."(7)

Nonetheless, Stead demanded of the residents the same things that he asked of himself, and the chairman was in the hospital most of the time. Phil Bondy, doing a lumbar puncture in the middle of one long night on-call, turned around to find the boss watching over his shoulder. Although longing to return to the din of the house staff dormitory for at least a few hours of being horizontal if not asleep, instead he spent the next thirty minutes discussing the case with Stead, who then wandered to another ward in search of new patients and more residents needing instruction.

After Stead, or Beeson when the chairman was away, took morning report, the real work of the day began with ward rounds. The faculty member attending on each service walked from bed to open bed accompanied by an army of students and the house staff, who wore starched white uniforms with shirts buttoned to the neck both winter and summer.

A student or intern presented each case without notes, describing the basic findings. "These discussions were usually Socratic, with the senior doctor questioning his juniors and leading them to come to their own conclusions." For the students and house officers these moments were either filled with terror if they were unprepared or ignorant, or else provided an opportunity for them to display an understanding of the disease in question either by recalling memorized text or, more rarely, displaying a real knowledge of the patho-physiology of the illness. For Beeson and the rest of the faculty, the debates held on rounds and the unsolved clinical questions that remained were the substance of the problems they took to their research labs for investigation.

When Stead began to recruit faculty for Grady, he wanted Beeson early, not only because he knew that Paul's Red Cross service exempted him from the draft, but more importantly because he remembered him as an excellent teacher and a promising investigator with credentials in the new discipline of infectious disease. Beeson was already committed to the study of infection after his experience at Rockefeller and Salisbury, and heeded Weiss' advice that the South would be fertile ground for clinical research in this field.

When starting at Emory, he still puzzled over the huge outbreak of hepatitis among the soldiers to whom he had given convalescent mumps plasma in England. Although the incidence of mumps did eventually decline, the men had certainly not been helped by the attack on their livers. Max Finland, one of the early investigators to specialize in infection, had suggested in 1939 that a virus might be responsible for hepatitis following serum inoculation, but Beeson and his co-workers had been unable to prove this claim in their own cases. At the time, the only transmissible hepatitis known (now called hepatitis A) came from contaminated food.

Shortly after he arrived at Emory, Beeson was having lunch one afternoon with a medical student who mentioned a patient on the ward who had what was being called toxic hepatitis. The sick man had been hospitalized three months before with burns, and had been treated with tannic acid, the suspected cause of his liver disease. Beeson asked the student to find out if the patient had been given blood during his first illness, and then made certain by examining the records himself. He went to the medical records room and looked up all the other recent cases of toxic jaundice and hepatitis, discovering six more—all of whom had been transfused. Because blood and blood products were starting to be given with regularity, the finding that hepatitis often accompanied transfusion was a significant one.

Stead saw to it that the discovery was rapidly reported in the widely circulated *Journal of the American Medical Association* in the spring of 1943; it was a major announcement.(8) Beeson had recognized that the most distinctive feature of this type of jaundice was a long delay between exposure and the onset of symptoms, suggesting an infectious process derived from blood. Soon, it was accepted that toxic hepatitis or jaundice following transfusion (now hepatitis B and C) was caused by specific viruses, just as Finland had suggested. As a clinician, Beeson was recognized around the country for establishing the link between transfusion and infectious hepatitis.

It was during this time that the compelling Beeson style of teaching, remembered lovingly by all of his students, began to be noticed on, but not limited to, the medical wards. When the problem was infection, his advice was solicited from attendings and residents on all the hospital services. The cardiologist Willis Hurst, who came to Emory in 1950, recalls, "His teaching on ward rounds and conferences was masterful and gentle, his style more reserved than Stead's. He was, we suspected, a bit shy. He was never intimidating and gained the immediate respect of the students, house staff and colleagues. His immense knowledge was always evident."(9)

Early in the fall of the first year at Grady, the person who had been running the bacteriology lab quit and Beeson was asked to take over supervision of this progressively more important function. Because he had continued Janeway's practice of examining the culture plates himself at Salisbury, the task of determining the specific bacteriological causes of various infections from around the hospital was not new to him. His review of the culture plates and identification of the various species of bacteria became a popular stopping place for students following morning rounds.

After the interns had collected urine, sputum, pus or drainage from a wound, they brought it to bacteriology for culture, where each specimen was marked with the patient's identification number, source, and date of collection. Under hoods in the lab, a dab of the infected material was scooped out on a tiny, flame-sterilized wire loop. It was then either smeared onto six-inch shallow, round glass culture plates filled with blood-agar, or incubated in test tubes of other culture media, before all specimens were carefully stored. Important conditions favoring the growth of various organisms were controlled, including pH, temperature, and presence of oxygen, so that colonies of the offending bacteria could be grown and identified.

Sometimes Beeson was able to name the illness simply by examining the colonies on the plates and in the test tubes, because subjecting each specimen to various conditions limited the possibility for survival in culture to one type of organism. More often, students gathered around him as he sat at a monocular microscope and examined the glass slides smeared with the product of the culture and then colored by gram staining. Various pictures of disease-causing bacilli appeared: Cocci, singly or in chains; pink and blue rods; sometimes organisms within cells or with little tails called flagella could be identified. By the time Beeson took over the bacteriology lab at Grady, if the organism could be named, the disease could often be treated effectively.

By 1943, the penicillium molds growing in the Midwest, having been chemically encouraged to ferment faster, began to yield a pharmacologically pure product that could be injected into humans. There was enormous excitement at the Emory Medical School when it became known that Dr. Beeson had been asked by Chester Keefer on behalf of the Office of Scientific Research and Development to distribute the new drug in the Southwest.(10) For several months, the local physicians attending every patient with an infection possibly susceptible to penicillin consulted the expert at Grady.

Since the bacteria had never been exposed to the drug, and therefore had not evolved resistance against its effect on their cell walls, Beeson doled out the precious compound in tiny doses of five thousand units (compared to the millions of units now required). Only a few months earlier, those patients almost certainly would have died without the drug.

Unfortunately, Beeson, with little information or first hand experience actually using penicillin, and trying to decide over the phone with another doctor who to treat, didn't always choose correctly. One practitioner calling from Southern Georgia attempted to get treatment for a patient with syphilis, and was denied the drug with the comment "there is no evidence at all that penicillin can be used to treat lues." This, of course, was an error, though one of few. With the advent of commercially available penicillin, and the other antibiotics that soon followed, internists became successful at treating diseases that before had been poorly managed by surgical drainage or excision of the infected area.

The changes in Beeson's professional life were no more profound than those at home. There was an active social life among the faculty; dinner parties were frequent and exhilarating. Many of the new professors and residents had known each other in Boston, and they all made new friends quickly. No sooner had

Paul and Barbara become accustomed to each other and to life in this new environment, when they had to get use to the idea of becoming parents. As Barbara's pregnancy advanced, she left the blood bank and they moved to a house on Lanier Boulevard, which really was a boulevard, the landscaped strip down the middle lined with huge magnolia trees. John Beeson was born at Emory University Hospital in January, 1944; both baby and mother were hospitalized for ten days. About the same time, they hired Mary, the first of several black women who worked in the household.

Mary was a big woman and afflicted with one of the several plagues that then attacked poor black people in the South: hypertension. This predilection for high blood pressure was probably related to a combination of factors, including poor diet high in sodium, obesity, stress—physical and emotional—and genetics.

Huge numbers of patients were also seen at the Emory Division of Grady with widely-spread miliary tuberculosis, syphilis, typhoid fever, black widow spider bites, and occasionally even rabies. The white Harvard-trained doctors had to learn a new set of diseases and a new vocabulary to work successfully in the black out-patient clinics. One of the residents, on hearing from a female patient, "I ain't seen nothing for two months" (meaning that she had not menstruated), sent her to the ophthalmology department.

Mary, not yet forty, didn't make it to the clinic at all, however. Her daughter called Barbara one day to report that her mother had been taken to the hospital with a heart attack in the middle of the night, and there she died two days later. Dr. and Mrs. Beeson were the only white people at the emotional Baptist funeral.

They had the same kind of relationship with Lilly, who came after Mary died, and who was surprised when she was invited to use the family bathroom. Years later, visiting from New Haven, Barbara went to see Lilly at her house, and asked her about freedom rides, sit-ins, and marches, and the politics of Martin Luther King, who was then emerging as an important leader. With considerable insight, the long-time domestic worker said, "We're going to have an awful lot of hate."

Peter Beeson was born in 1946, a year and a half after his brother. It appeared that the Beeson family was going to be in Atlanta for a while, a thing not certain when they had first arrived new to the South, academic medicine and each other. At the urging of the Steads, they decided to spend ten thousand dollars and build a house on Atlanta's north side. They chose an area on the edge of town with an excellent school system. Barbara helped supervise the construction of a house on North Druid Hills Road, complete with a tree house for John and Peter in the back yard, and a shallow pool in the front yard where she taught them to swim.

Barbara, consumed with the responsibilities of a young faculty wife and mother, was a partner to her husband as he started at Emory, as she was at every moment of his long career. Because of a heavy work schedule herself, toddlers John and Peter were sometimes left in Lilly's charge, and when their boyish energy had bothered her enough she sometimes commanded, "Go on down yonder!"

By the time they were in nursery school, it was clear that John was a musician and Peter a good athlete. Neither boy was ever interested in becoming a doctor. From a very early age, John loved nothing more than music, and listened to so much of the Metropolitan Opera on the Sunday afternoon Firestone Theater radio program that he learned Italian. Between the beds in the boys' room was a wind-up Victrola that they were allowed to play after one of their parents read them a bed-time story.

The children were quiet and not a nuisance in the evenings when their father brought papers home to work on while he sat on the living room couch, a habit he continued as an editor through several volumes of the most important textbooks of medicine. The family never did get around to converting their extra bedroom into an office as they sometimes planned. Most evenings when they didn't have other faculty or house staff for dinner, the living room was piled with papers, books and drafts of work in progress. Beeson was careful from the beginning of his academic life to leave both clinical matters and hospital politics out of the house. When Barbara asked if there were any problems as he arrived home in the evening, he invariably responded, "Nope."

❖ ❖ ❖

Gene Stead was driven to produce not only a strong clinical program at Emory, but to continue his own basic research in cardiovascular physiology and to provide an atmosphere that fostered similar work for the rest of the faculty. As the program was being developed during the war, Alfred Blalock, an important Johns Hopkins surgeon, visited Atlanta and recommended to Stead that he both apply for an Army grant to study the hemodynamic effects of blood loss and trauma and, more important, that he send Jim Warren to New York City where he could learn the emerging technique of cardiac catheterization.

At Columbia, Andre Cournand and Dickenson Richards, later Nobel Prize winners for this work, had perfected a thin, double lumen catheter, stiff but flexible enough to pass through a vein into the heart. This catheter and the techniques for using it allowed investigators to measure pressures and gas saturations in the heart and great blood vessels that before then were not known.

Warren returned from Bellevue Hospital armed with the catheters, and the department secretary sent the grant application off to the Army. She mistakenly typed the forms with a decimal off by a factor of ten in requesting funds to build, equip and operate the lab. Happily, the error favored Emory, and the Army, seeming not to notice, provided the inflated sum. Thus, Stead and his faculty had more than enough money to build the third cardiac catheterization laboratory in the world.

While Stead, Warren and Myers wanted to learn about cardiac function and hemodynamics, Beeson was interested in another killer disease then common on the Grady wards, subacute bacterial endocarditis. Patients with this infection on the valves of their hearts suffer fever from continuous bacteremia, and often embolization of clumps of organisms producing symptoms remote from the heart. Prior to antibiotics, endocarditis was nearly always fatal. Beeson recognized the opportunity to learn about the illness by sampling blood simultaneously from the heart, arteries and veins of infected patients during cardiac catheterization.

Because the concept still didn't exist in 1943, informed consent was not obtained from patients for these tests. Though the researchers were only sampling blood, there was still a small risk from the procedure itself. Writing for the Final Report of the Advisory Committee on Human Radiation Experiments in 1995, Beeson said:

> All I could say at the end was that these poor people were lying there and we had nothing to offer them and it might have given them some comfort that a lot of people were paying attention to them for this one study. I don't remember ever asking their permission to do it. I did go around and see them, of course, and said, "We want to do a study on you in the x-ray department, we'll do it tomorrow morning," and they said yes. There was never any question . . . [I]f I were ever on a hospital ethics committee today, I wouldn't ever pass on that particular study.(11)

The cardiac catheterization laboratory was in a small room off the x-ray department at Grady, and was especially busy on week-ends when people were most likely to be injured. Before sophisticated image intensifiers and computers, patients lay supine on a simple table under a long, horizontally mounted fluoroscope while the procedure was begun. The staff all wore red goggles to accommodate their eyes to dark before the fluoroscopic study could begin. This slowed down movement and created the odd sensation of doctors and nurses paddling around the dim room wearing their clothes in a strange sort of waterless swimming pool.

During one such examination, as the staff gazed awkwardly down into the fluoroscope, the catheter took an unexpected turn as it went through the right atrium and out of the heart. Uncertain about the anatomy, but feeling sure they had managed to perforate the heart, doctors, nurses and technicians all fell silent as Stead was summoned to save the patient, and them. The more experienced chairman determined that the catheter had simply passed through the inferior vena cava and into the hepatic vein, causing no harm to the patient or the much relieved staff.

By the end of the war, Beeson and his collaborators, with the help of Elizabeth Roberts, the capable technician Stead had provided for his lab, were now producing research of the highest quality. While he continued to publish more routine clinical research on observations concerning chancroid, rat bite fever and murine typhus fever, in the lab he produced definitive work on bacterial endocarditis.(12)

It was already known that, even though bacteria from infected heart valves had constant access to peripheral blood, they were also continuously being removed by some then-unknown mechanism. It stood to reason that if the bacteria were removed by certain organs, one could expect to find fewer bacteria in the venous blood just passed through that organ than in the heart or in arterial blood. If, on the other hand, some bactericidal action of blood itself were responsible for removing or killing the organisms, there would be no difference in the colony count (a measure of the degree of infection) between the samples.

Six patients were examined in the course of cardiac catheterization, and blood samples obtained from the heart, the femoral artery and several veins. Beeson iced the paired specimens as they were drawn, rushed off to his lab, plated them out and began their incubation. The results showed the number of bacteria was highest in arterial blood, lower in the vena cava and lowest in the hepatic vein just after blood had passed through the liver. The accidental passing of a catheter out the hepatic vein several months earlier now permitted obtaining blood from this vessel easily, and provided proof that bacteria were removed from circulating blood in the liver.

Prior to antibiotics, patients with syphilis and other infections were often treated with fever therapy, another of Beeson's interests. In Europe this was commonly done in "fever cabinets" using steam to elevate body temperature, but in the United States fever was usually produced by the intravenous injection of typhoid vaccine. Russell Cecil's *Textbook of Medicine*, by this time having replaced Osler's text in common use, reported the usefulness of this technique, which produced fever because of the bacterial pyrogens found in many micro-organisms.

Several investigators had noted that, in order to maintain a fever for the amount of time required to cure lues, more and more vaccine had to be injected, sometimes several hundred cubic centimeters. Using an experimental model that he had developed in rabbits, Beeson demonstrated that the reticulo-endothelial system (since identified in the mid 1980s by sophisticated immunology as the mononuclear phagocyte system, comprised of closely related cells of bone marrow origin) found in the liver, spleen, bone marrow and elsewhere, was responsible for removing the pyrogens, thus requiring more vaccine to produce the fevers.(13) Underlining the importance of the liver in this process, he separately reported that patients with cirrhosis of the liver, and therefore diminished hepatic function, had an exaggerated response to injected typhoid bacterial pyrogen.(14)

Beeson began presenting these research papers at scientific meetings. Before the minute sub-specialization in medicine that is now carried to such extremes that some investigators spend a career studying and treating one disease, most internists were generalists. The principal national meetings for internal medicine were for many years held along the boardwalk at Atlantic City. The gatherings involved a junior organization, the American Society for Clinical Investigation (called the young Turks) and the senior Association of American Physicians (the old Turks).

All the greats of internal medicine attended the event, which was first organized by a handful of influential physicians of the nineteenth century, including William Osler and Beeson's Dean at Penn, William Pepper.

The first meeting was held in Washington, D.C. in 1886, and stayed in Washington until 1911 when it moved to Atlantic City, remaining there for more than fifty years. As late as the 1930s, William Henry Welch, one of the fathers of the unique curriculum at Johns Hopkins School of Medicine, could be found ankle-deep in sand in front of the Haddon Hall Hotel, wearing a two-piece bathing suit and cap, a cigar clamped firmly between his teeth while he discussed some clinical problem with a colleague. Later, after Donald Trump made the location a less appealing gathering place and the associations moved to other cities, the conventions were still called the Atlantic City meetings.

From the beginning, the Atlantic City meetings were much more than scientific presentations. While the founders of the AAP had wished to advance the science and practice of medicine, they also hoped that their society (and later, the "young Turks") would avoid medical politics and concentrate on the free exchange of information and important research. The organizations, which included both physicians and basic scientists, were small enough so that most of the members were friends, with a collegial trust in the science being presented. While there were sometimes minor jealousies, there was little guile and no self-promotion.

Just as important were the personal assessments of potential residents and junior faculty offered by colleagues between sessions in the Terrace Room of Haddon Hall, on the Steel Pier at lunch time or in the restaurants and bars along the board-walk. Senior faculty often took their promising residents and fellows with them to the event, always held the first week in May.

Beeson, invited to go with Weiss, attended his first Atlantic City meeting in 1939. They stayed at Haddon Hall, and among other important talks heard John Paul of Yale present another in his series of papers on polio, work that later enabled Jonas Salk to produce the first polio vaccine. Beeson remembered that first meeting in the history of the AAP:

> The elderly black elevator operators, nice middle-aged dining room waitresses, and so forth, made it feel like coming home each time. Because the owners were Quakers, it had no bar, but the Brighton Hotel next door made up for that. The sequence of a day of enjoyable meetings, and informal discussions with old friends, as well as glimpses of the great men of that time, followed by a Brighton punch and then a lobster at Hackney's and the walk back along the boardwalk were a mar-velous combination of events.(15)

For a young man seriously interested in an academic career, the Atlantic City meetings were not only enjoyable, they were essential. All of the real business of general internal medicine was conducted at these meetings, and therefore membership, beginning with the Society for Clinical Investigation, was required.

Beeson, by then an Associate Professor, was elected at the time Stead served as secretary of the "young Turks." When Stead became vice president, Beeson took over the job of sec-retary. After a three-year term, he was invited to join the coun-cil, composed of a few members who ran the organization. Once more he followed Stead, this time to the vice president's job.

These positions were important in overseeing the organization, but also visible in the sense that the officers sat on the stage during scientific presentations and became recognized by other members. Although he was by this time a well-known figure in academic internal medicine and the scientific community, Beeson characteristically never forgot to take a treat of salt water taffy back to Atlanta for his sons, who remember eating most of the contents of the huge box as soon as they opened it.

By the end of his first several years at Emory, Beeson was growing a national reputation in infectious disease, both as a consequence of his clinical skills and work in the lab on endocarditis, hepatitis and fever. He was invited to serve on the Armed Forces Epidemiological Board investigating epidemics at bases in remote parts of South Dakota and Utah.

Another member of this board was Barry Wood, then still at Barnes Hospital in St. Louis. During these years the two infectious disease specialists became close and trusting friends. After one meeting of the board in Washington D.C., they spent a morning in the visitor's gallery of the U.S. Senate before going to watch the other Senators play the New York Yankees. Since one of Wood's ten letters at Harvard had been in baseball, Beeson got a good lesson in the real beauty of a baseball game.

In 1946, he traveled to Japan on behalf of the Board to help Japanese medical schools reorganize and to investigate epidemics after the devastating bombing of Hiroshima and Nagasaki. There were then few accurate scientific predictions about the effects of these events on diseases in the irradiated environment; medical problems that were to occupy Beeson late in his career.

The Emory Dean resigned in 1945 and the medical school, not wanting to mount a long national search—expensive even then—appointed the only local choice, Dr. Stead, to replace him. Although Emory, and the medical school especially, was generously supported by donations from Robert Woodruff, President of the Coca-Cola Company, it was still a Southern school with a small, though growing reputation.

The President of the University had just requested ten million dollars from the Board of Trustees for the School of Medicine, a huge sum at the end of the war. The job of running the medical school was tedious and occupied with the details of how to raise and spend such a vast amount of money. In an October, 1945 letter to the University President, Dean Stead described the medical school's financial needs, observing that they were responsible for providing highly skilled services to a part of the community that was economically the least productive. He noted that his budget would soon become inadequate to pay for developing technology; he proposed adding staff and wanted to create new pediatric and psychiatric units.

Finally, he explored the inadequacies of their physical facilities as well as the potential political liabilities at Grady Hospital, and raised the possibility of moving the medical school to an extensively remodeled and enlarged University Hospital on the Emory campus. In quietly recommending such a move, Stead noted that the rapid growth of both private and public hospital insurance made a university owned teaching hospital fiscally attractive.

These were not small projects and though Stead retained his position as chairman of medicine, more and more of the daily tasks of running the service fell to Beeson. Stead, a teacher and clinical investigator, didn't like being the dean. His dedication and endless compassion for patients is reflected in many of his aphorisms later collected by students, like this beautiful description of the proper relationship between a doctor and a sick person:

Tact, sympathy and understanding are expected of the physician, for the patient is no mere collection of symptoms, signs, disordered functions, damaged organs and disturbed emotions. He is human, fearful and hopeful, seeking relief, help and reassurance. To the physician, as to the anthropologist, nothing human is strange or repulsive. He cares for people because he cares for them.(16)

A year of being Dean at Emory was too much for even the tireless Stead, and he removed himself from the unwanted burden of administration by accepting the Chair of Medicine at Duke.

Stead's announcement in the spring of 1946 that he would be leaving Atlanta the following January threw confusion, if not panic, into the staff. His personality was so strong that, as sometimes happens to an organization with a powerful leader, the department had become firmly associated with the chief.

Beeson's national presence had continued to grow with Stead's during the mid forties, though, and in 1946 he had become co-editor of *The Yearbook of Medicine*, another high-profile position which helped to make him a candidate for the chair. The new dean, Hugh Wood, acted quickly to restore stability to the medicine service and suggested to the President of the University that, at a salary of ten thousand dollars a year, Beeson be appointed Professor and Chairman of the Department of Medicine as of September 16, 1946. But he wasn't left as chief of much, since Stead took most of the best faculty and several residents with him to Duke. Lamenting this, Beeson complained to Stead just before he left, "You're taking all the best people. What am I going to do for a chief resident?" With his usual excellent judgment of character, Stead recommended Phil Bondy, who Beeson agreed was the perfect choice for the job.

Aside from his logistical responsibilities—running the medicine service, organizing the house staff, and making rounds with Beeson, all still done in the careful, time-consuming manner taught so thoroughly by Soma Weiss—Bondy acquired an office and a lab. Beeson and his secretary Betty Pharr had moved into the space vacated by Stead, and his old office was remodeled into a lab for the new chief resident.

Bondy was interested in endocrinology and metabolism and was measuring protein-bound iodine (then the technique for determining thyroid function). He employed a method using equipment he housed in a closet. The technician who did this work weighed two hundred fifty pounds, requiring Bondy to keep his desk in a corner of the cramped room or be trampled.

While the experiments were in progress, C.N.H. (Hugh) Long, on the McGill faculty while Beeson was in medical school and later a well known endocrinologist before being named Dean at Yale, visited Emory and was impressed both with Bondy's research and his chairman's skill at running the department. Because Beeson wanted an endocrinologist on the faculty at Emory, he and Long arranged a fellowship at Yale for Bondy, who returned from New Haven to join the Emory faculty in 1948.

By 1949, Beeson was elected to the Association of American Physicians. A friend of his from Boston with the unlikely name of T. Duckett Jones, cornered him between sessions outside Haddon Hall during the Atlantic City meetings that year. The news Jones had to share, known within the medical establishment at medical schools between Boston and Washington, D.C., but not yet in Atlanta, concerned the National Institutes of Health. The rapid scientific development and mass production of penicillin during World War II had convinced government planners that the federal funding of medical research was a priority likely to yield quick rewards.

The Committee on Medical Research (part of the wartime Office of Scientific Research and Development) was dissolved after the war, but its ongoing projects and budget were transferred to the fledgling National Institutes of Health in Bethesda. With that transfer, the NIH budget grew from one hundred eighty thousand dollars in 1945 to four million two years later. By 1950, that budget was more than forty-five million dollars a year, about fifteen million of which went to grants given outside the institutes.(17) "You'd better know that there is going to be plenty of money available for research, and it's time to get in applications for as much as you want," Jones confided to Beeson on the boardwalk at Atlantic City.

When he returned to his small office, still in the basement of the "Colored Nurses Home," but now with knotty pine wainscoting covering at least half of the plain walls, Beeson himself began filling out the simple few pages of an NIH grant application for the study of fever. This work, which now requires pages of documentation and can take months, was finished quickly and typed by Betty Pharr; there were no copy machines, FAX machines, or computers for word processing.

The application process was simple and in Bethesda where the requests were sent, the funding process was equally simple. Officials in charge of the NIH Division of Research Grants ". . . showed a common pattern in respecting the sovereignty of the medical profession and local medical institutions. While the functions of government were expanded, the sphere of political discretion was deliberately restricted. In NIH the mechanism for restricting political control was the required approval of grants by panels of experts drawn from outside government."[18]

These panels of specialists who review what has become the mountains of proposals received by the various institutes, and rank the order of funding, are now called study sections. Serving on a study section today is an important, demanding job, but in 1950 the task was much simpler. To begin with, the science was less complex and the number of applicants tiny by modern standards. Furthermore, the informal panel of outside advisors assembled by the NIH all knew the applicants intimately, knew their interests as well as the research they were doing, and knew their capabilities; they all knew each other from Atlantic City.

Because he was trusted to produce meaningful results, Beeson's grant applications were quickly funded, as were most of the others submitted by members of his department. These grants, also tiny by today's standards, were used only to fund the laboratories of the principal investigators for their own research, or work being done in those labs by residents and fellows. There was no creative bookkeeping diverting funds for other uses in the department or the medical school.

About the time of this success, Beeson had two other important invitations. On July 12, 1950, he was appointed Associate Dean at Emory, responsible for the clinical departments at Grady as well as routine matters while Hugh Wood was out of town, something increasingly likely to happen to deans. The only reservation expressed by the various other department heads when Wood consulted them about this appointment was Beeson's own likely increased absence from direct clinical responsibility. Although the Chief of Medicine and Associate Dean initially thought this unimportant, he discovered later that the apprehensions were warranted. For the time being, though, he managed not only the department but the growing line of supplicants outside his office door. In addition, he managed the second important invitation, first delivered in 1948, to be an editor of Tinsley Harrison's new text, *Principles of Internal Medicine.*

Harrison, then Chairman of Medicine at Texas Southwestern Medical School, was a frequent visitor to Atlanta because his sister was married to Art Merrill, Stead's great friend and the Grady expert on renal diseases. Merrill had been important in helping Stead to organize the popular "Sunday School" during the war, a teaching conference held between 9:30 and 10:30 Sunday mornings, convened then so that the local internists and Army doctors from nearby Lawson General Hospital could all attend and not miss church.

Harrison admired Stead and may have offered him the editorial job before he asked Beeson—despite misunderstanding Stead's work in cardiac catheterization, a technique he believed unlikely to add much knowledge of cardiovascular physiology. Cecil and Loeb's *Textbook of Medicine* then dominated the market, but Harrison planned a different kind of internal medicine text to challenge the traditional form.

By the time Beeson joined the editorial board, which also included George Thorn, Max Wintrobe, Raymond Adams and William Resnik, Harrison had determined to organize the new book by first presenting clinical manifestations of diseases, then basic biology and, only then, specific presentations of illnesses. This system was well received, and soon Harrison's textbook rivaled Cecil and Loeb in popularity among medical students and practitioners. But it was a lot of work.

Because correspondence was either by phone or mail, and because there were so many authors involved, the editors' job was not only continuous but required meeting several times a year to plan and review manuscripts together. All of the editing work was done longhand, in pencil, along the margins. These gatherings were always held for a few days after the Atlantic City meetings, sometimes in New York City at the offices of the publisher, McGraw Hill, but occasionally in more beautiful and relaxed places like the Grand Teton National Park in Wyoming.

During the mornings of a December 1948 editorial meeting held in the Tetons, manuscripts were examined, discussed, and copy-edited by the entire group. From time to time, there were harsh criticisms, and more than once an entire manuscript was turned over to a new editor for revision, or even rewriting by a specialist in his department. Even so, they were cautious about hurting each others' feelings while they worked together in the morning hours.

In the afternoons, though, they had fun. One day Beeson, Wintrobe and Harrison all took a high mountain horseback trip together, through Cascade Canyon to Lake Solitude. The medical students of that era would have been surprised to find their heroes so relaxed, away from the wards with their wives and children or riding, wearing work shirts and jeans, in the high country of Wyoming. Beeson remained an editor of Harrison's *Principles of Internal Medicine* for almost five years, through two editions, but stopped that work in 1952 when he moved to Yale and took over a department that he considered too huge to allow enough time for editing a major text.

The Emory medicine program continued to attract excellent faculty and residents, including Ivan Bennett, Beeson's last Chief Resident at Grady. Bennett, attractive, glib and with an intelligence recognizable even as a sophomore medical student working part-time in the lab, was an excellent clinician who became Professor of Pathology at Johns Hopkins and later Deputy Director of the Office of Science and Technology of the President.

In 1951, Bennett was working on fever with Paul Beeson in the basement labs at Grady, where the major interest was still in bacterial pyrogens as a principal cause of febrile reaction to the injection of various biological substances.(19) They noted that these large, polysaccharide molecules were relatively resistant to heat and even to autoclaving, explaining the fevers that patients developed while Beeson was doing the antipneumococcal serum research at Rockefeller. Working alone, Beeson also began to investigate the relationship between fever and white blood cells, research that eventually was to lead to his most important scientific discovery.

Another of the Chief Residents, Daniel Hankey, who spent time investigating leptospiral meningitis with his chief, had been at Boston City Hospital along with Linton Bishop, who also moved to Grady as a resident. Both of these practitioners remember Beeson not only as a great bedside clinician and teacher, but for his gentle manner with both students and patients.

During professor's rounds in 1951, an intern presented to Beeson and Hankey the case of a young woman hospitalized on the polio ward. Without examining the patient himself, but only hearing the story of her illness, Beeson said kindly that he felt the patient did not have polio and should be transferred back to the general medical ward for more investigation; she had leptospiral meningitis.

Bishop, who as a student during the war had been given

the great honor of saving urine from the few patients who had been given penicillin so that it could be distilled and the recovered drug re-used, is now almost eighty and retired; he still declares, "Paul Beeson is my hero." This feeling of inspiration Beeson imbedded in his students and colleagues was a quality that endured for his lifetime.

By 1951, Beeson had earned a wide reputation as a clinician and investigator. Furthermore, he was recognized by other doctors at places like the Atlantic City meetings because, in his role as secretary of the young Turks, he sat before the audience on the stage during presentations.

At these meetings in May of 1951, Beeson went into the large men's room at the Haddon Hall Hotel, and was surprised to hear two men at the urinal discussing the retirement of Frances Blake, Chairman of Medicine at Yale. One of them said, "I understand Beeson from Emory is more likely to get the job than Gerry Klatskin." The speaker, a faculty member at Yale named Paul Lavietes, was dismayed when he turned around to find Beeson himself emerging from a stall. Immediately recognizing him, Lavietes came over and apologized, although Beeson thought the whole thing unlikely and forgot about the incident.

In the fall of that year, Hugh Long, the Yale Dean who had visited Emory and admired the program, called to invite Beeson to interview for the job of chairman. The curriculum vitae that he submitted to the Board of Permanent Officers at Yale in consideration for the Ensign Professorship and Chairman of the Department of Medicine included by this time forty-two papers, sections of five books, and membership in eight national societies.

Although he had been considered for other jobs (Chairmanships at McGill and Colorado, Dean at Vanderbilt), Beeson had not previously been tempted to leave Emory. Salary was always an issue, of course, but a minor one as the stakes were so small; even departmental chairmen in internal medicine were being paid only between ten and fifteen thousand dollars a year in

1950.

This time, however, he took the train in early November from Atlanta to New Haven, and was met at the station by the Chief of Surgery, Gustav Lindskog, also chairman of the search committee. Over the next few days, Beeson discussed the position with Long and a few others on the Yale faculty. While a contemporary search for a department chair might take months, and include negotiations not only over salary and space, but also a job for the applicant's spouse and private school for their children, in 1951 that was it. Beeson returned to work at Emory and again heard nothing for several months. When Long did finally call to offer him the Ensign Professorship of Medicine, Beeson said only, "good" and accepted the position.

When Paul telephoned Barbara at home to tell her that he'd been chosen for the Yale job, there was a moment of silence on the other end of the line as she anticipated the move. She had two small children in school, a comfortable life in a house they had built, and in nine years she had come to enjoy Atlanta. Barbara did remember her happy girlhood in New York State, but that isn't really New England, with its special brand of manners and social structure. Moving to New Haven, where the chairman's duties would be magnified, along with the duties of the chairman's wife, took a moment of adjustment.

Barbara wasn't the only one who had to make modifications; Emory was losing its second world class chairman of medicine within a few years. The impact of Beeson's departure was expressed in a January 1952 letter to him from Dean Hugh Wood:

> I feel depressed on turning on the Dictaphone to acknowledge your letter of December 15. . . . Your achievements here have been of such a superb nature and we have so long looked to you as the captain of the medical team and relied on your sound judgment in the planning for the entire school that one doesn't readily

adjust to getting along without this tremendous asset.
. . . Everyone from the President to the last non-faculty employee deeply regrets your leaving.(20)

It wasn't only the dean and faculty that expressed their deep feeling for Beeson. The president of the senior class wrote to him saying, "We value our association with you as being one of the most memorable phases of the past four years." The Emory Medical School Class of 1951 dedicated their graduation booklet to Beeson. In March of 1952, leaving his family in Atlanta until the end of the school year, Paul Beeson moved into the house staff quarters of the New Haven Hospital.

CHAPTER 8

Medical schools became sprawling, complex organizations that now saw their missions as threefold: research,
education and patient care (usually in that order). Full
time faculty increased 51 percent between 1940–41 and
1949–50....And during the next decade, full-time positions doubled....The tremendous increase in physicians
in teaching, research, government and other institu-
tional positions took place while the ratio of doctors to
population was little changed....The concentration of
medical work in hospitals and doctor's offices, the
growth in demand for personal health services, and the
declining availability of private practitioners made it
possible for doctors to increase their volume of practice
dramatically. The average private physician in 1930 saw
about fifty patients a week; by 1950 he saw more than
one hundred....They were not involved in a zero sum
situation. Rather, the power of the medical system as a
whole increased.

Paul Starr, 1950(1)

Bob Petersdorf, a senior medical student about to become a
Yale intern, sauntered into the New Haven Hospital cafeteria
at about 8:00 AM one March morning of 1952. He passed a classmate on the way out with a cup of coffee, who mentioned that

Bob had missed meeting the new chief of medicine by an hour. Dr. Beeson, about whom no one at Yale aside from the most senior faculty knew very much, had been surprised, his friend volunteered, to find the cafeteria so empty of students and house staff at that time of day. Petersdorf, already known as one of the most promising and ambitious senior students for his roundsmanship and research, was at the top of the class and had been picked to be a Yale intern by John Peters who was appointed acting chair of medicine following Blake's retirement. While there was hard work and prestige in Petersdorf's internship appointment, there was no salary.

1952 was the first year of the national internship matching plan, a ranking system designed to match senior students with hospitals they chose for internship and the institutions that also chose them. Medicine had grown so large that the era of "old-boy" department chairmen deciding among themselves where to send students had become inefficient. The matching plan replaced what had become a chaotic individual application process often characterized by the promise of more intern jobs than hospitals had positions, or by commitment by students to a particular hospital which they might desert at the last minute for a better offer.

However, as it was the first year, everyone cheated and professors told their favored students to pick them first, promising a match. Thus, Petersdorf and the other interns of the 1952 class were assured of jobs at Yale by John Peters before Beeson came to New Haven. Petersdorf was doing a clerkship on the Ear, Nose and Throat service that spring and was on call every other night. He made sure to get up early for breakfast the next morning.

Because his family was still in Atlanta, the new Ensign Professor lived in the house staff quarters of the hospital and ate most of his meals in the cafeteria with the students, interns and residents. The young students and residents were used to a more formal and distant Yale faculty; no one remembered ever seeing Francis Blake, wearing his stiff white collar, coat, tie and rimless glasses, anywhere near the cafeteria. So, when Bob Petersdorf, even then self-assured, lit a cigarette, grabbed a cup of coffee and wandered over to sit down with the only doctor in the place wearing a long coat at seven A.M., he wasn't too certain what to expect.

Beeson had an idea, though, about the student. He recognized him as the young man he had noticed persistently poking his head out from behind a curtain during the student skit held several days before, smiling slyly at the audience. The precocious Petersdorf, already an army veteran, had become interested in medicine after being assigned the job of presenting the venereal disease lectures and movies to incoming recruits at Fort Bragg, a task he accomplished between rounds of golf.

At Yale, he had been working with the faculty internist Louis Welt on human renal metabolism. Soon, his conversation with Beeson turned to these investigations and the young man's plans for his future. The student was surprised that, even though they had just met, the new chairman was not only willing to talk to him but actually seemed interested in his career. The almost-an-intern said he thought he wanted to teach in a medical school. Forty-four years later, when he accepted the AAP's 1996 Kober Medal, Professor Robert G. Petersdorf remembered what Beeson had told him that day: "...'the secret to success in [academic medicine is] to get one's hands dirty in the laboratory,' a lesson I never forgot."(2)

The laboratory was far from Beeson's own mind that spring. Like Gene Stead at Emory, the new chairman had inherited some problems. The Yale department of medicine was well established and, with eighteen full-time faculty members, Beeson considered it a huge, administrative maze. Francis Blake had been the only chairman for thirty years. Part of that difficulty associated with the transition from old chairman to new was sadly resolved by providence when Blake, only two weeks after retiring, had a myocardial infarction and died at the age of sixty-four.

His career had started, like Beeson's, at the Rockefeller Institute in Oswald Avery's laboratory, and had also been dedicated to the study of infection. Shortly after becoming a professor in 1921, Blake had recruited another young Rockefeller clinical scientist to Yale, John Peters.

Peters, a dour Presbyterian with a rigid personality, had worked with Van Slyke at Rockefeller on problems of endocrinology and metabolism. Tolerated by Blake as an equal, Peters ran his own medicine service, which he controlled completely, including the appointment of his own fellows, as well as making all the clinical decisions concerning hospitalized patients with illnesses related to metabolism. In 1952, Peters was already recognized as one of the world's leading authorities on clinical chemistry. He had expected to replace Blake as chairman.

Jack Peters openly opposed the new chairman. He did not welcome Beeson either personally or professionally, and continued to run an endocrinology and metabolism service that, while nominally a part of the medicine department, was nearly independent of it. One of his fellows from this era, Arnold Relman, later Editor of *The New England Journal of Medicine*, recalled a passionate loyalty to Peters on the part of his own students, a loyalty that was reciprocated. But to the rest of the medical world, including Beeson, Peters was often indifferent, if not hostile.

The Blake Medicine Library, about the size of an ordinary family living room, was used for the weekly late-afternoon departmental meetings instituted by Beeson. The faculty convened around a long table to discuss department business, with the chairman seated at one end. Peters, however, didn't join the rest at the table, but sat ominously against a wall behind Beeson, not saying anything—deafening in his disapproval.

In a reversal of protocol, but hoping to include him in the running of the department, Beeson sometimes visited the older man's office over the first several months, seeking his advice and attempting to form at least a workable relationship with the difficult Peters. He failed.

The day he consulted Peters about the appointment of two outstanding local physicians to the clinical faculty (then called visiting men), Beeson knew that the politically liberal but personally sour Peters was beyond his friendship. One of these candidates, William Resnik, was a nationally known cardiologist and an editor of *Harrison*. Even so, Peters turned his back, snorting that neither of the selections was worth having on the staff. Beeson appointed the deserving clinicians anyway, and for years both of them attended very capably on the wards at Yale.

After six months he gave up on Peters, leaving him to his own interests, which included not only metabolism but broad social aspects of medical practice. The slight and craggy-featured Peters held convictions, both clinical and social, that were unusual if not unique for a doctor in the early 1950s, and not always well tolerated beyond the immediate academic environment of New Haven.

Though at least emotionally separated from the former acting chairman, if not rid of him, Beeson was reminded daily of his presence because that year's chief resident, like the rest of the house staff, had been appointed by Peters. Sylvester Ryan, son of a prominent New England federal judge, did help to establish the Beeson style of running the department, however. Certainly a Peters partisan, Ryan fell into the routine of morning report with the new chief exactly at eight o'clock, and—at least publicly—supported him.

During the activities of the day, however, Al Feinstein, another intern that first year, heard the Chief Resident sometimes echo Peters' unflattering opinion of Beeson, whom he apparently considered to have usurped a position rightfully his own. Donald Seldin, a Peters fellow who became the long-time chief of medicine at Texas-Southwestern Medical School in Dallas, believes that, "There is no question that Dr. Peters wanted

very much to be a Chairman of a Department of Medicine. . . .
I would guess that he did not hold Paul in high regard. It is my
impression that he knew very little about Paul in any academic
capacity. . . . "(3)

Each morning, though, Ryan dutifully gathered various residents from the wards—Fitkin, Howard and Winchester—and
assembled them all in Beeson's office on the first floor of the
New Haven Hospital, looking out on a huge walnut tree in the
courtyard facing Howard Avenue. With his secretary Betty Pharr
(also imported from Emory) in the only adjoining office, the
chairman took morning report himself, as he had been taught
to do by Soma Weiss.

Beeson sat behind a glass-topped desk, rolling a letter-opener
around in his fingers, while the patients admitted during the
night were presented to him by the residents. Laboratory tests
had become more sophisticated since Beeson's own house officer days, thanks largely to Peters and Van Slyke's masterful
Quantitative Clinical Chemistry. However, history and physical
examination remained central to the process of diagnosis.

The impact of technological innovation was slight, in spite
of cardiac catheterization and even early angiography.
Laboratory values, x-ray results and physical examination were
expected to be reported efficiently by the sleep-deprived residents. Long-windedness was abbreviated by an impatient tap-
ping of the letter-opener.

The house staff soon learned that, while their new chairman didn't like mistakes, he tolerated them as a function of
learning. What he could not tolerate was thoughtlessness. When
it was uncovered that a patient had been treated unkindly, as
happened the day a resident referred to a homeless, alcoholic
patient as "a thirty-five year old bum," the letter-opener snapped
unhappily to the desk, and the room quieted while the offending resident searched in vain for an escape. This happened
rarely, a testimony to both residents and chief, but when it did
occur it was remembered for the life of the perpetrator.

While establishing himself as the chairman, Beeson also had to continue a long distance family life and find a place to live other than the house staff quarters in the Howard Unit. These domestic tasks were made easier when Barbara began making trips to New Haven on the overnight train from Georgia. A house was discovered on Rimmon Road in Woodbridge, a suburb popular with the medical school faculty. In July Barbara, John and Peter moved to Connecticut, into a house they were to occupy for the next thirteen years.

The mortgage on this two-story colonial was made affordable by an increase in Beeson's salary as chairman to eighteen thousand dollars a year. While surgeons and even internists in private practice were able to earn much more money, income in the academic community was not a central issue; the rewards for teaching and research in a university were considered ample compensation. Furthermore, salary scales in American life were then generally un-inflated by creation of the surplus value that necessarily accompanied the later growth of huge communication networks and mass marketing.

For example, Stan Musial, the great St. Louis outfielder, hit .376 and thirty-nine home runs in 1948 before signing a new contract for twenty-eight thousand dollars, then the largest amount of money ever paid a Cardinal player. That year the Chief of Surgery at Yale, Dr. Lindskog, earned about the same. In the early 1950s, the two greatest hitters in baseball, Ted Williams and Joe DiMaggio, routinely hit over .300 each season, and neither one made one hundred thousand dollars a year. Until 1956, when he batted .353, hit fifty two home runs and was the American League's Most Valuable Player, even Mickey Mantle was modestly paid. By such standards, the Beeson family was comfortable and satisfied.

Leaving the house she loved and the easy, sultry Atlanta life she had grown used to was an unspoken hardship for Barbara, but their new place on five acres of land at 194 Rimmon Road, Woodbridge was a remedy. The house, in a big open yard, was comforting to approach up the short driveway that led to the simple front porch. Behind a huge outdoor stone grill glimmered a pond the size of a football field, busy with frogs and turtles entering and leaving. Beyond it was a small barn at the edge of a deep conifer wood. By the second year, this yard was the scene of a huge summer party for the department of medicine house staff, an event that became a center piece for the entire year.

Inside, the house was small for a family of four, but comfortable even before several additions. Initially, the dining room had to double as a guest bedroom, and the living room was therefore occasionally conscripted for meals. Before an extra bedroom was added, John and Peter shared a room on the second floor. As in Atlanta, there was no study to begin with, so Beeson continued his evening practice of editing manuscripts longhand on the couch in the living room. The first year, that work included preparations for the Atlantic City meetings, where Yale's John Paul (with the collaboration of Dorothy Horstmann) presented more of his research on the polio virus. As the Beeson years at Yale were beginning, the era of the iron lung in hospitals was coming to an end.

Based on years of epidemiological data, Paul and Horstmann demonstrated that antibodies to polio viruses developed faster and in a higher percentage of people living in crowded, unsanitary conditions than those living more affluent lives. At the 1952 Association of American Physicians meeting, Paul concluded his paper by saying:

> By improving conditions as we do today, infants are spared and . . . this infection is being postponed, not eliminated. In those diseases which are severe, efforts to protect children from infection by avoiding exposure to a disease for which there is no artificial active immunizing agent, as in poliomyelitis and hepatitis, may mean postponing the evil day, and this is a dubious proce-

dure. The price we pay is having mumps after puberty, German measles in young married women, and even poliomyelitis in young adults and we should weigh this price carefully.(4)

That summer, more children died of polio than of any other infectious disease. The predictable and feared summertime epidemics of the crippling illness had been of interest to medical researchers ever since Thomas Rivers began to study viruses at the Rockefeller Institute in the 1920s, well before he offered Beeson the life changing job on Avery's pneumonia service. Albert Sabin at Rockefeller had grown the virus in cultured human brain cells as early as 1936, but not until the early 1950s did Jonas Salk managed to combine three strains of the killed polio viruses into one injectable vaccine.

Probably no event in American history testifies more graphically to public acceptance of scientific methods than the voluntary participation of millions of American families in the 1954 trials of the Salk vaccine. The methodological conscience of epidemiologists had demanded that these trials be double blind: Neither doctors nor teachers, neither parents nor children, knew whether the children were receiving vaccine or placebo. And when on April 12, 1955, epidemiologists at the University of Michigan announced that the vaccine worked, pandemonium swept the country
. . . . The magic of science and money had worked.(5)

◆ ◆ ◆

While the American public prepared to celebrate the eradication of polio, Dr. Beeson himself made ready to become a patient in the New Haven hospital. After about a year at Yale, and by then clearly established as the chairman in charge of the department's research, teaching and care of hospitalized patients,

Beeson woke up one night with a shaking chill, fever and another bladder infection. This time he was alarmed. While he had repeatedly developed acute cystitis since childhood, the cause was still uncertain and he now worried about what would happen to his young family should he become ill, disabled or even die. Cystitis was one thing, bacteremia another.

Beeson consulted the Yale urologist Marvin Harvard, who eventually made the diagnosis of a urethral-sigmoid colon fistula—part of the congenital defect—explaining the life-long recurring infections. Although Harvard recommended that this abnormal connection be repaired, it wasn't going to be simple and, in the process, Dr. Beeson was going to experience the other view of the bedside.

Before an operation could be done, the urologist wanted to see the rest of Beeson's renal system. More than twenty years before the invention of computed tomography (CT scan) and magnetic resonance imaging (MRI), this meant doing an examination known as an intravenous pyelogram or IVP. After the dye was injected and the kidneys had been seen on x-rays, Harvard told his patient that, in addition to the fistula, a mass had been discovered in one of his kidneys and further diagnosis required surgical exploration of the organ in order to insure that he did not have a malignant tumor. After all, there was little reason to undergo a complex series of operations correcting the fistula only to die of a renal cell cancer.

A flank incision is a painful business, and even though the cyst was benign, Beeson suffered through a week in the hospital and several more at home before the operations to repair the fistula could even begin. During the last six months of 1954, while these procedures were being performed by Harvard and Beeson's friend, the surgeon Gus Lindskog, the new Chief Resident in Medicine, Tom Amatruda, attempted to run the medicine service.

The faculty helped. The nephrologist Lou Welt, Elisha Atkins (whose interests were eclectic but included infection), Gerry

Klatskin (one of the first hepatologists to routinely perform liver biopsy), Phil Bondy (the endocrinologist from Emory who had come with Beeson to Yale, only to be completely obstructed by Peters), and the brilliant Ivan Bennett (Beeson's last chief resident at Emory who also moved to Yale with him) all attended on the wards, took morning report and helped run the administrative functions of the department of medicine.

Still, in July when the incoming interns and residents arrived, Beeson was lying in a stiflingly hot hospital room trying to keep up with the running of his service through the reports of the able chief resident, interrupted occasionally by shots of morphine. In addition to the faculty, Amatruda remembers being assisted in his duties by the twin terrors Bob Petersdorf and Al Feinstein. In 1954 they were assistant residents and both had natures that would today be called assertive.

The job of Chief Resident was, at that time, clinical as well as administrative, and designed to prepare a young physician for an academic life in teaching and research. While not guaranteeing success, appointment to such a post in an important academic center like Yale, with a mentor like Beeson, was a promising start to a university career. Over the past fifty years, as chairmen of medical school departments have been forced out of the labs and clinics into entirely administrative roles, Alvan Feinstein laments that their chief residents have become "appointment clerks."

Beeson was a patient in and out of the hospital for six months, and Amatruda functioned admirably as his surrogate. The disabled chairman did not go into his lab and, while he managed regular trips to his office between operations, he accomplished little beyond keeping up with the routine work. He did, however, experience being a sick person. He waited anxiously for his surgeons to appear on rounds, assuring him that he was recovering from one of the four operations it eventually took to repair the fistula. Finally, by the beginning of 1955, Beeson was back in his office, running the department, making rounds and working at the bench in his lab.

One of the early adjustments required of him and of the other new faculty members, was to the unique style of medical education at Yale. There were no grades, and no examinations except the National Board Examinations all the students took at the end of their second and fourth years.(6) Such a system required rigor on the part of faculty members who, without the milestones of tests or grades, found other means to determine what each particular student was absorbing from the experience of medical school. Performance on ward rounds was one measure and, if not quantifiable, at least it was an indication of the knowledge of a specific topic as well as the style and demeanor of each student. The Winchester and two Fitkin wards at Yale were the large, open units then typical of community or state funded teaching hospitals. Each housed twenty or thirty patients in ranks of bed after curtained-off bed. Teaching rounds with an attending physician were both a chance to learn and to display knowledge.

John Peters was famous for making rounds on the metabolism service with a herd of fellows, residents and students galloping behind him, desperately trying to hear what he said. His habit was to speak only to the person he addressed, in a whisper, and from a distance of a few inches. This made it nearly impossible for anyone else to hear him, a situation he apparently enjoyed.

On the other hand, the opinionated endocrinologist never left a doubt in his students' minds as to why they were doctors. When his residents complained about an especially vituperous patient, an unpleasant man who whined at them about everything from hospital food to the quality of their attentions, they took Peters to his room on rounds and were surprised that their teacher, receiving the same nasty treatment, said nothing. When the residents asked why he tolerated such abuse from the fellow, Peters answered, this time loudly enough for many to hear and remember, "Because he's sick."

When Peters mumbled "Good morning" to patients on rounds, he always touched them and asked how they were doing. If the patient, hospitalized with some horrible illness, complained about an incidental, minor pain in the big toe, Peters jerked around, demanding of the residents, "What are you doing about his big toe?"

Although Beeson's attitude toward patients was exactly the same, something Peters never appreciated, his style was much different. Tuesdays and Thursdays after morning report, Beeson left his office with the residents and students assigned to his service, walked past the Fitkin Amphitheater, and climbed upstairs to the wards where he consulted for two hours—all year long.(7)

There are several methods for making teaching rounds: very softly, like Jack Peters; with great volume and demonstration of learning; competitively and with the recitation of minutiae; or as Beeson did it, with an attempt to comfort the patients while leading the younger staff to a deeper understanding of the illness at hand and its effects on the sick person. This last method is high art, not easily learned and difficult to sustain day after day. After all, the students are forever merely students.

Beeson approached the bedsides of these patients, who were exposed on all sides and confronted by a crowd of people they barely knew, and immediately sat down. He had come to believe, possibly from his practice experience in Ohio, that standing by a patient's bedside places the doctor in a position of dominance that makes many ill people uncomfortable. He wished to place them at ease and so he reduced the distance between them by sitting unhurriedly, an act that suggested interest in each patient, rather than the disease, being discussed.

As the resident presented the history, physical examination, laboratory and x-ray findings, a task that sometimes took a while, Beeson said nothing. He allowed the younger doctors to discuss the problem themselves, develop a differential diagnosis, and argue about what made one possibility more likely than another. If speculations behind the curtains drawn around the bed grew too outrageous, Beeson gently guided it back toward reason. Sometimes, he said nothing at all, or simply agreed with the diagnosis and what was being proposed to manage the illness. Occasionally, he differed altogether, as in the case of a third-year medical student admitted late one night in 1953.

The student was Sherwin Nuland, later a Yale surgeon and gifted writer, who had been brought to the emergency room with a very high fever and, the admitting resident thought, an enlarged spleen. The temperature elevation alone wasn't a great worry, but Nuland was clearly sick and a spleen that can be palpated expands the possibilities in several nasty directions. Because they didn't know what was the matter with him, the residents did what they often did then (and now)—they gave him antibiotics and started to work-up the fever.

"I was evaluated from one end of myself to the other, carrying a diagnosis of either mononucleosis or hepatitis—no one being sure which. After about three days like this the Professor came to make rounds, examined me briefly, looked at his retinue and pronounced 'This boy had a strep throat a few days ago, but he's fine now. He can be discharged.' I don't suppose this is a major triumph diagnosed by Dr. Beeson, but what impressed me most was the gentleness with which he treated his residents when he had shown them to be in error, and his certainty."(8) For these qualities, Beeson became known at Yale as "Cool Paul."

George Thorn, who had become chairman at the Brigham Hospital after Weiss' death, came to visit Yale at Beeson's invitation. He showed a different method of rounding to the students, most of whom felt a keen competition with their Harvard fellows. On one of the Fitkin wards, the residents had admitted the complex case of a patient they suspected had Cushing's syndrome, a rare abnormality of adrenal metabolism. It was Thorn's specialty.

The house staff had researched the topic in exhaustive detail, knew all of Thorn's own publications on the subject, and spent the first forty-five minutes of a proposed two hours with their visitor describing the case. When finished, they all sat down rather pleased with their erudition, and waited to learn what Thorn would teach them about the disease. "Oh, this fellow doesn't have Cushing's," Thorn said, "what else do you want to talk about?" Unhappy that they had *nothing* else prepared, the residents floundered until it was time for their visitor to discuss his work with cortisone at Grand Rounds.

Medical Grand Rounds is an intellectual event. While most institutions have their own style, in general it was (and remains) a formal affair done according to a protocol, with emphasis on scholarship and a thorough review of a topic. For example, when a case of special interest to Alvan Feinstein was to be discussed in January of 1953, his chairman sent him a typed note requesting that he be present to comment, aware that the resident would have never for a moment considered being anywhere else.

George Thorn was masterful at this kind of presentation and, before the full one-hundred-seat Fitkin Amphitheater, he explained his own experience with the recently synthesized drug cortisone in treating a variety of diseases: rheumatoid arthritis, lupus erythematosus, glaucoma and glomerulonephritis. Although the talk was not basic science, it was the kind of clinical investigation meant to capture the attention of an audience at Grand Rounds.

Following the applause, Beeson stood and, as was customary, asked for comments. He first recognized the local authority, Dr. Peters, who "leapt to the stage, hitching up his belt like a prize fighter entering the ring. 'What you have just heard,' he announced, 'is nothing more than a catalog of ships.' (It is necessary to know that Peters, son of a noted classicist and Egyptologist who was also the Episcopal Bishop of New York State, was referring to the [Iliad], in which each warship of the

Greek force attacking Troy is cataloged, together with its contents). Paul Beeson looked pained and Thorn was nonplused."(9)

This sort of behavior exposed Peters as the remnant of an important man, perhaps unable either to inherit a new era or part with the old. Indeed, he had often privately confessed that he would not publish another edition of his lucid, beautifully written *Quantitative Clinical Chemistry* because the field had expanded too much.

Peters had problems outside of medicine as well, related to his liberal political views and sponsorship of an early proposal for national health insurance. Although many in the medical school shared these ideas, including Elisha Atkins (but not Beeson), most were circumspect. Senator Joseph McCarthy was on the hunt for communists in academia, and Peters' high profile and occasional enemies made him an easy target.

Hal Holman, a Yale medical student who had been a member of the progressive Association of Interns and Medical Students, claims that Peters, ". . . did not harbor true leftist views of economic or social organization. In his personal behavior he was somewhat arbitrary and dictatorial." This view is supported by Donald Seldin, not only a Peters fellow but also his friend, who is even stronger and more convincing in support of his former mentor: "The accusations were ridiculous. In the best sense, Dr. Peters was a patriot. He was devoted to the nation and was constructively involved in improving the healthcare system at a time when there was virtually no safety net of any kind. He contributed to the formulation of the Wagner-Murray-Dingell bill [modifications to the social security system] and was active in the Physician's Forum in developing a national health policy."

Nonetheless, Peters was named a Communist:

> . . . and on the basis of anonymous information he was discharged in 1953 from his position as consultant to the U.S. Public Health Service on its study section for metab-

olism. This was despite the fact that he had received loyalty clearance in 1949 and in 1952. His case, supported by professors from the Yale Law School and a former U.S. Attorney General, was carried through to the Supreme Court, and resulted in complete personal vindication. To his great sorrow, however, the court failed to rule decisively on the fundamental constitutional question of the right of an accused person to face and cross-examine his accusers.(10)

Throughout this trial, Peters was steadfastly supported by the entire faculty in medicine, including Beeson who, when he occasionally thought about politics, described himself as an Eisenhower Republican, a position he and Barbara both later dramatically abandoned.

In their June 6, 1955 opinion reported prominently on the front page of the *New York Times*, the Supreme Court restored the security clearance that Peters had been denied by the Loyalty Review Board. However, the brief, written for the majority by Chief Justice Warren, failed to address the constitutional question of the right of an accused person to face and cross-examine his anonymous accusers, the issue that had been the central point for Peters and his supporters.

Jack Peters, not an easy man, but an intense teacher and passionate physician, collapsed while making rounds at Yale and soon died in the fall of 1955, just before he was to retire. One imagines him arranging this himself, back to a wall, surrounded by his students and fellows, in whispers.

◆ ◆ ◆

Beeson inherited not only Jack Peters from Blake, but a dedicated and experienced—although very traditional—faculty. Medical education was changing rapidly, though, and money for research was available at the cost of postage to the NIH in Bethesda. The tendency toward sub-specialization had begun, and the Yale Department of Medicine was forced to add faculty members with more focused interests than only general internal medicine.

While recognizing this requirement, Beeson was reluctant to abandon his lifelong view that internists should be generalists. By 1954, this position, learned from both his father and Soma Weiss, was difficult to defend, and new fellowship-trained faculty members were hired. Beeson himself, and the Yale department, were now in a position to recruit from the best talent available. He spent a large part of his time at the Atlantic City meetings each May closeted with friends including Barry Wood and Walsh McDermott (with whom he shared an NIH study section assignment). He sought residents and fellows to add to his growing faculty, and promoted his own trainees for fellowships and faculty positions elsewhere. Vernon Lippard, the Yale Dean who replaced Long shortly after Beeson moved to New Haven, supported these activities with both rhetoric and money.

Margaret Lennox, daughter of one of the founders of electroencephalography, William Lennox, was the closest thing Yale then had to a neurologist, a discipline already highly sub-specialized. She was an excellent encephalographer, who ran the EEG lab in the basement of the hospital. She understood epilepsy, but her training had been largely in psychiatry. In 1951 she quit to take a research fellowship in Denmark, and not only left her husband Gerry Klatskin behind—then at least a slightly scandalous thing to do—she also left a busy EEG lab and epilepsy clinic without any sort of neurologist.

Beeson, inquiring about a replacement, called on the well-known Columbia physician Houston Merritt at his summer house near New Haven. This father of American neurology quickly recommended one of his own students, thirty-one year old Gil Glaser. Glaser, uncertain about the possibilities for a one-person neurology section, took the job but was thankful when Merritt promised to keep a position open for him at the

New York Neurological Institute in case the new program failed. It didn't.

By 1954, Glaser had established an accredited training program in neurology at Yale and, over the years, trained about a dozen department chairmen. The young neurologist was soon joined by other sub-specialists, including Aaron Lerner, a dermatologist recruited from the University of Minnesota who was interested in basic science. By 1958, Lerner had described the chemistry of both melatonin and melanocyte stimulating hormone, two major discoveries with wide impact not only for dermatology but also neuroscience.

At the time he discovered melatonin, Lerner (possibly at the urging of his more poetic wife) suggested naming the hormone related to light and circadian rhythms "Yalen," but the proposal was rejected by the stuffy Board of Permanent Officers at Yale. In the current environment of health food fads that promise melatonin might cure or regulate a clinic full of maladies, the university may now wish they had consented—or perhaps not.

As the department added more faculty, it also grew in other dimensions. Space was always an issue (one cardiologist's lab was in a remodeled coat closet off the Fitkin Amphitheater), and was relieved only slightly when the West Haven Veterans Hospital opened. The private Memorial Unit was constructed, allowing attending staff to admit insured private patients. Residents had an opportunity to care for these patients, as well as for the non-paying patients admitted to the renamed Yale-New Haven Hospital.

All of the faculty, with the exception of the Dean, were entirely indifferent to the funding sources for the care of any of these sick people. The faculty and house staff were paid a salary by the medical school; this income was not linked to nor influenced by months spent attending on the wards, number of patients seen or procedures performed, number of research paper published nor volume of work done as measured by any other scale. Patients were admitted through the clinics, emergency room, or privately, and taken care of by the same attending physicians and the same house staff regardless of their type of insurance—or lack thereof. Research funds were allocated only to research activities specified by a grant, and not shifted by bookkeepers into other budgets.

Such administrative issues always impose upon the time of a department chair. Beeson expected this. What he did not necessarily expect was the growing line of petitioners that never seemed to shrink outside his office door. Although the Southerner Betty Pharr moved back to Atlanta after only two Decembers in New Haven, and was replaced by the capable Betsy Winters, Beeson still ran the entire department with only a secretary.

The tasks were far beyond those of a routine secretarial job. Winters was responsible not only for scheduling appointments, phone calls, typing and mimeographing—the general business of running the office—but she also managed NIH grant applications, intern and resident applications, and medical student evaluations as well as monitoring the queue outside Beeson's door. Whenever people showed up, regardless of rank, Winters found a way to coax a few more minutes out of the chairman's schedule for them to be seen. Because the program was becoming so popular, and because he insisted on interviewing applicants for house staff positions himself, this task alone kept Beeson at his desk until late in the day.

Near the end of 1953 Paul and Barbara again became parents, this time of a daughter, Judy. Barbara's pregnancy and the baby's birth were smoothed by the hiring of an older Irishwoman to help care for the house and children. By then, the house had been remodeled to accommodate both the growing family and the increasing social obligations of the department chairman and his wife; obligations that were not minor.

The Beesons were busy entertaining, often giving weekly dinner parties for faculty members and their wives all care-

fully seated by Barbara in an attempt to avoid the conversa-
tion-stifling talk of only medicine between the men. This usually worked, and personal relationships grew warm and friendly
within the department, including wives and children. Barbara
began to notice more frequent remarks around the table, or
later at coffee in the living room, about her husband's influence, not only at Yale, but in academic medicine nationally and
internationally.

The lawn parties at the Rimmon Road house became a tradition and included every member of the house staff and their
families. A rope had been hung high in a tree next to the pond,
and the Beeson children were joined by the rest of the kids
swinging over the water, letting go of the earth like the soon-
to-be-launched astronauts, sailing joyfully into space, time and
splashdown. The giant rock grill was used to cook hamburg-
ers while the adults divided into softball teams for a game
umpired by the chief. A badminton court was set up on the
lawn, along with a game of croquet. Beeson was regarded as a
fiendish croquet player; other competitors playfully berated
him when they were unfortunate enough to see their own balls
sent flying to the other end of the lawn.

This summer event was anticipated all year, as was the
annual Christmas eggnog party the Beesons hosted at one of
the medical school amphitheaters. Paul was responsible for
making the eggnog punch while Barbara coordinated John,
Peter and the housekeeper in an assembly line production of
dozens of small sandwiches. Though these events were all carefully planned, they were so unaffected, happy and inclusive
that in addition to the faculty camaraderie in medicine and
research, the department of medicine became a social unit with
commitment to each other.

◆ ◆ ◆

There are a few people in any discipline so capable and charm-
ing, so intelligent, fluent and responsive, that they are imme-

diately noticed by all those around them as unique. The dermatologist Aaron Lerner holds that it is also a great advantage to be physically attractive. Barry Wood (who shared with Beeson the practice of editing in the family living room, though, in addition, he permitted his children to watch television as long as they wore headphones) was one of these rare people in medicine, and Ivan Bennett was another.

When he was a student at Emory, Bennett became interested in Beeson's laboratory investigations; he interned at Grady and then did work in pathology at Johns Hopkins before a medicine residency with Stead at Duke. He was Beeson's last chief resident at Emory and moved with him to Yale, connected as academic doctors were then. Because he was familiar with Beeson's scientific techniques, Bennett was able to help Liz Roberts, the technician also brought from Emory, set up the new lab for the investigation of not only infection but fever itself.

Since his first work at Rockefeller with type specific antisera, Beeson had been curious about the source of fever. While it was known that bacterial endotoxins (lipopolysaccharide substances arising in the cell wall of the organism itself) produced temperature elevation, fever was associated with a host of non-infectious diseases as well.

His research on patients receiving typhoid vaccine for the treatment of syphilis at Emory produced not only high fevers (a condition known to inhibit growth of micro-organisms) but also high white blood cell counts, and had raised the question of whether the leukocytes themselves were related to the rise in temperature. To study this possibility, Beeson developed a method for harvesting pure populations of the several types of white blood cells, and the leukocytes were injected into the ear veins of rabbits. In a paper titled "Temperature-Elevating Effect of a Substance Obtained from Polymorphonuclear Leukocytes" published in the *Journal of Clinical Investigation* in 1948, Beeson described this research for the first time:

Fever occurs in many different types of diseases, including such diverse entities as infection, neoplastic diseases, hemolytic crises, vascular accidents, and mechanical injuries. The way in which these various diseases affect temperature regulation is unknown, but the suggestion has been made that some agent, liberated from injured cells, acts on the cerebral thermoregulatory centers and disturbs their function.

The present work was done in an attempt to find in cells of rabbits a substance which, on intravenous injection into normal rabbits, would cause a rise in body temperature. Four cell types were tested: erythrocytes, lymphocytes, large mononuclear cells (macrophages) and polymorphonuclear leukocytes. Only one of these— the polymorphonuclear leukocyte—caused fever. . . . The rise begins in 10 to 15 minutes, and reaches its peak within an hour.

When a suspension of polymorphonuclear leukocytes is subjected to mechanical lysis (by shaking with glass beads) and then centrifuged, the supernatant fluid is fully active in causing fever, whereas the cell residue has no effect. The fever-producing property disappears after heating. . . . The active substance does not dialyze through a cellophane membrane. . . .

It seems possible that the liberation of material such as that present in the polymorphonuclear leukocyte of the rabbit plays a role in the pathogenesis of fever in certain diseases of man.(11)

The short four-paragraph paper was included in the proceedings of the American Society for Clinical Investigation, but it was not accepted on the program for presentation that year. However, the discovery that there existed a fever-producing chemical substance *in the white blood cells themselves*, not from some external source, was a major scientific contribution not appreciated at all when the work first appeared. Like Fleming's mold and Avery's transforming pneumococcus, for many years Beeson's fever-producing substance remained closed in a journal that no one read.

No one, that is, except Beeson, Ivan Bennett, the technician Liz Roberts and, later, Elisha Atkins and his students. In an elegant series of experiments published in 1953, Beeson and Bennett reported the first chemical characterization of this fever-causing substance that they began calling endogenous pyrogen, now classified as the cytokine interleukin-1 or IL-1 Beta.(12,13)

These studies expanded Beeson's original research and demonstrated that endogenous pyrogen, while heat-labile, was not destroyed by several enzymes nor suppressed by cortisone, and that it was highly concentrated in polymorphonuclear cells, but present in other cells as well. Repeated injection of the substance did not produce tolerance (as did the injection of typhoid vaccine) and the effect could not be augmented by blockade of the reticulo-endothelial system, also differentiating endogenous pyrogen from endotoxin. Beeson's original report of this concept-changing work is almost never referenced, but it is included in the bibliography of a long paper entitled "Pathogenesis of Fever" published by Atkins in 1960, and was known, of course, to workers in his laboratory.

In the late 1960s, the Yale medical student Charles Dinarello began to work on biochemical mechanisms of fever with his teacher, Elisha Atkins. When Dinarello moved to the NIH, rapid advances in immunobiology allowed him to help develop the concept of cytokines, a class of compounds whose synthesis is stimulated when white blood cells recognize microbes. Although there has been some controversy about what cell is the richest source of IL-1, it is now generally accepted that both monocytes and polymorphonuclear leukocytes produce several different polypeptides that are intrinsically pyrogenic. Dinarello, who along with Atkins, has done as much work as anyone to characterize these substances chemically, credits Beeson's 1948 abstract as the first report of a cytokine:

> This abstract is, in my opinion, the first report of an endogenous substance from a cell which possessed a dramatic biological response when injected into an animal. Upon re-reading this, his discovery has all the characteristics of a cytokine and more importantly, these qualifications are still required today. . . . 1) that the biological activity (fever) is not due to endotoxins, 2) the cell source(s) be identified, 3) the substance is a soluble product and 4) [includes] some physical characteristic (in Paul's case the destruction by heat and being non-dialyzable). These are the hallmarks of cytokine biology. Hence this abstract ranks as perhaps the very first report of a cytokine. . . . Like many "breakthroughs" in science, it was not appreciated for what it really was at the time but with retrospective examination, one can see how this abstract contained the birth of cytokine biology. Also, like many "firsts" it was rejected.(14)

Of Beeson's one hundred twenty-two publications, the discovery of endogenous pyrogen, the first cytokine, is certainly his most significant contribution to science. Not long after this work was done, Beeson arranged for Bennett to join the Johns Hopkins faculty, Petersdorf (who, with Beeson's urging, had given up smoking) to go to Harvard for a residency with Thorn, and Al Feinstein to join the labs at the Rockefeller Institute.

A farewell dinner was held at Mory's, the New Haven restaurant famous for the Whiffenpoofs, a photograph of George Bush as a Yale baseball player, much-carved tabletops, passable food and plenty of strong drink. None of the Yale faculty present that night remembers the food or the photograph of a little-known Texas Congressman, but they all remember "Alvan

Feinstein playing his guitar and singing 'The British Workman's Grave' and Professor Beeson, using segments of his vocabulary previously unknown to others, calling repeatedly for encores." That moment aside, the Yale faculty was now leading the way not only in clinical medicine, but was producing science and scientists that were among the best in the world.

In 1957, the major scientific and technical achievement was not thought to have come from Yale or even the United States, however, but from the Soviet Union. On October 4, the Soviets launched Sputnik 1, a Volkswagen-sized unmanned satellite, and agitation infected North America. In a series of legislative moves that resulted in "the space race," Eisenhower, who maintained a soldier's skepticism about what he called the military-industrial complex, was forced to pour money into space and weapon technology.

Because the mutual paranoia between the United States and Russia had been enthusiastically nurtured by both Joseph McCarthy and Joseph Stalin, so great a Soviet technological advance produced an even greater, and sometimes bizarre, reaction in the U.S. Among the strangest results was the hurried construction of basement bomb shelters in suburban homes all over America.

Americans sought to protect themselves, in spite of diplomat George Kennan's later admonition ". . . that the weapon of mass destruction is a sterile and hopeless weapon . . . which cannot in any way serve the purposes of a constructive and hopeful foreign policy. . . . A defense posture built around a weapon suicidal in its implications," he went on to say, "can serve in the long run only to paralyze national policy, to undermine alliances, and to drive everyone deeper and deeper into the hopeless exertions of the weapons race."(15)

Even so, the Russians were orbiting the earth and the United States wasn't, a situation that made people, including sophisticated academic families such as the Beesons, nervous. They constructed a cement block bomb shelter in the basement of the house on Rimmon Road, and stocked it with cans of food and a flashlight.

Although the effects of an atomic blast and radiation were certainly well known, the national paranoia demanded action. Building contractors were added to the list of beneficiaries of the Cold War. Like most of the others in basements and back-yards, the Beeson bomb shelter rapidly found better use as a storage room. Neighbors turned shelters into wine cellars and woodworking shops. Regardless, Paul and Barbara, like many Americans, had both been led to a new political consciousness as a consequence of the Soviet advances.

For Beeson himself, this awareness took several forms. The first opportunity appeared one morning during the commute from Woodbridge into New Haven with Elisha Atkins. Atkins, known for the range of his interests, had studied history and literature as a Harvard undergraduate. He came to Yale from Barry Wood's laboratory, and was often seen at noon strolling the Yale campus green in conversation with a student or fel-low, sometimes about research, but just as often about any sub-ject from Greek classics to liberal politics. When his colleagues, inside struggling to write grant revisions or finish experiments, caught sight of him during these excursions, they were curious about how Atkins so effortlessly produced work better than their own.

Beeson and Atkins, introduced originally by Barry Wood in Atlantic City, shared a warm friendship through a common interest in infection. They often rode to the hospital together from their houses a mile apart in Woodbridge. When his friend began to discuss the futility of imagining personal survival fol-lowing a nuclear attack, Beeson's relatively conservative, but not then very well-examined, convictions were challenged. As the conversation in Atkins' little car became more focused on specific politician's positions—and the defroster could no longer keep up with the vapors on the windshield—Beeson had to admit that a cementblock room in his basement offered little protection from either a nuclear blast or irradiation.

Gil Glaser also scoffed loudly at the idea during a departmental lunch meeting. After a few weeks of debate, Beeson withdrew from the fray with his better informed friend and pleaded, "Lish, let's not talk about this any more." Instead, he began to seek a more constructive contribution for the Yale department of medicine to make in world affairs.

Beeson soon found his opportunity in the form of the Atomic Bomb Casualty Commission.(16) The ABCC had been in operation since soon after the bombings of Hiroshima and Nagasaki, when sixty-four thousand civilians were killed immediately or soon died from radiation exposure. Beeson knew about the Commission not only because of his contact with the National Research Council which supported it, but also because of continued contact with his old neighbor from across the street in Wooster, James Neal, who had become a geneticist in Ann Arbor and an ABCC consultant.

A member of the National Academy of Sciences involved in the long-term study of radiation among the survivors in Japan, Keith Cannon, visited Yale. He discussed not only the terrifying scientific results that the Commission had already collected, but problems the Academy had with its continued funding. Beeson, during the spring 1958 meeting, proposed that Yale provide the medical staff for the operation of the ABCC, a model similar to Harvard's staffing of the epidemiological hospital at Salisbury, England. Beeson, the poker player, found money and support from Dean Lippard for this adventure, and began sending staff to Japan. The program had benefits in addition to the obvious scientific ones; the staff were mostly draft-eligible young men who, as ABCC members, could join the U.S. Public Health Service and satisfy their military requirements.

The first to go on this exciting mission was the young chief of medicine Beeson had installed at the VA, Bill Hollingsworth. Both Hollingsworth and his wife Dorothy were doctors, and Bill had experience in hematology and radiation biology. He

Paul Beeson stumped in 1910 at age two in Livingston, Montana.

The first Alaska Engineering Commission Hospital (foreground) next to the cabin where the Beeson family lived during their first year in Anchorage.

The second Alaskan Engineering Hospital built in Anchorage, Alaska in 1917.

Flexible Flyer sled dog "Ruff" and eight year old Paul Beeson, Anchorage, 1916.

Twelve-year old baseball player Beeson, Anchorage, 1920.

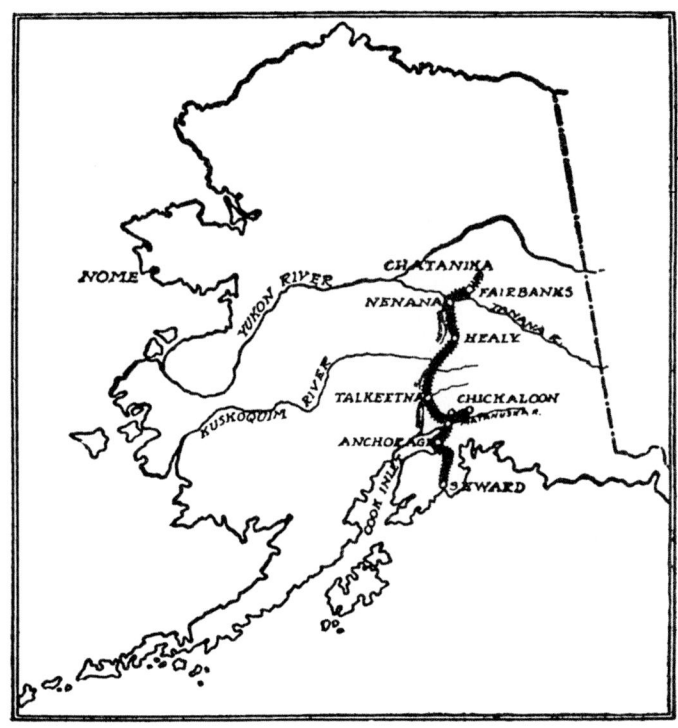

A map of the location and route of the Alaska Railroad.

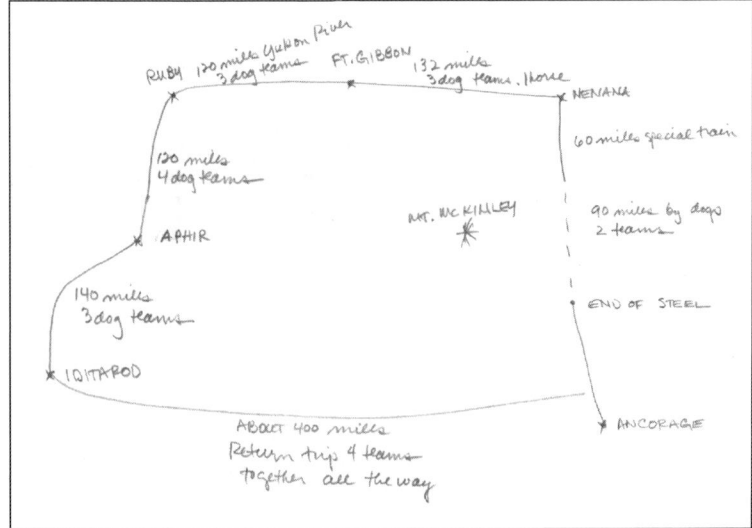

A hand-drawn map of the route of that John Beeson took on
the Iditarod trip in 1921.

John Beeson returning from Iditarod with Leonard Seppola and his dog team,
February 23, 1921.

John (still wearing toupee), Martha, Harold and Paul Beeson
in Anchorage, 1924.

Martha, Paul and John Beeson at their summer cabin outside of Ketchikan, Alaska in
1929.

Paul and Harold, Ketchikan,
1929.

Staff of the Rockefeller Institute in 1937. Front row: Oswald Avery is second from left and to his right is Thomas Rivers. Row 2: Kenneth Goodner is first on the left. Row 3: Beeson is first on the left next to Cornelius Rhodes. Rene Dubos is fourth in the same row, and to his right is Walther Goebel; Rebecca Lancefield is eighth.

Paul Beeson as a fellow at the Rockefeller Institute in 1937.

Some of the Harvard-Red Cross Hospital Staff at Salisbury, England in 1942. Barbara Neal, second from right, standing next to her future husband. This photograph was taken the day Beeson left to return to the United States.

July 10, 1942 wedding in Snyder, New York.

Emory University Department of Medicine faculty and house staff in 1942-43. Row 1: Harris, Lentz, Cargill, Hickam, Stead, Beeson, Freedman, Brannon, Warren. Row 2: Miller, Paullin, Kern, Golden, Armour, Holland, Cook, Rogers. Row 3: Brown, Haltom, Pressley, Hooten, Burge, Mays, McGinty, Stanley.

Two doctors: Paul Beeson and Walsh McDermott in Atlantic City (about 1960).

Barbara and Paul, Atlanta, 1943.

Meeting of Harrison's *Principles of Internal Medicine* editors at Grand Teton National Forest, December, 1948. Beeson, Max Wintrobe and Tinsley Harrison.

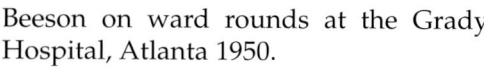

Beeson on ward rounds at the Grady Hospital, Atlanta 1950.

Summer party at the Beeson's house on Rimmon Road in 1957. Robert and Pat Petersdorf in foreground. Steve Malawista is to the left of Bob Petersdorf.

Paul Beeson as croquet player, 1957.

Yale University Department of Medicine faculty and house staff, 1964. Row 1:
Papac, D'Esopo, Granat, Cross, Weinerman, M. Calabresi, Goodkind, Finch,
Ebbert, Alexander, Bondy, Beeson, Ferris, Glaser, Spiro, Klatskin, Epstein, A.
Lerner, Feinstein, Rosenbloom. Row 2: Arndt, Gaudio, McDonald, Chanco,
Friedewald, Frank, Perillie, Thayer, Kaplan, McGuire, P. Calabresi, Frieda Gray,
Frank Gray, Scheig, Kennard, Snell, Witorsch, Eisenfeld, Wittenberg. Row 3: M.
Lerner, Taylor, Dillard, Atkins, Turner, Gregory, Peter, Vietzke, Lande, Elsas,
Fearon, Savin, Aach, Tate, Burns, Chick, Higgins, Fierer, Sachs. Row 4: Conn,
dePapp, Barlow, Kra, Lefkowitz, Granger, Gorden, Heller, Philip, Landowne,
Powell, Nomura, Kaplan, Braverman, Malawista, Karas, Binder, Kravetz,
Collins. Row 5: Fuhrmann, Hayslett, Berkman, J, Higgins, Schilder, Amatruda,
Kantor, Briggs, Godley, Seligson, Creasey, Cohn, Levitin, Godar, Fischer, Bertino,
Innes, Prien, Briggs, Groch, Goffinet, Weinstein, Kessner, Talley. Row 6: (left)
Talner, Pettinger, Coleman, Lubs; (right) Pincus, Sulavik, Egan.

1962 Atlantic City meeting surprise celebration of Beeson's
tenth year as Chairman of Medicine at Yale. Barbara,
Tinsley Harrison and Paul.

Reunion of Beeson's Chief Residents at Yale at the 1986 Association of American
Physicians Meeting in Washington, D.C. Seated: Bondy, Freedman, Beeson,
Petersdorf, Burrow. Standing: Amatruda, Ryan, Schimmel, Johnson, Nolan,
Kahler, Ferris, Lubs, Conn.

Max Finland and Beeson at Finland's eightieth birthday celebration held at Harvard, March 25, 1982.

Paul and Barbara Beeson with Bill and Dorothy Hollingsworth, at their home in La Jolla, 1992.

Paul Beeson as Distinguished Physician at the Seattle Veterans Administration Hospital in 1978.

later published some of the earliest, and best, data on the harmful delayed effects of radiation in man.(17)

This assignment became a sought-after appointment, both for the experience of bringing sophisticated statistical clinical research to the ABCC program itself, and because Hollingsworth—and those who followed him—all trusted that Beeson would continue to support their career development after the interruption of two years in Japan.

◆ ◆ ◆

Dedication to the careers of students, residents and faculty is a labor-intensive activity. The students, who often entered medical school with no idea about what clinical medicine truly involved, were sometimes overwhelmed when they found out. Patients admitted to teaching centers in the late 1950s were often so sick they could not be cared for in a community hospital, and the mortality rate was as high as ten percent on the Yale medicine wards. These patients were hospitalized for long periods, and the house staff and students developed relationships with them not available in today's technology-rich, day-surgery and out-patient environment.

An intern from 1958 remembers his young female patient with meningitis being treated with the new technique of injecting intrathecal penicillin, the drug infused into spinal fluid through a lumbar puncture needle in order to achieve high concentration at the site of infection. This was a procedure advocated by Beeson, who recommended that, even though she was improving, the spinal taps be continued until the patient was completely without fever.

An arithmetical error was made by the nurse preparing the infusion, and instead of ten thousand units of penicillin, the intern pushed in one million. The patient convulsed and died. The intern, who had been taking care of the young woman since her admission, also collapsed. Beeson was called by someone still left standing, and immediately came to the ward. He gathered both nurse and intern and took them into an empty room. After the tears slowed and a little calm had been restored, he explained to the two young people that errors are certain to be made in the care of the desperately ill, and that everyone involved in their care assumes part of the responsibility for what happens on the wards—the triumph and the loss. By involving himself in the accident, and reminding them that it was he who chose the treatment, Beeson comforted the nurse and intern at least a little, and let them know they were supported. Next, they told the family exactly what had happened. There was no lawsuit.

When the occasional intern was found sobbing at a conference room table in the middle of the night because she couldn't stand the uncertainty of a patient's condition, the choices of treatment and the threat of death, Beeson was called. When a student needed an internship recommendation or a resident a fellowship, when a faculty member was not awarded a grant he expected, or when unanticipated lab results were reported by a technician, Beeson was consulted. The line outside his office grew longer. He arrived home later for dinner. His children grew suddenly older.

The life of a busy program director at a university center was truncated at home even in 1958, and Paul was a little surprised that his daughter was already nearly five years old. Judy Beeson, bundled up by the housekeeper went toddling outside to the frozen pond. She was hoping to play in the snow with her brothers but expecting to be sent right back inside. At age five, she could not have grasped the complexities of why the fresh air outside the house was better for her than the somehow stale air inside, where it was cozy. However, her mother had learned this rule as an absolute from her own mother in the fields of Snyder, New York, so Judy scraped her boots through the snow to the edge of the pond where her two teenage brothers flew around, skating.

Peter, pretending to be a member of the New York Ranger

hockey team, went as fast as possible. His older brother John, perhaps listening to the Schubert sonata playing in his mind, was a more languid skater. Neither of them paid much attention to their baby sister who, after a while, plopped down in the snow and waited for her father to get home from wherever it was he went each morning.

When he finally did arrive, she watched him walk out on the pond near the spring inlet where the ice was known to be thinner and jump up and down a few times, testing its safety before herding the children in to dinner. When they had eaten and Barbara took Judy up to bed, the two boys went off to their room to finish their homework for classes at the Amity Regional High School. Paul picked up his stack of editing.

That spring, Judy's riding lessons began. Her mother, an enthusiastic horsewoman, had tried to interest the boys in this activity, but failed. Judy loved the animals from the first day, and soon took lessons twice a week. While the entire family enjoyed swimming in the pond during the summer, Peter and John were dropped off by their father for lessons at Yale on Saturday mornings while he made rounds, and then went to wait for him in his office. They sat in the outer office of the dignified Betsy Winters without much curiosity about their father's growing stature in medicine.

Inside the office, the piles of paperwork grew higher. In order to protect the residents and junior faculty from burdens of worry about money, a subject known to make Beeson's eyes crinkle in displeasure, the chairman did all of the administrative work himself. The rest of the staff was left alone, like Dukes, to take care of the patients and do research.

Administration of the department included negotiating faculty salaries individually with each member, a practice that eventually produced unbalanced overlaps and paid some assistant professors more than their seniors. In addition, there were traps involving not only salary but retirement benefits. Before IRA's and more formal retirement programs, extra money was not always included for the beneficiaries of a named chair, for example, or other salary derived from a source outside the Dean's Office. A professor might wind up with a substantial salary by being appointed to an endowed chair, but later he would find no retirement benefits included.

These budgetary decisions were made by Beeson and the Dean without regard to house staff salaries, which were still so low as to be inconsequential. Just because they weren't a major part of the budget, however, didn't exclude the house staff from demands on the chairman's time. Because they knew he was fair and completely honest, if a little shy and reserved, they brought him problems as major as fellowship choices and as minor as the best way to treat hiccoughs.

Though his time actually working in the lab was shrinking, Beeson still had enthusiasm for research, and was happy when McDermott called one afternoon proposing a new society for the study of infection.

The spirit of the Atlantic City meetings, what now would certainly be called an old-boy network, was one of trust and cooperation but was being eroded by an increase in sub-specialization. Anxious to preserve the intimacy of a small society of friends dedicated to a common interest, McDermott and Barry Wood had discussed forming a small group for informal meetings of intimates working on problems of infection.

Wood, by then at Hopkins as Professor of Microbiology and Vice President for Medical Affairs, McDermott and Beeson agreed to form this society and began referring to the group by the inelegant title of the "Pus Club." The first meeting was arranged to be held at Rockefeller. Students and friends were invited and a program was proposed. The principals became alarmed that a name like the Pus Club might be coolly received at the staid Rockefeller Institute, and alternative suggestions were solicited.

The resident Bob Fekety remembered the venerable Interurban Clinical Club, founded by Osler, that all three professors belonged to, and reasoned that the launch of Sputnik and the space race propelled organizational names into a new geography. Thus, going Osler a solar system better, he suggested the Pus Club be officially called the Interplanetary Society, a group that still meets occasionally and is still usually referred to by the more vulgar name. Beeson, McDermott and Wood were the only three official members of the organization, but most of the people they trained through several generations of investigators consider that they also belong.

About the time the Pus Club was preparing for its first meeting, Paul's father was getting ready to retire. In 1957, John Beeson had been taking care of the sick for fifty-five years and, at the age of eighty-five, he wanted to leave the Beeson Clinic and Wooster. Harold had already become interested in international medicine and had taken a job with the State Department, so John and Martha were free to live where they chose. On the day he left Ohio, the eldest Dr. Beeson saw patients in his office until noon, then packed his own car and drove with his wife across the country to La Jolla, California, into retirement.

By 1958, John Beeson's younger son was fifty, past the age Osler considered the prime for scientific contribution. Indeed, the majority of Nobel Prizes are awarded for work done before the recipient is forty-five. Paul needed a break from his growing department and its progressively more tedious administration. He found this opportunity in London at the laboratory of Professor Derrick Rowley.

George Pickering at St. Mary's Hospital Medical School, later Regius Professor at Oxford, had written suggesting the St. Mary's group at the Wright-Fleming Institute shared Beeson's research interests. Yale's Dean Lippard was an enthusiastic proponent of sabbaticals, and so Gerry Klatskin was named acting chairman and the house on Rimmon Road was rented for the year. Sixteen years after Paul and Barbara had returned from London during the war, the Beeson family prepared to sail again for England, this time not on a freighter but on the Holland-America Line.

CHAPTER 9

The Seventy-First Annual Session [of the Association of American Physicians]: Atlantic City, New Jersey, May 6 and 7, 1958. President William S. Tillett described the future. . . . What at that time would appear on the program of an Association meeting? First, the effects of radiation. . . . As bacteria in recent times have adapted themselves to antibiosis. . . . Tillett prophesied that we may be obliged to become resistant to fallout. . . . Next, Tillett considered the aging process. . . . His third category was mental illness. . . . The essential basis for psychotherapy would be found, he believed, "in the field of demonstrable organic biochemical and/or metabolic defects." Finally, Tillett discussed the replacement of damaged tissues with normal tissue from living humans. . . . "so with control of the new principles making practical replacement of all tissues or whole organs. . . . "

A. McGehee Harvey, 1958(1)

*A*fter they docked at Southampton in July of 1958, the five members of the Beeson family, with some of their belongings for the year, crammed themselves into a car left for them by Frank Epstein. Another of John Peters' fellows, Epstein had finished a sabbatical at one of the London medical schools in 1957 and had arranged to sell his Morris car to the Beesons before returning to the United States. They drove north to London and found a house to rent in the Highgate district, where they enrolled the children in school. Judy, only five years old, gagged on the disagreeable English nursery school meals of lumpy mashed potatoes and grilled liver. Teenagers Peter and John were installed at the venerable Highgate School, which they were impressed to discover had been founded in 1565.

Their father promptly returned to bench research at the Wright-Fleming Institute of Microbiology, a little building adjacent to St. Mary's Hospital and Medical School in Paddington. Derrick Rowley's laboratory in this Institute, named for Fleming, discoverer of penicillin and Wright, who had introduced antityphoid vaccine, was a convenient place for doing basic research in infectious diseases.

Beeson anticipated the return to solitary days in his own small laboratory, where he could do his own investigative work without administrative distraction. He obliged himself to no clinical responsibility either, even though his friend George Pickering was chief of the medical service at St. Mary's.

Long interested in the urinary tract and kidney infection, Beeson had written about both the hazards of catheterization of the urinary bladder and the causes of experimental pyelonephritis.(2,3) It was perhaps his own experience with recurrent urinary tract infection that stimulated this research, an interest that was to occupy his entire sabbatical in London.

In a series of papers with Lucien Guze, Larry Freedman and Heonir Rocha at Yale, Beeson had shown that obstruction of the ureter of the kidney or injury to the renal medulla rendered the kidney susceptible to *Escherichia coli* infection, whereas lesions in the cortex of the kidney did not. Working alone in London, Beeson began a series of experiments to investigate why the kidney is so vulnerable to coliform bacterial infection.(4)

He first demonstrated that, while suspensions of other tissues did not influence the bactericidal activity of serum against *E. coli*, the presence of kidney tissue suspended in serum allowed the bacteria to continue growing. Because both antibody and the complement system are required in the bactericidal action of serum, Beeson studied the effect of complement on renal infection.

The complement system of plasma proteins interacts with antibodies enabling phagocytes to ingest and destroy bacteria. Complement, now known to involve many proteins, may be activated in several ways to coat the surface of a pathogen, enhancing phagocytosis through opsonization. When complement proteins bind to a pathogen, thus opsonizing it, the bound proteins both recruit phagocytic cells to the site of infection and lyse microorganisms by creating pores in their membranes.

The complexity of this system was unknown in 1958. Beeson eventually proved that the protein then identified as the fourth component of complement was inactivated by ammonia. Since renal cells form ammonia from glutamine and some amino acids as a part of acid-base metabolism, it is added to the tubular urine, thereby making the kidney susceptible to bacterial infection because of the inactivation of complement.

With Freedman, he later showed that stimulating ammonia formation by the kidney increased the susceptibility of treated rats to bacterial pyelonephritis, a different way of looking at the same problem.

This was the kind of investigation that Beeson most enjoyed, actually doing the clinically suggested work at the bench himself as he had been taught to do by Oswald Avery at the Rockefeller Institute. It was the sort of individual research he had been able to do less and less frequently at Yale while his administrative responsibilities had grown, a predicament that was to confound growing numbers of clinical investigators.

As academic advancement became increasingly predicated on publishing, rather than teaching ability or clinical skill, and money for research became more readily available, the manufacture of science became its own industry. Not surprisingly, many departments began to expect or even require a certain volume of publications before promotion was considered. To facilitate advancement, the number of authors on papers grew from one or two to several and then many. While the importance of exceptional individual work was sometimes recognized, the length of a curriculum vitae itself acquired an independent value.(5) During his sabbatical year in London, Beeson exulted in a rediscovered ability to do his own research without distraction.

Shortly after arriving in London, he did acquire one other new responsibility, however. He received a letter from Walsh McDermott inviting him to consider taking on a new job, this time as editor of the great competitor to the Harrison text, the *Textbook of Medicine* edited for many years by Russell Cecil and Robert Loeb. After the first few years at Yale, he had realized how much he missed editing and hoped that even a huge faculty, by then distended to forty members could, with difficulty, be managed efficiently enough to allow new work.

When McDermott contacted him from Cornell in 1958 with the information that Loeb was retiring, Beeson did not feel overwhelmed by the idea of a return to editing a textbook. McDermott had become a close friend through shared interests in infection, membership in the "Young" and "Old Turks," and assignments together on NIH study sections. Though he was slightly disabled by the tuberculosis acquired as a medical student, and just at that time moving from internal medicine into the School of Public Health at Cornell, McDermott was a leader in the study of infectious disease and he was a capable administrator and exacting editor.

Beeson was also recognized as a gifted editor, not only for his prior work on Harrison's textbook, but also because of the lucidity of the writing in his own publications and a formidable ability to improve the prose of his residents and faculty. Manuscripts thought ready for submission to a journal by their authors were likely to be returned from a trip across the chairman's desk with more red ink than intact sentences.

In a note at the top of page one, he once instructed Professor Alvan Feinstein "to read *Strunk and White* and use more active verbs." Larry Freedman had the same experience when Beeson assigned him the task of writing a chapter for Lou Welt's new nephrology textbook; he wrote some, gave it to Beeson, then started over, salvaging a few sentences from what he had thought was a polished product.

Robert Loeb himself favored Beeson as his replacement, a choice endorsed not only by McDermott but also the editor-in-chief at Saunders, the publisher. Because McDermott had already helped to edit the infectious disease section of Loeb's last edition, his friend from Yale assumed that the spine of the book would read McDermott and Beeson. However, McDermott objected, saying strongly that an internist, not a physician specialized in public health, should be the first author of one of the two most-used textbooks of medicine. For the next five editions of Cecil and Loeb, medical students all over the world looked up from their desks to the bookshelf, and found the answer to most of their questions in a comprehensive textbook of medicine edited by Beeson and McDermott.

The book made an enormous contribution to the education of these students, and was a primary reference for all physicians; it also sold well and supplemented Beeson's still small salary by doubling it. Though he accepted the editorial job from London, the real work of editing did not begin until he returned to Yale. The first Beeson and McDermott edition of the *Textbook of Medicine* was the eleventh, published in 1962.

Daily life for the Beeson family in London was more leisurely than it had been in New Haven. St. Mary's Hospital was a thirty-minute Underground ride from Highgate, an easy commute for Beeson. The children were excited by their opportunity to live in a different and older culture. Peter was especially thrilled, shortly after they arrived, to discover the tomb of Karl Marx in a cemetery near the Highgate School.

The boys' experience attending the school, however, was

not quite so thrilling, especially at first. Shortly after John and Peter entered the day school at Highgate, the Headmaster invited Paul and Barbara to his home for tea. He advised the parents to encourage their children to engage in the activities of the school as if they would be there for their entire high school education.

While this was probably sound counsel, it was initially difficult especially for the younger Peter, who required a tutor. After the day's classes he did extra work with this tutor until he was able to catch up with the demands of the more rigorous English "public school" educational system which, in the second form (eighth grade) included levels of mathematics, Latin and foreign languages not expected of students in New Haven.

In the beginning, "the school seemed dank, musty and old, and all the masters stern and unforgiving", thought Peter, who had a patriotic concern for being able to represent his country well. His own master, "a crusty older Englishman with a gruff veneer," adjusted the requirements for him, and helped him through the first few weeks of classes.

Beeson, recognizing that his younger son was slightly lost in his new environment, spent an hour or two every night at the start of the term helping Peter catch up with the subjects he did not understand. The thirteen-year-old boy learned a little about the research his father was doing at the same time. John, the musician, had an easier time finding his place, but after a few weeks of classes, soccer, horseback riding and musical programs all of the children adjusted well to their new schools, though Judy never did acquire an appreciation for grilled liver.

Although Beeson had been hesitant to take the sabbatical year in London, worried about abandoning his department and people he felt were dependent upon him, he soon settled into a relaxed life without a faculty to manage. Barbara, always adaptable and quick to make new friends, took to the British habit of daily visits to the neighborhood green-grocer, butcher and baker. During the late 1950s, it was still an easy tube ride into London for plays and concerts. Most week-ends, if there weren't athletic events for the boys or riding lessons for Judy, the family toured the countryside around London in their Morris.

The opportunities for a richer family life were part of the sabbatical freedom. Paul and Barbara rejoiced when they could return to Stonehenge and the hospital at Salisbury where they had first met, and planned a spring trip across the English Channel to visit some of the rest of Europe.

The day they set off for France, Judy developed a fever. The crossing from Dover to Calais took four hours, and by the time they reached Paris, the child was clearly ill. The Beesons checked into their hotel room and went immediately to bed. The next morning a French maid came to clean their room while the family was still in it, took one look at Judy and announced that she had the measles. Professor Beeson had to agree. Though spotted, the little girl wasn't so sick that the rest of the trip, south through Monte Carlo, to Pisa and Rome, had to be abandoned. They eventually returned to Highgate for another two months before they sold the Morris and sailed back to New York on the QE II.

◆ ◆ ◆

By 1960, the administration of a major department of medicine such as Yale's had become much more than the chairman and one secretary could manage. A business manager was added to the staff, and took over fiscal responsibility for the department, as well as management of the growing volumes of reports that NIH and other funding agencies expected.

Even this increased manpower did little to allow Beeson the freedom for laboratory research and unhurried individual meetings with students he had so valued at Emory and during his first years at Yale. He became a clever and capable administrator, but never the kind of merciless program director later bred out of competition for money, faculty and patients. He had returned from London devoted to sabbaticals, and encouraged his faculty members to find a place for study when they were eligible, but he himself was plunged straight back into the morass of departmental administration that had plagued prior to his trip to London.

The Yale Department of Medicine had joined the first rank, competing with Harvard, Johns Hopkins and Columbia. A 1964 general article about Yale in *Newsweek* describing the medical school as "good, if not outstanding," brought this quietly outraged December 14 response from John Bowers, who had been dean at two medical schools, member of the Atomic Bomb Casualty Commission and later, President of the Macy Foundation: ". . . . The medical school at Yale has consistently ranked as one of the top schools in the country, with an excellent faculty and students. . . . Recently a distinguished colleague at a New York medical school told me the Department of Medicine at Yale was unquestionably the most outstanding in the country—and neither he or I are sons of Old Eli."

Beeson continued the habit of interviewing all the candidates for house staff positions himself. Yale took about twelve interns a year, most of whom stayed as assistant residents in general medicine, while a few moved to fellowships in specialties. The competition for these positions was, if not fierce, at the very least, demanding. Since most applications came from the most outstanding students graduating from the best medical schools each year, Beeson looked for ways to reduce inquiries and interviews by students he knew would not be competitive.

He had been receiving too many applications from Harvard graduates who were in the middle of their class or lower and would not be considered for the coveted internships at Yale, so he wrote to the dean at Harvard requesting that he encourage only students ranking in at least the top quarter of the class to consider matching at Yale. The following May at the Atlantic City meetings, a Harvard Associate Dean cornered at him at

Haddon Hall complaining that, considering the institution, these students from Cambridge deserved particular consideration. Beeson disagreed, and the two left the hotel through different doors. Reducing the volume of applicants would prove impossible.

He discovered that restarting bench research in the laboratory was just as difficult. Beeson had tried, when he came back from London, to again begin his own investigations in the laboratory of Fred Kantor, then recently returned to Yale and working in infectious disease. Beeson had given the address for NYU's newly elected Alpha Omega Alpha members in the spring of 1955, first met Kantor, one of the initiates, and offered him a residency.

During that year, the young resident went to Beeson's office with the outline of his plans for an academic career. The chairman, who was usually noncommittal when asked simply "Dr. Beeson, what should I do?" happily helped Kantor apply for and win a Helen A. Whitney fellowship in allergy at NYU, then one of the leading institutions for the study of immunology.

When he returned to the Yale faculty, the talented Kantor received a career development award from NIH, and with grand ideas and ambitions, reapplied to renew the grant at the end of three years with an expanded agenda. He was turned down. Devastated by the unexpected rejection, and questioning his suitability for an academic career, Kantor reported this failure to his chief. Beeson "smiled that very subtle smile and said, 'You know, you're very upset, disappointed and angry. Sleep on it a day or two, then ask them for the pink sheet. You'll find there are some important things they have to say. You know, my first paper on white cells and fever was turned down,' he told me."

Kantor did as he was instructed. When he received the pink sheet summarizing the study section's review of his application, Kantor read, "This fellow has gone off the deep end and expanded everything." In the end, he rewrote his application, dividing it into three more reasonable sections, all of which were funded separately.

While Kantor's lab was, therefore, very well supplied with money, the department chairman was still short of time. When Beeson tried to return to his own bench research after the London sabbatical, he failed. From that point on at Yale, Beeson's research was limited to collaboration with students and other faculty members, a situation that left him progressively more frustrated. Working alone in the lab all day long, relating research work to clinical problems, was something that he had loved to do, but satisfaction slipped from the experiments as they became another hurried duty.

One of the clinical problems that had long absorbed Beeson was fever that lacked a clear explanation. He had first started to puzzle about this problem at Emory, continued at Yale, and by the time of his sabbatical had collected over a hundred cases of patients admitted to the general medical service with prolonged, unexplained fever.

When Bob Petersdorf became the chief resident in 1957, Beeson asked him to begin working out the details for a paper describing one hundred of these patients with an illness of more than three weeks' duration and episodic fever of more than 101 degrees, who remained undiagnosed after one week in the hospital. This work was published in 1961 as "Fever of Unexplained Origin." It was an article that nearly forty years later remains one of the most frequently cited papers in all of medical literature.(6)

When he was visiting professor at Vanderbilt several years after the paper was published, students took Beeson to the departmental library and showed him the bound volume of *Medicine* containing the article. It didn't have to be looked up to be found; the pages were thumbed from so many readings that the yellowed edges stood out on the side of the book.

Although the Department of Medicine at Yale was known especially for infectious disease, throughout his tenure there

Beeson remained a firm champion of the generalist in internal medicine. But as the department continued to grow, more and more faculty were added with fellowship training in sub-specialities—a nearly universal trend by 1960.

The hematologist-turned-rheumatologist Bill Hollingsworth took over as Chief of Medicine at the Veterans Hospital. Other young specialists joined him on the faculty: Steve Malawista in rheumatology, Stuart Finch and Robert Levine in hematology, and Howard Spiro in gastroenterology. Al Feinstein returned to invent the discipline that by 1968 he began to call clinical epidemiology.

While the department expanded both in depth and scope, some people left. The vast majority of Beeson-trained academics found careers in the best medical schools in the country; twenty-seven of these went on to hold major administrative positions at other universities, including departmental chairmen and deans.(7) Bob Petersdorf, perhaps the most notable, became internationally known as Chairman of Medicine at the University of Washington, then later Dean at the University of California at San Diego, President of the Association of Medical Colleges, and an editor of *Harrison*. All of these academic physicians continued to train their own students and house staff in the image of their teacher, valuing patient care, instruction of house staff, and clinical research above their own advancement.

Beeson promoted the fortunes of his students rather than himself. He helped even when he couldn't place them securely at Yale. When it was sometimes required that an unproductive faculty member, a poor teacher or failed researcher leave the department, the chairman often first found him or her another position and then announced that he would not stand in the way of the opportunity. This kind of delicacy in his relationships with people earned him the respect and devotion of even the people he had to let go.

In 1961, there was some concern that the chairman himself

might go. When Loeb retired from the College of Physicians and Surgeons and turned over the editorship of the *Textbook of Medicine* to Beeson and McDermott, the new editor was also approached about replacing Loeb as chair of the department at Columbia.

When they noticed their chief begin taking trips to New York City, Bill Hollingsworth recalls that the younger faculty members in New Haven worried that he might be getting ready to leave Yale. As Hollingsworth remembers the episode, Beeson turned down the prestigious job in part because it paid even less than the meager salary he was earning at Yale. In addition, Barbara had been quite clear from the beginning of their marriage that she was willing to "move anywhere but New York City," a factor certainly more convincing than the money, although funding for his department was always an issue.

Hollingsworth also recalls that "The department budget in money allocated by Yale University was only $250,000. Like most faculty members, I never saw a copper cent of Yale money for myself or for my programs during 13 years at Yale. Almost everything we did was paid for by grants we solicited competitively from the NIH. My grants even paid for the phone bill!"(8)

The dean did, of course, have a budget to pay faculty salaries, which was negotiated with department chairmen each year. At the end of the discussions about what to pay faculty members in the department of medicine, Dean Lippard sometimes volunteered, "and we will increase your salary by a thousand dollars next year too, Paul." Beeson never made more than twenty-eight thousand dollars a year at Yale (about what Stan Musial made in 1948), despite the fact that, by the time he left Yale in 1965, the yearly departmental budget was two and a half million dollars.

While there were many successful white men in medicine during the Beeson years at Yale, women and minority students were not a major presence there or in most medical schools until much later (in the 1960s, women were usually fewer than ten percent of a class, with only a faint sprinkling of Asians and African-Americans).

The medicine service at Yale did have female faculty members, however, and usually a few women interns or residents. One of these, Lisa Steiner, Beeson first met when she was an exceptional editor of the *Yale Journal of Biology and Medicine* as a student. Marge Lerner, Marie Louise Johnson, Margaret Albright, Dorothy Hollingsworth and Frieda Gray all held positions in Beeson's department. While not a large percentage of a faculty that grew to sixty-five full-time members by 1965, women did at least have a place in the Department of Medicine at Yale, where they were treated as fairly as the men.

As the success and size of the department continued to grow, so did Beeson's own prestige, both at Yale and across the nation. This was not the result of self-promotion, but happened as a natural function of his unassuming manner and what Lew Landsberg and the rest of the house staff ". . . debated endlessly as the nature of the 'Beeson mystique.'"

> What was it, we wondered, that contributed to the aura of greatness that surrounded this man? When Beeson walked into a room everybody stood up. His very presence imbued the department of medicine at Yale with an organic unity that was felt by third year clerks and full professors alike. No one wanted to appear unworthy in behavior, demeanor, or medical knowledge in the eyes of Dr. Beeson. I remember vividly, as a freshman medical student, attending grand rounds. . . . Dr. Beeson always sat in the front row and although he commented only occasionally his presence dominated the amphitheater. It was this experience . . . that directed me to a career in academic medicine. . . . (9)

While charismatic leaders like Soma Weiss, encyclopedias of

medical knowledge like Robert Petersdorf or innovators like Alvan Feinstein have a talent for acquiring this sort of following, what was Beeson's gift? Both Landsberg and Tom Ferris call it an ineffable quality; a combination of graciousness, shyness, diligence and the intense desire to always do the best that can possibly be done for another person, that characterized Paul Beeson—qualities recognized by his students.

Faculty colleagues benefited as well. Shortly after Charles Cook came to Yale as the chairman of pediatrics, he was asked to attend his first meeting of The Yale-New Haven Hospital Board. Cook, inexperienced in his new role, found himself in the midst of the final discussion about how to reorganize the care of pediatric emergencies—something the board had been considering for many months.

Surprised, the newly appointed chairman was opposed to the changes on good grounds and said so, but the discussions had gone on too long for minds to be changed, and Cook's negative vote was the lone dissent. He felt "betrayed and depressed at the turn of events on one of my first days on the job," emotions that increased throughout the meeting.

Beeson, whom Cook didn't know, was actually to be the beneficiary of the new organization in that the about-to-be created Ambulatory Service run by the department of medicine was scheduled to take over care of pediatric emergencies. As the meeting drew to a close, Beeson asked that the vote on pediatric care be reconsidered. While he made it clear that he disagreed with Cook, the new professor of pediatrics had been hired, he said, to lead that department. He convinced the board to postpone judgment on the question. Eventually, Cook's position prevailed. While some might have been offended or annoyed by this turn of events, Beeson continued to support Cook, sometimes even inviting the pediatrician to take morning report with the medical residents.

Travel is part of a department chairman's job. In addition to committee work for academic societies, study sections at NIH and research meetings, Beeson was now invited to deliver named lectures around the United States, Canada and Europe. As editor of Cecil and Loeb, he was, by 1963, considered one of the leading internists in the world. He had been elected to the American Academy of Arts and Sciences and awarded the Fiftieth Anniversary Gold Medal at Peter Bent Brigham Hospital.

While demanding, this kind of status did not distract him from what he still considered his primary missions of teaching and patient care. At Yale, he continued to take morning report himself in his office at eight o'clock, he still attended on the wards throughout the year, and he gave the annual introductory lecture to the third year medical students as they began their clinical training.

At each lecture, a gravely ill person was chosen from among the hospitalized patients and brought to the Fitkin Amphitheater. As students who had studied only basic sciences, the twenty-four-year-olds about to enter the wards for the first time had little understanding of the disease being presented. Neither was it their professor's intent, on these fall afternoons, to teach them details of the specific illness as he slowly and carefully interviewed and examined the patient.

What a comfort it was to these bewildered students when they were then told:

> . . . as your acquaintance with clinical teachers grows, you will observe that although each of them has special knowledge and experience in some area of clinical medicine, they make no pretense of knowing it all. You will also find that clinicians frequently disagree, and that each of them comes to wrong conclusions from time to time. . . . Biochemists and pharmacologists have "hard" facts to propound. We, on the other hand, deal with such commodities as pain and nausea. We must accept any kind of problem. We cannot insist on working with inbred strains of people, we cannot control the envi-

ronment from which they come, we know that their recollection of past events is faulty, and we cannot reduce
them to sub-cellular fractions to determine what is going
on. . . . We live, therefore, in an atmosphere of doubt
and uncertainty, and make our decisions and take our
actions on the basis of probabilities. . . .

So these are some precepts you must consider: Give
each patient enough of your time. Sit down; listen; ask
thoughtful questions; examine carefully . . . be appro-
priately critical of what you read or hear. . . . Follow the
example set by William Osler: "Do the kind thing and
do it first."(10)

The tone of this concern for the students extended to former
and current residents. In a letter to Al Feinstein after he had
sent the younger man to do research at the Rockefeller Institute,
Beeson wrote, "Do keep me informed about developments. I
am much interested in what happens to you."

Not too much later, after a former resident was briefly married and then divorced, his onetime chief wrote him a note that
followed the advice Osler had recommended to medical students. The hand written letter read, "It was thoughtful of you
to tell me your news. I am indeed sorry to hear it, but admire
your ability to look squarely at the situation and come to a def-
inite conclusion, with what seems to be minimum harm to both
parties."

He demonstrated the same compassion in caring for the last
illness of Yale's President Whitney Griswold after his operation for colon cancer. When there was no further surgery to recommend, and really no treatment at all except morphine, Beeson
was consulted and several times a week made house calls. This
went on for about three months and, although there wasn't
much to offer the sick man, the visits were comforting to Mrs.
Griswold and her daughters. The afternoon that her husband
became comatose, Mary Griswold called Beeson, who rushed
from his office to be with his patient as he died.

In spite of obligations, the Beesons found some time every summer to continue their trips back to Barbara's family's summer house in Dorset. The drive across New York State and Ontario was a long one with three children, but the pine-needle-strewn lane leading to a simple raw lumber house guarded by a totem pole carved Barbara's sister Jane, promised at least a few weeks of ordinary family life. The room above the boathouse in the isolated and peaceful Lake of Bays country provided Beeson a perfect opportunity for uninterrupted work, editing and thinking about clinical research projects.

In an era of word processing and Internet access, the tedious process of editing a highly technical, two-thousand-page medical textbook by hand seems a task similar to Tolstoy's writing *War and Peace* with a quill by candlelight. Parked in the big empty room over the Dorset boathouse, alone at a desk with stacks of manuscripts and reference books on the floor, Beeson edited the text in longhand. In fact, he liked this sort of isolated scholarship; he considered it a benefit of academic life, not a burden.

By now there were associate editors, Phil Bondy (endocrine and metabolic diseases), Cornell's Fred Plum (neurology), and others, but Beeson and McDermott read every submission themselves. They asked old friends Frank Horsfall, who had become Director of Sloan-Kettering Institute for Cancer Research in New York, and Rene Dubos, still at Rockefeller, to write brief forewords.

Because communication was slow, the work went on all year, and as soon as one edition was completed, labor began on the next. In this way, along with occasional meetings in New York or Atlantic City, a new edition of Cecil and Leob came out about every four years.

The senior editors learned early that it was a good idea to occasionally change contributors, as professors with hefty obligations tended to resubmit chapters soon outdated. Perhaps surprisingly, they had little difficulty receiving the manuscripts on time, and as the honor of contributing to the text was prized, threatening phone calls in search of late submissions were rare.

All this work was done at the same time that Beeson continued his other duties. He attracted the best students and house staff to Yale, conducted daily business as chief of medicine, supervised the clinical and research activities of sixty-five full-time faculty members and their technical staffs, and still participated in the summer departmental party and softball game at his house each year. It was too much psychology, bookkeeping and business administration.

◆ ◆ ◆

When Larry Freedman returned to Yale from Europe after getting out of the army, he brought with him a twenty-year old German-Jewish bride. Since they had been married in England, Larry's mother gave a reception at a small apartment in New Haven where, for the first time, the young and very worried Rina Freedman met Paul and Barbara Beeson.

Rina already knew that these were people her new husband and all of his friends depended on and deeply admired. As the child of survivors of World War II who had escaped to Israel, Rina, who eventually became a psychoanalyst, was alert to the implications of the event. The young European woman was accustomed to being self-sufficient and cautious; she searched the room, and the Beesons in particular, for signs of the social ranking and narcissism she feared she would find in her new American home. She discovered none of these kinds of warnings.

Instead, she found kindness, honesty and disarming charm. Barbara gave the new couple a bone china figure of a horse as a wedding gift. Rina, who knew her to be both an animal lover and a horsewoman, interpreted this present as Barbara's giving something of herself.

Like that of the rest of the young residents and staff, Freedman's salary was a bleak sum. Regardless, all of the staff stayed. The power that Beeson exerted was not through intim-idation or promises, and certainly not through money; he pro-vided something much more difficult and rare. The residents and faculty came to Yale and stayed at Yale, not only because of the quality of the work being done, but because of Beeson's reliability and fairness. Rina Freedman, though, quickly iden-tified the seductive and slightly unsettling aspect of both Paul and Barbara Beeson's influence over people. It was, especially for someone who became a psychoanalyst, that they uncon-sciously became parent figures.

But of course the Beesons were already parents. John and Peter had, after their experiences at Highgate, attended the Hopkins School in New Haven and then entered Yale as under-graduates. Judy was still at home.

At the age of fifty-five Beeson was discouraged to find that his year's absence in London had changed little of the admin-istrative demand he faced. The students still needed him, the residents wanted him and the faculty demanded him just as they had before his sabbatical.

Tom Ferris was the chief resident in 1963 when someone announced during a hospital conference that John Kennedy had been assassinated in Dallas. In general, people remember where they were that day. Later, alone in his office considering the death of the promising young president and perhaps realizing his own limits, Beeson pondered ways by which he might lessen the burden of his non-clinical chores. As the money for running the department now came principally from sources outside the medical school, these obligations were more and more duties that had little to do with the patient care, clinical research, or medical student education that had attracted Beeson to acade-mic medicine twenty years before. No matter how he examined the problems, he saw few solutions.

He was unused to this predicament. When people came to him with their own problems, he expected to help them find an answer and he was usually successful. Not long after the annual Christmas party that year, Beeson invited several confidants to a meeting at the Rimmon Road house. He was seeking their advice about how to reduce his administrative burdens.

No one remembers exactly who attended the meeting, but all agree it included Beeson's closest friends, experienced academic physicians who would give him honest advice. The chairman explained a problem they well understood: he didn't have enough time. He wondered how some of the administrative work might be divided, and suggested first having the intern and resident applicants interviewed by all the faculty members rather than only by him. He proposed an assistant department chairman, different ways of taking morning report and making rounds, new schemes for seeking funding and different relationships with the dean's office. He wondered if someone else could spend more time with the medical students, take over editing papers and grant applications, or at least help listen to the house staff's endless personal problems.

He found little help. The others could not agree to any of his suggestions, or offer better solutions, not because they were unwilling but because Beeson had been too successful. It was proposed that he have someone else take morning report, but that was the one thing, of course, he considered central to his job. He was stuck.

This was not a flash of insight on Paul Beeson's part. In declining the several other offers of chairs and deanships, he had recognized the limits of his administrative abilities and his growing distaste for the size and complexity of the department he was running. He already knew that the style of clinical investigation he loved was being supplanted by the pure science of molecular biologists, immunologists and geneticists: researchers spared the responsibilities of taking care of patients.

In addition, rumors of an expanded war in Vietnam were beginning to send tremors, and then rumbles, through universities. Medical students were not exempt from the disquiet, and began to advise undergraduates about health strategies for avoiding the draft.

The cost of caring for patients was increasing, and while the Kerr-Mills Bill passed by Congress was a step toward Medicare, it had not solved the problem of universal coverage. It turned out, that Medicare and Medicaid didn't solve the problem either, although these programs delivered more money to providers and institutions.(11)

The reasons he had loved academic medicine were rapidly disappearing. The lab was gone. The students and house staff, even the wards, were fading away.

By the end of the summer of 1964, Beeson was considering a second sabbatical at Stanford as one possible solution to his growing predicament. The annual summer party was a great success that August, picking up his spirits. The incoming class of interns, including ringleaders Lewis Landsberg, Richard Lee and John Forrest, decided to name themselves the "Fitkin Ironterns", implying both loyalty to the department and their indomitable spirit. They had made tee shirts to wear to the party bearing the new name. Their enthusiastic faces revealed their joy, and the pride they took in being Yale interns on the medicine service, as they warmed up for the softball game. It may have been that game that led to the meniscal tear in Beeson's knee and another surgical experience.

Arthroscopic surgery was yet to come, and so in January of 1965 Beeson's knee was opened by an orthopedic surgeon and repaired. During the several days of recovery in the hospital, then required for what is now an outpatient procedure, Beeson's secretary brought the mail to his room each afternoon.

He was surprised to receive a letter from George Pickering, who had moved to Oxford, labeled confidential. His old friend from the London sabbatical wrote that Leslie Witts, the Nuffield Professor of Medicine, was about to retire, and Pickering wondered if Beeson might be interested in having his name entered as a candidate to succeed him. The salary was 4,500 pounds a year, about half what he made at Yale.

In this offer, Beeson saw a solution. The Department of Medicine at Oxford was small and organized in an English way—diffusely. Research would be possible. The wards were intimate. Students and house staff were accessible, and there was time for tea in the afternoon. When he told Barbara about the inquiry, and the suggestion by Pickering that he come to visit Oxford, she told the children that she was going along because she expected Paul to take the job.

Pickering arranged for Beeson to be invited to serve on the selection committee to choose a new Vice Chancellor at the University of Nottingham. This was a way of getting the Beesons to Oxford without attracting too much attention. Pickering was wary of taking any candidate through the John Radcliffe Infirmary himself because, as Regius professor, the act alone would cause speculation and rumor. So with another consultant, Beeson toured the department where he found forty beds, four house officers and five faculty members.

Pickering did take him to Magdalen College where the Nuffield Professor was automatically a fellow. It was a companionable collection of old stone buildings and tutors not far from the hospital. Witts had lab space that would become available, and the administrative work would be much less than at Yale. The entire situation appealed to both Paul and Barbara, and when the formal offer came from Pickering, Paul promptly accepted.

But there was one catch. Beeson, one of the great names in medicine, didn't have a British medical license and it appeared it would be difficult to get one. The British did not accept the National Board Examination, so it seemed that Beeson might be asked to take a licensing exam that included basic sciences, an idea that did not appeal to the fifty-six year old professor.

However, Pickering discovered that several Canadian provinces, including Alberta, would give reciprocity for Beeson's McGill degree and the National Boards. Paul flew to Alberta, paid a fee, acquired the license immediately and sent it to

Pickering at 13 Norham Gardens, Osler's old house, where the Regius Professor lived. When Pickering was informed that Beeson's credentials had been accepted by the General Medical Council, he wired his friend in New Haven who made plans to tell his department that he was leaving Yale. In this way, the Chair of Medicine at Yale obtained a license recognized in England.

Only Bill and Dorothy Hollingsworth were forewarned of the Beesons' impending departure. During dinner at the Faculty Club one spring night in 1965, Paul and Barbara excitedly told their friends about the decision to move. The two couples went to a concert together at Woolsey Hall, but midway through the evening both the Hollingsworths began to weep, and had to leave.

An announcement soon went out from the department office that a special meeting was to be held in the Fitkin Auditorium, but said nothing about the subject. There was no other warning, other than the fact that Fred Kantor noticed that Bill Hollingsworth was slightly edgy that day. With all of the faculty and house staff present, some standing at the sides and back of the room, Beeson sat in front of them and quietly said he would move to Oxford that July. No one said a word.

Their shock was not simply that the chairman was leaving. By 1965, many heads of departments sometimes sat in the chair only long enough to make it comfortable—or uncomfortable—for their successor. Beeson had become so strongly identified with Yale, and so personally responsible for the department of medicine, faculty, staff and students, that his departure seemed like a death. In fact, Rina Freedman had understood this problem clearly when she recognized the Beesons as parental figures. One simply could no longer run huge departments in the same paternalistic way as they would small ones, no matter how altruistic the leader.

The shocked staff gathered in small groups afterward, wondering what this development meant for them personally and for Yale. Kingman Brewster, who had replaced Griswold as the President of the university, wondered too, and called Dean Lippard to discover why Beeson was leaving and to determine if his mind could be changed.

As the news of his appointment as the second Nuffield Professor of Medicine leaked out across the profession, letters of congratulations began to arrive from around the world. Beeson answered each one. It is an example of his value to individuals that almost two hundred people wrote to him when they learned he was leaving Yale. Deans and department heads, family and students, friends from around the world all sent letters congratulating him on his new appointment. But they were always with some personal note of sorrow that he was going away to England, and with an acknowledgment of his influence on their training, career, research, and life as physicians.

As an example, from the Yale faculty in epidemiology, John Paul explained:

> This is a sad letter for me to be writing; indeed it will be a sad day for all of us when you leave Cedar Street. . . . And yet I can sympathize greatly with your desire to get back to a small department and to doing the kind of clinical work which it is hard to achieve here, and is probably going to be more difficult in the future. . . . I must find some unembarrassing way of expressing my personal feelings toward you. At the beginning of our friendship I immediately began to appreciate your sterling qualities beyond those as a superb professor of medicine; but as a parent, as a stimulating guide of young men, and many other characteristics in which you are certainly in the top rank.

Ivan Bennett, who moved frequently and often between disciplines, wrote from Baltimore where he had become the Director of the Department of Pathology at Johns Hopkins, observing:

> The situation that has developed in this country more and more means that a department . . . is constantly expanding, that a chairman of a department has less and less time for contemplation and careful thought without interruption, and that the majority of the activities of a department are likely to be determined by the momentum built up by various programs of the NIH, etc. which make money available in such large quantities. . . . Well, I am grateful to you, I owe you more than I will ever be able to repay, and knowing you . . . has had a profound influence on me, on my thinking and on my way of life.

There was some concern, too, about why he was going to Oxford. Albert Snoke, Executive Director of the Grace-New Haven Hospital, sent a note to the dean in April 1965, concerned about Beeson's successor. Snoke wrote, "the Department of Medicine has undoubtedly been shaken to the roots by Paul's decision," but at the same time he wondered why he was leaving. "I am sure that part of it is his desire to be in a different type of atmosphere, but I am also suspicious that part of his desire is to get out of the type of environment and responsibility we have placed on him."

In August of 1965, an announcement appeared in the *Journal of the American Medical Association* describing Beeson's Oxford appointment, and noting how uncommon it was for another country to import teachers for important positions. This was a period in Europe when "the brain drain" saw many teachers and research scientists leaving for the United States; passage in the other direction across the Atlantic was not only uncommon but enthusiastically welcomed by the British. The *JAMA* article went on to comment:

There is, of course, an interesting similarity between the new Nuffield Professor, and the Regius Professor of Medicine at Oxford from 1905 to 1919, Sir William Osler. Although Osler was, and remained, a Canadian, and Beeson was born in the United States, both men graduated in medicine from McGill University in Montreal— a proud achievement for that university. Both men held important posts in academic medicine in the United States of America. Both men were responsible for highly influential textbooks of medicine. Now, just 60 years after his famous predecessor, Dr. Beeson and family are organizing passports, suffering inoculations, packing books, and planning itineraries.

For the Oxford Medical School Gazette in 1965, Robert Loeb told Beeson's new medical students and faculty they were getting a "Stimulating teacher, skilled scientist, able administrator and wise physician.…" All of the dozens of letters and articles praised Beeson in the same way, recognizing not only his abilities, but the humanism of Osler that he had continued to exemplify.

Perhaps the sweetest and most poignant of these recognitions came not from important scientists, former students or faculty members, but in a letter dated June 23, 1965 typed by a physician in private practice on Dixwell Avenue in New Haven. Dr. Fred Smith, who was black, sometimes came to Yale for rounds and had admitting privileges at the New Haven Hospital:

Your leaving Yale to go to England is no longer news— yet there is still a gnawing unacceptance of it within me. I shall miss you—not for the medical give and take which for obvious reasons we never experienced. Nor was there any warm, personal interchange between us. I shall miss you for the pleasant smile and nod as we would meet in the hallways, for the short discussions we had on the few things common to us, like children and school choices. These small things made me feel I was accepted into the Yale family and gave me that sense of dignity so many Negroes talk about, nowadays. For these things, I shall remember you. Accolade of the world in your chosen field you already have. However, I make mine to you as a kind, perceptive, and understanding human being.

CHAPTER 10

One of the major choices any society must make is how
far to go in equalizing the access of individuals to goods
and services. Insofar as this is a question of social choice,
one cannot look to economics for an answer. What economic analysis can do is provide some insights concerning why the distribution of income at any given
time is what it is, what policies would alter it and at
what cost, and what are the economic consequences of
different distributions....

. . . many nonpoor seem more willing to support a
reduction in inequality in the consumption of particular commodities (medical care is a conspicuous example) than toward a general redistribution of income. In
England, for instance, everyone is eligible to use the
National Health Service, and the great majority of the
population gets all of its care from this tax-financed
source. At the same time, there is considerable inequality in other aspects of British life...

Victor Fuchs, 1972(1)

𝒫aul, along with Barbara and Judy prepared to sail again for
England. He was unable to take along the gift of a desk that the
Yale faculty members presented to him, inscribed "To Paul
Beeson from his department at Yale, 1965." He did travel to

Atlanta once more to accept the Emory Medical School Alumni Association Award of Honor before leaving. John had just graduated, and Peter was still in college, beginning to learn about the unwise war in Vietnam from Yale Chaplin William Sloan Coffin, and so neither of the boys made the trip.

There were two other family members that went along, a dog called Molly and a cat named Sally. The cat was actually being repatriated, having been acquired in England during the Beeson's sabbatical year. Both animals required quarantine in Southampton for six months before being allowed to join the family in an apartment on the Oxford High Street. Barbara, attentive to all creatures from the time of her childhood in Snyder, went nearly every week to the port city simply to pet the dog and hold the cat, trying to insure their health and relative happiness in the unhappy situation.

Just across from the front entrance to the Botanic Gardens in Oxford, the square tower of Magdalen College rises in Gothic authority one hundred fifty feet above the High Street. The architecture itself implies an essence of English scholarship and learning that dates from thirty-four years before Columbus discovered America. In spite of the grandeur, book-lined rooms seen through narrow windows seemed inviting to the Beesons as they walked past the college in the evening and across Magdalen Bridge, learning their way around a city with a recorded history from the thirteenth century. The flat where they first lived, however, was neither inviting nor grand but in fact cold, dingy and gray.

A block west of the college, on the same side of the High Street, the Beeson's little flat was located above some shops near a stoplight. Twelve-year old Judy, who had the front bedroom, sometimes looked unhappily out her window into the inquiring gaze of passengers on top of the momentarily stopped double-deck buses. She took one of these buses herself to the Headington School for Girls. Though the education was excellent, she wasn't fond of the unflinching British discipline and regimentation, a distaste that persisted when she moved to the Oxford High School for Girls.

Beeson himself had to accommodate to the Oxford method of teaching medical students and a departmental organization quite different from the American system. Medical students were accepted into one of the Oxford colleges and spent their first three years studying basic sciences with tutors, along with all the other undergraduates of that college.

Until World War II, fourth year Oxford students then transferred to one of the teaching hospitals in London, where they completed three years of clinical clerkships. In fact, prior to 1940 at Oxford, there was really no serious clinical teaching of medical students at all.

While Osler made rounds at the John Radcliffe Infirmary in the first decades of the century, and saw private patients for which he charged dearly, the Oxford medical students continued to go to London for clinical training until it became unsafe during the Battle of Britain. By the time Beeson arrived in 1965, a large percentage of Oxford medical students were staying at the Infirmary for clinical instruction, where they were joined by students from other undergraduate colleges in London and elsewhere.

Beeson noted early in his tenure that studying chemistry and physiology in the rooms of a tutor ill prepared the students for their first experiences with living patients on the clinical wards. He knew a system used in both the American and Canadian medical schools that introduced college graduates to clinical medicine both early and gradually in the medical school curriculum.

There were other adjustments to be made as well. Whereas for almost twenty years as chairman of departments at major universities in the United States, Beeson had enjoyed both authority and influence, the Nuffield Professor of Medicine had a title. The faculty of four other consultants were all senior, mature physicians, devoted to Leslie Witts. They had well-developed research programs and clinical interests of their own, as well as established relationships with doctors in the community who referred them patients.

Beeson arrived respected in infectious disease and famous in medicine as the author of a major textbook, but with little real control over the running of the Nuffield Department of Medicine, one of five medical services (called firms) at Oxford. The other university service was the Regius firm of George Pickering; the National Health Service ran the three additional firms that admitted patients to the Infirmary.

All five firms operated small clinical services. The Nuffield firm admitted to the Thomas Willis and Richard Lower wards, each with about twenty beds.(2) Admissions usually came when a firm was "on take," the British expression for admitting cases through the emergency room or clinics, which they did in rotation. Such a system did not lend itself to any centralized administration, nor even to a method for conducting morning report, which Beeson at first attempted but soon had to abandon because four days out of five there were no admissions.

In addition, Beeson sometimes had trouble managing the autonomous consultants of all five firms. Even though they met for consideration of mutual problems, few of their long-established procedures were easily changed. The "on take" method of admitting patients to the various services in some kind of rotation presented continuing controversy. The firms took turns admitting patients on specific days, but because certain days such as week-ends were busier than others, and because some firms had more staff and students, inequities were inherent in the system.

After one difficult meeting, characterized by a misunderstanding in which Sidney Truelove seemed to agree to a modification of the system but then changed his mind, Beeson himself typed an uncharacteristically strong memo complaining about the method for admitting patients and offered a solution.

They all finally agreed, but in the process feelings had been trampled. Two days later, a distressed John Ledingham was moved to write to Beeson, "I write this letter instead of talking to you, because I would like to add a note that might be difficult to say—and that is to tell you that there is *no man* who could command the affection, respect and admiration that you command with us all...." According to ancient British traditions, the five firms and all the consultants operated quite independently, although there was some central control of the budget, most of which was derived from a single source.

The Nuffield Benefaction was the major grant given to Oxford by William Morris, Lord Nuffield. "Willie" Morris started his career operating a bicycle shop on Longwall Street in Oxford. He began to make motorcycles and by the time Osler arrived in England he had started to build cars. By 1912, he was massproducing the Morris Oxford. These cars, with a characteristic bull nose, sold well, and Morris became known as the Henry Ford of England.

Apparently, Osler owned a car that required frequent repair, a service provided by the neophyte auto mechanic Morris, who was something of a complainer, if not a hypochondriac. So in return for a car that operated properly, Osler looked after Morris' health. The two men became friends.

Both Osler and Morris it seems, were on occasion rather fun-loving, and enjoyed each other's company. In fact, until Osler's death in 1919, they were often referred to around the City of Oxford as the "two Willies." Lord Nuffield did not forget his debt to Osler, and bequeathed a large part of his fortune to the university, funding, among other things, five chairs in the medical school.

The Nuffield Committee for the Advancement of Medicine, which included the Nuffield Professor of Medicine, determined how this money was spent. The Regius Professor, a title dating from the reign of Henry VIII, also sat on the committee of about a dozen people. These trustees had complete authority to decide how to spend the income and capital out of the trust, and to set the agenda for the meetings.

At the time it was announced in the Nuffield Committee minutes that Beeson had replaced Witts as professor of medicine, the Curator of the Chest reported that "the recurrent income of the Nuffield Benefaction from 1965-6 can be assumed at not less than 200,000 pounds per annum." With authority to spend money and set the agenda, the trustees did have collective authority, but of a far different nature than Beeson had known at Emory or Yale.

Beeson established the tone and administered the budget, but the clinicians in the Nuffield Department did not require the same sort of handling the larger, more diverse and frequently more dependent faculty at Yale had required. The Nuffield firm consultants included Sidney Truelove, said by Pickering to be the best gastroenterologist in England; Sheila Callender, already famous in hematology; and the epidemiologist Donald Acheson, who created the Oxford Record Linkage project (directly supported by the Ministry of Health) to investigate patterns of illness in large populations.(3) Acheson, a rigid Irishman, later served capably as Chief Medical Officer of the National Health Service. These accomplished and slightly insular British doctors required little more of the Nuffield Professor than his regular participation at the meetings of the trustees.

Soon after he arrived, Beeson did have the opportunity to add Hans Krebs to his faculty. Krebs, whose work in sub-cellular energy metabolism won the Nobel Prize in 1953, was about to retire from Oxford as the Professor of Biochemistry, but wanted to continue his research.(4) In a demonstration of the pettiness that George Pickering found especially distasteful but common in the basic science departments, the rest of the biochemistry faculty wanted his lab space more than they wanted the former chairman. Beeson had about fifteen hundred square feet of space converted to laboratories for Krebs. He moved into the Nuffield Department, and along with the others in his group, including several Yale visitors on sabbatical, was added to the collegial atmosphere created by the new Nuffield Professor of Medicine.

Pickering, a strong, perceptive and clever administrator, had sought to bring Beeson to Oxford because he knew his strengths, but he was careful to make sure his friend was informed about potential obstacles. In March of 1965, Pickering sent to New Haven copies of the forms Truelove and Acheson had submitted in application for the chair to which Beeson was appointed, "so that you can see what manner of men they are." At the same time he acknowledged his problems, writing, "When I came here . . . the issue in Oxford was a moral one. It seemed to me then that Oxford had every card in the pack to make a first rate medical school . . . [but]the Nuffield professors were all out for themselves; they would not share their toys; they hated each other and the non-professors; there was little intercourse between the museum [basic science] departments and the infirmary departments."

The Regius Professor knew he needed help in creating an environment that fostered cooperation between the powerful, long-isolated basic scientists and the clinicians, as well as between the members of the various clinical firms. He also knew his man. The letter ended, "However, the key post is medicine and I do feel that what we need is a man of character and integrity, a first class physician whom his colleagues and the young will respect, a good scientist and above all a man who will inspire the young to advance their subject and take trouble over helping them. It is for these reasons that we invited you."

Beeson took the Oxford job because he was worn out with the administrative work at Yale and realized that advancing in the traditional sense, or even moving laterally to another American medical school, meant doing more at his desk and less in the lab and on the wards. He understood the way in which he had become quite trapped at Yale:

Here I was, with another decade to go before the conventional age of academic retirement. That offer from
Oxford was just a godsend as far as my personal enjoy-
ment was concerned. I'm not a good executive, and I
wouldn't be the best man to run one of these big departments now. But what I acquired from my own training,
and valued so highly, was going around like Soma Weiss
did, seeing patients and being intensely interested in
them and talking about them—in that way being an
example of a clinical teacher for my teachers and house
staff. And that's why young people used to like to go to
Atlantic City and listen. . . .

He began to attend on the wards within a week of his arrival.
From the High Street, it is only a right turn and about a mile
down Woodstock Road to the John Radcliffe Infirmary campus.
A circular drive with a huge fountain containing a statue of
Triton, son of Neptune, leads to a front door that looks more
like the entrance to one of the venerable Oxford Colleges than
a hospital.

The Nuffield Department office, wards and labs were down
a long main corridor across the back of this two-hundred-year
old building. Even without morning report, Beeson was thrilled
to make rounds with a few, very capable young doctors such
as Jim Holt, Witts' last registrar, and a handful of medical students. It was Holt who discovered that an Englishwoman flown
back from America and hospitalized for six weeks at the
Radcliffe Infirmary with fever of unknown origin wasn't sick.
She had married an American, but was so homesick she had
contrived the temperature elevation as a route out of the United
States. Once she was home in England, the fever vanished.
While neither Holt nor Beeson figured out how she did it, they
did have enough time to devote to her problem and to help
her recover. For Beeson at Oxford, there was leisure, time to
talk to patients and to think about their illnesses with the stu-

dents before returning to his office, now lacking a line of worried supplicants.

While Beeson acquired Leslie Witts' Chair and Registrar, he did not inherit his secretary, who had also retired. Before long, however, Phyl Woolford, who had been secretary in another Nuffield department and had started her career as a nurse in the Infirmary, interviewed for the vacant position. Because she was competent and experienced, she got the job, also adding her little dog to the office staff. The animal spent each day under her desk. Even with the occasional interruption of excited barking when the dog was surprised by an unexpected noise, Beeson and Woolford together were able to accomplish all of the administrative duties required of the small department.

In the afternoons, at tea time, the professor usually spent an hour with his D. Phil. candidates discussing their projects, or attended the research seminars held on Wednesday afternoons. At first, these meetings attracted only Nuffield Department members, but like much (though not all) of the American style Beeson imported to Oxford, the exciting speakers and ideas soon attracted participants from all over the university. He was also able to expand on Witts' attempt to merge the efforts of all five medical firms by sponsoring the evening meeting of the heads of these services to discuss mutual problems.

One of these long unsolved dilemmas, the smooth entry of undergraduates moving from the rooms of their tutors onto the wards, eventually resulted in Beeson's creation of an introduction to clinical medicine called the "bridge course," a project which occupied him for the first several years at Oxford.

In the October 1966 minutes of the Nuffield Committee, he introduced this subject saying, "The pre-clinical departments are making certain changes in their degree courses, omitting much that is pertinent to training for medical practice, and are teaching about their disciplines as independent subjects. They plan then to participate with the clinical teachers in a so-called 'bridge course' of perhaps six months duration, to take students over the gap between the basic sciences and the study of man and his diseases." Finding this much cooperation between the basic science and clinical departments was a task inhibited by years of British tradition, part of the obstruction to teaching for which Pickering had imported Beeson to surmount.

In addition to a smaller, more focused administrative burden and increased opportunity for direct clinical teaching, there were two other privileges attending the Oxford move. The Nuffield Professor was automatically a Fellow of Magdalen College, and the always shy Beeson found a mid-day pleasure in driving the mile from the Radcliffe Infirmary back to High Street and through the gate into the college. He passed the kitchen and climbed the few stone steps up to the common room.

In 1458, when Magdalen was built, the architect thought it prudent to place the fellows common room on the floor directly above the only reliable source of heat then available, the kitchen stoves. This mahogany common room filled with comfortable leather chairs and couches was a perfect place to read the *London Times* and enjoy a glass of sherry or conversation with other scholars about their work. The historian A.J.P Taylor was there most days, as was Hugh Sinclair, an eccentric student of medical history.

Beeson might have wondered, however, about the seesaw-like board spanning the open end of a horseshoe-shaped arrangement of overstuffed chairs. By lifting one end, this device was employed to slide the sherry decanter across the gap at the open end of the horseshoe so that the last tutor wouldn't have to trouble himself to get up and carry the bottle to the other side.

Beeson often ate lunch at Magdalen, and attended the monthly meetings of the tutors, although he said so little the others sometimes called him "the quiet American." In the early afternoon, he had plenty of time to return to his office and to the other opportunity lost at Yale: research.

Oxford is a magnet for recipients of various scholarships, including the Rhodes, offered by the British. Beeson found that these young doctors stimulated him once more to work on clinical problems in the lab. With the Australian Tony Basten and others, he began to explore mechanisms of eosinophilia, a hematologic response to parasitic infections such as trichinosis, certain allergic conditions and some neoplastic diseases.(5,6)

This type of white blood cell, named for its staining properties when examined by light microscopy, was poorly understood then, and though Beeson's group showed that the lymphocyte controls eosinophil response, it remains, even now, a mysterious player in the workings of the immune system.

At a recent conference on eosinophils Peter Weller's forward notes:

> Dr. Beeson brought to his investigations a broad clinical and scientific knowledge. He was well aware of the disease associations of eosinophilia. He remembered the time when lymphocytes were ill-understood and recognized simply as a unitary type of small compact mononuclear leukocyte. Modern immunology has refined, and continues to delineate, the functional diversity and complexity of lymphocytes, despite their nominal morphologic similarity and simplicity. Dr. Beeson, a pioneer in laying the ground work for much of our current studies of eosinophils, has wondered whether the morphologic unity of eosinophils belies a greater diversity of function. . . . What are the evolutionary benefits to having eosinophils?(7)

The editorial work on the *Textbook of Medicine* continued too, and brought Walsh McDermott to Oxford as the eosinophilia research was beginning. Ken Johnson, one of the chief residents from Yale, who was considering an appointment at the University of Washington, turned up at the same time seeking his former chief's advice about taking the job.

At tea, Johnson was introduced to McDermott who was still

Chairman at the Cornell School of Public Health. The young epidemiologist recalled that Beeson phoned him the next day saying, "I've just returned from taking Walsh to the airport. He will write you, offering the directorship of the epidemiologic research unit in his department at Cornell. You can bring your own team." When his former resident expressed surprise, Beeson added, "Ken, don't shilly shally in making a decision." Johnson thought, "Shilly shally, you've just told me about it. He hadn't said 'Take the job' but I sensed he thought I should, and subsequently, I did."(8)

◆ ◆ ◆

After a year in the High Street flat, the family gratefully moved to a house at Boar's Hill, just outside of Oxford. The roomy, furnished place had an enormous main room with a big fireplace, perfect for the eggnog parties the Beesons liked to give for faculty and house staff at Christmas. There were enough bedrooms for visits from Peter and John, as well as other American friends who found Oxford a convenient place to stop.

What the house lacked, however, was a kitchen. The place the previous English residents had thought was a kitchen was, in reality, a tiled room containing a primitive sink and a cold marble slab—the only refrigeration. The arrangement was unusable, and the Beesons had the room rebuilt to accommodate American appliances Barbara had had shipped to England.

In addition to being more comfortable, the house was convenient to the riding lessons and horse shows that occupied both Barbara and Judy's time. Barbara bought her daughter a horse, and riding her own mare Cecil, the two of them spent most week-ends competing in shows or cantering across the English countryside.

Judy never adjusted to the British educational system well, however, and especially disliked a teacher she shared with her friend, Susan Juel-Jensen. In celebration of the gunpowder plot conspiracy on Guy Fawkes Day November 5, she was invited to her classmate's house for fireworks to be set off by Susan's father. The children didn't come in from the garden after the firecrackers were ignited. Later, they were discovered to have made a figure of their teacher and stuck pins in it. The next day when the woman fell and broke her leg, the girls were horrified.

Judy took little interest in the English boys, but she did enjoy trips to Scandinavia and France with Peter when he came to visit, trying, in conversation with his parents, to make sense of the expanding war in Vietnam.

In 1967, Peter left Yale with a degree, no plans, and eligibility for the draft. Like most college students at that time, Peter had trouble believing in the "Domino Theory" and couldn't support the war in Vietnam. Neither did he feel going to graduate school simply to escape the draft was an honorable solution.

When he was accepted into the Peace Corps, he declined an assignment in Korea because he didn't think the war would be over in the two years of Peace Corps service. "I did a lot of thinking and moaning about the lack of alternatives for myself. I didn't want to go to Canada, and I didn't want to go to a war where I might die, and that I didn't believe in. There wasn't any really right thing to do as I saw it, and so I was sort of paralyzed."

Peter's parents, able to see the problem from England, had a more unobstructed view of Vietnam than many parents of their generation, but no real solutions to offer for their younger son's dilemma. John had been actually inducted into the army before being found ineligible and discharged. He was looking for work as a musician in New York, though with little success.

Peter, confused and worried about his choices, repeatedly wrote to Boar's Hill complaining about the injustice of his situation. His parent's politics had begun to move to the left; both had supported Kennedy and then Johnson, but not the war the two Democrats had intensified. They also wanted Peter to decide himself what to do. "My father was increasingly impatient and sent a couple of strong letters telling me to make up my mind."

Finally, out of options, Peter enlisted, and went to Officers Candidate School before being sent to Long Binh as an infantry lieutenant assigned to the program designed to win the "hearts and minds" of the Vietnamese villagers.

In the hamlet of Long Binh there was, in fact, little evidence of war aside from an occasional misdirected rocket. The 90th Replacement Battalion built schools, taught English and helped to raise pigs with the Vietnamese villagers. Peter felt that he was part of a Peace Corps of sorts after all. He, and his parents, later agreed with the opinion of Barbara Tuchman who, writing of the Vietnam War in 1984, said, "What America lost in Vietnam was, in one word, virtue. The follies that produced this result begin with continuous over-reacting: in the invention of endangered 'national security,' the invention of 'vital interests,' the invention of a 'commitment' which rapidly assumed a life of its own, casting a spell over the inventor."(9)

One night around a dinner table in a hut at Long Binh, Peter began to discuss this view of the war with another young officer recently graduated from West Point. Positions were taken, voices raised, and soon the conversation turned to shouting as beliefs collided. The moment symbolized an entire generation.

The pall of the war and his children's problems didn't affect Beeson's responsibilities in the United States. He traveled frequently across the Atlantic, leaving Oxford by Buck's Travel Overland Taxi for Heathrow, flying back several times a year to attend meetings. In 1966–67, he was President of the Association of American Physicians, and in 1968 was elected to the National Academy of Sciences, both rare honors.

He also served on the Board of the Scripps Institute, which allowed him easy opportunity to visit his aging and frail parents in La Jolla. Both were past ninety, and John, the frontier surgeon who had often discovered that he was the final opportunity between a sick patient and death, was himself failing. Paul's mother Martha had grown forgetful.

Beeson occasionally stopped at Yale on these visits to the

U.S., where he found the medical school changed, and Phil Bondy, who had replaced him as chairman, with his hands full:

> ...concern that the Oxford move would remove Paul Beeson from the American academic mainstream turned out to be totally unfounded. If anything, he became even more influential . . . his time in England coincided with the Vietnam War, a time when children rejected their parents, young people were generally alienated from their elders and from the government those elders supported, and medical students and house staff tended to view their professors as natural antagonists . . . he certainly would have been miserable as a leader during a period when challenge-the-leader was the order of the day, particularly at volatile private universities such as Yale.(10)

Because they were in England, neither he nor Barbara suffered the mind-hardening political schism between generations that came to characterize America during that period. Beeson was deeply concerned, however, over politics within the community of academic internal medicine when he gave his presidential address, "The Academic Doctor," at Atlantic City in 1967.

More and more interested in the social aspects of providing medical care, he had come to admire the British National Health System. At the same time, he had growing apprehension about trends in university departments of medicine inclined towards more specialization on one hand and molecular research, rather than clinical investigation, on the other.

His controversial speech at the "Old Turks" meeting summarized these two problems and helped define an academic debate of the next two decades:

> Our rapid expansion was made possible because the American people became persuaded . . . that better health could probably be obtained by investing a great deal of

money and manpower in medical research. We in academic medicine agreed with this notion, and gladly accepted the assistance that came with it. . . .

It is important to recognize . . . that this great expansion was financed only to augment our research output. Our two other traditional responsibilities were scarcely affected at all, for we continued to deal with about the same number of medical students and with about the same number of patients in our teaching hospitals.

Certainly the net effect of events in the past 15 or 20 years has been good. . . . Despite that, I have chosen on this occasion to talk about certain trends that trouble me. These trends fall into two categories which are interrelated: one is the increasing tendency of academic physicians to devote most of their time and thought to laboratory research; the other is their ever growing clinical specialization. I don't see how these tendencies can fail to have detrimental effects on our competence as physicians and as teachers of clinical medicine.(11)

Beeson and some of his colleagues realized that the growth of technology and increased biochemical sophistication made the body of medical knowledge too vast to allow real expertise in more than one corner of a discipline. But the fact that "we have forever passed out of the era of clinical teachers who could deal with all branches of clinical medicine" saddened those who had trained when such teachers were the norm because it weakened relationships between the healer and the sick. The ideal of a real generalist caring entirely for each single patient exemplified by John Beeson and Soma Weiss, had been lost. At the same time, in medical schools radicalized by progressively more aggressive students privileged to be there instead of Vietnam, health care was democratized.

Paternalism, inherent in a system of medical care largely

founded on clinical acumen, became unfashionable. Patients were first allowed and then encouraged to participate in decisions about both the nature of their care and of their doctors. Increased numbers of women and minorities were admitted to medical schools, broadening the profession and access to it. Students and patients had greater autonomy.

More information, though sometimes it was simply camouflaged advertising, began to circulate outside of the traditional medical community. Patients became consumers. No longer were they willing to simply receive the opinion of doctors, who became providers. A fear that the health-care system would be destroyed by socialized medicine, always sponsored by the American Medical Association, grew as students advocated egalitarianism.(12)

Such democracy, while popular and just, weakened the subtle, magical qualities of a profession that brought their own potency to healing the sick, or if not curing at least calming them. Once the mysterious hidden power of allopathic medicine was exposed as incomplete, patients helped create a new magic of alternative therapies often based not on evidence or science, but folklore, myth and the wish for hope sometimes denied by a more biochemical and physiological truth.

The second contentious issue Beeson raised in the presidential address concerned molecular biology. As an advocate for clinical research in departments of medicine and opposed to the growing trend towards pure science, Beeson was swimming upstream. Even during his address, he noted the disapproval of Don Seldin, who was building a department at Texas Southwestern focused on molecular medicine.

Seldin, whom Beeson knew and admired, had been considered for the Yale faculty shortly after Beeson took the chair. He had expected to be hired with the rank of associate professor, a demand his mentor John Peters had found laughable, and dismissed with a terse *amour propre*. So he remained at Southwestern. Seldin represented a growing group in academics who foresaw increasing the emphasis on molecular biology as the most profitable direction for research in departments of medicine. It is, however, difficult to have a personal relationship with mitochondria, a disjunction that caused Beeson to mourn the neglect of clinical research as the cost of funding pure science.(13)

When he returned to the small and quiet Oxford, Beeson directed his attention away from these meta-issues and back to the more manageable ones associated with running his firm and supervising his fellows' research. He did manage to assemble enough consensus among the basic science faculty to launch the "bridge course," which included clinical pathology and an introduction to clinical medicine focused on history, physical examination and laboratory evaluation.

These lessons taught young students who knew the biology found in books to listen to the patient's story and hear the entire message. In the same way, they learned to auscultate a chest and hear the cleverly camouflaged abnormal sounds that sometimes came from a sick heart. The Krebs cycle, vital in biochemistry but irrelevant on the wards, was forgotten as medical students learned to care for human beings.

Eventually, a five-hundred-thousand dollar grant was obtained from the Commonwealth Fund for this course, which Beeson never considered a complete success. However, with some modifications over the past twenty-five years, the Oxford "bridge course" has survived and is still a principal component of the introduction to clinical medicine in the fourth year. While he did not revolutionize the curriculum, this contribution to students beginning their ward clerkships was meaningful and lasting, and Beeson is still remembered for bringing the idea to Oxford.

The Nuffield Department of Medicine continued to attract both fellows looking for research projects and established physicians on sabbatical. One of the latter, Thomas Stamey, a urologist at Stanford, knew Beeson through their mutual interest in urinary tract infections.

Stamey was already a respected department chairman in 1967, but before submitting two papers to *Nature* that year, he wisely first submitted them to Beeson. "There was hardly a line that had less than 4 or 5 corrections; it was a humbling experience for a chairman who had already written a few reasonable papers. Paul did these corrections in such a wonderfully gentlemanly way that I have always felt tremendous gratitude. . . ."

The urologist learned another lesson while at Oxford that he published in a 1995 monograph about making difficult choices in the treatment of prostate cancer:

> I have another reason for trying to present this controversy in a way that will help patients make a choice. I learned 25 years ago from Professor Paul Beeson . . . that each of us, when faced with a serious illness beyond our comprehension, *unknowingly* become childlike, afraid and look for someone to tell us what to do. It is an awesome responsibility for the surgeon to present the options to a patient with prostate cancer in such a way that he does not impose his prejudices. . . . (14)

While Beeson was immediately able to join in the research projects and manage the business of the Nuffield Department of Medicine, George Pickering had rightly foreseen that his greatest contribution at Oxford would be in building cooperation and trust *by his example*. He sometimes did this in ways that were curious to the English.

Derek Hockaday, a young consultant on another of the medical firms, came hurriedly to see the infectious disease expert one afternoon a few days after his wife's hysterectomy at the gynecological hospital near the Radcliffe Infirmary. He was worried about his wife's fever and lethargy. The young husband was frantic that his wife didn't seem to recognize him. When Beeson rushed to see her, he found her septic, and arranged an urgent transfer to the Willis Ward.

It was a serious breach of British protocol to snatch another consultant's patient and move her to a new hospital without discussion, but Beeson believed the situation dire, and he was right. Thirty years after his wife survived this nearly fatal illness, Hockaday still told the story unable to contain his tears.

The ability to foster trust and sponsor cooperation made him a valuable asset to Pickering, who wanted Beeson to succeed him as Regius Professor after his early retirement in 1968. Pickering and others were frustrated to learn that the Regius Professor, appointed by a special emissary of the Queen, was required to be a citizen of the empire.

Being an American did not prevent Beeson from deep involvement, though, on several committees, one studying plans for the new John Radcliffe Hospital to be constructed at Headington and another evaluating a reorganization of the administration of teaching hospitals sponsored by the Minister of Health.

The traditional British way of running their medical schools had become too ponderous to keep up with rapid advances in bio-technology. At a time in the United States when departments were growing almost exponentially, Beeson could not add one new consultant position to the faculty out of funds from the Nuffield Benefaction.

His clinical and administrative responsibilities increased when Richard Doll was appointed the new Regius Professor. Doll, an epidemiologist who had proven the hazards of cigarette smoking, was not a clinician, and so the ward responsibilities of running the Regius firm fell largely to Beeson. He also found himself asked to sit on a growing number of committees, but the duty was not oppressive.

The responsibilities of the Nuffield Committee were broad, though, ranging from incorporating the recommendations of the 1970 Green Paper modifying the relationship between the National Health Service and Oxford University at the Infirmary, to a request by M.S. Dunhill, Director of Clinical Studies, for an electric typewriter.

◆ ◆ ◆

In 1969, David Durack graduated from medical school in Australia and was named a Rhodes Scholar. Because he wanted to do both a house officer's job and research at Oxford, he applied to Magdalen College and to the Nuffield Department of Medicine. When he finally reached Oxford after the long journey by ship, the traditional way for Rhodes Scholars to travel to England, he immediately started in on what he recalls as almost endless work.

His first assignment was to the male, or Lower, ward. To get there, he had to pass Sir Hans Krebs' lab. It was formidable enough for a new graduate who only weeks before studied the great man's metabolic pathway, but then he was confronted with the terrifying figure of Sister Elizabeth Howells—"Sister Lower." Although the doctors wrote the orders on patient's charts, the stolid Sister Howells was the final authority on every other subject, a truth undisputed by the house staff. Absolutely in charge of the ward, the head nurse was asked daily by the six foot, two inch Durack, "Sister, may I make rounds now?" "Yes," she enunciated crisply, "welcome to the ward."

One of Durack's early problems was how to admit quickly and inconspicuously the head of one of the colleges, a very large man having noisy DTs. Beeson was available to the inexperienced house officer, and quickly arranged for a private room at the back of the ward while helping to calm the Oxford Don and begin his treatment. After a week in the hospital, his dignity recovered, the man was discreetly returned to his duties.

Durack was impressed with his professor's quiet way of teaching on rounds, a method that often included saying something slightly surprising or controversial and then just leaving. Shortly after the Australian started on the wards, a wasted, febrile and very ill-appearing patient was admitted with pain in his back. During professor's rounds, the man was presented as a case of cancer of the pancreas. When asked his opinion about the patient's clubbed fingers, Durack agreed with the diagnosis of pancreatic cancer and thought the clubbing a secondary event.

Beeson, who had looked in the patient's eyes and seen flame-shaped hemorrhages, correctly diagnosed endocarditis, and then returned to his office without further comment. When blood cultures were positive the next morning, proving endocarditis, Beeson asked the junior house officer how the patient should be treated. "I was ready by then," recalled Durack. "I'd read the book overnight and proposed twenty million units of penicillin a day, to be given for six weeks." Beeson recommended half a million units four times a day. "He didn't push it. He just went off."

This moment formed a basis for the next fifteen years of Durack's important research, asking questions of antibiotic therapy such as "What is the right dose? What dose would work? Does it matter what the dose is, and how did we ever get to the point of saying twenty million units of penicillin for six weeks was correct anyhow?"

After a year on the wards, Durack took his scholarship into the laboratory for three years of research toward a Doctor of Philosophy degree. In addition to Beeson, it happened that there were several prominent American researchers working in the Nuffield labs with Krebs at the same time: Alexander Leaf, Frank Epstein, Lou Welt, and later Bob Petersdorf. It was a wonderfully exciting environment for the twenty-five year old Durack to enter this world under Beeson's guidance, a little like walking with Socrates into the agora.

Beeson and Durack developed a reliable model for producing bacterial endocarditis in rabbits, and conducted experiments describing the morphology of the vegetations, survival of the bacteria in the lesions, and the efficacy of antibiotic prophylaxis against the infection in patients with valvular heart disease.(15,16,17)

The prophylaxis issue was important clinically. Over the thirty years since the first dose of penicillin had been given at the Radcliffe Infirmary, the prescription of antibiotics had become arbitrary and ill conceived. Durack and co-workers showed that, unless serum levels of antibiotic were maintained at a therapeutic level for a prolonged duration, prophylaxis failed. Ineffective treatment promotes mutations that protect bacteria from antibiotics, and despite warnings, such mutations have continued to produce virulent, resistant strains and new illnesses.

For Durack, who was invited to the Atlantic City meetings to present one of the papers, it was the beginning of a valuable and important career. Bob Petersdorf was so impressed with the young Australian that he asked him to be his own chief resident at the University of Washington in Seattle.(18)

While this work was being completed, Beeson's parents had a car accident. He flew back to La Jolla to help them. The state police found that John Beeson had improperly driven through an intersection, and recommended that the ninety-six year old give up his license. Paul hired a driver for them, and supervised their move into a retirement apartment.

About fifteen months later, in May of 1969, John Beeson died. When their father was admitted to the Scripps Clinic Hospital with a myocardial infarction that proved fatal, Harold left Beirut for Heathrow, where he met his younger brother for the flight back to California. By the time they arrived, John Beeson was comatose. Both of his physician sons found it difficult to sit in the room with him, waiting.

When his father died after a few days, Paul woke his mother to tell her, but she had become so confused that the following morning she didn't remember that her husband of seventy-one years was gone. Martha lived another two years, becoming gradually more demented, and needed care in a nursing home after John's death.

The death of parents is a landmark in any life, and the nature of Beeson's publications after this time reflect a shift in his attention from specific clinical research to concern about broader social and political aspects of medicine. The publication of Duff and Hollingshead's 1968 book *Sickness and Society*, based on research done at Yale and highly critical of both medicine and hospitals, also influenced this change in his interests.

At the time he reviewed the book, however, Beeson found the authors guilty of sensationalism, misuse of data, and, perhaps worst of all for the gifted editor, too much "gossipy detail." But demonstrating his always open mind, he did "...conclude by conceding that there are bases for many of the things the authors deplore, and that we all hope for a better world." Not finding an example of how to discover that world in the book, Beeson went looking for it himself.

He began to write not only about the importance of clinical research, and a generalist approach to medical care, but how to train doctors and improve the last years of patient's lives. He became interested in the developing field of geriatrics, a discipline not even named as the bookend to pediatrics when he was in medical school.

Anticipating the debate over assisted suicide that was to erupt twenty years later, Beeson's essay "Quality of Survival" is a masterful summation of the arguments against euthanasia.(19) He correctly identified the codification of legal policy as an error in this controversy, and pointed out that once physicians are identified as possible executioners rather than healers, their trust relationship with patients is abandoned. At the same time, he advocated death with dignity and rejected aggressive treatments for the hopelessly ill. Killing patients is not the same thing as helping them to die.

As one path to these goals, he continued to admire and recommend the British National Health Service, then widely feared in the United States as an example of socialized medicine. He responded to an essay in the *London Times* critical of the NHS by writing, "To work well, a hospital must be a tight-knit community of people who respect one another and enjoy working together."

Beeson delighted in telling his American friends that the NHS system did work well and provided a good standard of care for everyone. He found it especially interesting that, while there were only eight thousand specialists in the U.K., there were then two hundred and eighty thousand in the U.S. The ratio of family doctors to specialists in the two countries was reversed. He recognized that, to achieve this kind of better balance in the United States, "Some agency will have to take charge; and of course the federal government is the most likely one. Wouldn't it be gratifying, though, if we [the medical profession] could exhibit the statesmanship and self-discipline to do it ourselves?"

While Beeson's interests expanded in the 1970s, so did the list of his honors. He was made a Master of the American College of Physicians and became a Charter Member of the Institute of Medicine, a branch of the National Academy of Sciences. Five universities, including Yale, McGill and Oxford awarded him honorary degrees. In 1973, the Infectious Disease Society of America gave him the Bristol Award, their highest honor. That same year he won the Kober Medal, the rarest prize for an internist.

Even this list did not prepare him, though, for the letter in a plain envelope he found sitting on the kitchen counter when he arrived home on November 20, 1973. Sir Keith Joseph, Secretary of State for Social Services, wrote explaining:

It is my privilege to write to inform you that Her Majesty the Queen has been pleased to appoint you to be an honorary Knight Commander of the Most Excellent Order of the British Empire. This honour, to the bestowal of which the Government of the United States of America have agreed, is conferred by Her Majesty in recognition of the very valuable services which you have rendered as Nuffield Professor of Medicine in the University of Oxford.

Robert Lord Platt, former President of the Royal College of Physicians, wrote pointing out that this was no ordinary honor. In the carefully constructed British hierarchy, a Knight Commander is a significant distinction and takes precedence over more ordinary knighthoods. Beeson was no more impressed with this ranking than Osler had been when King George V made him Sir William in 1911. Still, he was very pleased to receive an honor given to very few Americans.

Because Americans do not kneel before the Queen, a ceremony was arranged for December 12 at Admiralty House. Paul, Barbara and Judy, accompanied by the Pickerings, went to receive the parchments and medal proclaiming his knighthood. Beeson, the first American to be made honorary Knight Commander in twenty-five years, joined his countrymen Vannevar Bush, General Mark Clark and Yehudi Menuhin on a very short list of those being so recognized.

Dozens of letters and telegrams began to arrive from all over the world. Just as had happened when he left Yale, the people around Beeson, both friends from the U.S. and colleagues in England, wanted to send him congratulations and praise. The letters reflect an admiration beyond the simple wish to acknowledge the honor; they convey a feeling of respect and love for Beeson denied to most people. It is the sort of esteem reserved not for a doctor or scientist, but for a teacher—someone who has shown us how to live.

One short note from George Godber, former Chief Medical Officer of the NHS, concludes, "This is going to give enormous pleasure to your friends in British medicine. I've never heard of any doctor being so honored before. The first man to stand rightfully beside Osler. You won't believe that being the modest man you are, but the rest of us know."

By the time he was knighted, Beeson was already making plans to return to the United States. Though his years at Oxford had been among the happiest of his career, several forces pulled him back across the Atlantic, including his children.

Judy had graduated from high school and entered Washington University in St. Louis. One afternoon before she left, she warily approached her father announcing her intention to "smoke some dope," perhaps as a way of preparing herself for the anarchy of American university life. To her surprise, and as an example of his wisdom in managing young people, her father did not protest, but allowed her to make her own decision.

Peter had started Cornell Law School, and John's calling in music, a career that eventually took him to the Metropolitan Opera, was underway. The attractions of family were powerful, and furthermore, the Veterans Administration had just then created an opportunity for senior academic physicians to continue teaching beyond the usual age of retirement. The major impetus to leave England, though, was a push not a pull, and came from changes at Oxford and from within Beeson himself.

The plans to build a new Oxford University Hospital had occupied the Nuffield Committee and Beeson since he had arrived. By 1973, David Weatherall was ready to succeed as the Nuffield Professor, and the new John Radcliffe Hospital was nearing completion in Headington. In a characteristically unselfish decision, Beeson concluded that the person who would be in charge of the Nuffield firm in the new hospital should lead the effort from the outset.

In order that Weatherall could move the Nuffield Department of Medicine to Headington, Beeson retired two years early. Remembering the conversation when he called to discuss this plan, Weatherall, now the Regius Professor at Oxford, said, "I think that he loved Oxford in many ways, and that it showed the generosity of the man not to make it difficult for his successor in any way."

In March of 1973, Beeson announced his intention to return to the U.S. in September of 1974, allowing plenty of time for an easy transition to the new hospital.

Sometime previously, the Chief Medical Officer at the Veterans Administration had contacted Beeson, telling him that the V.A. Distinguished Professorships had been established, and suggesting that he could accept a nomination for the program anytime. Only one person had then been appointed, William Castle. The offer included a pay increase, important because Beeson never did reach even his modest Yale salary while at Oxford, as well as the location of his choice. Paul and Barbara considered moves to several university-affiliated V.A. hospitals around the country, and finally chose Seattle both because Bob Petersdorf was the Chair of Medicine at the University of Washington and because the weather wasn't too hot.

Awe-inspiring medical technology has combined with egalitarian rhetoric to create the impression that contemporary medicine is highly effective. Undoubtedly, during the last generation, a limited number of specific procedures have become extremely useful. But where they are not monopolized by professionals as tools of their trade, those which are applicable to widespread diseases are usually very inexpensive and require a minimum of personal skills, materials, and custodial services from hospitals. In contrast, most of today's skyrocketing medical expenditures are destined for the kind of diagnosis and treatment whose effectiveness is at best doubtful.

Ivan Illich, 1976(1)

Judy returned to Oxford from St. Louis and helped her parents prepare for the move back to Seattle. This time, the entire family, including the pregnant mare Cecil, made the trip home across the Atlantic by plane.

Beeson arrived to discover a huge university in a metropolis spread out along Puget Sound and spilling into suburbs on both sides of Lake Washington. In the forty-six years since he had abbreviated his undergraduate education and entered McGill Medical School a year early, Seattle had become a fash-

231

ionable West coast city that in 1974 was entering another period of rapid growth. New buildings were sprouting downtown like dandelions in the cement cracks, and entire new communities had shot up around the Sound as Boeing, recovering from a slump in the airplane industry, began to manufacture planes as fast as possible.

Paul and Barbara, hoping to continue the semi-rural way of life they had enjoyed at Boar's Hill, found a little farmhouse in what still bordered horse country on Avondale Road in Redmond, east of Lake Washington. Because of timing and bureaucracy, Beeson's journey back to Seattle and the V.A. Hospital had taken five years to negotiate. As he moved from the drizzle of Oxford to the drizzle of Western Washington, he prepared to begin the final phase of a medical career devoted to patients and students.

He had been contacted by the Veterans Administration about the Distinguished Physician position in June of 1969, long before he was prepared to leave Oxford. H.M. Engle, then the V.A. Chief Medical Director, helped create this program in 1968 when William Castle was assigned at the West Roxbury V.A. In fact, Castle's departure from Harvard seems to have been at least part of the motivation for creating a plan to employ influential physicians beyond the usual age of retirement. The program not only extended the teaching lives of those appointed, but also provided an income late in their careers to supplement lifetimes of slender academic salaries.

In his early letter to Beeson, Dr. Engle told him that he would be nominated for one of the five funded positions whenever he was available, and included the official description of the program, which stated, in perfect government language:

The position of Distinguished Physician is established to enable the Veterans Administration to use the talents of outstanding medical scientist educators. Distinguished Physicians are those who have made significant contributions to medical science and have attained exceptional professional stature over long and distinguished careers.

The Distinguished Physician, though located at a particular VA hospital, will serve on a VA-wide basis as a consultant, lecturer, or in other teaching capacities. . . . He should have no major administrative responsibilities.(2)

Between Castle's appointment to the first of these positions and the time Beeson was actually ready to leave Oxford, the program had selected several other Distinguished Physicians, including Tinsley Harrison in Birmingham and Max Finland in Boston.

In August of 1971, when Beeson finally decided to take the position in Seattle, he had heard nothing more from the Veterans Administration. He knocked softly on the back door of the process when he wrote to Castle, asking his old friend, "I wonder if I could make a confidential inquiry, about the status of the V.A. Distinguished Physician program. As you know, in 1969 I had a very nice letter from Dr. Engle, inviting me to accept one of these.... Since then, of course, Dr. Engle has left the V.A, and I know that budgets are tighter than ever, and I wonder if this program is still being implemented, etc." In a hand-written note avoiding secretaries, Castle told him about the new appointments and promised to inquire further nearer the end of Beeson's tenure at Oxford.

By July of 1972, Bob Petersdorf, as Chair of the Department of Medicine, wrote the Dean at the University of Washington asking permission to make the necessary arrangements for the appointment with the V.A. Central Office, a dense bureaucracy.

Petersdorf called his former chief "one of the most distinguished physicians in American Medicine," and reminded the dean that Beeson had already been honored by the Board of Regents of the University of Washington as their 1968 Alumnus Summa Laude Dignatus, even though technically he wasn't a graduate. "Most of all," Petersdorf closed, "he is a marvelous man who will add tremendously to the intellectual atmosphere not only of the Department of Medicine and the V.A. Hospital but of the entire University." By the end of May 1973, the new Chief Medical Director at the V.A. contacted Beeson at Oxford naming him Distinguished Physician at the Seattle VA starting October 1, 1974.

Robert Van Citters, long-time Dean at Washington, acknowledged the appointment in a letter to Beeson sent in July, 1973. "All of us here look on your coming as a mark of great distinction for the school and the community," wrote Van Citters, who went on to describe a fiscally healthy medical school that had recently completed a period of rapid growth and that enjoyed a national reputation for excellence in research.

In a candid paragraph revealing some of his problems, and foreshadowing the much greater dilemmas to plague teaching hospitals that were two decades ahead, he added:

> However, we continue to have major problems in the clinical areas. We have never developed a substantial following, and we are inept in the basic skills required to generate the necessary referral practice. The great majority of our doctors seem to be entirely willing to sit around and wait for patients to come in and touch the hem of their gowns. One manifestation of this is an abysmal census at both our hospitals, and this at a time when more patients are needed for our teaching program and for meeting the fiscal requirements of the program as well.

As Beeson prepared to help the University of Washington Medical School correct these clinical deficits, Barbara was anxious to continue the life she had known as a child in rural New York and had rediscovered outside of Oxford. Their new location on ten acres across Lake Washington was perfect. Although the house itself needed remodeling, there was pasture for Cecil and her foal, and near by trails to ride. Redmond was still little more than a village, and the two lanes of lightly-traveled Avondale Road provided an easy commute to the University and the V.A. Judy decided to transfer from St. Louis to Central Washington University to be closer to her parents, now in late middle age, but Paul and Barbara were alone with the horses in their new home. They were happy to avoid the hot summers of Atlanta and the snow of New Haven, so the rains of Seattle did not discourage them.

The chief of the medicine service at the Seattle V.A. was Phil Fialkow, known for his work in genetics and later as Dean of the Medical School at the University of Washington. In his new, unfamiliar role as something other than the chief of a service himself, Beeson went to see Fialkow a few days after he arrived. They discussed the duties of the Distinguished Physician, purposely left undefined by the Veterans Administration.

Fialkow did not demonstrate the shock he must have felt when his new faculty member asked to attend on the wards for six months of the year, but just nodded his head in agreement. Busy researchers considered it a chore to make rounds with students and house staff for even one or two months of the year, and so having one of American's greatest internists on the wards for half the year delighted the taciturn Fialkow. "I was out of laboratory investigation," Beeson said later, "and I liked to see patients and house staff and students, so that's what I did."

In his new office across the hall from Fialkow's, Beeson's days acquired a new pace. When the V.A. chief was away, residents were thrilled to give their morning report to the first man who had learned the practice from Soma Weiss, its inventor. Most mornings after rounds, he returned to his office where he continued to edit Cecil and Loeb's textbook through the fifteenth edition, published in 1979. This tedious and time-consuming work was still being done entirely by hand.

Initially at least, he had the help of his loyal Oxford secretary, Phyl Wollford, who moved to Seattle when the Beesons returned to America. However, she was sharing an apartment near the V.A. Hospital with a woman she described later as "a bit of a 'dipso' who kept a jar of cannabis in the fridge." Already homesick, she soon became discouraged with the odd roommate as well, and went back to England, leaving most of the work to the editor himself.

Beeson still had national obligations to study-sections of the NIH, the National Research Council Institute on Aging and the Merck Foundation, and continued to travel. He persisted with editing journals, now focusing on geriatrics rather than the new kind of internal medicine that was progressively dividing itself into smaller and smaller sub-specialties. However, he was also free to indulge his greatest joys, going to grand rounds at the University and the V.A., making rounds with students, and occasionally sneaking off to lunch with Bob Petersdorf.

Departments of medicine had grown to hundreds of people by the late 1970s, and required full-time administrators who were unable to do much else. Instead of a line outside the chairman's office, an appointment book grew black with names written in ball-point pen into each fifteen minute time-slot, reservations carefully tended by a secretary parceling out dates far in the future.

For the students and house staff who were able to stand at the bedside on the V.A. wards with Paul Beeson, listen and watch while he discussed the illness and then examined the patient, the process connected them to those generations of healers who went to care for the ill without much technology, but with a dedication to helping each person in whatever way they could.

CT scans, MRI and angiography, complex biochemistry and virology, new generations of antibiotics, micro-optics, minute sub-specialization and a nosology that demanded treatment for every abnormality had taken over clinical teaching, removing the more senior faculty from the intimate daily details of education. The new, self-perpetuating technology established the appearance of an immediate and unambiguous, potent certainty.

In describing the power this technology confers on doctors, Eric Cassel deplored a reductive oversimplification in the definition of illnesses that had begun to create in patients the expectation of immediate, perfect cure. "In using technological methods," Cassel goes on, "physicians mistakenly believe they can reduce uncertainty by changing the patient's problem to one for which there is a technological answer."(3) For Beeson, the questions, not the answers, remained the quintessence of medicine.

It shocked the chief resident one day to receive a paper in the mail from Beeson reviewing a debate in cardiology that had been presented on ward rounds several days earlier, but not resolved. The surprise was that the professor had taken serious note of the discussion, and that he had troubled himself to look up an important reference and send it to him. He was accustomed to attendings who, hurried by circumstances, retreated to their labs after rounds, closed the door on their clinical problems and went to work on research or another grant application.

Expectations had changed in medical schools, and clinical teachers like Weiss, Stead and Beeson had all but disappeared by the late 1970s. By then, few would have agreed with Osler's aphorism, "There are, in truth, no specialties in medicine, since to know fully many of the most important diseases a man must be familiar with their manifestations in many organs."(4)

In the mid-1980s, digital angiography, new generations of faster CT scans, and then MRI, had made possible such exquisite pictures of almost every organ that few secrets remained about anatomic abnormality in diseases. New problems could be introduced, of course, when images obtained for some complaint discovered unrelated and clinically irrelevant normal anatomic variants, or other changes with uncertain significance to the patient. Though he appreciated the beauty of the technology, Beeson lamented this pattern of patient care, and continued to write convincingly in support of the generalist.

As sub-specialty medicine grew to the point where more than two-thirds of doctors who passed the American Board of Internal Medicine examination went on to fellowship training, Beeson gave up on his concept of the internist as generalist. But he didn't abandon the idea; he moved it to a new arena. As a member of the Institute of Medicine's National Institute of Aging, he began to write about the generalist in geriatrics.

The specific care of the old, not even mentioned by Osler when Beeson was in medical school, troubled many of the committee members because it seemed so ignored. The medical education of the late 1970s continued to focus on basic science, high technology and tertiary care, all laudable pursuits in Beeson's way of thinking, but neglectful of the most rapidly growing and dependent segment of the population—the elderly.

Noting the demographic shift and the increase in expensive, highly technical care as well as the long-term care older patients required, Beeson observed:

> Certainly no one denies that all trainees today come in contact with a great many elderly people. But these old people have been admitted to our teaching hospitals for diagnosis and treatment of acute serious illnesses. The aspect that is being slighted is a special characteristic of the needs of the elderly: the kind of continuing (lifelong) medical care required for people who have multiple, chronic, progressive disabilities. To get a "feel" for this kind of medical care is hard for any of us in the academic world and almost impossible for students and house officers, who change from one inpatient service to another every few weeks.(5)

Anticipating changes in medical training that would not appear for a decade, he offered some remedies for the problems of caring for the aged. He suggested an introductory course in clinical training that included the teaching of ambulatory care by sociologists, psychologists, economists, and home nurses; it was an Oslerian kind of "liberal education in medicine." He argued that medical schools should affiliate with chronic care institutions and train academic teachers specifically in geriatrics.

In short, he proposed a new kind of generalist. While the old sometimes do need technical solutions to specific problems, Beeson noted that they more often need "simple help in getting the right kind of dentures, proper spectacles or assistance with a walker." The programs in family medicine that eventually grew out of this period have, in many important ways, achieved these goals.

The problem is certainly not solved, however. The final report of the ad hoc committee on Leadership for Geriatric Medicine of the Institute of Medicine, National Academy of Sciences, came to Beeson in draft form. He sent it back covered with proofreaders' marks, noting, "an old editor finds it almost impossible to resist penciled suggestions about wording, and some thoughts about the substance of the report." He found the draft redundant, too long, and full of "hand wringing frustration that doesn't seem terribly persuasive." He argued for support of teachers in geriatrics and something specific to teach, not "meandering around with a lot of ideas and half-hearted advocacy for a variety of strategies. . . . "

The report eventually published in the *New England Journal of Medicine* observed, "currently, the 12 percent of the U.S. population that is over the age of 65 accounts for more than 33 percent of physicians' time, 25 percent of medications, and 40 percent of acute hospital admissions."(6) The authors described special needs of the aged, citing frailty, incontinence and confusion as part of the multiple-systems disease states requiring long-term care, and they offered some solutions. Interestingly, their proposals included many of Beeson's original suggestions for a liberal medical education.

At the same time, Beeson criticized his profession for the kind of mistakes marring the report of the Presidential Commission on Heart Disease, Cancer and Stroke (Debakey Commission), "…a classic of the kind of myopia that the medical establishment of the mid-twentieth century confused with visionary ideals. No one . . . ever asked whether other diseases, such as those affecting children, or diseases that could actually be cured, might be more worthy of federal effort."(7)

On the other hand, he still found admirable substance in modern medicine, and defended the clinician against McKeown's attack in *The Role of Medicine*. This author, arguing for emphasis on public health measures much as Illich had done in the more heretical *Medical Nemesis*, seemed to Beeson "disapproving of the whole system of medical care, clinical teaching, and biomedical research that prevails in the world today."(8)

He praised the long-term analysis of health problems in the book, but found it filled with "massive and unjustified overkill." As he always did, Beeson recognized an imperfect world in which clinicians, sometimes enlarged by technology, tried to take care of individual patients one at a time.

◆ ◆ ◆

America's equilibrium changed when Ronald Reagan was elected president in 1980. Post-industrial free-market capitalism allowed the inflated economy of the Carter administration to expand in many directions simultaneously. If, as Barbara Tuchman claimed, America lost her virtue in Vietnam, during the decade of the 1980s she lost her balance, and fell into the sanctification of greed.

Part of this fiercely profit-driven, uncontrolled growth occurred on the east side of Lake Washington. The farmhouse in Redmond became surrounded by construction and fronted what was becoming a major highway. Farms turned into housing developments in a few months. As Barbara's riding trails disappeared, she worried that nothing would be left but pavement, and went to City Hall hoping she would not unearth plans for further development. She found nothing but growth.

In reaction, she began to attend public hearings, including several in downtown Seattle focused on low-cost public housing. Before too long, she was helping her neighbors write requests for environmental impact statements and working to organize media campaigns calling for restraint.

Barbara Beeson, former conservative, became a well-known, tireless environmental activist. Still, the Redmond golf course became another shopping mall. While she remembered her grandfather's theory that one should "pull yourself up by the bootstraps and do it on your own," she also realized that she was "fortunate, had an education and opportunity that just doesn't always happen now. We have been lucky, but many people haven't been blessed in this way, and part of it has to do with a political system in this country that puts money someplace other than where it can really help people."

As the village of Redmond, home of Microsoft, turned into a bedroom community of new millionaires, the Beesons moved farther out of town and built a new house with enough surrounding land for Barbara's horses.

The Reagan years also brought the concept of defense through a bankrupting kind of military buildup. Nuclear weapons came into particular favor. The Republican position on military strategy was sounded clearly during the presidential debates, and shortly after the 1980 election, Physicians for Social Responsibility was resuscitated in opposition to nuclear proliferation.

Doctors had initially founded PSR at the time of intense political organizing two decades earlier, and had successfully lobbied the Kennedy administration for an end to atmospheric testing of nuclear weapons. Plutonium 239 and other long-lived radioisotopes released by these blasts were being measured in soil samples around the world. Several governments recognized the risk, and above ground tests came to a halt by international agreement in 1963.(9)

During Reagan's first term, political factions became more confrontational when the United States and the Soviet Union began the manufacture of megaton nuclear weapons for use both as deterrents and as bargaining chips in the conduct of international affairs. Aroused by this headlong rush into hazardous policy, Helen Caldicott, a charismatic Australian pediatrician, began to rebuild PSR into a lobbying force against nuclear proliferation.

A compelling speaker, Caldicott was soon joined by other prominent physicians including Jonas Salk, Benjamin Spock, Oliver Cope and Herbert Abrams. Over the course of a few years, PSR grew into one of the six largest medical organizations in the United States. The movement, which initially focused on the health effects of testing, deployment and first strike potential of nuclear weapons, trained physicians to speak about the uncontrollable hazards associated not only with their use, but with their manufacture.

In 1981, the Australian delivered Grand Rounds on this horrifying subject at the University of Washington. Beeson was in the audience as she itemized the effects of a one-megaton blast over downtown Seattle, including the immediate liquefaction of people and things over several miles, as well as the long-term mortality from cancers induced by the radiation.

Beeson sat listening intently in the over-filled auditorium. As an academic physician, he had spent his life trying to educate young men and women in the best methods for saving patient's lives, or at least comforting them when they could not be saved. The kind of slaughter Caldicott described prompted the usually apolitical Distinguished Physician to think as he had never thought before about the discrepancy between his work as an individual and the political realities that were being created for all citizens of every country.

Beeson began to read about isotopes with half-lives of thousands of years, blast effects equivalent to more tons of TNT than had ever been used in all wars, and millions of immediate and long-term deaths from radiation. In short, he learned about the potential for devastation of the earth by nuclear war.

That year Beeson was seventy-three years old, an age when most successful people are contracting their life's work and becoming more conservative. It is a measure of Beeson's always open and absorbing mind that he, instead, expanded his. This was not an easy transition. He was accustomed to an academic life in charge of a department, and to setting the agenda; he was used to being the teacher.

The immediately influential Seattle chapter of PSR rapidly attracted several thousand members, but the core of the organization was a group of about twenty people who had learned political organizing in medical schools during the radical 1960s. What was Paul Beeson, Chairman of Medicine at Emory and Yale, Nuffield Professor at Oxford, and Honorary Knight Commander of the British Empire, doing with a collection of former hippies?

He never asked himself that question. Convinced that producing, deploying and testing nuclear weapons was a moral and practical error for all the world's countries, Beeson wholeheartedly joined the effort to oppose proliferation. He began to barnstorm around the country, lecturing with other doctors who graphically articulated the "bombing run," a description like Caldicott's in Seattle, of what a one-megaton blast would produce in other American cities.

He was a featured speaker in lobbying efforts large and small, local and national, against the escalation of the nuclear threat. Because he was so famous, so scholarly in appearance, and so softly eloquent, people listened. This participation cemented the resolve of the younger members of PSR.

Passionate young professionals proficient in organization

did much of the work of PSR. Schooled in the peace and freedom marches of the 1960s, these former medical students were
dedicated to addressing the nuclear threat as a public health
issue. Local chapters of the organization grew quickly, attracted
money and were immediately able to put on the mantle of
respectability then still assured to groups of physicians.

In addition, the speakers knew the issues well, and were
able to present a graphic, scientifically accurate picture of nuclear
destruction. Unencumbered by bureaucracy, agile, and with a
clear, simple message, PSR employed the "end run" tactic of
quickly scheduling large public educational events using pictures and speakers to show the results of nuclear conflagration
in targeted cities. At the same time, they lobbied local elected
officials individually and in city councils, state assemblies and
congress. They were very successful, and the reserved, cautious
Paul Beeson quietly occupied the center of the maelstrom.

Although this political transformation may have seemed
out of character, especially for those at Yale who had known
him as a moderate Republican, the substance of Beeson's concern was a constant. He had, after all, recognized nuclear threat
as a folly both qualitatively and quantitatively different from
conventional weapons when he volunteered Yale's medicine
faculty as staff to the Atomic Bomb Casualty Commission.

Stuart Finch, one of the Yale hematologists involved in those
early epidemiological studies, also became a PSR spokesman on
the hazards of irradiation. In writing about the August 6, 1945
explosion of the 12.5 kiloton Hiroshima bomb and the 22 kiloton Nagasaki detonation three days later, Finch noted, "It is now
clear that the most important late medical effect of atomic bomb
radiation exposure is the increased occurrence of cancer."(10)

Beeson quietly testified at hearings before the Seattle City
Council and the Washington State Legislature, as well as traveling to cities as far flung as San Diego and Nashville. The
debate grew progressively more one-sided.

Partly because of the efforts of groups like PSR, ordinary

people became more and more convinced that the myth of personal survival following any nuclear exchange was illogical and dangerous. Beeson himself had recognized this when he had sheepishly abandoned the tiny cement block bomb shelter in the basement of the Rimmon Road house years earlier. But as sometimes happens, those perpetuating the folly were increasingly consumed by it.

Nowhere was this tragic error more manifest than in the person and policies of Thomas K. Jones, a former Boeing engineer appointed by Reagan to be Deputy Undersecretary of Defense for Research and Engineering, Strategic and Theater Nuclear Forces. For PSR speakers such as Beeson, T.K. Jones was difficult to take seriously. However, so much money and energy were being spent advertising the myth of individual survival after a nuclear exchange, an idea so clearly an illusion, that PSR speakers were handed an ideal "straw-man."

Jones' real job was to reconfigure the Federal Emergency Management Agency, a body composed largely of earnest federal bureaucrats, former firemen and military personnel responsible for disaster relief, into a civil defense force with the solitary mission of insuring survival after nuclear war.

Although Jones himself seems to have honestly believed that common citizens would actually live through hundreds of megaton nuclear explosions, much of the agency's effort was directed at the survival of the government itself. Whatever the real motives, T.K. Jones continued to promote ideas few took seriously, and he became a character in the Doonesbury cartoon strip when he claimed " . . . that nuclear war was not nearly as devastating as we have been led to believe."

He said, "If there are enough shovels to go around, everybody's going to make it." The shovels were for digging holes in the ground, which would be covered somehow or other with a couple of doors and with three feet of dirt thrown on top, thereby providing adequate fallout shelters for the millions who had been evacuated from America's cities to the countryside. "It's the dirt that does it," he said.(11)

In Seattle, the folly was exposed further when the contract for a plan to empty the city at a time of nuclear threat was obtained by PSR. The relocation plan proposed evacuating five-hundred thousand people on short notice, moving them to remote parts of the state, prompting one rural politician to observe, "If you bring all those people from Seattle to Grays Harbor County, the loggers will shoot them."

The plan assumed that those without transportation across the mountains could be moved in buses, but was broadly ridiculed for including in the calculations those trolleys dependent on overhead power lines.

The debate would have been comical had it not been for the gravity of the risk being studied, not to mention three-hundred-fifty thousand dollars the draft evacuation plan cost Seattle.

At a public meeting reported in the *Seattle Post-Intellegencer* April 11, 1982, Beeson was quoted saying that everyone "agreed on one thing: Once a nuclear confrontation starts it can't be stopped. It'll escalate to an all out exchange."

PSR preached that limited nuclear war, and the hope of individual survival after such a conflagration, was not possible; it was a public health problem taken to global limits. Eventually, T.K. Jones vanished, and FEMA returned to the more sensible burden of trying to manage the effects of natural disasters.

Beeson continued his activism after his final retirement from the V.A. in 1981. The seven years added to his career by the Distinguished Physician position had allowed him not only to discover teaching through politics, but to return to a kind of medical education he had prepared for and had loved all of his life: the demonstration of how to care for the sick through the bedside instruction of young doctors and medical students.

Throughout his professional life, Paul Beeson rarely lectured to people. Rather, he showed them how to be a doctor. He had an intuitive grasp of what Wittgenstein meant when he wrote, as the final proposition in *Tractatus Logico-Philosophicus*, "Whereof one cannot speak, thereof one must be silent." Students learned from Beeson by *watching* him.

At the last Grand Rounds that he presented as Distinguished Physician in December of 1981, the medical house staff gave their teacher a certificate which read, "In appreciation of Dr. Paul Beeson for his contributions in teaching and encouraging the pursuit of the highest ideals of a physician: scholarliness; humility; compassion; and integrity."

The two chief residents on the medicine service then stood and said:

> He has been our teacher, our council, and our friend. He has taught us through his vast experience and knowledge, but he has also taught us by his example. As a living example, he has taught us through his enthusiasm, humility and the genuine concern for the teaching of students and house staff, and toward the care of patients. In short, he is the kind of physician all of us aspire to be.

He hung the framed certificate in his study, next to the document of his knighthood.

Ben Belknap, then Chief of Staff at the Seattle V.A., added his praise in noting Beeson's departure. Writing to the Chief Medical Director at the V.A. Central Office, Belknap recounted his contributions in the usual way such accomplishment is recorded, but he added:

> It is, however, in the wards, the corridors, the nurses' stations, the physicians' offices, the many conference rooms and the lunch tables of this hospital that Paul Beeson will be missed most acutely . . . residents and

staff physicians, medical students, nurses and patients have benefited equally from his dedicated presence. Speaking for all the employees of this facility, we would like to express our gratitude for the opportunity of having this unique man among us for such an extended period.

CHAPTER 12

The independent small businessman is firmly rooted in the American imagination. His misfortune is that he is much less firmly rooted in the American economy. As large corporations have risen to dominate economic life, the myth and the ideal of the entrepreneur have persisted. . . . Bureaucratic professionals seem anomalous even though they now represent the overwhelming majority of professionals in the modern world.

In the twentieth century, medicine has been the heroic exception that sustained the waning tradition of independent professionalism. Physicians not only escaped from corporate and bureaucratic control in their own practices; they channeled the development of hospitals, health insurance, and other medical institutions into forms that did not intrude upon their autonomy. But the exception may now be brought into line with the governing rule.

. . . the last decades of the twentieth century are likely to be a time of diminishing resources and autonomy for many physicians, voluntary hospitals, and medical schools.

Paul Starr, 1982(1)

Two events startled Beeson after he retired in 1981. First was the news that his dearest friend for more than thirty years, Walsh McDermott, had died suddenly in the bathtub at his summer house. McDermott, founder of the "Pus Club", long-time co-editor, and confidant had himself retired from Cornell in 1975, but continued in public health as an advisor to the president of the Robert Wood Johnson Foundation, a charitable fund with broad interests in medical education and scholarship.

"Walsh and I were continually chatting on the phone or meeting," Beeson recalled after his colleague died. "We formed a very close and wonderful friendship. His death was an awful shock to me."

Gone was the voice on the other end of the phone sharing the work of Cecil and Loeb; gone was the research on tuberculosis and other infection discussed honestly and without pretense at the Pus Club; gone were the parties and introduction of promising residents between meetings in Atlantic City.

Not only was a professional relationship lost, but so was a shared ideal of the embodiment of academic medicine. Beeson and McDermott agreed that "we have been experiencing advances in medical science and technology at a pace just steady enough but just slow enough that our institutions have failed to make adjustments that would be in the best interest of medical education."(2)

Throughout the decade of the 1980s, as mergers and acquisitions consolidated so much of American commerce, the pace of technological advances in medicine quickened enough to make the packaging of health care attractive to investors. The changes that marketing and corporate profits introduced into traditional doctor-patient relationships were broadly recognized, and soon resulted in the cries for health-care reform that emerged in 1990.

The epidemic spread of AIDS and other sexually-transmitted diseases, drug-resistant tuberculosis and new, more virulent infections convinced planners that health care was necessary for everyone, if for no other reason than the control of disease. However, by the elections of 1992, a populist call for universal health coverage and access to care had been co-opted by politicians as a sound-bite.

While the Clinton administration did make a serious, ambitious attempt to re-design the entire health care system and provide universal coverage, they underestimated the resolve and influence of insurance companies and for profit HMOs opposing the scheme. The forces that profited from the health care industry manufactured formidable opposition to change.

In the market place, access became constricted, costs increased and technological solutions began to replace the intimate relationships between doctors, nurses and patients that formed the basis of medical practice from before the time of the Flexner Report. Instead of the welcoming, soothing voice of a nurse or receptionist answering the telephone in doctors' offices and hospitals, patients responded to the cues of a computerized answering tree. This contraction spilled into all of medicine, even academics.

With the death of his dearest friend and the open calendar of his own retirement, Beeson's daily intimate interaction with students ceased. Nevertheless, he continued to think seriously about them and about the problems of teaching medicine that had occupied his life. He observed that, in spite of great progress, both the teaching and the learning of medicine had become less satisfying as an unintended consequence of success.

As the mass of knowledge expanded, medical schools became university medical centers, incorporating charity hospitals that passed into the control of salaried clinical faculty. Universities were forced to assume financial responsibility for funding some teaching activities out of endowments, research grants, clinical fees and income derived from hospital services. The precious qualities of academic life, characterized by the leisure to think about each patient's complaints, to concentrate on teaching and learning from students and colleagues, then to transpose problems of illness found on the wards into clinical research efforts, evaporated in the steam of financial constraint and obligation. Academic medicine was becoming less than academic.

Before this time, no matter what the demand for insured medical goods and services in America, there was always supply. The standards for using the goods and providing services had largely been established within medical school faculties. Now, forced to compete for patients in an environment increasingly dominated by for profit HMOs operating with the advantage of huge economies of scale, university medical centers adopted strategies similar to these corporations. In short, the autonomy of academic doctors vanished.

The second shock was far from tragic, and came in the form of a letter from Elisha Atkins surprising him with news of a four-million-dollar Beeson Chair established at Yale. Atkins, who "had some family money he never showed," had attempted to keep the endowment anonymous, but finally had to tell his former chief:

> I am writing to tell you I have done something you may not approve of—but it will have the enthusiastic support of so many of your old disciples during your years here at Yale that you will simply have to accept it. With some funds that have passed on down through the family, I have set up a chair in your name. . . . I needn't tell you how much joy it gives Libs and me to bring you back to Yale in this fashion. Though to us who were lucky enough to have been there then, you were never really gone, at least in our better efforts to carry on what you have given us by your example.

In a letter of February 2, 1981, Yale President Giamatti announced the appointment of the young infectious disease expert Richard Root as the first Paul B. Beeson Professor of Medicine at Yale.

More honors followed, always prefaced not only by respect for his achievements in science, but also by deep appreciation and affection for the tenderness he had shown his patients and the purpose he had given to all his students.

In 1981, the University of California at San Francisco presented him with the Gold Headed Cane, an award recognizing great physicians. The Radcliffe Infirmary named the Beeson Ward in his honor the next year. This ward provides for geriatric rehabilitation, a tribute appropriate to Beeson's late interests in the problems of aging.

In 1985, the University of Washington established the Paul Beeson Award, presented each year by the house staff to the teacher they find exemplifies and encourages the highest ideals of a physician. The care of all those around him—students, patients, faculty—had always been Beeson's goal.

In that same year, the year that Physicians for Social Responsibility shared the Nobel Peace Prize, he accepted the first annual Paul Beeson Peace Award from the Washington Chapter. They chose him as their model champion of peace and disarmament.

Another sorrow overtook Beeson in 1985; his brother Harold died. Standing in the Montana night in 1910, John Beeson had predicted that his older son would live to see Halley's comet come again when he was an old man, but Harold was gone a year before its reappearance.

Beeson himself underwent another operation, a total hip replacement, not long after. He was a little surprised that, in spite of his early recurrent urinary tract infections and several major operations, his own health, and Barbara's, remained good. The news of infirmity and deaths of friends, however, had started to arrive with the daily mail.

Both Paul and Barbara remained involved in politics. PSR struggled on as a lobbying force for control of nuclear weapons, and for clean-up of contamination around nuclear sites such as Hanford and Savannah River. Beeson remained an active icon in the organization, still strong twenty years after its rebirth.

While the collapse of the Soviet Union appeared to diminish nuclear threat, the actual hazard had never been greater. In many former Soviet states, unmonitored weapons and plants containing long-lived isotopes, vulnerable to seizure or purchase by radical factions around the world, alarmed peace activists and their sometimes unlikely allies.

Beeson attended the 1997 PSR Annual Dinner held in his honor. At the same dinner the following year when he was ninety, he listened carefully as former CIA Director Admiral Stansfield Turner described the staggering task of trying to re-bottle the nuclear genie.

The navy, curiously, had produced a number of "peace admirals" and other high ranking officers who knew enough about both nuclear physics and risk to agree that the weapons threatened their owners as much as the targets. The authority of these outspoken experts gave the anti-nuclear crusade new resolve. Though Beeson gave up speaking publicly for PSR, his dedication to the organization provided a kind of inspirational glue, binding together these doctors and others committed to improving their community and their world.

He also assumed some of the secretarial duties generated by Barbara's community organizing in Redmond. "She spent the first half of our marriage following me around, so it's only fair that I give her preference now," he said, while answering her mail.

In addition to work as an editor, Beeson wrote about medical education, changes in the nosology and treatment of some diseases, and care of the aged. He also entered the debate over reform of health care. In a 1993 essay that, ironically, heavily quoted his old antagonist Jack Peters, Beeson recalled the history of the 1937 Committee of 430 Physicians.(3) This group of doctors, many internationally known academics, advocated a far-sighted national health policy that would have insured care for all Americans. Peters, in addressing the American College of Physicians in 1938, had said, "The social responsibility of medicine, as I see it, is to provide to all classes of the population medical care of the highest quality. . . . "

Although fifty-five years later Beeson found reasons to be hopeful about fulfilling that vision, at about the same time he also wrote, "We must recognize that we inhabit a frighteningly unstable planet."(4)

That unstable planet was on his mind when he spoke to medical students and house officers about the changes he had seen over sixty years as a doctor, and when he participated in conferences about medical ethics, health-care reform and aging. Attempting to understand the conflict between a progressively more industrial culture in medicine, and the nature of the human urge to observe, to know and to comfort, occupied his later years.

In her book that included interviews with Beeson, Sharon Kaufman observed, "...that medicine is driven by means, not ends . . . [and that] devices, tools and procedures dominate our thinking. Their use is not informed by a shared cultural mandate which considers their long-term social worth or their ability to alter the meaning of nature and culture."(5)

Though elderly and physically more frail, Beeson maintained an ability to engage his listeners deeply and to inspire a faith, not in medical science and technology, but in the simple wish to care for sick patients.

Geriatrics became his forum as Beeson pursued and investigated these issues. In 1995, The John A. Hartford Foundation, The Commonwealth Fund and The Alliance for Aging founded the The Paul Beeson Physician Faculty Scholars in Aging Research Program. This well-funded program offered major grants to junior faculty committed to academic careers in aging-related research.

Beeson Scholars investigated specific problems of the aging brain such as Alzheimer's disease, as well as sociological problems including elder abuse and the assessment of the older driver. Their web-site said of Beeson, "He has profoundly influenced the career paths of many young physicians, who now form the core leadership in geriatric medicine. He is a physician who exemplifies the William Osler tradition of excellence. . . . "

He reiterated his belief that geriatric medicine is a vehicle for the generalist in his address to the 1996 Beeson Scholars when he told them, "I note that the people who conceived and funded these scholarships stated clearly that they wanted also to bring about improvement in the total health care of older people—to learn more about the diseases of old age, and to enhance the quality of life of old people."

When he accepted their Annual Award at the 1998 meeting of the American Geriatrics Society in Seattle, nearly two thousand people stood to applaud him—the sort of crowd that used to convene for the Atlantic City meetings. At about the same time, in an uncharacteristic expression of glee over the failure of another person, Beeson felt his belief in the generalist was vindicated when Don Seldin's residency program dedicated to sub-specialization and molecular medicine failed to fill its available positions.

In January of 1997, the man who helped define the standard of care in internal medicine and geriatrics endured his own encounter with the transformations in American medicine. He had noticed a change in a pigmented area of his forehead, and on biopsy the pathologists reported malignant melanoma. His physician recommended a wide excision and graft: surgical procedures requiring general anesthesia.

In elderly males especially, the combinations of drugs used in anesthesia sometimes makes urination difficult after such an ordeal. Following discharge from his overnight hospitalization, Beeson couldn't avoid a trip back to the emergency room for catheterization. His long history of bladder difficulty increased his risks for catheterizing himself at home, especially when the problem persisted for several months.

Even using sterile precautions that he fully understood, he developed urosepsis and was readmitted to the University of Washington Hospital with shaking chills and a fever of one hundred four. Fortunately, he responded to new antibiotics, and after a frightening few days, recovered. He did not, however, approve of the commercial care he had received at the hospital, nor of some of the new generation of physicians who hurried into the room, wrote in the chart and hurried out.

By the last week-end of May that year, Beeson was well enough to attend a meeting of the Interplanetary Society held in his honor at Port Ludlow, Washington. Most of the sixty participants had been trained by Beeson, McDermott or Wood, or by someone from one of the several subsequent generations of their trainees.

Whereas speakers at the initial meeting held forty years earlier discussed topics such as the best choice of an antibiotic to treat a specific illness and methods for culturing certain bacteria, at Port Ludlow the research was sub-cellular. Studies were presented that investigated "Activation of the neutrophil respiratory bust oxidase" and "Progress in gene therapy for chronic granulomatous disease," as well as various topics related to AIDS and antibiotic resistance to drugs.

Rather than culture plates and test tubes, research in infection by then involved manipulating retrovirus vectors for inserting genes into human stem cells or studied super oxide enzyme systems in membranes during phagocytosis. All of the participants were concerned about the rapid rate at which bacteria and viruses had learned to protect themselves against treatment, a problem not really even considered at the first Pus Club meetings.

The Port Ludlow participants all felt related to that earlier work of the society, however, through its remaining founder. Bob Petersdorf and Dick Root concluded their dedication of the event to Beeson writing, "The impact of his honesty, integrity and commitment to inquiry, and his vision and humanity will continue to inspire us all for many generations to come."(6)

Thirty-six awards, elections, degrees and even a title came to Paul Beeson over the six decades of his career. The one that he learned about in early 1996, though, pleased him most. With the encouragement of several of the "Fitkin Ironterns," his last group of interns at Yale, the Department of Internal Medicine named the Medical Service at Yale-New Haven Hospital in honor of Dr. Paul B. Beeson, recognition shared with only one other internist in America; the Medicine Service at Johns Hopkins is named for William Osler.

The physician-moralist Edmund Pellegrino calls profession "The voluntary self-imposition of higher than ordinary standards." Paul Beeson's life is a testimony to this ethic, and to all that is most valuable in the canon of medicine. From his childhood on the American frontier to a place beside the few great physicians of the century was a solitary journey, and a passage that might have made a less thoughtful person confuse himself with the mission. Paul Beeson remained the same man throughout his life of dedication to patients and students. He was ready to learn from Oswald Avery when the chance came in a New York City basement restaurant. He absorbed the humanism and dedication of Soma Weiss on the wards of the Brigham Hospital. The attention he paid to clinical hints in patients with fever led him to the description of endogenous pyrogen. The gifts he gave to house staff and faculty at Emory, Yale and Oxford were returned to him as love and respect. He prepared the minds of all the doctors who read his books, scientific articles and essays, and are to this day his students.

On the edge of the twenty-first century, the predictions of Paul Starr that medicine will become progressively more industrialized seem probable. Even so, there remains a longing for patients to tell their stories and for doctors to hear them. While Wall Street and biotechnology companies drive treatments, and insurance companies drive the industry of health care, patients and doctors struggle to recover their relationship with each other, a relationship defined by healers who had far less to offer. Still, there remains the example of Paul Beeson sitting beside a patient on an open ward, surrounded by students, listening to the clues, fears, and questions embedded in the story of a single sick person.

END NOTES

CHAPTER 1

1.   Osler's aphorisms have been published in several places. The direct quotations used throughout this book are usually taken, as in this case, from William Osler, Aequanimitas: With other Addresses to Medical Students, Nurses and Practitioners of Medicine, 3rd ed. (Philadelphia: The Blakiston Company, 1932) 30. Elsewhere I have quoted a special edition of Osler, Councils and Ideals (Birmingham: The Classics of Medicine Library, 1985).

2.   Abraham Flexner, Medical Education in the United States and Canada, (New York: Carnegie Foundation for the Advancement of Teaching, [Bulletin no. 4], 1910). This publication was based on Flexner's visit to every medical school in North America, and was an investigation invited by the AMA. "The Flexner Report" established standards for medical education, strengthened the best schools, which were usually associated with universities, and helped to extinguish the fraudulent ones.

3.   Byron Beeson, The Beeson Family (Marshalltown, 1898) 7.

4.   Much of the specific information about John Beeson and his parents is taken from a thirteen page letter Harold wrote to his brother Paul dated November 26, 1981.

5.   Paul Starr, The Transformation of American Medicine (New York: Basic Books, 1982) 108.

6.   Livingston Enterprise Souvenir (Livingston: Enterprise Publishing, 1976) 2.

7.   Harold Beeson (1981) 4.

8.   Harold Beeson (1981) 5.

9.   Harold Beeson (1981) 11.

10.   On page 151 of Paul Starr's book cited above, he describes these "pesthouses" as places where patients with contagious illnesses were segregated from the main hospital population. This was done not only to try to contain the spread of the diseases, but also to improve the look of the institution's statistics by reducing the mortality rates in the hospital itself.

11.   Bernadine Prince, The Alaska Railroad (Anchorage: Ken Wray's Print Shop, 1964) 2. This carefully researched two-volume book, containing hundreds of perfectly presented black and white photographs, was loaned to me by Robert Hocker, who homesteaded in Alaska after World War II. When the second Alaska Railroad Hospital was torn down in the early 1950s, the Hocker family salvaged some of that lumber to build their own house.

12.   Prince 23.

13.   Prince 75.

14.   Young Pentland, "Reviews," review of The Principles and Practice of Medicine, by William Osler, The British Medical Journal, June 18, 1892: 1310–11.

15.   Harvey Cushing, The Life of Sir William Osler (London: Oxford University Press, 1940) 59.

16.   This story, including the heroics of the lead sled-dogBalto, is told in Kenneth Underman's book The Race to Nome (New York: Harper and Row, 1963).

17.   Elizabeth Ricker, Seppala (Boston: Little, Brown, 1930) 269–270.

18.   Much of the information concerning the dog-sled trip to Iditarod was written by Harold Beeson in a letter to Paul dated July 6, 1971, including this quote from page 5. This letter was later used as the basis for Paul Beeson, "Rushing the serum to the Rescue: A Long House-Call," Resident & Staff Physician, April, 1990: 99–102.

CHAPTER 2

1.   Osler (1985) 142.

2.   Paul Dorpat, Seattle Now and Then ,2nd ed.(Seattle: Tartu, 1984) 109. This volume compares photographs of Seattle taken in similar locations first in the late nineteenth and then the late twentieth centuries.

3.   Osler (1932) 57–58.

4.   W.H. Jackson, Handloggers (Anchorage: Alaska Northwest Publishing Company, 1974) 76.

5.   Paul Beeson, "Reflections on Teaching and Medical Education," Background paper for University of Washington Medical School Workshop 2, March 4–5, 1993 and Workshop 3, June 18–19, 1993: 2.

6.   Osler (1932) 452.

7.   Starr 130.

8.   George Butler, A Text-Book of Materia Medica, 6th ed. (Philadelphia: Saunders, 1908) 13. Butler's text went through many editions, and offered information about the chemical nature of manufactured therapeutic compounds as well as botanicals. The last paragraph of his introduction to this edition is a curious praise of Christian Science, in which he attributes natural healing to the presence of "curative agents with which the laboratory of nature has been mercifully stored."

9.   Russell Cecil, Textbook of Medicine, 6th ed. (Philadelphia: Saunders, 1943). Paul Beeson and his friend Walsh McDermott took over the editorship of this textbook, which first appeared in 1927, with the eleventh edition published in 1963, but of course began working on it earlier. Beeson and McDermott continued through four more editions, to be joined by James Wyngaarden in their final edition, the fifteenth, published in 1979. As they studied or looked up obscure information, most medical students from those years remember seeing the name Beeson on the spine of their textbook of internal medicine, a final authority on many subjects for students, faculty and practitioners.

10.   Rene Dubos, The Professor, the Institute, and DNA, (New York: Rockefeller University Press, 1976) 109. The story of Oswald Avery and the discovery of type-specific serum therapy for treatment of pneumococcal pneumonia, and the now little-remembered role Avery played in the identification of DNA as genetic material, became an important part of Paul Beeson's life when he went to the Rockefeller Institute in 1937.

11.   Beeson (1993) 2–3.

12.   William Osler, The Principles and Practice of Medicine, (New York: D. Appleton and Company, 1892) 38.

13.   Beeson (1993) 3.

14.   Cushing 235.

15.   Beeson (1993) 4.

16.   Wilder Penfield and Herbert Jasper, Epilepsy and the Functional Anatomy of the Human Brain, (Boston: Little Brown, 1954). This volume summarized Penfield's remarkable experience at Montreal, where he operated on hundreds of awake patients and was the first surgeon to map the cortical representation of motor, sensory and language functions in man. The operating room he designed was copied almost exactly by his resident Arthur Ward when he became Chief of Neurosurgery at the University of Washington in 1948, and was the same room Ward and George Ojemann used when they taught their residents, including the author, to do an operation for the treatment of epilepsy as originally conceived by Penfield.

17.   Starr 116.

CHAPTER 3

1.　Lewis Thomas, The Youngest Science: Notes of a Medicine watcher, (New York: Penguin Books, 1995) 12–13.

2.　Beeson (1993) 5.

3.　Fluid and electrolyte balance began to have real clinical meaning after Donald Van Slyke invented the bulky but reasonably accurate "Van Slyke Apparatus", allowing simplified measurements of carbon dioxide in blood. The publication of the two volumes by JP Peters and DD Van Slyke, Quantitative Clinical Chemistry, (Baltimore: Williams and Wilkins, 1931 and 1932) applied German analytical methods to clinical chemistry and permitted more routine examination of serum electrolytes. Prior to their better methods, electrolytes were measured by extraction from large volumes of serum, ashing it and then weighing the product, a procedure requiring days, and not accurate. Jack Peters was well known for this work by the time Beeson arrived at Yale in 1952.

4.　By the time he finished his internship at Penn, Beeson knew that he had few surgical skills, and this later became a problem as he entered general practice where some surgery was required. In The Autobiography of William Carlos Williams, (New York: New Directions, 1948) 77, Williams (who graduated from medical school at Penn in 1906) comments on his year as an intern at French Hospital in New York: "I remember Eugene Pool accosting me when my time in the French was finally up and asked me what I was going to do. It was he who had given me the name 'the boy surgeon' when he had come upon me one day as I was trying to dissect out a Bartholin cyst abscess. 'One thing I'm not going to do,' I told him, 'and that's surgery.'

'Why not?'

'I don't fancy a life spent dabbling in people's guts.' "

Both Williams and Beeson found internal medicine more interesting than surgery, and neither man wished to dabble much with intestines.

5.　Beeson (1993) 6.

CHAPTER 4

1.　Dubos 26–27.

2.　Frank Horsfall, Kenneth Goodner and Colin MacLeod, "Type specific anti-pneumococcus rabbit serum," Science 84 (1937): 579.

3.　Simon Flexner, The Evaluation and Organization of the University Clinic, (Oxford: Clarendon Press, 1939) 18.

4.　Dubos 33.

5.　Sarah Reidman and Elton Gustafson, Portraits of Nobel Laureates in Medicine and Physiology, (London: Abelard-Schuman, 1963) 67–80.

6.   Dubos 88.

7.   Oswald Avery, Colin MacLeod and Maclyn McCarty, "Transformation of pneumococcus types induced by a desoxyribonucleic acid fraction isolated from Pneumococcus Type III," Journal of Experimental Medicine 79 (1944): 137.

8.   Colin MacLeod, "Oswald Theodore Avery 1877–1955," Journal of General Microbiology 17 (1957): 543. Although shy in public, Avery was passionate and precise in private conversation. Often fragments of discussions appeared more than once, and students memorized some of his soliloquies, which they named the "Red Seal Records" after a brand of musical recordings then considered the best available.

9.   Cecil 108.

10.   Paul Beeson and Charles Hoagland, "Use of calcium chloride in relief of chills following serum administration," Proceedings of the Society for Experimental Biology and Medicine 38 (1938): 160.

11.   Cecil 123.

12.   Cecil 1035–1037.

13.   Charles Hoagland, Paul Beeson and Walther Goebel, "The capsular polysaccharide of the Type XIV pneumococcus and its relationship to the specific substances of human blood," Science 88 (1938): 261.

14.   Selman Waksman was born in a small town in the Ukraine and emigrated to the United States at age eighteen. After obtaining an undergraduate degree in agriculture from Rutgers in 1915, he received a Ph.D. in biochemistry from the University of California, then began work in soil bacteriology with his student Rene Dubos.

15.   James Hirsch, "William Barry Wood, Jr.," Biographical Memoirs, vol. 51 (Washington, D.C.: National Academy of Sciences, 1980) 390.

CHAPTER 5

1.   Cecil xii

2.   Sharon Kaufman, The Healer's Tale, (Madison, The University of Wisconsin Press: 1993) 211–212.

3.   John Duffy, The Healers: A History of American Medicine, (Urbana, The University of Illinois Press: 1976) 289–290.

4.   Kaufman.

5.   Eugene Stead, "Soma Weiss at the Peter Bent Brigham: Steering a new course." The Pharos, 59 (1996): 19–20.

6.   William Hollingsworth, Taking Care, (Chapel Hill, Professional Press: 1994) 275, 283.

7.   This blue leather-bound volume with no publishing history includes

the eulogies of several speakers at a memorial service for Weiss held at the Harvard Medical School March 19, 1942. The quote here, taken from the section entitled "The New York Years" by Eugene DuBois, is on page 12.

    8.   Hollingsworth 143.

    9.   Stead 20.

   10.   Beeson (1993) 10.

CHAPTER 6

    1.   Sarah Reidman and Elton Gustafson 79.

    2.   James B. Conant, My Several Lives, (New York, Harper and Row: 1970) 265.

    3.   Paul Beeson, "Factors Influencing the Prevalence of Trichinosis in Man." Proceedings of the Royal Society of Medicine, 34 (1941): 585–589.

    4.   Paul Beeson, "Trichiniasis." The Lancet, 241 (1941): 67–72.

    5.   Paul Beeson and David Bass, The Eosinophil, (Philadelphia, Saunders: 1977) v.

    6.   Conant 263, 264.

    7.   TF McNair Scott, Paul Beeson and William Hawley, "Paratyphoid B Infection." The Lancet, 244 (1943): 487–495.

    8.   Paul Beeson, George Chesney and Allan McFarlan, "Hepatitis Following Injection of Mumps Convalescent Plasma." The Lancet, 246 (1944): 814–819.

    9.   Paul Beeson, TF McNair Scott, "Clinical, Epidemiological and Experimental Observations on an Acute Myalgia of the Neck and Shoulders; Its Possible Relation to Certain Cases of Generalized Fibrositis." Proceedings of the Royal Society of Medicine, 35 (1942): 733–740.

   10.   J. Willis Hurst, The Quest for Excellence, (Atlanta, Scholars Press: 1997) 77. Hurst's book describes the history of the Department of Medicine at Emory Medical School, and includes invaluable material about both Beeson and Stead while at Emory and other periods in their lives.

CHAPTER 7

    1.   A. McGehee Harvey, The Interurban Clinical Club (1905–1976, (Baltimore, The Interurban Clinical Club: 1978) 265–266.

    2.   Hurst 70.

    3.   The two last letters Weiss wrote to Beeson are dated October 25 and December 29, 1941. He details the opportunities available for an assistant professor interested in infection, but doesn't attempt to influence the choice. Both letters were typed by Evelyn Selby Stead, including the letterhead, a brief "Peter Bent Brigham Hospital, Boston, Massachusetts."

4.   Hurst 73.

5.   Philip Bondy, Recollections, (New Haven, The Advocate Press: 1996) 227–228.

6.   Kaufman 165.

7.   Bondy 231.

8.   Paul Beeson, "Jaundice Occurring One to Four Months After Transfusion of Blood or Plasma." Journal of the American Medical Association, 121 (1943): 1332–1334.

9.   Hurst 125.

10.   In 1940, President Franklin Roosevelt appointed Vannevar Bush Chairman of the National Research Defense Committee; Conant of Harvard (trained as a chemist) was one of the Committee members. In 1941, this body became a subdivision of the Office of Scientific Research and Development, a group meant not only to promote research but to solve defined problems. The Committee on Medical Research, also part of OSRD, but working through the National Research Council, was largely responsible for administering medical research during and just after World War II.

11.   Advisory Committee on Human Radiation Experiments: Final Report. (Washington, U.S. Government Printing Office: 1995) 145.

12.   Paul Beeson, Emmett Brannon and James Warren, "Observations on the Sites of Removal of Bacteria from the Blood in Patients with Bacterial Endocarditis." The Journal of Experimental Medicine, 81 (1945): 9–23.

13.   Paul Beeson, "Tolerance to Bacterial Pyrogens." The Journal of Experimental Medicine, 86 (1947): 29–38.

14.   Albert Hayman and Paul Beeson, "Influence of Various Disease States Upon the Febrile Response to Intravenous Injection of Typhoid Bacterial Pyrogen," The Journal of Laboratory and Clinical Medicine, 34 (1949): 1400–1403.

15.   A. McGehee Harvey, The Association of American Physicians: 1886–1986. (Baltimore, Waverly Press: 1986) 399–400.

16.   Galen Wagner, Bess Cebe, Marvin Rozear, E.A. Stead, Jr.: What this Patient Needs is a Doctor. (Durham, The Editors: 1981) 13.

17.   Starr 342–343.

18.   Starr 351.

19.   Ivan Bennett and Paul Beeson, "The Properties and Biological Effects of Bacterial Pyrogens," Medicine, 29 (1950): 365–400.

20.   Hurst 135.

CHAPTER 8

1.   Starr 352, 359.

2.   Robert Petersdorf, "Acceptance of the 1996 George M. Kober Medal,"

Proceedings of the Association of American Physicians, 108 (1996): 408–409. The Kober Medal, the Association's highest honor, identifies the recipient as one of the few great physicians in the country. Bob Petersdorf, who became an example of the best in academic medicine, must have listened very carefully indeed to the advice of his mentor. He certainly got his hands dirty in the lab; his Curriculum Vitae is sixteen pages long, without the four hundred sixty-nine publications.

3.   Letter from Donald Seldin, M.D. to the author, June 1, 1998. Seldin, also a past president of the AAP and a Kober Medal winner, is largely credited with building Texas-Southwestern Medical School from a minor center after World War II into one of the best institutions in the country. Seldin heavily promoted pure science and basic research in departments of internal medicine, as opposed to clinical research.

4.   Harvey (1986) 519.

5.   Starr 347.

6.   Yale still gives no grades and no examinations in the medical curriculum until the end of the final year. Students are required to present a senior thesis and to pass the National Board exam, a standardized test given to all medical students, in order to graduate.

7.   Currently in most medical schools, no faculty member attends on the wards more than one or two months of the academic year. The work of the chairmen of these enormous departments, especially in internal medicine where the faculty members often number several hundred, is entirely administrative. After a brief period in such a position, most chairmen could not responsibly attend very ill patients on the wards. At the 1997 meeting of the Interplanetary Society, Dr. Jonathan Ravdin, current Chair of the Department of Medicine at Minnesota, read a paper describing his job, duties totally unrecognizable to the older physicians in the audience. Most of them, including Beeson, felt the task of chairing a large, modern department better suited a person with a business degree than one in medicine. When popular magazines publish lists of the best physicians in the country, they unknowingly refer largely to the reputations of institutions and departments rather than the individuals they name, who often no longer even see patients.

8.   Letter from Sherwin Nuland, M.D. to the author, July 30, 1997. Nuland is author of several excellent books, including *How We Die*, an explanation of just that.

9.   Letter from Franklin Epstein, M.D. to the author, June 10, 1997. Dr. Epstein, a Peters fellow, is now the William Applebaum Professor of Medicine at Harvard.

10.   Max Miller, "John P. Peters: 1887–1955," Diabetes, 6 (1957): 99–103.

11.   Paul Beeson, "Temperature-Elevating Effects of a Substance Obtained

from Polymorphonuclear Leukocytes," Journal of Clinical Investigation, 27 (1948): 524.

12.   Ivan Bennett and Paul Beeson, "Studies on the Pathogenesis of Fever: I. The Effect of Injection of Extracts and Suspensions of Uninfected Rabbit Tissues upon the Body Temperature of Normal Rabbits," Journal of Experimental Medicine, 98 (1953): 447–492.

13.   Ivan Bennett and Paul Beeson, "Studies on the Pathogenesis of Fever: II. Characterization of Fever-Producing Substances from Polymorphonuclear Leukocytes and from the Fluid of Sterile Exudates," Journal of Experimental Medicine, 98 (1953): 493–508.

14.   Letter from Charles Dinarello, M.D. to the author, April 15, 1998.

15.   George F. Kennan, The Nuclear Delusion. (New York, Pantheon: 1976) 7.

16.   The Atomic Bomb Casualty Commission was set up in 1947 by what was then called the Atomic Energy Commission (now the Department of Energy) and directed by the National Academy of Sciences - National Research Council. This long-term study was designed to determine the dose-response relationships between radiation exposure in the Japanese survivors of the bombing and later health effects.

17.   William Hollingsworth, "Delayed Radiation Effects in Survivors of the Atomic Bombings," New England Journal of Medicine, 263 (1960): 481–487.

CHAPTER 9

1.   Harvey (1986) 535–536.

2.   Paul Beeson, "The Case Against the Catheter," The American Journal of Medicine, 24 (1958): 1–3.

3.   Paul Beeson, Heonir Rocha and Lucien Guze, "Experimental Pyelonephritis: Influence of Localized Injury in Different Parts of the Kidney on Susceptibility to Hematogenous Infection," Transactions of the Association of American Physicians, 60 (1957): 120–126.

4.   Paul Beeson and Derrick Rowley, "The Anticomplementary Effect of Kidney Tissue," The Journal of Experimental Medicine, 110 (1959): 685–697.

5.   In an effort to justify this sort of academic world view, a neuro-surgery resident in the mid 1970s promoted the mathematical, and thus scientific, formula "n + 1 is better than n" to justify padding his CV with weak science. Because they tend to be so busy and distracted from the intellectual rigor demanded by basic science research, surgeons are, in general, slightly more guilty of this ruse than internists.

6.   Robert Petersdorf and Paul Beeson, "Fever of Unexplained Origin: Report on 100 cases," Medicine, 40 (1961): 1–30. In a January 1998 note to

Beeson about a current publication concerning tuberculosis as the cause of FUO, Petersdorf wrote, "You will be pleased to know that our paper is still the gold standard and that this author characterizes us as 'giants in the field of infectious disease.' There is even an old quote from Ivan [Bennett]."

7. Hollingsworth 7–12.

8. Hollingsworth 178.

9. Letter from Lewis Landsberg, M.D. to the author, September 18, 1998. Landsberg is Chairman of the Department of Medicine at Northwestern University School of Medicine.

10. Paul Beeson, "On Becoming a Clinician," On Doctoring, ed. Richard Reynolds and John Stone (New York: Simon and Schuster, 1991) 173–178.

11. Starr 365–374.

CHAPTER 10

1. Victor Fuchs, Who Shall Live? (New York, Basic Books: 1974) 22.

2. Thomas Willis (1621–1675), was Professor of Natural Philosophy at Oxford and wrote the most complete and accurate account of the nervous system of his time. In the preparation of his text Cerebri Anatome, Willis was aided by Richard Lower (1631–1691). Lower himself was the first to understand that blood absorbed air (Priestly didn't isolate oxygen until 1772) when passing through the lungs.

3. The Oxford Record Linkage project was established as a large, population-based epidemiological project similar to the Framingham Study conducted over many years outside of Boston.

4. The Krebs, or citric acid cycle, is a series of chemical reactions required for the oxidative metabolism of glucose to carbon dioxide and water. It is an essential part of energy metabolism in man and most higher animals.

5. Anthony Baston and Paul Beeson, "Mechanisms of Eosinophilia: II. Role of the Lymphocyte," The Journal of Experimental Medicine, 131 (1970): 1288–1305.

6. Paul Beeson and David Bass, The Eosinophil. (Philadelphia, Saunders: 1977).

7. Renato Cordeiro, Redwan Moqbel and Peter Weller, eds., New Perspectives in Eosinophils. Role in Inflammation Associated with Allergy, Asthma and Parasitic Disease. (Rio de Janeiro, Memorias Instituto Oswaldo Cruz: 1997) 6.

8. Letter from Kenneth Johnson, M.D. to the author, July 5, 1998.

9. Barbara Tuchman, The March of Folly. (New York, Ballantine: 1984) 374.

10. Hollingsworth 193–194.

11.   Paul Beeson, "Presidential Address: The Academic Doctor," Transactions of the Association of American Physicians, 80 (1967): 1–7.

12.   In fact, with the failure of health care policy reform in the early 1990s, and the growth of for profit HMOs and insurance company management of patient populations, the real threat to medical care came from unregulated capitalism.

13.   The debate between Beeson and Seldin continued and expanded. As he prepared his own presidential address for the AAP meeting in 1981, Seldin sent Beeson a draft of the paper. They did not agree on the "Boundaries of Medicine," the title of Seldin's speech. Beeson sought a broad definition, including care of the elderly and considerations about nuclear war, whereas Seldin argued that "medicine is a narrow discipline." The positions taken by these two important academics helps define the differences between the art and the science of medicine at the end of the twentieth century.

14.   Thomas Stamey, "Prostate Cancer: Who Should be Treated?," 1995 Monographs in Urology, 16 (1995): 3–16.

15. David Durack and Paul Beeson, "Experimental Bacterial Endocarditis: I. Colonization of a Sterile Vegetation," British Journal of Experimental Pathology, 53 (1972): 44–49.

16.   David Durack and Paul Beeson, "Experimental Bacterial Endocarditis: II. Survival of Bacteria in Endocardial Vegetations," British Journal of Experimental Pathology, 53 (1972): 50–53.

17.   David Durack, Robert Petersdorf and Paul Beeson, "Penicillin Prophylaxis of Experimental S. Viridans Endocarditis," Transactions of the Association of American Physicians, 65 (1972): 222–230.

18.   Such alliances and appointments helped determine academic careers. While perhaps a kind of intellectual nepotism, the relationships were based on proven talent; Durack was, after all, a Rhodes Scholar. Most of the academic internists of Beeson's era deeply mourned the loss of friendship and trust best characterized by the Atlantic City meetings—when the internal medicine societies actually convened there. While the methods for choosing house staff are now necessarily more democratic, a certain community has been lost—the difference between a handshake and a contract.

19.   Paul Beeson, Quality of Survival. (Oxford, Oxford University Press: 1972).

CHAPTER 11

1.   Ivan Illich, Medical Nemesis. (Toronto, Bantam Books: 1977) 13.

2.   The original unpublished memorandum was presented in a slightly different form by James Eckenhoff, "Commentary: 20 Years of the VA's

Distinguished Physician Program," Academic Medicine, February 1990: 94–95.

3.   Eric Cassel, "The Sorcerer's Broom: Medicine's Rampant Technology," Hastings Center Report, 23 (1993): 32–39. To emphasize that the irresistible growth of technology is related to the inflation in medical economics, Cassel quotes the aphorism, "To the man with a hammer, everything is a nail."

4.   Osler (1985) 10.

5.   Paul Beeson, "Training Doctors to Care for Old People," Annals of Internal Medicine, 90 (1979): 262–263.

6.   John Rowe, Esta Grossman, Enriqueta Bond, "Special Report: Academic Geriatrics for the Year 2000," New England Journal of Medicine, 316 (1987): 1425–1428.

7.   Starr 370. The 1964 Presidential Commission on Heart Disease, Cancer and Stroke was heavily lobbied by the Lasker Foundation to establish a national system uniting medical education, health care and research around these three categories of illness. The final recommendations of the commission were, according to Starr, determined in advance by the influential Lasker lobby, and ignored perhaps more profitable investment.

8.   Paul Beeson, "McKeown's The Role of Medicine: A Clinicians Reaction," Milbank Memorial Fund Quarterly, Summer (1977): 365–371.

9.   John Gofman, Radiation and Human Health. (San Francisco, Sierra Club: 1981) 495–506.

10.   Stuart Finch, "Occurrence of Cancer in Atomic Bomb Survivors," The Final Epidemic, eds. Ruth Adams and Susan Cullen (Chicago, Educational Foundation for Nuclear Science: 1981) 151.

11.   Robert Scheer, With Enough Shovels: Reagan, Bush and Nuclear War. (New York, Vintage Books: 1983) 18.

CHAPTER 12

1.   Starr 420–421.

2.   Beeson (1993) 13.

3.   Paul Beeson, "An Early Call for Health Care Reform: The Committee of 430 Physicians." The Pharos, 56 (1993): 22–24. Peters and the other early proponents of universal coverage were attacked by Morris Fishbein, long editor of The Journal of the American Medical Association, and a reactionary defender of the physician as entrepreneur. On behalf of the AMA, Fishbein repeatedly denounced any government involvement in medicine, often implying it was un-American. He eventually became so outspoken, however, that the Trustees of the AMA specifically prohibited him from making any public statements except on scientific subjects, and at the same time assumed supervision of his editorials on controversial topics.

4.   Paul Beeson, "Priorities in Medical Education," Perspectives in Biology and Medicine, 25 (1982): 673–687.

5.   Kaufman 14.

6.   Richard Root and Robert Petersdorf, "Dedication: to Paul B. Beeson, M.D.," The Journal of Infectious Diseases, 179 (1999): iv.

BIBLIOGRAPHY

Advisory Committee on Human Radiation Experiments: Final Report. (1995). (Washington: U.S. Government Printing Office).

Avery, O., MacLeod, C., and McCarty, M. (1944). "Transformation of pneumococcus types induced by a desoxyribonucleic acid fraction isolated from Pneumococcus Type III," *Journal of Experimental Medicine*, 79, 137.

Baston, A., and Beeson, P. (1970). "Mechanisms of Eosinophilia: II. Role of the Lymphocyte," *The Journal of Experimental Medicine*, 131, 1288–1305.

Beeson, B. (1889). *The Beeson Family.* (Marshalltown).

Beeson, P. (1941). "Factors Influencing the Prevalence of Trichinosis in Man." *Proceedings of the Royal Society of Medicine*, 34, 585–589.

Beeson, P. (1941). "Trichiniasis." *The Lancet*, 241(2), 67–72.

Beeson, P. (1943). "Jaundice Occurring One to Four Months After Transfusion of Blood or Plasma." *Journal of the American Medical Association*, 121, 1332–1334.

Beeson, P. (1947). "Tolerance to Bacterial Pyrogens." *The Journal of Experimental Medicine*, 86, 29–38.

Beeson, P. (1948). "Temperature-Elevating Effects of a Substance Obtained from Polymorphonuclear Leukocytes," *Journal of Clinical Investigation*, 27, 524.

Beeson, P. (1958). "The Case Against the Catheter," *The American Journal of Medicine*, 24, 1–3.

Beeson, P. (1967). "Presidential Address: The Academic Doctor," *Transactions of the Association of American Physicians*, 80, 1–7.

Beeson, P. (1972). *Quality of Survival.* (Oxford: Oxford University Press).

Beeson, P. (1977, Summer). "McKeown's The Role of Medicine: A Clinicians Reaction," *Milbank Memorial Fund Quarterly*, 365–371.

Beeson, P. (1979). "Training Doctors to Care for Old People," *Annals of Internal Medicine*, 90, 262–263.

Beeson, P. (1982). "Priorities in Medical Education," *Perspectives in Biology and Medicine*, 25, 673–687.

Beeson, P. (1990, April). "Rushing the serum to the Rescue: A Long House-Call," *Resident & Staff Physician*, 99–102.

Beeson, P. (1991). "On Becoming a Clinician." In *On Doctoring*, ed. Richard Reynolds and John Stone (New York: Simon and Schuster).

Beeson, P. (1993, March 4–5, 1993 and June 18–19). "Reflections on Teaching and Medical Education," *Background paper for University of Washington Medical School Workshop 2 and 3*.

Beeson, P. (1993). "An Early Call for Health Care Reform: The Committee of 430 Physicians." *The Pharos*, 56, 22–24.

Beeson, P. and Hoagland, C. (1938). "Use of calcium chloride in relief of chills following serum administration," *Proceedings of the Society for Experimental Biology and Medicine*, 38, 160–162.

Beeson, P., and McNair Scott, T.F. (1942). "Clinical, Epidemiological and Experimental Observations on an Acute Myalgia of the Neck and Shoulders; Its Possible Relation to Certain Cases of Generalized Fibrositis," *Proceedings of the Royal Society of Medicine*, 35, 733–740.

Beeson, P., Chesney, G., and McFarlan, A. (1944). "Hepatitis Following Injection of Mumps Convalescent Plasma," *The Lancet*, 246, 814–819.

Beeson, P., Brannon, E., and Warren, J. (1945). "Observations on the Sites of Removal of Bacteria from the Blood in Patients with Bacterial Endocarditis," *The Journal of Experimental Medicine*, 81, 9–23.

Beeson, P., Rocha, H., and Guze, L. (1957). "Experimental Pyelonephritis: Influence of Localized Injury in Different Parts of the Kidney on Susceptibility to Hematogenous Infection," *Transactions of the Association of American Physicians*, 60, 120–126.

Beeson, P. and Rowley, D. (1959). "The Anticomplementary Effect of Kidney Tissue," *The Journal of Experimental Medicine*, 110, 685–697.

Beeson, P., and Bass, D. (1977). *The Eosinophil*, (Philadelphia: Saunders).

Bennett, I. and Beeson, P. (1950). "The Properties and Biological Effects of Bacterial Pyrogens," *Medicine*, 29, 365–400.

Bennett, I., and Beeson, P. (1953). "Studies on the Pathogenesis of Fever: I. The Effect of Injection of Extracts and Suspensions of Uninfected Rabbit Tissues upon the Body Temperature of Normal Rabbits," *Journal of Experimental Medicine*, 98, 447–492.

Bennett, I., and Beeson, P. (1953). "Studies on the Pathogenesis of Fever: II. Characterization of Fever-Producing Substances from Polymorphonuclear

Leukocytes and from the Fluid of Sterile Exudates," *Journal of Experimental Medicine*, 98, 493–508.

Bondy, P. (1996). *Recollections*, (New Haven: The Advocate Press).

Butler, G. (1908). *A Text-Book of Materia Medica*, 6th ed. (Philadelphia: Saunders).

Cassel, E. (1993). "The Sorcerer's Broom: Medicine's Rampant Technology," *Hastings Center Report*, 23,32–39.

Cecil, R. (1943). *Textbook of Medicine*, 6th ed. (Philadelphia: Saunders).

Cordeiro, R., Moqbel, R., and Weller, P. eds. (1997). *New Perspectives in Eosinophils. Role in Inflammation Associated with Allergy, Asthma and Parasitic Disease.* (Rio de Janeiro: Memorias Instituto Oswaldo Cruz).

Conant, J. (1970). *My Several Lives.* (New York: Harper and Row).

Cushing, H. (1940). *The Life of Sir William Osler.* (London: Oxford University Press).

Dorpat, P. (1984). *Seattle Now and Then*, 2nd ed. (Seattle: Tartu).

Dubos, R. (1976). *The Professor, the Institute, and DNA.* (New York: Rockefeller University Press).

Duffy, J. (1976). *The Healers: A History of American Medicine.* (Urbana: The University of Illinois Press).

Durack, D., and Beeson, P. (1972). "Experimental Bacterial Endocarditis: I. Colonization of a Sterile Vegetation," *British Journal of Experimental Pathology*, 53, 44–49.

Durack, D., and Beeson, P. (1972). "Experimental Bacterial Endocarditis: II. Survival of Bacteria in Endocardial Vegetations," *British Journal of Experimental Pathology*, 53, 50–53.

Durack, D., Petersdorf, R. and Beeson, P. (1972). "Penicillin Prophylaxis of Experimental S. Viridans Endocarditis," *Transactions of the Association of American Physicians*, 65, 222–230.

Eckenhoff, J. (1990, February). "Commentary: 20 Years of the VA's Distinguished Physician Program," *Academic Medicine*, 94–95.

Finch, S. (1981). "Occurrence of Cancer in Atomic Bomb Survivors." In *The Final Epidemic*, eds. Ruth Adams and Susan Cullen (Chicago: Educational Foundation for Nuclear Science).

Flexner, A. (1910, Bulletin no. 4). *Medical Education in the United States and Canada*, (New York: Carnegie Foundation for the Advancement of Teaching).

Flexner, S. (1939). *The Evaluation and Organization of the University Clinic.* (Oxford: Clarendon Press).

Fuchs, V. (1974). *Who Shall Live?* (New York: Basic Books).

Gofman, J. (1981). *Radiation and Human Health.* (San Francisco: Sierra Club).

Harvey, A.M. (1978). *The Interurban Clinical Club* (1905–1976). (Baltimore: The Interurban Clinical Club).

Harvey, A.M. (1986). *The Association of American Physicians: 1886–1986*. (Baltimore: Waverly Press).

Hayman, A. and Beeson, P. (1949). "Influence of Various Disease States Upon the Febrile Response to Intravenous Injection of Typhoid Bacterial Pyrogen," *The Journal of Laboratory and Clinical Medicine*, 34, 1400–1403.

Hirsch, J. (1980). "William Barry Wood, Jr.," *Biographical Memoirs, vol. 51*. (Washington, D.C.: National Academy of Sciences).

Hoagland, C., Beeson, P., and Goebel, W. (1938). "The capsular polysaccharide of the Type XIV pneumococcus and its relationship to the specific substances of human blood," *Science 88*, 261–263.

Hollingsworth, W. (1960). "Delayed Radiation Effects in Survivors of the Atomic Bombings," *New England Journal of Medicine*, 263, 481–487.

Hollingsworth, W. (1994). *Taking Care*. (Chapel Hill: Professional Press).

Horsfall, F., Goodner, K., and MacLeod, C. (1937). "Type specific anti-pneumococcus rabbit serum," *Science 84*, 579.

Hurst, J.W. (1997). *The Quest for Excellence*. (Atlanta: Scholars Press).

Illich, I. (1977). *Medical Nemesis*. (Toronto: Bantam Books).

Jackson, WH. (1974). *Handloggers*. (Anchorage: Alaska Northwest Publishing Company).

Kaufman, S. (1993). *The Healer's Tale*. (Madison: The University of Wisconsin Press).

Kennan, G. (1976). *The Nuclear Delusion*. (New York: Pantheon).

Livingston Enterprise Souvenir. (1976). (Livingston: Enterprise Publishing).

MacLeod, C. (1957). "Oswald Theodore Avery 1877–1955," *Journal of General Microbiology 17*, 543.

Miller, M. (1957). "John P. Peters: 1887–1955," *Diabetes*, 6, 99–103.

Osler, W. (1892). *The Principles and Practice of Medicine*. (New York: D. Appleton and Company).

Osler, W. (1932). *Aequanimitas: With other Addresses to Medical Students, Nurses and Practitioners of Medicine*, 3rd ed. (Philadelphia: The Blakiston Company).

Osler, W. (1985). *Councils and Ideals*. (Birmingham: The Classics of Medicine Library).

Penfield, W., and Jasper, H. (1954). *Epilepsy and the Functional Anatomy of the Human Brain*. (Boston: Little Brown).

Pentland, Y. (1892, June 18). "Reviews," review of The Principles and Practice of Medicine, by William Osler, *The British Medical Journal*, 1310–1311.

Peters, J.P. and Van Slyke, D.D. (1931 and 1932). *Quantitative Clinical Chemistry*, (Baltimore: Williams and Wilkins).

Petersdorf, R., and Beeson, P. (1961). "Fever of Unexplained Origin: Report on 100 cases," *Medicine*, 40, 1–30.

Petersdorf, R. (1996). "Acceptance of the 1996 George M. Kober Medal," *Proceedings of the Association of American Physicians*, 108, 408–409.

Prince, B. (1964). The Alaska Railroad. (Anchorage: Ken Wray's Print Shop).

Reidman, S. and Gustafson, E. (1963). *Portraits of Nobel Laureates in Medicine and Physiology*. (London: Abelard-Schuman).

Ricker, E. (1930). *Seppala*. (Boston: Little, Brown).

Root, R., and Petersdorf, R. (1999). "Dedication: to Paul B. Beeson, M.D.," *The Journal of Infectious Diseases*, 179, iv.

Rowe, J., Grossman, E., and Bond, E. (1987). "Special Report: Academic Geriatrics for the Year 2000," *New England Journal of Medicine*, 316, 1425–1428.

Scheer, R. (1983). *With Enough Shovels: Reagan, Bush and Nuclear War*. (New York: Vintage Books).

Scott, T.F.M., Beeson, P. and Hawley, W. (1943). "Paratyphoid B Infection," *The Lancet*, 244(1), 487–495.

Stamey, T. (1995). "Prostate Cancer: Who Should be Treated?," *1995 Monographs in Urology*, 16, 3–16.

Starr, P. (1982). *The Transformation of American Medicine*. (New York: Basic Books).

Stead, E. (1996). "Soma Weiss at the Peter Bent Brigham: Steering a new course," *The Pharos*, 59, 19–20.

Thomas, L. (1995). *The Youngest Science: Notes of a Medicine Watcher*. (New York: Penguin Books).

Tuchman, B. (1984). *The March of Folly*. (New York: Ballantine).

Underman, K. (1963). *The Race to Nome*. (New York: Harper and Row).

Wagner, G., Cebe, B., Rozear, M. (1981). E.A. Stead, Jr.: *What this Patient Needs is a Doctor*. (Durham: The Editors).

Williams, W.C. (1948). *The Autobiography of William Carlos Williams*. (New York: New Directions).